"It's a wonder the novel itself doesn't explode, but Millet's confident writing holds the center." —*The New York Times Book Review*

"*Oh Pure and Radiant Heart* provides catharsis and education while allowing us to bask in the humorous, poignant possibilities of *what if.*" —*The Believer*

"Delicate and beautifully handled, this is indeed a literary balancing act . . . When it's flying, this novel can be moving and wonderfully funny." —*Hartford Courant*

"Millet has written what might prove to be the year's finest urban fantasy . . . Sporting dark humor, caustic insight, and a genuinely disturbing denouement, [it] is a must-read for all fans of good literature—genre and mainstream alike." —*St. Louis Post-Dispatch*

"A brilliant form of cultural commentary." —*The Plain Dealer* (Cleveland)

"Complex and affecting . . . While its premise seems absurd at first, its message is anything but." —*The Washington Post Book World*

"That rarest of finds: a compassionate satire, with a terrific premise and writing that's so assured that readers should be lining up for admission to this dystopia . . . Her re-creations of the characters of the three physicists are stunning." —*The Christian Science Monitor*

"For all its frenetic energy and fiery satire, *Oh Pure and Radiant Heart*—part farce, part comedy of errors, part spiritual inquiry, part historical testimony, part love story—is an acutely sensitive novel, a work of many moods and modes, a richly dimensional, shrewd and humanistic tale in the manner of Mark Twain, Kurt Vonnegut and Haruki Murakami. . . . Uproarious and clarion." —*Chicago Tribune*

"Lydia Millet is da bomb. Literally. While the sixtieth anniversary of the Trinity test has seen an awe-inspiring proliferation of books about the atomic experiment, Millet's blackly comic fifth novel, *Oh Pure and Radiant Heart,* is more entertaining and insightful than a silo full of them . . . Though *Oh Pure and Radiant Heart* possesses the nervy irreverence of Kurt Vonnegut and Joseph Heller, Millet makes the subject matter her own, capturing the essence of these geniuses in a way that can only be described as, well, genius." —*Vanity Fair*

"In her brilliant and fearless novel *Oh Pure and Radiant Heart,* Lydia Millet takes a headlong run at the subject of nuclear annihilation, weaving together black comedy, science, history, and time travel to produce, against stiff odds, a shattering and beautiful work. **A-.**" —*Entertainment Weekly*

"Lydia Millet has written a funny, courageous and very human novel. A political thriller, a sci-fi romp, and a poetic meditation on history, *Oh Pure and Radiant Heart* confronts America's nuclear legacy and present lunacy with furious satire and haunting grace." —Sam Lipsyte

"*Oh Pure and Radiant Heart* showcases the many brilliant talents of Lydia Millet: her lovely lyrical prose, fierce intelligence, wicked sense of humor, and an imagination for reinventing history that is deserving of the greatest admiration." —Jill McCorkle

OH PURE

AND RADIANT

HEART

OH PURE

AND RADIANT

HEART

LYDIA MILLET

A HARVEST BOOK

HARCOURT, INC.

Orlando   Austin   New York
San Diego   Toronto   London

Requests for permission to make copies of any part of the
work should be submitted online at www.harcourt.com/contact
or mailed to the following address: Permissions Department,
Harcourt, Inc., 6277 Sea Harbor Drive, Orlando, Florida 32887-6777.

www.HarcourtBooks.com

First published by Soft Skull Press in 2005

Library of Congress Cataloging-in-Publication Data
Millet, Lydia, 1968–
Oh pure and radiant heart/Lydia Millet.—1st Harvest ed.
p.   cm.
"A Harvest Book."
First published by Soft Skull Press in 2005.
1. Oppenheimer, J. Robert, 1904–1967—Fiction.   2. Fermi, Enrico,
1901–1954—Fiction.   3. Nuclear physicists—Fiction.   4. Women
librarians—Fiction.   5. Santa Fe (N.M.)—Fiction.   6. Szilard, Leo—
Fiction.   7. Celebrities—Fiction.   8. Atomic bomb—Fiction.
9. Time travel—Fiction.   I. Title.
PS3563.I42175O37   2006
813'.54—dc22   2005023808
ISBN-13: 978-0-15-603103-5   ISBN-10: 0-15-603103-5

Text set in PB48PS
Designed by Scott Piehl

Printed in the United States of America

First Harvest edition 2006
K J I H G F E D C B A

Behold,
I have set before you an open
door, and no man can shut it.

—Revelation 3:8

CONTENTS

ACKNOWLEDGMENTS

❧ For their insight and critical help I wish to thank Jenny Offill, Kieran Suckling, and Kate Bernheimer. For their forbearance as readers, my thanks to Saralaine Millet and Maria Massie. And I am deeply grateful to Richard Eoin Nash for his perseverance and conviction.

For her help with the Japanese language and her hospitality in Tokyo, thanks to Nerissa Moray; for help and guidance in Hiroshima, thanks to Andrew Hill; and for her many social connections, thanks to Alycia Rossiter. For their kindness and interpretive skills, thanks to Kazue Moshi Ichi in Hiroshima and Keiko Shirahama in Nagasaki. Thanks to Hibakusha Tomei Ozaki for his eyewitness account of the bombing of Nagasaki.

Thanks also to Tonya Turner-Carroll and Michael Carroll for their gracious hospitality in Santa Fe, to Debbie Bingham for her help at the White Sands Missile Range, and Peter Galvin and Melanie Duchin for their knowledge of the Grateful Dead. I am also grateful to Brian Segee for his advice on Freedom of Information Act matters, Evelin and Mike Sullivan for their assistance with particle physics, and Ernest B. Williams, tour guide at the Nevada Test Site, for his inspiration.

I

THE MEANING OF
THE PORKPIE HAT

෧ In the middle of the twentieth century three men were charged with the task of removing the tension between minute and vast things. It was their job to rend asunder the smallest unit of being known to be separable from itself; out of a particle so modest there are billions in a single tear, in a moment so brief it could not be perceived, they would make the finite infinite.

Two of the scientists were self-selected to split the atom. Leo Szilard and Enrico Fermi had chosen long before to work on the matter, to follow in the footsteps of Marie Curie and her husband, who had discovered radioactivity.

The third man was a theoretical physicist who had considered the subject of the divisible atom among many others. He was a generalist, not a specialist. He did not select himself per se, but was chosen for the job by a soldier.

Thousands worked at the whims of these men. From Szilard they took the first idea, from Fermi the fuel, from Oppenheimer both the orders and the inspiration. They built the first atomic bomb with primitive tools, performing their calculations on the same slide rules schoolchildren were given. For complex sums they punched keys on adding machines. Their equipment was clumsy and dull, or so it would seem by the standards of their children. Only their minds were sharp. In three years they achieved a technological miracle.

Essentially they learned how to split the atom by chiseling secret runes onto rocks.

And it should be admitted, the concession must be gracefully made: in the moment when a speck of dust acquires the power to engulf the world in fire, suddenly, then, all bets are off.

Suddenly then there is no idea that cannot be entertained.

⤳ On a clear, cool spring night more than half a century after the invention of the atom bomb, a woman lying in her bed in the rich and leisured citadel of Santa Fe, New Mexico, had a dream.

This itself was not surprising.

To be precise it was less a dream than an idea in the struggle of waking up. She thought the dream as she began to rouse herself and she was left, after waking, with an urgency that had no answer. She was left salty and dry, trussed up in a sheet, the length of her a shudder of vague regret.

In the dream a man was kneeling in the desert.

The man was J. Robert Oppenheimer, the Father of the Atom Bomb. The desert was an American desert: it was the New Mexico desert, and the site was named Trinity. Oppenheimer named it that. He gave lofty names to all his works, all except Fat Man and Little Boy.

These details would be revealed to her later. At the time nothing had a name but the man.

The man's porkpie hat was tipped forward on his head and his pants were torn. His knobby knees were scratched and the abrasions were full of sand. She almost thought she could feel the sand against her own raw flesh, where the grains agitated. It may have been dust on the sheet beneath her, or, further removed, dust between the sheet and the mattress, a pea dreamed by a princess.

He was bent over abjectly, his face turned to the ground.

Then there was the flash, as bright as a thousand suns, which turned night into day. And on the horizon the fireball rose, spreading silently. In the spreading she felt peace, peace and what came before, as though the country beneath her, with its wide prairies, had been returned to the wild. She saw the cloud churning and growing, majestic and broad, and thought: No, not a mushroom, but a tree. A great and ancient tree, growing and sheltering us all.

The sight of it was poetry, the kind that turns men's bones to dust before their hearts.

At this point in the scene she confused it with the Bible. The man named Oppenheimer saw what he had made, and it was beautiful. But when he looked at it, the light burned out his eyes and turned him blind.

She saw the rolling balls of the eyes when he righted himself to face the tree, and they were white like eggs.

❧ Back then she knew nothing about Oppenheimer's life: not who he was, not the identities of places, not the fact that the sand in the scrapes in his knees would have been the sand of the valley with the Spanish name Jornada del Muerto, Voyage of the Dead. There were infinite details she could not recognize, infinite details beyond her awareness in her own half-idea, in the deep blind territory of what is not known to be known but is known all the same.

Also there was what she knew without knowing why she knew it, for example the phrase *brighter than a thousand suns*. She recalled these words without a hint of where they came from or how they had first been imprinted on her memory. She did not know what "brighter than a thousand suns" would mean, how a brightness so bright could be outdone. The eye is not equal to even one sun, she thought. Straight, unwavering, bold, the eye cannot abide it.

A thousand suns? The eye could never adapt.

Or maybe once it is blinded the eye is transformed, she thought, and ceases to be an eye at all.

How much is learned unconsciously? It must be vast, she thought. We sweep through fields of knowledge and later all we can see is the dirt that clings to the hems of our clothes.

Of course the scene itself, the dramatic idea that was not quite as unconscious as a dream, might have simply been a blurry cognitive rerun of any number of World War Two documentaries. It might have been a fragment from television, a black-and-white epic of scarred and pocked newsreels interspersed with propaganda footage from the Nuremberg rallies. She might remember young boys marching in synchronicity and jutting out their arms in salute; further she might recall the chilling but majestic banners hanging long and thin and several stories high above the seemingly endless crowds, their spidery symbols rippling like water in the wind.

And over this she might recall the droning, authoritative voice of a British narrator.

Afterward she remembered the name. She could not forget the name, in fact, in the way a bad jingle overstays its welcome, tinny and insistent, lodged in the neural pathways of the brain. It was a famous name, or a name that had once been famous anyway, before she was born when her parents were young, when *the Japs got what was coming to them,* and later still when the drunkard McCarthy was hunting down Communists.

It was Oppenheimer, J. R.

Also the words *The Father of the Atom Bomb.*

A few days before, in waking life, she had seen the name at a small garage sale in a driveway, on the yellowing pages of a dog-eared copy of an old magazine from 1948, titled *Physics Today.* At the garage sale she had purchased a trivet, and the trivet had been sitting on this magazine when it caught her attention. She did not need a trivet, and in particular she did not need a porcelain trivet decorated with watercolor-style renderings of the Seven Wonders of the Ancient World. But she felt a need to compensate the woman who was trying to sell it. The woman had a gentle gaze and a distracted manner and admittedly also a flipper for one arm.

Later, when she thought of the magazine cover, she also thought of printed words on the trivet: The Hanging Gardens of Babylon.

On the cover of the magazine was a picture: the porkpie hat perched on some pipes, possibly in a factory. Later she learned the porkpie hat had been a stand-in for Oppenheimer at the height of his fame. After Hiroshima and Nagasaki, when the bombs had been dropped, the war was over and the Father of the Atom Bomb was a hero, the hat actually posed alone for photographs.

As an ambassador, the hat had a simple message. It said: I am worn by a gentleman.

It said: We are all gentlemen here.

☙ In the scene that was not quite a dream she saw the man named Oppenheimer kneeling in the desert when the first atomic bomb went off, and he was wearing his characteristic porkpie hat.

The scene had other elements, such as a squirrel shaped like a long balloon, dragging its belly on the ground. The squirrel came before Oppenheimer and then it retired politely. The squirrel was not present when the mushroom cloud rose over the horizon on its slowly twisting stem.

Neither was her mother, who had also been in the dream when it was still a dream, before it drew itself out of a well of sleep. Twelve years old, her mother rode a blue bicycle along the top of a white wall. She saw not the color blue in the dream but only the word *blue, blue bicycle*. Her mother did not need to hold the handlebars and she was proud of this; her hands were in the air, flitting birdlike as she rode. From the ends of the bicycle handles sprouted bright-colored strips of plastic, and on her small fingers the little mothergirl wore bulging candy rings. Color was at her hands.

Watching the girl ride along the wall, almost dreaming, her heart broke that she had never known her mother when she was young. As she turned in the sheets, hot, almost waking completely, she thought: She will never be young again. None of us will ever, ever be young again.

She wanted to cry, but was more thirsty.

Nothing was present at the end of the scene. Squirrels, mothers, bicycles vanished. And the faint, dry aftertaste of it all was only a porkpie hat.

As soon as we know it, it is gone.

When she realized she was awake she also realized she was

sweating, and her shirt was sticking to her skin. She flicked on the nightstand lamp.

How this particular woman, Ann, would have looked to an observer then, a so-called peeping tom for example, staring in the window, was this: she was a white woman, young, small, with a thin, muscled torso and a delicate, fine-boned face. She was sweating and the rings of sweat under her arms, soaking her cotton tank top, made her look like a fresh army recruit in boot camp, someone new to obstacle courses and discipline. In the past, people had caught sight of her and called her "wholesome." They had said, many people on many different occasions—She's so wholesome looking.

Her husband Ben was next to her in bed, and she looked down at him in the dim light cast by the bedside lamp. It occurred to her that he was not the Father of the Atom Bomb. He lay sleeping; his face was collapsed. He had nothing to hide, or if he did he had no will to hide it, she thought. If something lay hidden, he slept beside it unknowing.

It also occurred to her that Ben was not only *not* the Father of the Atom Bomb but less a father than a child, at least compared to the man in the desert. Feeling poised on the brink of a discovery she knew, at the same time, she would never make, she thought the words *a baby*. The man in the desert had been as old as the hills but also ageless.

She studied her husband's dark hair with its few gray strands at the temples, the wings of his eyelids casting shadows across his pale cheeks, and was guilty: she had condescended to him. Even though he was sleeping and could not read her mind, he would never know it, true, but still it stood. There was an insult in that involuntary gesture of pity. She felt a pang of sorrow for both of them. But it was not childlike to be defenseless, she told herself: defenseless and weak are not the same, they are nothing alike.

No, she reassured herself as she got up and changed shirts, in fact it is the strong who feels no need to defend himself, any idiot knows that.

She padded to the bathroom and brushed her teeth absently, thinking that not having brushed them might be what was keeping her awake. Grainy teeth.

It is the weak who act ferocious, she thought, those small, yappy dogs, those tiny inbred dogs with high-pitched, shrieking barks, leash-straining, frantic, leaping savagely at huge placid Dobermans trotting past.

It takes courage, she thought, to be one in a multitude.

—The wine, she said aloud in recognition.

White wine made her maudlin.

Looking into her face in the mirror she flicked out the bathroom light and her face disappeared in the blankness of dark. Then, climbing into bed again, gently to keep the mattress from jiggling, she thought: We both lie here every night with secrets all around us.

The truth of it grazed her like a feather, brushing as faintly as a breeze but leaving a burn of feeling in its wake. We have no knives, no guns, no weapons, we have no armor at all, we lie here without barriers, near a paper-thin window, she thought, and shivered under the blankets. We are naked as the bulbs of flowers. We may not be children, we may not be innocent at all, but we will always be easy to hurt.

That was something of which she felt sure, as she looked down at Ben sleeping, propping herself up on an elbow on the sloping, fat pillow. Easy to hurt, nothing could be easier.

❧ Ben had been woken by her restless movement and was only feigning sleep. He was doing so in order to allow Ann to fall asleep again, in order not to prevent her from taking her rest. As he lay beside her knowing she was awake he wished to gather her up in his arms and put himself in her body.

But Ann did not always sleep easily and he knew this. He was worried about her sleeplessness, how it might age her before it was her turn to be old. Sleep, he had read, is even more important for health and longevity than a nutritious diet.

That there could be a time after her, a time when he was alone, actually made him cringe if he dwelled on it too long: how empty all the buildings would be, and the streets of cities. Cavernous and gray they would echo the sound of his voice.

Shuddering he pressed his face into her shoulder, and felt the sympathy of her leaning toward him, her cheek against the crown of his head. She still believed he was sleeping.

He breathed her skin and told himself a story to drift away. Once in the future, on the surface of the moon, there were thousands who raised their arms. They sang in a tone he could not hear, beyond the threshold of the human ear. But to look at them was enough: white like ghosts, their faces beaming, they were arrayed in great number, as far as the eye could see. Behind them the mountains of the moon rose up like pillars in the airless sky.

❧ She had grown up on a street where, at dusk on a calm day, a woman could stand on her front porch with a cocktail in her slim hand and hear the faint laughing splashes from seven swimming pools at once. Long, dark cars pulled into driveways with their silent engines purring, black men pushed lawnmowers, there were houses for finches like small wooden cathedrals.

There were even old trees with spreading limbs that shaded her as she played.

This street of green lawns on hills, velvet bands in the sky at dusk, and the smell of barbecue as the heat of the day rose away was not where Ben spent his formative years. Ben lived lifetimes of exhaustion before he was ten.

But when she was a child the ground had been steady beneath her feet, and in the spring and the summer she had grass stains on her tennis shoes. The tennis shoes had always been new, and as soon as they were gray her mother bought her fresh white ones. She picked crab apples from the trees in the schoolyard and played with the smiling girls across the street, whose parents came from Holland. They liked to perch pipe-cleaner tiaras on their heads and pretend they were queens and princesses. They dressed in old clothes that smelled of mothballs, which they fished from a wicker trunk in the play room, and pranced up and down the street on silver platform shoes with their flowing robes trailing behind them. They had sung loudly as they paraded down the street, sung at the top of their lungs.

The platform shoes, her mother had told her later, were all she had kept from the sixties.

Of course there had been slights, disappointments, the shock of the world. She had been left alone once or twice and felt abandoned, forgotten by others. She knew she was only a narrow slip of existence.

When the family dog was hit by a car she stood with her face to the wall for fourteen hours. —Do other kids kill themselves when their puppies die? she asked her father, wracked with sobs, having seen the dear brown body twisted against the curb. Laying the dog to rest on a bed of tissue paper in a liquor box he had told her —Not very often, honey.

So instead she nobly turned to the wall in mourning.

Her mother and her father had not interfered. They let her be noble and watery with grief in silence. Once, in passing, her mother stooped to kiss the top of her head in a benediction, and then moved around the room tidying and humming.

The house was sweet with cleanness and always the same, fans whirring on the high ceilings with their dark crossbeams. She and her brothers floated in the pool on blowup whales and alligators until their thin, sleek calves and bony shoulders were evenly toasted. Her mother, who often wore a string of pearls around her neck, liked to bake bread and the smell of the baking bread would waft through the open windows and over the lilac bushes.

Ben had never known anything like that.

She pushed her fingertips against his temple, stroking a wing of his hair. Then she flicked the light off again.

Innocent and ignorant, she thought sadly, turning to lie on her back, there's no real difference, actually we are both. Finally our ignorance consumes us, licking our backs with tongues of fire. And behind us the earth is left black.

What odd monsters will walk here after us, she wondered then, staring up.

She thought of them roaming the plains, the aftermen, their legs as tall as buildings but as thin as wire. She saw them bounding over the barren wastes like giant mosquitoes.

She wondered if they would be the leavings of men, the grandsons of robots, their veins and sinews delicate skeins of wire. Or if men had left nothing they might be the descendants of beetles and dragonflies. She tried to imagine their hearts, metal and polymer or muscle and blood.

And if there is memory then, if there is any recollection, it is our ignorance that will be remembered, she thought. Our innocence will be forgotten, our kittens will not go down in history.

A few minutes later, restless under the sheets, she thought: Secrets have lain waiting in matter, down through the centuries.

❧ The soldier who chose Julius Robert Oppenheimer as lead scientist for the Manhattan Project was General Leslie R. Groves. A West Point graduate and an engineer by training, Groves had built the Pentagon before he set to work building the A-bomb to win the war against the fascists. "I'm not prejudiced," he once said. "I don't like certain Jews, and I don't like certain well-known characteristics of theirs, but I'm not prejudiced."

Although he admired Oppenheimer he hated Leo Szilard. Convinced Hitler was working toward an A-bomb or would be soon, Szilard had persuaded Albert Einstein to sign a letter he wrote to Roosevelt in 1939. With this letter they alerted the president to the possibility of an atomic bomb and thus, rather lamentably for two pacifist academics, touched off the nuclear arms race.

Later, Groves tried to have Szilard imprisoned as an enemy of the state. "If there were to be any villain of this piece," he said, "I'd say it was Szilard."

He also wrote of Szilard, as marginalia in a book: "He was completely unprincipled, amoral, and immoral."

In 1948 Groves retired from military service to work in the private sector, as a Vice President of the RAND Corporation. He died in 1970 of heart disease.

❧ As for Szilard, he thought Groves was a moron. It was Szilard who made up the term *breeder reactor.*

❧ Finally Ann got up again because she was still turning in the sheets.

The floors were red clay tile and cool against her bare feet. As she walked noiselessly through the rooms she touched certain fixtures and furnishings, letting her fingertips drift over their surfaces: the candles on iron stands, which smelled of vanilla and orange, the soft, old wood of sideboards and shelves, the soft, fibrous paper of a lampshade that gave off a faint, warm glow. The walls of the house were hung with paintings lent or given to her and Ben by a friend who owned an art gallery, and their amber and gold oils were carefully lit. She pulled the sliding doors open and stepped outside onto the flagstone patio.

There was a mild night wind and a new moon. Sitting down on the edge of the fountain with gray shrubs and flowers around her ankles—sage, for instance, and lamb's ear, and a plant that Ben called hens 'n' chicks—she could smell basil and mint and lavender growing ten feet away. She knew the name of other flowers she could see faintly in the dark: columbine, sego lilies. Water in the fountain trickled, faint and itchy, and she listened. Her arms were bare and the breeze lifted the fine hairs.

She thought of the child. She had decided a few days ago to throw away her pills, the three weeks of estrogen, the single week of placebos. Ben had wanted her to do this for years. Boundless love, like the boundless sky, seemed easier to make than earn.

You made your own, of course. There was no guarantee of theirs.

Even if there were dangers, even if the rivers and seas and the fish that swam them were flowing with mercury, forests were being felled and deserts turned into strip mines, there was nothing to do but trust. If she had been given a choice before she was conceived, say to exist in chaos or not to exist at all: Chaos, she would have said. She would have said, not without sadness of course, still: let me come. Let me watch as all things fall apart.

There was no birdsong. It was the silence before dawn, when the birds do not sing, the stopped time after dreams in which men die with their eyes on the ceiling, throats aching with tears, arms leaden beside them on the cold sheets.

Later she would think that was the first time she ever understood the danger: the more beautiful a house, the more invisible the rest of the world.

❧ Ben, the husband of Ann, who at that moment was sleeping again, was a gardener.

He thought of himself first as the husband of Ann, and only second as a gardener. More than most husbands, possibly, he liked to be a husband. It was a vocation, whereas gardens were merely a hobby that paid.

They lived in Santa Fe, New Mexico, where they were surrounded by slick restaurants and boutiques, upscale art galleries and also those that catered to the tourist trade selling paintings of purple and pink desert landscapes, trinket stores that sold oxydized copper Kokopelli statues and coyote bookends and five-gallon hats and leather boots with six-inch fringes, celebrity refugees from Hollywood who kept toy ranches in the hills and liked to pretend they were cowboys.

In fact they lived less than an hour's winding drive from the city of Los Alamos, on the high pink and gray mesa with its juniper trees and piñon bushes, salvia and chamisa, a city that had barely existed before World War Two and where, from 1943 to 1945, hundreds of Manhattan Project scientists, working under Oppenheimer, had built the world's first atomic bomb and where, still, nuclear weapons were designed and redesigned, nuclear secrets kept and broken. They lived a little more than two hours from White Sands Missile Range in the Alamogordo desert, in the shadow of the Oscura mountains, home to a sea of flowing, shifting white gypsum dunes. Beyond the dunes in the fluvial-alluvial soil of the ancient Rio Grande valley had grown quietly, for thousands of years, giant flowering soaptree yuccas, globe mallow and fourwing saltbush and mint-green ethereal winterfat, jackrabbits and kit foxes and porcupines and herds of delicate galloping pronghorn antelope, until the predawn darkness of July 16, 1945, when a strange cloud blossomed over all of them.

⤳ What happened was, the night of the dream three men were born again. One was born in a motel room, one in a gutter. And the third was born again beneath a table that smelled of french fries and disinfectant, in a cafeteria at the University of Chicago.

2

❧ Oppenheimer lay on a bed in a motel in his expensive suit. He felt stunned and lay without knowing where he was, in a tingling and static dark. Finally, still queasy but also restless, he reached a hand out into the treacherous thick air and fumbled with objects on the nightstand. Flicked at what felt like the switch for a table lamp. Light blazed.

He was in a motel room, shoddy and dim. In front of him and above hung a box with an opaque gray screen, a glass screen of some kind on a black platform, protruding from the wall. Kidnapped? Could some enemy power—Germans, Japanese, even the Russians, those so-called allies—be watching him from the other side of that convex glass?

—Remain calm, he told himself.

He had been surrounded by soldiers at the countdown. No abduction would have been possible. He had just been there, crouched, waiting for ignition in the desert, in the dark, a little after five in the morning, his crowd of other geniuses surrounding him, holding their breath as he held his. And then the blast, that great and terrible flower, that sear of lightness lifting up the sky.

And now he was here.

But where was here, and why was he? He must have been injured by the blast. That was it. This was some kind of dark infirmary.

Plucking at his shirt he felt no pain, however, and there were no cuts or bruises: a head injury? Brain damage? Possibly he had simply been knocked unconscious and they had left him to rest in peace in this dim and ugly room, the best Socorro had to offer. But my God: what was that painting? It was outrageous! On the wall opposite, as he pushed himself up on his elbows to look, was a hideous watercolor of a girl child grasping a fistful of tulips.

It unnerved him. There was an offensive, crass quality to the thing. Something was wrong with the flowers in the young girl's pale orange bouquet, their pink-purple whorls and openings. Dead, dead wrong. It seemed geared to evoke the fantasies of a pervert.

If he was injured where was Kitty? They should have summoned her right away. He had to look outside. He had to know where he was.

He got up unsteadily and went to the door, whose faintly greasy knob featured an oddly printed DO NOT DISTURB sign, and jerked it open. Dark outside, and all he could see was a parking lot, vast, buildings in the background, all crowded close together, which he surveyed from a second-floor walkway. Civilian buildings, dense and well-used: this was not the mesa and he did not think it was Socorro.

He stumbled onto the walkway and made his way to the stairs and down them, where, in front of a door marked OFFICE, which was all too brightly lit but untenanted, he saw a newspaper box.

Ye gods, it claimed the price of the paper was 35 cents! He laughed aloud and leaned down to look through the clear panel and discover what marvel of the Fourth Estate might be worth this king's ransom. *The Santa Fe New Mexican.* Santa Fe, by God, he had always felt at home here. But a newspaper like this? It was slick.

Although, straightening up and looking around, he didn't know this part of this city, if it *was* Santa Fe: a slum, industrial, concrete and asphalt everywhere. He could pick out almost no trees in the darkness. It had to be a bigger place, possibly Albuquerque.

But good lord, the date on the paper was a joke too. March 1, 2003.

He was exhausted. He had been working long hours and forgetting to eat. This was delirium, thick and heavy on him as though a large man was pushing down on his shoulders from behind. Groves, possibly. He felt burdened. Yes: and the burden was intolerable, finally. Sleep was required. Look at him!—he might be mistaken for a hobo and thrown out of here on his heel. His clothes were wrinkled and needed to be pressed.

He squinted at the cars in the parking lot and though it was too dark to see well he thought their shapes were strange, the cars were small and strange, both sleek and complicated at once, jarring and shiny hulks. Maybe this was an Army outpost after all, one he had never known; possibly like the mesa it was a locus for the development of new technologies. Leave it, though: in the morning things would be clearer. Right now he was overcome by fatigue. He would go back to bed.

Veering away from the newspaper box to go up to his room again he suddenly smelled garbage, a rank, rotten smell, and then saw a kid walking by carrying a large flat box marked PIZZA.

—Excuse me? he asked the boy. —Did you see the date on this paper?

—What?

—The date on the newspaper here.

The kid leaned over and looked, nodded briefly.

—So what?

—Kind of an odd gag, isn't it? H. G. Wells?

—Sorry. I don't get it, said the kid, and shrugged before he continued walking, the pizza box on his shoulder.

—I mean what's the date today? called Oppenheimer after him.

—It's the first, said the kid.

—But what year?

—Get outta here, man, said the kid.

In the office he rang a bell, but no one came to the desk. Another of the gray-screened boxes hung on the wall. The counter featured machinery he had never seen before. Was this a foreign country? No: they were selling the *New Mexican* right outside. Still, hard to put his finger on it, but few of the objects on the desk looked familiar. He had spent time in many well-equipped offices over the past three years and never had he seen one like this. Flat dark adding machines lying there with buttons barely raised from their surfaces, another box with a screen that blared bright, near-royal blue, and white words stood out from it, holding tight and vibrat-ing, both at once. He could not read them; the glare of the light was too bright.

No one came to his assistance, but turning around to leave he caught sight of a calendar on the wall.

Again: 2003.

Stupid. How dare they allow this to happen to him, after all he had given them.

All he wanted was sleep.

～ For a while after the dream Ann did not think about Oppen-heimer, the so-called Father of the Atom Bomb, physicist and genius.

She had no reason to think about Oppenheimer in her waking life and she seldom remembered her dreams. When she did they tended to be dreams she thought were trivial: dreams in which her hair had been elaborately curled and was weighing down her head, dreams in which she had not been warned there was a test, dreams of wooden spoons, breadfruit, and once an angry monkey.

She did not think about Oppenheimer per se but she remem-bered the bent man and the death-light. She remembered waking up sweating, and staying up until the sun rose, and the bitter, dry aftertaste.

～ Szilard, in his first conscious minute in the new world, was kicked in the ribs by a freshman named Tad. Tad's real name was Thaddeus Baysden Newton III, originally of Columbia, South Car-olina, and currently of the Delta Kappa Epsilon fraternity, whose brothers were commonly referred to in the University of Chicago Greek community as Dekes, renowned for courageous beer swill-ing. Tad was wearing a bulky shoe on his size twelve foot and the fat man grunted loudly when the toe of it caught him sharply in the sternum, causing Tad to bend down and look under the cafeteria's formica-topped booth with the expostulation —What the fuck!

What Tad saw was a fat man, jowls drooping like a Basset hound's, lying on his side on the floor, bleary-eyed and disoriented.

—A fucking homeless drunk on the floor, man.

—What is the world coming to, said his fellow DKE, name of Gil short for Gilman, shaking his head in disgust.

They picked up their orange trays and trudged over to the next free table.

❧ When he was a boy Ben had read voraciously with a weak flashlight under a threadbare brown blanket: comic books, works of fantasy, science fiction, horror. On the other side of the flimsy wall his mother had been wracked with coughs as he read. His father, a kind man but short of words, had worked on the lot at a place that sold secondhand camper shells for trucks, as well as used appliances for RVs. He had a second job as a busboy, and a third as a night watchman. He slept only three hours in every twenty-four, from seven until ten in the morning, but he insisted he had never needed more.

Ben had sneaked into the movies through the back door where Gary the janitor smoked. Gary slipped him in after his cigarette break, and crouching he would find a place in the front row, his head tipped back beneath the screen's immensity.

He still daydreamed in boxes and fields of color, rich and perfect, the lines between them bold and black. There were few straight edges in the world of soils, shrubs, and trees, of pests, butterflies, and hummingbirds, in other words his professional milieu, so the satisfaction he derived there came not in exact, clean measures and angles but voluptuous patterns.

He thought often of his wife as he worked, and behind the work there was always a grateful peace, the peace of a man who has more than he expected to have. Sentimental only in this one reach of life, attempting in the rest a businesslike detach, he was prone to seek comfort in memories of his wife, recollection and anticipation. The first time her skin had touched his own the texture of the world had changed, grown warmer but also more expansive. He had felt permeable then; he had seeped into everything and everything into him.

The first trip they made together, after two nervous dinners, had been in a car that belonged to some of his friends. He remembered it clearly: a mid-sized sedan with a gray interior. They sat awkwardly side by side in the back seat. It was early fall and they were being driven south to a wildlife refuge named Bosque del Apache, an artificial oasis in the middle of the desert where they hoped to see birds. In the front seat his friends, an older, academic couple he had worked for who were amateur ornithologists, who kept immaculate life lists of all the birds they had seen, were talking about cormorants, and from cormorants they moved to herons and from herons to egrets. They told of bird-watching weekends in Patagonia, Guadalupe, and the Salton Sea, and of all the birds of North America that flew for thousands of miles each year in migration. Neither Ann nor Ben was educated on the identities and behaviors of birds, so they remained silent.

Over the murmur in the front they both floated away, both gazed out their windows at the rolling tan mountains and the light sky. And as they softened in their seats, carried over the blacktop impervious and aloft, as they rested on the gray imitation leather, Ann looked at Ben and moved her hand over the cool smooth slope of the vinyl seat to touch his wrist.

Fullness surged.

Of course he did have preferences beyond the fact of her existence; but that was all they were, a set of requests. Nothing was actually necessary beyond what he already had, any added pleasure or comfort he was willing to forgo if need be. In the center were the two of them, bound together, and what rotated, what clung, what distant satellite might orbit them in a faint attraction, far out from the core held fast, was mostly empty space.

❧ Before the Trinity test, the physicist Edward Teller—later known as the Father of the Hydrogen Bomb, a famously passionate advocate for the nuclear arms buildup—calculated that the heat of the first atomic explosion might be sufficient to ignite and consume the world's atmosphere. Subsequent calculations showed this was unlikely: there was only a three-in-a-million chance, the physicists in charge of the test decided, that the atmosphere would be ignited.

Enrico Fermi, however, who liked a good wager, made a jesting offer on the morning of the test.

"I invite bets," he said, "against first the destruction of all human life and second just that of human life in New Mexico."

Physicists are well known for their sense of humor.

❧ Oppenheimer's first full day at the motel was devoted to television. He located the remote on the bedside table, where it sat beside the enigmatic telephone with its sheet of intricate numeric instructions, and eventually by pressing the button marked POWER discovered its function.

There had been some false starts while he held the remote sideways and attempted to type on its buttons, pointing it randomly at the ceiling, the door, and his face. Finally, when he noticed it shared a brand name with the black box on the wall, he had moved it toward the box.

After that he lay on the bed staring at show after show, a barrage of stimuli his eyes and mind had never known, a primer in pop culture, a primer in history. The motel, though cheap, had free cable and non-stop movies.

He gathered that he was far away from where he had just been. He was no longer in Los Alamos in 1945; or alternatively he was no longer a self-steering mind but one lost, gone floating off its moorings. Carefully he reserved his judgment.

The next morning he emerged from his room into daylight and

lost himself in a larger panorama still, people, cars, and buildings flowing past as he strolled out of the motel lot and down the street. He looked at everything, but he spoke to no one. He was aghast.

⮞ Noteworthy in Ben, perhaps this is already clear, was his devotion.

⮞ In life Oppenheimer was a tall man, tall and gaunt, handsome with luminous blue eyes; he was a Jewish man who loved the Bhagavad-Gita, who held fast to his creed of Ahimsa: At least do no harm while he directed the making of the first weapon of mass destruction. He was an intellectual from the city of New York, the grandson of poor immigrants who became importers of suit linings, who became purveyors of ready-made garments in the city of New York. His delicate mother had a deformed hand, which she kept concealed in a long glove. He was the husband of a woman named Kitty who drank too much.

Oppenheimer died of cancer in 1967.

⮞ Then there was Ann: in good health, she was confident in her marriage, satisfied, and secure. She worked at the public library and gave to local and national charities, typically modest amounts in response to direct mail. She preferred gentle, reasonable solicitations to those that shrilled "This bunny was blinded by hairspray!" Of course, in recent times bad things were happening: planes flew into buildings and democracy was waning. War was everywhere erupting and as people multiplied obscenely and advanced on open space they were driving all the plants and animals extinct.

But much of this was far away. The world kept its distance.

Although she was sometimes withdrawn and thoughtful she had never been prone to depression, had never in fact suffered from any major affliction, disorder or syndrome described by the

American Psychiatric Association. In other words there was little in her makeup to presage disruption, little on which, subsequently, to look back and nod knowingly.

It was a day in March with low skies and rain threatening, and she had walked Ben to work on her way to the library. He was helping to design and plant a garden for a middle-aged couple who had just bought one of the largest adobe houses in east Santa Fe. It had been said that this man and his wife had been in business together in high finance on Wall Street, and together had perfected what she once heard described as "the art of the leveraged buyout." In fact they were practically the inventors, it was said, of the leveraged buyout.

She did not understand this. It did not sound like "inventors of the player piano." It did not sound like "inventors of the donut."

They had hundreds of millions of dollars at their disposal, Ben had told her, and so they had casually bought one of the largest adobe houses in east Santa Fe. Strictly speaking it was a mansion, not a house. She had seen the mansion long before, when others had owned it, and she liked the high adobe walls around it, the walls that were so thick that they themselves had roofs. She liked the old acequias that flowed beneath the house, some of which dated from 1700. She liked the hand-carved wooden gates and the apple trees; she liked the lilacs and sand plums that grew against the walls, scraping on the curved tiles when the wind blew.

But the inventors of the leveraged buyout found little to like in the house, despite the quickness of their purchase. One thing they did not like was the mansion's garden, so they bulldozed it. And then they hired Ben, along with a well-reputed Japanese landscape architect named Yoshi, to make them some new gardens.

Ben was often invited to the homes of clients after he had worked for them. He rarely accepted these invitations, and when he did it was always in consultation with Ann. And then, when Ann and Ben arrived at the dinner or cocktail party, the woman of the house would introduce him fondly to her guests—often, Ann had observed, with a proprietary air. —This is my gardener, the hostess would say, or "landscaper," or even "garden consultant" or "horticulturist," and once, with relish, "yard man."

And typically the man of the house would give Ben a brief sidelong glance, grudging and skeptical. If Ben and Ann were the only guests the host might clap him on the back and steer him through the house showing him the expensive items, stereos or plasma televisions or kitchen appliances in brushed stainless. He might do this casually, as though, despite the fact that he wished to give the tour, it was his wife who insisted on owning everything.

Once, while Ann lingered in the background, a husband had shown Ben the head of a Dall sheep he had shot in Alaska, now mounted on a peach-colored wall. He told Ben a story about the kill—a trek that had lasted for days, the report of which involved the timeless phrase *slithering on our bellies*—and then led him away to show him something else, leaving her in front of the sheep head. She stood there, without knowing it, for half an hour, gazing into the dark, dewy glass eyes where she wandered and lost herself. She felt the city receding behind her, its twinkling lights forgotten, felt herself leaving the city as she walked through the gates of the eyes. In the eyes there was welcome, an envelope of pity.

Oh sweetheart, they said, *you see, there's no more they can do to me.*

Finally the wife had come in from the living room to retrieve her. Ann had followed her in a daze past an altar to the goddess and a beadwork tapestry to where the guests sat drinking frozen margaritas and eating mixed nuts in the living room, beneath a vaulted ceiling with a tinted skylight. The women were clustered together on a black-and-white cowhide sofa, talking about how it felt to be Rolfed. The men stood outside the sliding doors on the patio, one of them flipping steaks on the barbecue with long tongs.

Ann was not afraid she would be stuffed and mounted.

Ben's employers often treated Ann as though she was a book-end to him, the two of them a matched set, both slight and shy, except with each other, and tending to smile gently when nervous. Moreover she was a librarian, which was felt to be quaint and properly humble, not unlike gardening.

It was a day with low, dark banks of thunderclouds that might produce dramatic storms, storms that would make the high desert turbulent, an epic country. She was looking forward to the smell of the rain, its cool fragrant breezes, and warm blankets tucked around her and Ben at night. The large adobe mansion was not far away from her small adobe house, and Ben had left his battered truck there the night before. So she walked down the long hill with him until they came to the mansion; she walked him over the bull-dozed soil, feeling the texture of mounds of fresh dirt beneath her feet, past a polished Mercedes and a dusky violet Jaguar to where his truck was parked, its doors and windows splattered with mud.

He kissed her on the lips and the eyebrow, and she turned and went up the hill and away.

❧ When he left the motel on his second morning, wearing his rumpled suit, porkpie hat and polished shoes, all of which he had found in a suitcase in the motel room closet, Oppenheimer stopped in the lobby first to ask for directions. A pimply clerk handed him a complimentary Santa Fe map on what appeared to be a paper placemat.

He folded the map carefully and placed it in his inside jacket pocket; then he asked the clerk how one traveled to Los Alamos on a limited budget.

As far as he knew all the money he had was the few bills in his wallet; he was in a city that had some of the attributes of Santa Fe and purported to be Santa Fe but barely resembled the mountain settlement of rounded adobe buildings and narrow, winding streets that he knew from half a century before. He was unsure of his situation and did not want to spend money on taxis.

The clerk apparently knew nothing about public buses. He said jokingly that if he stood beside the road with a sign that said LOS ALAMOS someone would eventually stop and drive him up the hill for free.

Oppenheimer nodded curtly. The clerk seemed surprised, but nonetheless, when asked, provided a piece of cardboard and a thick black marker.

Following his directions Oppenheimer made his way at a leisurely pace to the intersection of two freeways. Along the way he stopped in a drugstore, one far more extensive than any he had seen before. It offered, besides drugs and cosmetics, a vast selection of liquor, children's toys, kitchenware, an entire wall of refrigerated sodas, and miscellaneous containers of all kinds. Many of these containers were made of a hardy and translucent plastic, and he picked them up, palpated and sniffed them curiously. Finally he bought a pair of sunglasses for $3.99. He had rarely worn sunglasses before but the vivid brilliance of the sky was hurting his eyes.

After only five minutes standing at the side of the road he was picked up by a man in a torn shirt driving what looked like a race car. He was relieved at the brevity of the wait and slid jauntily, albeit on unsteady legs into the low-slung, deep seat. He was immediately faced with a worn sticker on the dash that read TWISTED SISTER. This left him feeling nonplussed.

The car moved fast when it jolted forward, far faster than any he had driven himself. The momentum was dizzying.

The driver had tied his long hair back in a ponytail and slicked down the front with pomade. He was apparently of a deeply religious bent since his upper right arm bore an intricate tattoo of St. George slaying the dragon, not with a sword but with what looked like an oversize Tommy gun. It jetted a spray of crimson bullets into the dragon's face. Oppenheimer gaped openly, first at the extensive ornamentation of his benefactor and then at the roads around them as they sped along, so slick, wide, and fast. The driver talked about Jesus for most of the drive, in highly laudatory terms, to which Oppenheimer, though distracted by the speed and the road, listened politely. Occasionally he interjected a comment on the Scriptures, which he had always read with great interest.

Just as they passed a sign that read LOS ALAMOS CITY LIMITS, however, the driver became agitated and began to talk also about righteousness, purity, homosexual Sodomites and finally those dirty Christ-killers the Jews.

At this point Oppenheimer asked in civil, if anxious tones to be let out, thanked the driver and began to wander through what was apparently the city of Los Alamos, though he did not recognize it.

The city was clearly no longer a closed community run by the Army, though the nuclear lab had still not thrown its doors open wide to the public. But more affecting than this administrative shift was the physical transformation. He had not admired the aesthetics of the cheap Army buildings thrown up in haste to house Project personnel—far from it—but what was this? He reviled what had taken their place.

The rutted mud streets had been replaced by wide, slick blacktop roads, clean and blank as an embalmer's slab. Rows of squat, bland buildings were set far back from these all-powerful, all-seeing avenues on flat, square lots scraped free of vegetation, the land itself robbed of shape along the sweeping roads, flattened by what must have been legions of heavy earth-moving machines.

The mesa had been a place of elegant and windswept isolation, a place where it was possible to be alone and feel the presence of God. He had wanted it to revert to wilderness one day. When the soldiers, the engineers and the scientists had all left he had wanted it turned back to open space, abandoned ranches and yellow grass and sage scrub or a small, bucolic town. He had wanted it to be a place that history had moved through once fleetingly, with no trace of the past blowing through the high silver branches of its solitary trees.

But the wide streets were treeless now. In place of trees there were telephone poles.

He wandered through the town looking at the cheap modern buildings, shivering in his shirtsleeves. He always forgot it was colder up here than down in Santa Fe. Finally he found himself at a small building labeled BRADBURY SCIENCE MUSEUM, and shuffled past the reception desk and across the carpet in a daze. He forgot to pay the price of admission but the presiding volunteer, overcome by surging schoolchildren, failed to notice or stop him. Inside he sat down in the first chair he saw.

It was a hard chair in front of a television monitor. Beside him sat an older woman in dark slacks and a red-and-white-striped blouse in some slick silky fabric that was far too small for the heavy slope of her massive, pearlike breasts. He glanced sidelong at her and thought: Madam, your burden is heavy.

It had always been his understanding that, in cases where there was such a rude superabundance of flesh, girdles were de rigueur. Women of a certain age in particular, he thought, did not even like to leave the privacy of their boudoirs without the support and decency of whalebone or a less expensive substitute. But then here there were young girls on the streets with their midriffs showing, their navels actually exposed to the open air. And more disturbing still, he had seen a boy whose massive bluejeans, in which he seemed to wade with difficulty as though treading through quicksand, actually commenced fully beneath the lower edge of his buttocks. It was an engineering marvel that they did not fall down— either that or a sleight-of-hand trick.

At that point a busload of schoolchildren ran loud and distracted behind him, bouncing from wall to wall, glancing only briefly at pictures and shouting taunts and mockeries at each other.

—That's so fake! yelled one of them barely a foot from his ear, as though even the idea of history was a trick.

Taunting a schoolmate, another boy said: —You fuckin' fag, then who's the big fat faggot now, huh bitch?

Oppenheimer sat frozen at his station for some time, pondering the obscenity. Out of the mouths of babes. They were a rough tribe, possibly juvenile delinquents. To call them ill-behaved would be an understatement; no doubt they were children from a specialized facility.

On the monitor he saw short videos—he had just learned the word *video* in his motel and liked it, a Latin verb in common usage, people actually said "I wanna see a video," he had learned, which literally meant, of course, "I want to see an I-see"—about the Manhattan Project. They showed the Trinity test and the use of the A-bomb on Hiroshima, and even he himself was pictured, right there in black and white, wearing his favorite hat, which he now held carefully on his lap.

He clutched the hat, his hands shaking uncontrollably.

He and the hat had been transported together.

On the monitor he saw the mushroom cloud. It had been captured on film, he realized with detachment, by Berlyn Brixner who had worked on the mesa in the Optics group, brought to Site Y by their mutual friend David Hawkins. Hawkins was a philosopher by trade but in wartime had accepted a position as the official Los Alamos historian. Oppenheimer had known they were making history; he had known this was a process that should be recorded, even then, and hired a scholar for the job. It was not a task that could be entrusted to the military. One thing for which he could take credit: he had never mistaken the endeavor for anything less than it was. He had never thought it was not important, that they would not, after some fashion at least, make history.

He remembered this man Brixner, the photographer, when he saw the mushroom cloud rising and blossoming on the monitor, small and contained. Brixner, Hawkins, Serber, Alvarez, Groves, all these men, different men, fat and thin, arrogant and modest, some with senses of humor, others dry as a bone. He had liked some of them and disliked others, but to all of them he had given his support, all of them had had his shoulder to cry on or his ear to complain into when the pressure was great, and that, at least, was something of which to be proud. All of them together: this was what they had made, all those millions, or in fact, if Groves could be taken at his word, *billions* of dollars. He remembered Hanford and the Columbia River, the river of sweet pink salmon and the plutonium flowing there.

That and the mystery of the young boy's trousers, held beneath his buttocks by some invisible force. These questions must be answered.

Watching the video he registered not the strange, anomalous cloud but the rest of what he had lost, the vacuum that was left. That was what it looked like at a glance. It was sucking a vacuum on the ground, blistering a hole in the sky. It was vengeance on them all: it was the unspeakable and the divine.

It had taken everything.

The people he had known, he'd been with yesterday, all gone, gone from him now or he was gone from them, a robbed soul, a victim. He felt it like a tearing loss, felt it weaken his knees as he sat there, how they had all disappeared in the blink of an eye, in the space between seconds. He felt at once the outrage of his absence from that scene he had made, the production he had authored, with its ponderous massive godhead looming over the land.

Kitty. Where was his wife? Was she dead now, or had she only forgotten him? And the children, taken. Where were they? He felt panic rising. Other people had known them, but not him.

All that was what it claimed to be, if this was the future and time had gone on without him.

They had worked together, he and all of these men. They had

striven so hard all these weeks, so earnest in the enterprise, laboring in a fever of concentration and letting their families fall by the wayside, knowing they were the priesthood of the atom. They had believed staunchly in Roosevelt before he died and in Niels Bohr, the great man, his own mentor, a scientist for peace. They had known they were fighting the good fight, but then again—it was clear to him now as the cloud rolled outward—by the same token they had believed everything, they had been like children. They had been willing to accept every word he said to them, he realized suddenly, and there had been no deception: he had believed the words himself. And yet while he was reassuring them, plying his logic and his wit and gracious speech—he would admit it, he rose to the occasion, occasionally even he with his mere gifts was capable of eloquence—he had actually known nothing.

That was what he saw now. All he had known was how to make science into faith, or at least that had been his pretension. He had known nothing, despite his erudition or maybe because of it, possibly the layers of information had smothered what lay beneath. He had known nothing at all, finally, and now his own ignorance stunned him.

He ran the footage from the Trinity shot repeatedly, pressing the button that started the video again and again. As he watched the shot, the cloud that transformed itself as it rose, he finally forgot about individuals, forgot about the others who had been there with him. At first he had remembered their gestures and habits, the texture of them had come home with startling force as he watched the cloud rise and burgeon, its pregnant violence spread rolling and tumbling over the sky, spectacular and obscene birth.

But now he was losing them as he began to see the cloud for what it was, grandeur and mass. It took so many forms: at first it was a dome, then a bell, then a jellyfish. People called it a mushroom cloud: he heard it all around him.

At first he had not fathomed its enormity. When he was there, although it had been awesome, it had also been too near to see clearly. He had seen close instead of clear. But still he knew it for what it was and it had struck to his heart and to the hearts of all of them.

And now the longer he watched the more clearly he saw it, as though from far away, through space and time that had left him. He forgot the families of the men, their wives and kids, all of whom he had met, most of whom he had known by name, handed drinks at parties or patted on the head—wives drinks, that was, and children heads. Their faces faded and his mind wandered to other matters, to vast sights and abstractions, darkness and light.

Finally what he recalled as he sat there, as he pushed the button and watched the cloud rise over and over, mesmerized, was a distraction, a tangent. He digressed, with the cloud rising before him on the small screen, and it struck him how hopeful he had been when he was young. As a child he had dreamed of heaven: even as a child, before he even knew the rigors of adversity, he had clung to the idea of another place, a flawless and gentle place beyond and after this one.

Despite what had been taught to him at the Adler school, the politely benevolent atheism, despite the secular learning of those he most respected he had still, as a child, dreamed of heaven almost rapturously. It had been a quasi-Christian heaven, possibly, he reflected as he sat watching the cloud. It smacked of the pearliness and sentimentality of Christian visions, not his own family's faith, such as it was, now that he thought about it. He had been assimilated even then: it had begun when he was very young.

But whether heaven was on earth or elsewhere, futurist utopia or a return to the garden of Eden, a worker's paradise or a rich man's material indulgence, he had held fast to this vision. Men could make an empire of peace, an empire of perfect comprehension. Somewhere, future or dream, this city of God must exist.

He wondered how old he had been, whether it was ten or

twelve, when he had first begun to cling to this. He wondered whether his last sandcastle on the beach had been built and washed away before then.

It occurred to him fleetingly that this might be a test, that his presence here, in what appeared at first glance to be a sterile and terrible future, was not real but only a test, a test of faith, moral fiber, a test of integrity.

At last the old woman beside him, disgruntled, complained loudly that he was "monopolizing the button." She heaved herself up from her chair and crept away swaying. Stray children wandered over and sat down but they quickly became bored with his trigger finger and he was left alone at the monitor, motionless and staring.

After an hour or two—it might have been longer, he did not know—he began to cry.

This was contrary to his usual practice. He wept, like most adult men, so rarely that there were often years between outbreaks.

Finally another visitor to the museum, a young woman wearing open-toed suede sandals, put a sympathetic hand on his shoulder as he sobbed. She stood behind him and watched with him patiently as the mushroom cloud rose and blossomed first tens, then hundreds of times; she shook her head sadly at the blossoming, touching and rubbing his shoulder gently but firmly.

At first he was taken aback by this intrusion, by the sudden intimacy and forwardness of the gesture, but presently he became grateful for it. The hand was warm and soft and linked him to a person who, unlike all the others he knew, had not yet disappeared. When she squatted down behind him to watch the screen at his level he could see the shape of her head reflected in the monitor, the braids on either side of her face and the long earrings whose complicated beadwork swayed with the slow movements of her shaking head.

She left with a final pat to his shoulder and the whispered word *Peace.*

He was greatly comforted by this.

Later, telling of his encounter with the woman at the museum, he would repeat the phrase *She had such a generous heart!* In fact he would always be moved by the smell of patchouli, which in and of itself he found fairly unpleasant, because it reminded him of kindness.

After that he left the museum and walked through the streets looking for his old house, which he failed to locate. Kitty and the children had been living there only the day before yesterday. Only the day before yesterday, this was where he came home to, this but not this, here but not here, and his wife and children were no longer wife and children: all they were was all gone.

If everything he knew had not been swept away they would be living here still. When he came to the place where he guessed his house had once been he sat down on a bench, his hat beside him, and wept again. His eyes were dry but his throat rasped with sobs.

A passing youngster lobbed a quarter onto his hat brim.

After three cups of coffee and nine cigarettes in a nearby dive he walked to the lab complex and inquired after physicists and engineers and even secretaries and file clerks he knew, hoping one of them would still be present, working there. He wracked his brain for the names of the youngest employees of the Project, the ones he'd known when they were in their very early twenties, who might feasibly still be around, postponing their retirement because they were wedded to their work. But not surprisingly none of the names he gave to security were recognized, and finally they turned him away.

❧ Firsthand accounts of the Trinity test make clear it was a sight that could never be captured by photography or by words. It was a moment that had to be felt in the stomach, seen with the eyes. The singularity of the sight of the first atomic bomb is clear in all descriptions by the physicists who were present. It turned scientists into poets.

Enrico Fermi wrote: *Although I did not look directly towards the object, I had the impression that suddenly the countryside became brighter than in full daylight.* Robert Serber wrote: *At a height of perhaps twenty thousand feet, two or three thin horizontal layers of shimmering white cloud were formed.* Luis Alvarez wrote: *My first sensation was one of intense light covering my whole field of vision.* Victor Weisskopf wrote: *The path of the shock wave through the clouds was plainly visible as an expanding circle all over the sky.* Phillip Morrison wrote: *I observed an enormous and brilliant disk of white light.* Ed McMillan, the test director, wrote: *The whole surface of the ball was covered with a purple luminescence, like that produced by the electrical excitation of air.*

❧ Oppenheimer read his own comments about Trinity too. He read the line his other self, the shell of self that had witnessed the explosion and continued living in its own time, had apparently selected from the *Bhagavad-Gita* to describe the experience. It was a line that had been famous, almost as famous as he himself, the line *I am become Death, the Destroyer of Worlds.*

He saw himself pronounce these words on film. On the grainy gray film stock he was a white-haired old man, old beyond his years, careful and worn, his eyes misty.

❧ Every night Ann walked alone. She walked home, she walked down the street, she walked to meet Ben at a restaurant or a friend's house or occasionally a bar. She made sure that she walked alone.

As she walked she became all abstract.

The opposition between the small and the big, the *idea* of the minuscule and the idea of the vast, she thought, is not far removed from the opposition between the mundane and the sublime.

And if the question were asked: What is more real, the mundane or the sublime? most would hesitate before they gave an answer.

On the one side details: say, the aftermath of a breakfast, dirty chipped plates in the sink, their rims encrusted with egg yolk. Against this, the unnameable: small aching heart with boasts, what can you know? Outside the cage of everything we ever heard or saw, beyond, outside, above, there lies the real, hiding as long as we shall live, there stretch and trail the millions of names of God burning across the eons. When all through this our end will come before we even know the names of us.

For many the egg yolk prevails.

☙ He did not know what was real but for the time being, until he got his bearings, he allowed himself to believe what was being proposed: he had been displaced in time and the man whose story had been told in history books, this other impostor self, therefore could not be and had never been him. How could it? Here he was: this was he.

He also read other people's descriptions of him. He pored over these, attempting to glean from them a sense of his own wonder secondhand. He was disturbed by one description of him "swaggering" as he left the Trinity site after the test, as he stepped into the car. He felt that this comment was unfair. He was not, and never had been, a man to swagger. He would not have strutted like a cowboy from a sight like that.

He was downcast for some days at the betrayal of intimates. Haakon Chevalier had written a novel featuring Robert himself, thinly veiled, as a cruelly rendered protagonist, an arrogant and self-deluding intellectual. This drew from him a shaken and wounded astonishment. Haakon had been a close friend, or so he had believed: but in fact to judge from the text Haakon had not known him, had not known him at all, clearly. And then there was the report that Teller, during what appeared to be a right-wing political witch hunt in the 1950s, had spoken ill of him and doomed him to a senescence of obscurity.

Reading these accounts of the past, accounts that he read as though they were fiction, he was struck dumb by the spite of people, which was sadly not outweighed by the charity of others, no matter how generous it might be.

He knew he had been robbed but he was not sure exactly what had been stolen from him.

❧ Leo Szilard, brilliant gadfly, meddler, inventor, physicist, molecular biologist, friend of Einstein, inveterate seeker of patents, crusader for peace, amateur policy analyst, writer of exceedingly dull fictions, and would-be savior of the world, was born in Budapest, Hungary, in 1898. There, the oldest of three children, he lived in a house designed by his uncle Emil, which looked like a fairy-tale castle. In the garden of the castle Leo played with his brother and sister and their cousins. Later, in the wake of the fall of Bela Kun, persecution and war following him, Szilard left Hungary for Berlin, Berlin for London, London for New York. Szilard was always one step ahead of catastrophe.

After curing his own bladder cancer with a self-designed course of radiation treatments, Szilard died suddenly in 1964, in La Jolla, California, of a heart attack.

He had moved to La Jolla for the sunshine.

❧ Unlike Oppenheimer, Szilard did not dwell on his former life, his former ties, his lost family when he found himself transplanted into the twenty-first century. This was partly because none of his personal ties had been too close. He had always been too busy with destiny to have much truck with minor details of emotion and sentiment.

Instead he immediately set himself the task of catching up on history, ravenously, tirelessly, processing information at a high rate of speed and storing it for reference in the near future. He was instantly as busy and as full of zeal, as unfazed and as tunnel-visioned as he had been in the 1940s.

∾ The walks that Ann had begun to take soon became, if not a compulsion, at least a necessary hinge. It was hills that she liked, hills and hidden corners.

She set herself tasks of thinking when she left on a walk, small tasks such as: What counts as mundane? If mundane just means "Of, pertaining to, or typical of this world" how is it that over the years the mundane has become allied with the trivial?

The word *mundane* derives clearly from the Latin *mundus,* the world. Why is the world—which after all is all we have—so much maligned? Why does familiarity breed contempt? When she thought of being familiar she thought of bed, and Ben. There was no contempt there but it was certainly the case that when they were first together there had been a voluptuous turbulence, now settled into routine.

She knew this was *just what happened.* She knew that Ben liked the routine and had been relieved to trade uncertainty for stability, and she did not mind. But why desire had to change when the new became old she did not know and walking by herself she lamented it. When there was not less love why was there always a slacking off?

She stopped to watch a thin coyote trot across the road and disappear in a thicket and decided it was this: that familiarity breeds not contempt but affiliation, and affiliation is the opposite of urgency, of focus and ardor and intent. Affiliation is a linking of arms in which the subjects move forward side by side. Because they are looking ahead into the world, watching the road and making sure not to stumble, they no longer look each other in the eye.

Thus the opposing tension of two people standing face-to-face dissipates.

∾ As soon as he had raised himself from the gutter and wandered through downtown Santa Fe long enough to assess his surroundings, pat down his pockets to discover a wallet fat with cash, and secure a hotel room, Fermi collapsed.

For several days he existed in a state that might fairly be described as mild catatonia, sitting on the edge of his hotel bed and staring.

∾ Contingencies. Had the German military had access to an A-bomb during what they call World War Two, it is unlikely that strategic planners in the Third Reich would have forfeited the opportunity to drop said device on an English or American city.

Had the physicist Werner Heisenberg, who was heading the Nazi A-bomb program, decided to use graphite instead of so-called heavy water to slow down neutrons in his chain reaction experiments, the Germans might well have beat the Americans to the bomb.

Had Fermi and Szilard, when they discovered that graphite could be used for this crucial purpose, published their findings, Heisenberg would have known about graphite.

It was a man named George Braxton Pegram, physicist at Columbia University and an avid tennis player and canoeist, who told Fermi and Szilard not to publish.

This might, among other functions, serve as a parable for those who do not believe in the power of the printed word.

Evidently the mundane is by nature massive, even all-powerful. Once a few particles can exterminate people by the billions, never again can it be argued that small and trivial are in the same family.

∾ The public library was a sanctuary. Ann liked the calmness of the stacks, which she felt as the presence of thousands of minds, many sympathetic. In the silence she sometimes thought she could detect a low hum, all of them murmuring.

On the day in question, however, the sanctuary was no protection.

Around two in the afternoon the other librarian stepped out to lunch. Moments later a thunderclap sounded and heavy rain drummed on the roof. Ann leaned on her counter listening to the rain and wondered what Ben was doing, whether the inventors of the leveraged buyout were calling him into the kitchen for tea. Or maybe he was going to sit sketching at the drafting table with Yoshi the landscape architect. They did not speak each other's language and they had no interpreters, Ben had told her. Hence instead of talking they drew on a paper, and passed it back and forth politely, bowing their heads. They were polite men, Yoshi meek, Ben quiet, both of them eager to please.

She was thinking about this when Mr. Hofstadt came to her desk with one of his reference requests. Mr. Hofstadt was a man in his early fifties with thinning red hair and thick bifocals and liver spots on his trembling hands. He was partial to Ann, whose shyness he saw as a welcome. For months he had been coming to Reference every other day. His questions had become increasingly arcane, in fact it seemed to Ann that they were arbitrary. He had sought information on the natal chart of one of the lesser Marx brothers and on volcanism along the Mid-Atlantic Ridge; once he had told her he was studying the life cycle of hermaphroditic gastropods. On that occasion he had rested his elbows on the counter, leaned in and confided in her, in a wheedling voice, —In, for example, *Lymnaea stagnalis,* the pond snail, the penis is located immediately adjacent to the vagina. Not so the apple snail!

Ben had suggested more than once that Mr. Hofstadt was desperate to keep her by his side and encouraged Ann to deflect Mr. Hofstadt's questions. He saw sinister possibilities. But she was a reference librarian and in general she did not mind humoring a patron, though sometimes, when there were other patrons waiting, she would concede defeat early and tend to them.

As the rain pattered on the roof and windows Mr. Hofstadt interlaced his fingers, leaned forward to place his elbows on the counter as usual, and asked her how to find out how many children with blond hair had been born in 1983.

—In this city? she asked. —Across the country? Or globally?

But before he could answer another man burst through the front doors, drenched. He was a long-haired man, darkly tanned with a weathered face; he wore a green Hawaiian-print shirt blaring with leaves and parrots, canvas shorts, and flip-flops on his broad feet. Her first thought was that he must be chilled by the rain. She noticed his calves were muscular but his midsection was flabby. Finally she saw he was holding a weapon, which she took for an instant to be a plastic toy. It looked absurd to her, a boxy gray thing in relief from the world around it.

In fact it was not a toy, or at least it was not in the category of toy that graced the aisles of children's stores, but, as Ann would later learn, a Heckler & Koch submachine gun.

When the long-haired man waved it, and Mr. Hofstadt dropped out of sight in front of the counter, she decided to give the gun the benefit of the doubt, though it struck her as ridiculous. She raised her hands tentatively and waited for instructions, feeling awkward and somehow guilty of her own awkwardness. The man with the gun was muttering something, but she could not make out the words.

He looked around, not aiming the gun purposefully; it drooped in his hand, pointing down at the floor. Mr. Hofstadt was moaning a prayer that went *No-no-no-no-no-not-me*. Ann's heart raced and her face felt cold and separate from her head. When the man began to walk toward the counter she stretched her hands a little higher and, fluttering and hiccuping inwardly, resolved to try to be serene. She thought *Death be not proud* and also *Jack be nimble, Jack be quick*. The man's wet rubber flip-flops squeaked and slapped against his wet heels. Then he stopped in front of her and she could hear Mr. Hofstadt warbling in fear at his feet.

He looked to his right and left and then leaned toward her and whispered. There was garlic on his breath.

—Watch out.

Quickly he turned to Romance Paperbacks, on a revolving rack, and let loose a volley of bullets.

The noise was loud and shocking, and she forgot her vow of serenity, knees shaking, and dropped to the floor like Mr. Hofstadt before her.

It was silent for a few minutes after that, and when she rose hesitantly from her crouch the man with the gun had run off. She leaned forward to peer down over the counter edge and saw he had left his wet flip-flops behind. Dirty water pooled in the shallow hollows left in the rubber soles by the balls of his feet and his heels.

Mr. Hofstadt, squatting beside them, was staring up at her, his hands shaking uncontrollably. From the trail of gasps and shrieks she could tell where the man with the gun had gone: he had run past Romance Paperbacks and past Mystery, past the shelves of General Fiction and into the children's books section. Luckily, she thought reflexively, all the children were in school.

She called 911 and said, —A man with a gun is in the library. He has fired several rounds.

Then she went around the counter and kneeled down beside Mr. Hofstadt, who was panting and gasping. Her own mouth was dry, drier, she thought, than she recalled it ever being in the past. She was afraid Mr. Hofstadt had suffered a heart attack.

And while she was fanning his face with her hand, urging him to tell her how he felt, there was another round of gunfire.

❧ At this time Ben was digging a ditch for an irrigation hose, yet he, in contrast to her, was not thirsty. Santa Fe was seven thousand feet above sea level, and in the summer in particular, working at elevation, the sun could drain him of what felt like life itself but was more precisely water. So he had made a concession to this and underneath his plain work shirt, usually a cotton T-shirt, white or drab or gray, without logo or design, there hung against his hard and bony back a flattened water bottle with a long, thin tube extruding, actually less a bottle than a bladder slipped inside a black foam sleeve. In the store they had called it a "hydration kit," a plastic bag made for hiking and shaped to fit the contours of the back. From this he could sip as he shoveled, hoed, or knelt on his kneepads to plant. He kept it inside the shirt so that its faint and insulated coldness lay touching the skin.

When he was bored with his work he lived in scenes. Sipping the plastic-tasting water he might be a pioneer on a far planet, sowing the seeds of future life in angry fields, sustained only by the vein of liquid. Or he might be a plant himself among the plants, drawing rainwater into his barely mobile body.

Sometimes he imagined the son he would have, because he wished for a child as though it was too much to ask, as though it was a unreal dream, as some men wish for wealth or fame.

❧ At lunch in a Mexican restaurant Oppenheimer looked up from his plate of beans and saw Fermi walking toward him as though in his sleep. He rose from his seat so fast that he hit the table and spilled his beer, and they looked at each other across the bright room as the beer cascaded off the table edge.

❧ As she learned after the police came jogging in wearing their riot gear, a ricochet off a pipe had hit the gunman near the base of his skull. He had died quickly beside a display of Navajo baskets.

It had happened too fast for them to save him or, as one of the policemen said jauntily, the carpet.

Mr. Hofstadt had not had a heart attack but a panic attack. He got up as soon as the policemen came in, then waited for the Crime Scene Unit and hovered behind them, bulgy-eyed and avid, as they taped off the corner of the room. After that day he would seldom return to the library, and when he did it was not to ask her questions but merely to check out a few books, mostly whodunits, quickly and wordlessly.

So she never found out how many blond babies were born in 1983.

They closed the library that afternoon so that the police could come and go without obstruction. She stayed at the phone, away from the bustle and the eyewitness interviews, until late in the afternoon, when she walked over to the children's books section, hesitant and stepping lightly. A policeman and a forensic pathologist tried to tell her how to "sanitize the area," but she could not discern the meaning of the words from their sound. She looked down at the man with the gun and felt dizzy.

He was not *the man with the gun* anymore, in fact, because he had dropped the gun before he died. The police had picked it up and bagged it as evidence. He looked casual to her, a man who had tripped and fallen some time ago and was now lying on the carpet by choice, idly recalling an untended detail: a dog unwalked, a sink of dishes uncleaned.

She thought: When I die there will be an envelope without a stamp, or worse an envelope with no address, with no name on it, even. They will have to open it to determine its object, and who knows what they will find? She shuddered at the idea that some wrong detail might slip unintended beneath the wrong eyes.

She thought: Maybe this fear is what keeps some people from writing letters at all.

One of the parrots on his shirt, red and yellow and beady-eyed, was upside-down. By means of its precarious perch on the shirt and its long tail feathers it led her eyes to the wound on the side of his head, where the hair was not dry and light. Instead there was heaviness there, the inside like worms, and it was wet.

She glanced away again, and a few minutes later they lifted him onto a gurney, covered him and rolled him outside and into the coroner's van. She had the feeling of watching television, then of being inside television, inside bad television, in fact. She watched the van pull down the drive and stop at the lights down the street. Then she turned to her fellow librarian, asking: —Was there something I could have done?

The other librarian, a portly vegan named Jeff with a brown ponytail, shook his head and reassured her. She was unconvinced. He stepped away to talk to a reporter, though he himself had been occupied eating a tofurkey sandwich on rye, lettuce, mustard, extra lite organic soy mayo, when the tragedy occurred. Ann had not spoken to the media and she did not plan to, but Mr. Hofstadt had talked at great length to a reporter from Channel 2, in sweaty agitation.

It was a loose, spare day. After the police and the reporters and Jeff had all left she felt the library to be empty, emptier than it should be. At the same time it was cloying: it was empty and suffocating at once. The metal shelves, the windowsills, the curtains, the tables and chairs and counters were washed with an unfamiliar veneer, somehow altered and not how they used to be. Their surfaces could not be trusted; who knew what they hid?

They were the last fixtures to be seen of the world, the last sight seen.

Above him as his heart slowed there had been long fluorescent tubes and beside him, open on a table, had been a children's book called *Make Way for Ducklings.*

The last sight seen could not be designed, she knew, and this stung her, it grieved her, it made her beg secretly. It should be an entitlement, she thought, at least this should be guaranteed, shouldn't it? Even if everything else was chaos. That you could be outside, under the sky at night, seeing the white blur of stars that was the Milky Way. Because why should it be that this was what you got, your last touch of anything, the instant then, the instant of disappearing forever, why should that be fluorescent tubes and formica tabletops?

Anyway, she thought further, no one dies too well.

This was not a comfort.

She went to the bathroom, and standing at the sink washing her hands she thought: Heaven is an idea, but it does not follow that an idea is heaven. Still, it seems likely that in ideas, she thought, and only in ideas is there heaven. It can't be found in plain sight, where most of us live, she thought, because we have teemed over the surface of the world and stained it. Rich people look for heaven in Bali or Key West but poor people have to find it between the fingertips and the frontal lobe: cigarettes, booze, crack and heroin.

The library bathroom was fairly pleasant and none of these were in evidence.

❧ Ben was brought out of his trance rudely when Lynn came to talk to him.

—It's Yoshi. He just does not want to understand my needs. I really can't talk to him.

—I'm sorry to hear it.

—So I was wondering: Could you talk to him for me? Like always? I can't deal. I mean really.

He did not think it was a good idea. Yoshi was in the next room, so he said softly, —I'm sure you can find a way of understanding each other.

—You know why it is? He doesn't respect me. I think it's that, you know, Asian woman thing. They're totally subjugated. *They bind their feet.*

❧ Whining for a good death was weak when even a good life was a tall order. At the same time she felt imploring, and asked universe to hand out good deaths for everyone. What harm could there be?

Though her parents had died in an accident not too long since, she had not seen the accident or the death. They had only been reported to her. It was a secondhand death and had stayed that way, the abstract removal of parents who themselves, in recent years, had abstracted themselves. It had still wrenched her but she saw it differently at different times: it was fluid so the shape of it did not loom. Sometimes it was a sad blur, other times it was violent and the soles of her feet tingled up from the ground at the thought.

But this had been near, near and real like a slap.

She closed the plastic blinds on four windows in a row and said to herself self-consciously: And then he was lucky. She was thinking of her grandmother, now dead, who had by her own admission lived decades too long. For her grandmother, in the years before she died, the ground itself had ceased to be stable and balance could not be regained: the world shook and trembled and her hands followed suit, her unsteady hands, quavering voice, even the laws of gravity had let her down. Her skin was white and powdery as moth wings. Once lucid briefly, she had pulled Ann down close to her on the pillow and whispered, with wet eyes: —It isn't me anymore. I'm all gone.

Even disregarded and packed away, she thought, in a home with the other old ones, in a home with the other defunct, we cling with our bodies in shreds to the smells, the branches dipping in the wind, the old worn pads of our fingers: the same fingers we have had all our lives.

And the light in the air.

The bodies, she thought, those sad oxen, tired, they beg us to go free. *The bodies beg us to go free.*

She sat down near a magazine rack and paged through a *People*, blankly and without engagement. She could think of nothing to do, nothing that would occupy her. Her hands hung useless and she was surprised by a rush of adrenaline followed by restlessness.

At certain moments of shock or stupefaction it is clear, she thought, that doing anything is a waste of time, that effort itself is a waste. Doing something appears more wasteful than doing nothing, while only doing nothing seems safe. This may be because something is always, at base, a distraction from nothing. Paradoxically *nothing* is full, whereas *something* is often surprisingly empty; yet in *nothing* all things are possible, whereas in *something* there are limits on all sides.

And it is possible to relax into nothing, let nothing envelop you like a love.

❧ Fermi was even more lost than Oppenheimer himself, but this mattered less than the obvious fact that it was him. It was Fermi, his old friend.

He had never been so relieved in his life.

❧ Ann left the building thinking of herself as *a woman who had witnessed a shooting.* Then she amended this: she was *a woman who had heard a series of loud noises, i.e., shots, one of which produced a death.* A subsequent amendment: *Violent death.*

It did not occur to her to interrupt Ben at work. She was distracted and instead of going home she got into her car and drove up into the mountains, pulling off the shoulder where a trailhead led into the forest. It was still raining, with an occasional low shiver of thunder; she got out of the car anyway and began to walk, between tall ponderosa pines on a brown bed of needles and cones.

She walked fast, wanting to drain herself of what felt like a morbid, even lurid excitement. Whether she was pressed onward by fear or exhilaration was not obvious to her and this made her furtive and shameful even as her legs moved. The texture of the day, of time itself on this day, it seemed to her, had been altered, roughened and sharpened, and it occurred to her that she would be far safer as a tree among trees. Upright and unbending, her feet frozen and locked in soil, she would be solid and surely without confusion.

She looked up into the ponderosas and saw how long and bare their trunks were, how their riddled columns of rust-red bark soared up around her without branches for what she thought must be seven stories, eight or nine or even ten, to the height of tall buildings. Even though she walked and they were stationary she wanted to make herself vertical like them, stiff like them, like them surrounded by fellows, strengthened by an impassive and silent army.

❧ Ben was also contemplating trees. He was considering the arrangement of trees in part of the garden, and how the sunlight fell on them.

To Ann lighting was everything. She liked to place frayed and beloved objects in careful positions, making sure the surfaces of scuffed old tables, worn rugs and torn chairs were never lit bleakly from above but always illuminated gently by sconces and floor lamps containing bulbs of dim wattage. She avoided bright lights both at home and in public places.

Recently she had refused to go to a home store with him. It made her feel bleak, she had told him. She often looked at the others standing in line to pay for their hardware products: here fat Stan with his two-by-fours, paint thinner and level, there Larry with the ear tufts holding his drill bits and royal-blue air conditioner filter, swaying and moaning as they plodded heavily in single-file down a dull concrete road, cheap home-improvement wares piled up high in their carts like the spoils of a sad war.

He asked her why she felt this way at the home store but not buying groceries. She said the grocery store was better because it held the prospect of giddiness, impulse and lightness.

Men felt that way buying hardware, he had said.

Her lighting arrangements were directed toward soft handling.

She had to flatter things, manmade things that fell short, as they almost all did. The ugly had to be treated gently, as though it was sick.

❧ She kept walking even after she was soaked, touching her arms in their wetness, fingers against the cold slick skin. She felt bereft of ideas except for one that said Move forward.

After an hour she turned back shaking, her hair ropy and dripping down her back. She picked her way over tree roots gnarled and jointed like bones on the muddy trail.

She thought now, instead of *Move forward*, only *Be warm and dry again*.

When she got to the car she turned on the heater full-blast. She drove back down the mountain, teeth chattering, and toweled off at home, in the bedroom. She changed clothes, bundling herself in wool and denim. But she was still afraid she would begin to think morbidly: morbid thoughts would come to her unbidden. That she could not control what she thought was horrifying to her, though it had never been before. With all that was external and beyond control it seemed at least that thoughts should be a modest self-determined privilege, but no, not even *there* was relief. Everything overlapped and nowhere was privacy.

Finally she called Ben and left a message on his cell phone, asking him to meet her when he got off work. Then she got into the car again and drove to an expensive restaurant, frequented by tourists but owned by a friend.

It was late afternoon and the cocktail-hour crowds were beginning to wander in. She warmed herself by the fire and then sat on a stool at the slick, varnished bar and ordered a glass of wine. John, the owner's son, was behind the bar; she told him what had happened. He took her hand in both of his, which she did not mind although she was not overly fond of him. But then he made a suggestion about her *chakras* and she was required to be tolerant. Her hand itched and felt like a prisoner.

When he moved away to pour drinks she sipped her wine slowly, red this time. She could feel the spreading heat from the hearth, and the rain steady overhead.

She was about to ask for a second glass when she noticed a man sitting a few stools down. He wore a plaid shirt and jeans, and a belt with an ungainly silver buckle. The clothes hung on him; his body was gaunt. He was in his early forties, she guessed, with a prominent, aquiline nose, close-cropped dark hair and large, light eyes under his thick eyebrows.

He had a martini at his elbow, and was smoking a cigarette from a pack of Lucky Strikes beside him on the counter as he paged through a large-format, square paperback book. The book seemed to her to be compelling him almost unnaturally, so rapt was he as he read it, so hunched over and beadily focused. When he glanced up he reminded her of a gangly baby bird—an ostrich maybe, though he was elegant, not absurd.

—May I trouble you, John, he said, and fingered the stem of his martini glass.

—Sure.

He had a nervous, angular charm. His clothes were shabby and the colors on the shirt struck her as slightly garish but despite this he seemed genteel, with an air of easy privilege. She noticed the title of the book he was reading: *Oppenheimer.*

But in fact it was not until later that she thought consciously of the name in her dream and connected the book with the dream. At the moment of seeing the title, *Oppenheimer,* she felt only a faint flick of recognition.

As he turned back to his book his eyes moved past her face and she looked away quickly. But he paid no attention to her; he had caught sight of someone coming in the door and was beckoning him over. It was a compact, balding man who brushed past her in his wet trench coat, sat down on the bar stool next to the martini drinker and began to speak rapidly in Italian.

The first man listened closely, nodding, until the Italian calmed down and paused in his speech, looking around for the bartender. Then he said to him, in English —I'm glad to see you're feeling better, anyway.

They were quiet, and then the first man went on —For the rest, I don't know, Enrico. I have no idea. If I were a strictly religious man . . .

He paused again, and the two of them sat staring at the mirror behind the bar. She saw their faces between the shelved bottles, somehow both animated and stunned. The Italian was elfin with a long nose, and his hairline receded almost to the crown of his head.

—. . . I would think it was punishment.

—Ridiculous, said the Italian. He had a heavy accent.

—But that's when your recollection ends too, isn't it. After the flash.

—Yes.

—And this, he lifted the book. —Have you read your own biographies?

—I just read a book by my wife.

—Laura wrote a book?

—Several. One of them was about me.

—And what did it say?

—The bomb ended the war, et cetera. It was published in the year that I died. You know, if I believe these books, I only had nine more years to live?

—It's like a bad joke, isn't it.

—You lived until '67. But the government turned against you.

—The ungrateful bastards.

—Let us get out of here, yes? I need a good walk. And I always hated that smell.

He gestured toward the ashtray.

—Well, I will concede, said the first man slowly, —these cigarettes taste terrible.

There was a pause. The Italian relaxed briefly and smiled.

—You shouldn't smoke anyway, he said. —I read it in a book: you're going to come down with cancer.

They laughed.

The first man stubbed out his cigarette, put some money down on the bar, tucked his book under his arm and clapped the Italian on the shoulder.

—Whatever it is, is it just us, or are there others here too? he asked, and they moved past her and out the door, into the rain.

When they were gone she turned to John, who picked up the first man's ashtray and began to wipe it.

—Did you hear what they were saying? she asked him, incredulous.

—Nah, game's on.

—Do you—did you know those men?

—Nah, not really, he said. His eyes were small. His puffy lips and cheeks gleamed and from under his pink Oxford cloth collar wafted a detergent smell, Tide, thought Ann, or Era, stiff, strong and white. —The tall one started coming in here last Friday and he's been here every single day since. Pain in the ass. Guy smokes like a chimney. I told him it was against the law to light up in the restaurant and he laughed his head off! Thought I was joking. Then he offered to pay the fine himself if we got one. He asked me how much it would be and said he was good for it. Finally I had to pull out this thing for him. Afraid he was going to ash on the mahogany. The guy's Eurotrash or something.

—I don't think so, said Ann. —I mean he speaks English with an American—

John's girlfriend, sitting two stools down with a beer in hand, leaned over and confided in her.

—That guy had a completely dark aura. I swear. It was practically a *smog*.

—Oh.

—Browns, grays, blacks. The only positive color I saw was yellow, light yellow. The color of intellect.

—Wasn't he reading—

—But the browns are *very* murky: selfishness. And the gray symbolizes, like, narrow focus. He's cold and he's got this kind of like, real anal retentive thing going on, but like he tries to hide it? And like the black in the aura's just the absence of color. Probably depression. He's totally depressed and under this big like *weight* of something. He's got work to do. Healing work.

—The poor man.

—There's a lot of negativity there.

—Oh. You know I should probably—

—Whereas *your* aura is very positive. I see a lot of pale blue, and even some gold. That's so special! Gold is *rare*.

—Oh, she said again.

But her voice trailed off. She was looking out the window past John and his girlfriend, wishing the men had not disappeared so soon. She was gazing at where they were not.

Already then, she was wishing she had followed them.

❧ Ben cherished arrangement over lighting. A simple rectangle containing small, neat squares, distinct from each other by texture or color, could actually evoke in him a sense of sudden and overwhelming fullness.

Enclosed and separated fields that lay beside each other perfectly, shapes that fit together, these were something at once unbearably contained and triumphantly uncontainable. He often thought he might have found another outlet for the expression of this had he been born wealthy, or even middle-class, to a family with bourgeois aspirations. But he had always had to work, even before it was legal. When he was ten he had apprenticed to a carpenter and by the time he was twelve he was already working on custom furniture, sculpting and sanding the details on desks and tables.

The work was hard for his thin, small hands, and at night the fingers, the wrists and even the elbows would ache. Several cuts with saws had reshaped the ends of his fingers, giving the pads a rippled texture, deep lengthwise rifts even thirty years later.

So he was still young when he discovered shapes and the satisfaction to be gained from them. Arrangement in a confined space, say a garden bordered by road, brought with it a sad thrill, because as soon as he saw the beginning of the perfect he could always also see the end. The perfect was never even perfect at all, but invaded by its opposite.

❧ Szilard embarked on the long journey west and south by bus. He had wished to take the train, but was shocked to discover it too expensive. Though far from sentimental and even further from emotional, he had always trusted his instincts. In the midwest he was alone, and though alone did not bother him it had strategic limitations.

He knew beyond a shadow of a doubt that he would find others where he was going.

❧ Leaving the bar, wondering as she walked whether she would see the two men again, it occurred to Ann that an idea could not always be packaged in words, but that did not make it less true. What puzzled her was how ideas that vibrate with life, with beauty and with truth, could change into weapons when they became knowledge. Ideas may be sun on the water, but then as knowledge they turn fierce, *as bright* or *brighter than a thousand suns.*

❧ A young man in the 1920s, Enrico Fermi went through a phase of wearing knickerbockers and a Tyrolean jacket. He would later exchange these for what his wife Laura called a "too-tight suit." He was short-legged, stocky and athletic, and on hikes in the Italian mountains he always insisted on being first: faster, stronger, more capable than others. He was far more arrogant about his physical prowess than his aptitude for physics. Laura, who would write his biography shortly before his death, was Jewish. They left Rome four months after Mussolini published the *Manifesto della Razza,* which stated "Jews do not belong to the Italian race."

Fermi died of cancer in 1954.

❧ The man with the gun had not been homeless, from some far elsewhere or without friends or relatives, as Ann had first assumed. He was the scion of a well-known Albuquerque family with political connections. His uncle had once run for mayor, the newspaper said, and lost by only a few hundred votes.

His mother, Mrs. Lopez, came to see Ann at work. She was a white-haired apple doll with rosy cheeks and bright, darting eyes. She asked if they could talk privately, so Ann asked a volunteer to take her place at the counter and led Mrs. Lopez back past the children's books section and the square of new carpet. They drank a cup of lemon tea in the small staff kitchen, standing beside the sink. Mrs. Lopez did not wish to sit down.

Mrs. Lopez apologized for her son, whose name was Eugene, and for his gun. She wanted Ann to know that Eugene had been mentally ill, in fact he had suffered from schizophrenia.

—But he was also a warm person, a warm and wonderful person, his *real* self.

—I'm sure he was, said Ann softly.

Ann bore Eugene no ill will. Now and then she imagined the details he might have left behind, a dripping tap, refrigerator door standing open, plant drying out on a windowsill and dropping its leaves. She felt herself pulled toward these details, as though she herself was expected to correct them, needed in the spaces he had vacated by accident. It was always only later, apart from the details, that she remembered the Heckler & Koch.

But Mrs. Lopez was not content with the assurance. She told

Ann that when Eugene was eight he had built a cardboard rocket covered in tinfoil to fly his gerbil to the moon. The gerbil's name was Burpy.

Eugene had wanted Burpy to see Mars, Jupiter, and even Neptune, she reported sadly. She was lost in memory.

—Even Neptune, she repeated.

Burpy would conquer the skies, Mrs. Lopez told her. But reason had prevailed, she went on, and the gerbil had not been launched.

She told Ann that when Eugene had first become delusional and violent and one time lifted a knife to her throat, she often recalled the tender affection he had shown to animals as a small child. She remembered the gentleness of his hands as he picked up Burpy the gerbil and petted him softly, and how protective he had been of Burpy when other children handled the gerbil roughly.

She asked for more hot water for her tea, and Ann poured it into the mug from a spigot on the coffeemaker.

—When he was seven, said Mrs. Lopez, —he liked to design zoos. He would draw these zoos on newsprint, with drawings of all the animals that he wanted to put in them. He papered the walls of his bedroom with them! His zoo had something he called the Giant Animals Section.

The Giant Animals Section had featured dinosaurs, mammoths and, somewhat inexplicably, a toucan. Ann remembered the parrot on his shirt, and where the tail feathers pointed. Birds, brightly colored birds.

Then Mrs. Lopez asked what he had said, that is, what his last words had been.

—All he said was that the old ones were coming, said Ann.

Mrs. Lopez nodded, resigned, as though the old ones had been coming for a long, long time, as though she was so tired that she welcomed them.

If some good ideas are loved too much, Ann was thinking as

she got up to show Mrs. Lopez out, if they are loved too much and therefore known too well, if they are followed to their end, they can cease to be good. They can be *too much* of a *good thing.*

You can't treat an idea like a fact, she decided. You have to treat it like music.

As she was leaving Mrs. Lopez told Ann that she wanted her to attend the memorial service and hear the eulogies.

—Because, said Mrs. Lopez to Ann, and took her hand, —you were the last one to spend time with him. I don't want you to remember him that way.

Ann said yes, she would go, and Mrs. Lopez smiled at her and bustled out, blowing her nose. Watching her negotiate the doors, the doors of this building of books where her son had died, Ann thought: We have sought the wrong knowledge all these years. We have believed that knowledge should be accumulated, taking the form of many separate pieces. But this is not the knowledge that we need most. To be able to separate things was a skill that allowed us to survive when we were being hunted but not later, now, when all the animals that hunted us are dead.

❧ The Sunday after the shooting Ben went with her to the funeral in Albuquerque. They entered quietly as the service was beginning and sat immediately inside the church doors. Ann did not think she should pretend to have known the deceased. She wanted to be mouselike, polite and present but not intrusive.

There was no coffin, only a photograph of Eugene as a young man, framed and propped upright between heavy, large wreaths and tall sprays of daffodils and irises. His hair had been short and curly when the picture was taken, and his smile easy. He wore a suit and tie that clearly dated from the 1970s. Ann wondered if his mother had asked him to pose for the photograph, and if she had thought back then: One day I may need this when there is no more of him.

In the front pews the mourners seemed somber but not shocked, mourning but not grieving, except for a red-haired woman with freckles in the third pew, who sobbed.

The priest read, —Even so must the son of man be lifted up, that whosoever believeth in him should not perish, but have eternal life.

Increasingly Ann could not hear the priest because of the sound of the red-haired woman sobbing. The sobbing grew in volume till it was half-choked, raw and full of phlegm. It was so loud that other people were also prevented from hearing the words of the priest, and turned around and stared.

The woman finally stood up, quickly then, and scrambled out of the pew, banging along the row of seated mourners. She was bowing to their disapproval by leaving, Ann could feel it, but even in leaving they could not let her be: the awkwardness of her progress along the jutting row of knees drew scorn. There was a very soft murmur of irritation as she bumped along the knees, almost imperceptible. She ran past Ann and Ben, alone at the back, and let the heavy doors slam behind her.

Later Ben was talking to Eugene's mother on the receiving line—he had one of her hands in both of his and was leaning in close over her small white head, listening—when Ann's eyes strayed over the floral arrangements to a stained-glass window, purple and pink with white lilies on an emerald-green bank. She did not like it, she was thinking, she did not like the colors of Easter on the window because they were the colors of pre-filled Easter baskets at the drugstore, bursting with chemical additives beneath their plastic wraps. She did not like the stylized, curving lilies: they projected a clinical, professional indifference, and the light they let through was a feeble, trapped light.

Then she noticed something behind the lilies: the moving silhouette of a man's hat over hunched shoulders.

She excused herself and slipped outside, walking in a hurry

around the corner of the church to the window. There was no one there, only a gate that prevented her from going further and a ragged, weathered wooden fence topped with barbed wire, up close to the building's back wall. It ran beneath the window just a few inches from the crumbling adobe brick. Behind it were some rusted oil barrels, lying on their sides on the ground, a hub cap, and a waterlogged pile of colorful beach towels. There, on a rising wrinkle sticking out of the earth, was the face of Minnie Mouse streaked with dirt. There too was a smiling turtle.

But not enough room for a man to pass.

She thought she must have made a mistake: there must be several windows with lilies on them, behind which a man in a hat could have walked. She gazed past the oil barrels into a stand of pines, and saw nothing moving, not even the trees. It was still. Maybe the shape of the man had been a fluke of angles and sunlight, a shadow cast from far away.

Back inside she walked along the windows, but there was no other window with lilies. She did not know why it mattered to her that a man in a hat might have walked past the window.

Ben was still talking to Eugene's mother when she slipped back inside, or rather she was talking to him. After a while he clasped her hand and walked toward Ann. He had never met Mrs. Lopez before, Ann was thinking, and in all probability he would never see her again, but watching his face as he came nearer she recalled him telling her once that all grief was the same.

He had been weeding her yard while she read on a lawn chair. She had found him in the phonebook. Surrounded by what she knew, the gentle slope of the hill behind her house, the pale-green bluster of chuparosa bushes, snakeweed and grass, he was swallowed by home, he was natural there.

She herself held a paperback, a dog-eared, doleful Russian novel in which a gloomy family marched steadily toward death.

Despite this she kept smiling.

Later he commented on the book. He said the book had it wrong, that it was not happy families who were all the same and unhappy families who were different but the reverse.

And a while after that he had uprooted a spindly, homely plant with minute yellow flowers the size of pinheads, and held it out to her.

—These are called London Rockets, he went on softly. —They're an invasive exotic. As the name suggests they came from the Old World, all the way across the ocean. They never evolved here. They're tourists.

That night, lying awake, she had repeated "invasive exotic" to herself. She had repeated even "as the name suggests." She called him again the next morning and he said it was a relief to hear from her, because he had thought about it at some length and decided the yard was not finished.

It might not be finished for years, he said.

And now he came walking toward her leaving the frail mother behind the flowers and the photograph, and a white-gray light streaming through the Easter window.

The room was almost empty by then.

❧ The same night she curled into the fetal position and he held her cold toes in his hands to make them warm. They were lying in bed and she told him about the dream of the atom bomb, the squirrel, and her mother as a young girl. Days or weeks had passed since the dream, enough for her to forget how long it had been. She did not tell him she suspected herself of being half-awake when she dreamed it, of in fact thinking it more than dreaming, because she wanted to have been held hostage to the dream. She wanted to look passive, like someone who had received a bad gift but was polite to the giver.

The dream was embarrassing.

—I used to have dreams of mushroom clouds when I was thirteen, confessed Ben.

—But not since then.

—Never, said Ben. —There are too many other ways the world could end.

She gazed up into the mosquito net that hung from the beam above them on its circular frame, turning and turning back at a leisurely pace in the stream of quiet air from the fan. They had not unfurled the net; it hung above them knotted, gauzy and white, untouched, awaiting the plague.

She thought: being hurt and forgetting, the two easiest tasks in the world. Millions and billions we forget every day, we forget the others.

She closed her eyes to shut it out though there was nothing before them, nothing but the rotating net and the curtains in the dark. Between the two curtains was a strip of window, and outside a bluer, paler dark than the thick felt dark of the room. She thought: We can't even live without forgetting.

Ben put his lips behind her ear and then pressed them against her temple.

—I mean, what is there to be afraid of? he asked gently. —Endings? The end is simple. One day all of this will be gone.

❧ At work she studied the history of Los Alamos when she was not helping patrons. She found a book that contained a blurry photograph of two men: *Dr. J. R. Oppenheimer and General L. Groves,* it read, *Scientific and Military Leaders of the Manhattan Project.* They were standing beside the twisted remains of a steel tower. Oppenheimer wore a suit with a button on the lapel, and his hat shaded his features; General Groves was in an army uniform, a fat man with a caterpillar mustache and a babyish face.

The steel tower had housed the first bomb, the one exploded in the test named Trinity. It had stood a hundred feet tall and after the explosion lay crumpled on the ground. The sand had fused into a green glassy rock they called Trinitite.

When the "gadget," as they called it, exploded, Oppenheimer and another physicist named Kistiakowsky, who had designed the bomb's trigger, were watching from a control station five miles from Ground Zero. General Leslie R. Groves, along with physicists Fermi, Rabi, Morrison, and others watched from a base camp ten miles from Zero, Fermi through a hole in a board covered with welding glass. Physicist Robert Serber watched with the naked eye, twenty miles from Zero; physicist Luis Alvarez watched from a B-29, at a distance of about twenty-five miles. Leo Szilard, who had catalyzed the A-bomb project but subsequently been cut out by Groves, was not in New Mexico at all but at the University of Chicago.

There was a flash, there was a bright expanding disc and then a roiling ball of smoke, red and orange, which rose to more than thirty thousand feet on a purple column, growing and swelling and pushing out a wall of dirt in a vast ring on the land below it.

❧ Beneath the violet pillar, in the vacuum before the roar of the cloud, there came a soft sound that might have been heard by those who listened closely: the gentle sigh of an idea unbound.

❧ After the explosion all the men watching, the physicists and the technicians and the Army men, knew the world had changed and that this change could never be reversed. Science, like time, seems only to move forward.

Some of the men who saw Trinity had high hopes, others were chilled to the bone and would never recover. Groves said, rather optimistically as it turned out, "This is the end of traditional warfare."

Oppenheimer said later—maybe a little too neatly—that he'd thought of a line from the *Bhagavad-Gita:* "I am become Death, the Destroyer of Worlds."

Kenneth Bainbridge, the British physicist who was the official test director, shook Oppenheimer's hand and said only, "Now we're all sons of bitches."

Kistiakowsky said: "I am sure that at the end of the world, in the last millisecond of the earth's existence, humanity will see what we have just seen."

People living hundreds of miles away had seen the flash too. For them it was something quick and bright and inexplicable on the horizon. They were not told what it was until some years had passed. The day after Trinity, in fact, they were given misinformation. The New Mexico newspapers bore stories claiming the flash had been a munitions warehouse exploding—an explanation that came to them from the Manhattan Engineering District's PR man.

So the people saw the flash but could not see *in* the flash, as the scientists had, the shudder of history petrified.

❧ It had been out of the question, Ann saw, for the physicists of the Manhattan Project to abandon their *good idea* before they had followed it as far as they could. They were men on a road with no choice but to walk it: they only wanted to keep going.

And they adored the idea, pursuing it with a devotion they never considered could be anything but virtuous. With their minds they had fastened onto a secret, which went on and on forever and had never before been known.

Further they justified it this way: once the good idea was had at all, they said and knew, it would be had again. Across the globe the good idea would spread, and if they did not bring it to fruition surely someone else would do so instead.

Across the globe, they said, some other so-called geniuses, because they could, would take the good idea and run with it. And so, in perpetuity, the mere presence of so-called genius would guarantee the final efflorescence of knowledge.

❧ In the second book she flipped through there was another photograph of Oppenheimer, a portrait. He was hatless in it. She stared.

Stunned, she peered down at the photograph from different distances, different angles, trying to find points of distinction between the man in the portrait and the man who had been smoking at the bar. Finding none she began to mull it over: an Oppenheimer relative? Oppenheimer's son? She scoured the indexes of several books to confirm that he had a son, and he did, though she could not find a picture of this son as an adult. There were only baby pictures. The son, she read, lived in the hills of New Mexico, not far away from Santa Fe. He should be in his late fifties or early sixties, she deduced from the mention of his birth, and the man she had seen looked younger than that: but people age at different rates, the bar had been dimly lit, in fact the bar had been a hall of shadows.

It was a coincidence, certainly, she thought: first a bad dream about Oppenheimer, then a sighting of someone who looked just like him. Then it occurred to her that of course not, it was not a coincidence at all, and she felt ashamed of her simple-mindedness. She was exaggerating. Probably the man in the bar had borne a slight resemblance to the man in the photograph, and the rest she had fabricated. She had been affected more than she knew by Eugene and his death. She was looking for a mystery like a child who wished for a secret. She was on the brink of hysteria, even.

Oppenheimer also had a daughter, she discovered, but she had been subject to periods of depression and finally, with a broken heart, had killed herself.

It had been slow at the library since the shooting, so slow that Ann could spread out books on the Reference counter without interruption, smoothing her hands over the pages, the rounds of her elbows settled on thick cushions of paper.

The Manhattan Project had been housed, at first, in the Los Alamos Ranch School for Boys, where for decades spindly, pasty specimens from wealthy families back East had been sent to find hardiness, to grow robust and manly in the sun and pines. The school had been commandeered by the Army almost overnight, condemned, shut down, and unceremoniously cleared of all boys. Two scientists calling themselves "Smith" and "Jones" came to supervise the eviction. The school was also cleared of headmasters, faculty and staff, stunned, sad, and marooned, who left for the Manhattan Engineering District their garbage pails, pie plates, and mustard jars, their bunk beds, horses, and bales of hay.

Oppenheimer had chosen the site because of his fondness for the desert, she learned. She also learned that the scientists and their wives were under a security quarantine on the high, isolated mesa for the years they lived there, and could rarely venture outside. Partly due to the dearth of entertainment, the birth rate in Los Alamos was so high there were diaper shortages.

And though all traffic through the official gates of the supposedly high-security compound was strictly controlled, the children on the mesa regularly escaped to play outside the top-secret Site Y through unnoticed holes in the fences.

The next day she pored over pictures of the Trinity test in its first seconds, a black-and-white, stop-motion sequence of the rising and billowing mushroom cloud in the Alamogordo desert. She cast her eyes slowly over photographs of the Army barracks the scientists and their families had lived in, up on the mesa in World War Two, over Oppenheimer and his brother on horseback and scenic vistas of the Sangre de Cristo and Jemez mountains, snow-covered pines against a clear winter sky. She saw grainy, blurred shots of the bombs made at Los Alamos and then dropped on Hiroshima and Nagasaki.

The first bomb, called Little Boy, was rocket-shaped and used rare uranium 235. The second bomb was called Fat Man. It was rotund and used plutonium, which could be produced in bulk.

Finally she looked at portraits of the scientists themselves, rows and rows of men, many of them so-called geniuses. Among them was Fermi, a Nobel Prize winner and refugee from Mussolini. It was Fermi who had produced the first chain reaction in piles of graphite and uranium under the bleachers of Stagg Field at the University of Chicago. He was the one who had found a way to manufacture plutonium, the one who enabled the Allies to beat the Nazis to the bomb, and the one who made the bomb infinitely buildable.

He was also the spitting image of the short, balding man in the trench coat. His first name was Enrico.

When she saw the photograph of Fermi she closed the book she was reading and then deliberately, carefully closed the other books spread out at her elbows. She stacked them neatly in a pile beside her; she sat with her hands folded in her lap and watched the second hand tick on the clock on the wall. At five o'clock she made the usual rounds, flicking off lights and checking for stragglers, of which she already knew there were none.

Then she left.

❧ Though Oppenheimer would say later that implicit in the invention of the bomb was its use, while he directed the Manhattan Project he did not choose to frame it that way. Instead he chose to argue that the bomb, if its design succeeded, would be so terrible, so awesome in its power to destroy, that it would bring an end to all wars. Like no other weapon before it, the atom bomb would be an instrument of peace.

But for a brilliant man, Oppenheimer was relying on a surprisingly impoverished logic, the logic of a man attempting to rationalize. For clearly an undiscovered threat is no threat at all. For the idea of the bomb to emanate such awesome power, of course, the bomb would have to be used.

❧ Ben had promised Yoshi they would join him for cocktails at the mansion. He had promised Yoshi despite the fact that Ann rarely enjoyed a party, despite the fact that he knew this and usually tried to turn down such invitations, because Yoshi was uncomfortable with Roger and Lynn. Lynn was prone to ask him questions

about Japanese culture in a loud, carrying voice, stressing the sub-
jugation of women.

Ann was often anxious before social events but today she was
curiously indifferent. Stepping out of the shower she stood behind
Ben, who was shaving over the sink with a straight razor, and put
her arms around his waist. She saw the soft pinkness of their skin
in the mirror and the hardness of the tiles.

He turned to brush his foam-rimmed lips along hers and then
away again, and she stood on tiptoe and rested her chin briefly on
his shoulder, watching them in the mirror side by side. She marveled at their differences, how the two of them could be limited to
their separate spaces in air, their outlines distinct.

Letting go and crossing the room, dabs of white on her chin
and nose, it occurred to her that something was missing and she
stopped mid-stride, spinning on a heel, afraid for a split second she
had left it behind.

—Ben?

—Uh huh?

—Oh. Nothing.

The split-second had passed and she knew she hadn't forgotten anything specific: just part of her had vanished before she even
knew what it was. Something had escaped.

She stood still and tried to bring it back but could not. Instead
she thought of Roger and Lynn in their adobe palace, holding their
drinks in hands spangled with silver and turquoise, faces bored and
expectant. Usually she was alarmed when she thought of people
like that before she had to see them, usually it was dread, but now
she saw them in their element, certain that the ground would never
move beneath them unless they ordered it, and felt no apprehen-
sion. They were arrogant and they were right, they had always been
right: the world was safer for them than for anyone else. They
moved between adobe and a penthouse on Park Avenue and an
alpine chalet on Interlaken and a beach home in the British Virgin

Islands. The boards of their companies were peppered with men of girth with Pacemakers, men who had worked for tyrants. They would never be proven wrong.

Their smugness could be trusted, she told herself.

Always before this had bothered her, it had grated on her and rung with injustice, but now, oddly, it seemed like relief.

Then the next second, standing in the bedroom and looking back at the open door to the bathroom without moving, she saw the deep-blue tiles and caught a glimpse of a flash of metal as Ben flicked the razor along his jawbone. The relief was gone and she felt liquid, trembling from the center.

She had the fleeting recognition: I am not afraid of them now.

And then the next moment: Because I have more to fear.

She turned and opened the closet doors slowly and saw the worn shoes lying piled on the floor, the familiar grain of the closet door's wooden trim, the winter sweaters folded and piled sloppily on the shelf, a paper clotheshanger jacket that read *We* ♥ *Our Customers*.

Nothing routine could alarm her again: she was sealed off. Briefly this braced her, buoyed her up as though she'd won; but then the feeling was weak, with something dark and yellow behind it.

She thought: As long as I am surrounded by the life we all know. The life we all agree on.

❧ As they walked down the sloping street to the mansion Ben held her hand and told her that Roger and Lynn wanted waterfalls built for them, small hills and ponds sculpted in their garden. They wanted him to plant wildflowers that bloomed "at all times," lupines and Colorado columbine and penstemon and evening primroses and Indian paintbrush. —They have to bloom at all times, Lynn had said to Ben. When he told her that would require constant replanting and constant vigilance she shrugged. Also, he told her, there was the niggling problem of winter, the pesky revolution of the globe around the sun. She waved her hand and said —Fine! Just remember, we want them to be blooming at all times. Through the snow. If you have to heat the ground, whatever, put in heat lamps or whatever, just do it. As long as the lamps are hidden by leaves or something.

Roger wanted a one-hole golf course, Lynn wanted his golf course concealed with ornamental shrubs. Ann thought: The world we all agree on. With its terrible gardens.

She clutched Ben's hand and closed her eyes as they went down the hill, telling herself to let go of everything.

❧ Ben decided to stay close to her at the party to ensure she did not wander off as she sometimes did in clients' homes, wander off and stand alone in a dark walk-in closet where it was silent, or sit in an armchair in a neglected corner staring at some useless object she'd picked up off a shelf.

Because it was acceptable to pay attention to objects, and far easier than facing people she did not know, she would fasten herself to them sometimes to get away. Her lack of interest in the object was irrelevant: what counted was the envelope they made together, protected from intrusion.

❧ Caterers in white shirts and black bow ties carried trays of rich hors d'oeuvres through the crowd, goat cheese and rosemary and foie gras and puff pastries full of crab from the Bering Sea. Lynn took Ben by the arm and walked them through the other guests introducing him, and then Ann as an afterthought. Ann was not anxious, only pleasantly bored, but wished Lynn would not introduce her at all. She wanted only to observe the party, to watch the others from a quiet and concealed position.

After they had run the gauntlet they were given drinks and left in a corner to talk to Yoshi, who stood alone beside the beehive fireplace. He was smiling a slightly embarrassed smile and politely holding an untouched martini at arm's length. He said a few words to her, —Hello, my name's Yoshi, and then: —How are you?

But then he shook his head in apology when she tried to make small talk. He knew quite a few English words, Ben said, but it was difficult for him to string them into a sentence.

So Ben took him by the arm and led him to an alcove where there was a table and chairs. They sat down, Yoshi pulled a small lined notepad and a pencil from the pocket of his jacket, and Ben and Yoshi began drawing for each other. They had worked out a code of stick figures, which performed actions such as arriving at the door to the house or talking to each other in symbols: ! ? * $ #. Ben understood them quickly, and pointed out their meanings.

Now, Yoshi wrote, Roger and Lynn wanted a fountain in the front yard of the mansion, and they had commissioned one from a prominent Western artist, to be cast in bronze. This was a word Yoshi knew. —Bronze, he said. He had seen the sketches for it, and he could replicate them. He drew swiftly and efficiently: a horse with front legs flailing the air and an Indian warrior on its back, in full ceremonial headdress.

The horse would be rearing in the center of the fountain, and water would come spurting from his mouth. His mane would be flying wildly. The Indian would wield a tomahawk.

Behind her chair Ann heard a woman gasp and turned, panic rising. But the woman was only looking at another woman's raised left hand, which bore a diamond ring.

The woman with the ring, whose lips shone a peachy orange, said, —Yeah. Just Saturday. We were at Ten Thousand Waves actually.

—Really? A group tub?

—Yeah right. But seriously, he wants to go to lousy Maui!

She listened to them as the jarring sensation faded, replaced by safety, insulation. Privately she told herself: See? They are just the way they've always been. *Nothing has happened.*

These people, the ones I've never been able to stand, she thought, these people are the normal background noise of the world. They are a guarantee.

She thought: It is wrong but even not liking them, even not being able to *stand* them, all of a sudden I feel grateful.

❧ On the way home, three glasses of wine later, she held Ben's arm again, this time to steady herself. She had talked at length to an obstetrician who had his own country western band. They specialized in covers of Conway Twitty songs and played at weddings, baptisms and keg parties, he told her. But seldom bar mitzvahs.

She was proud of herself for talking to him.

—See? she said to Ben, one of her slippers falling off her foot, swiveling to scoop it up again with her toes. —I can do it!

Later, when he got into the shower to wash the cigar smoke from his hair, she left the house again and ran weaving down the street, arms wide and foolish, to lie on her back on the front lawn of a neighbor, hidden in a pocket of trees. The grass was already moist from the dew.

She gazed with blurred vision at a constellation of stars in the sky and thought: a drunk woman in a neighbor's front yard. Inside they lie in bed or do whatever else they're doing, and we don't know each other at all.

One of the books she had read about Oppenheimer claimed that it was at the moment of the first atom splitting that material things gained final ascendancy and took the place of God.

—But maybe God was just revealed, she whispered to the constellations, as though she possessed special wisdom, spinning and wet in the grass.

Before the mushroom cloud there had always been a dream of setting the human spirit free, a dream that the spirit could be loosed from its gates of skin, become airborne, ecstatic and undone.

And here it was at last: the mind of man.

3

❧ For several days after she saw the photographs of Oppenheimer and Fermi it was impossible for Ann to read about them. She woke up confused, woke up and was awake for less than a second one morning before she remembered her confusion. She had the nauseated, hollow feeling of someone struck by a loss.

She considered keeping everything simple, actually adopting the pose that everything *was* simple, adopting the pose and denying all evidence against it. It could work. Denial was a time-tried method, well-proven. She saw herself wearing blinders, willfully looking straight ahead. She wondered how long it took for horses who walked straight ahead without flinching under the whip to feel their front legs buckle beneath them.

❧ Although he had a relaxed manner and gentle posture Ben was inwardly in a state of constant vigilance. He had noticed the change and was watchful, always on guard against the sky falling.

He knew, like most of those on whom the sky has already fallen, that if the sky was, in fact, to fall there would be nothing he could do to stop it.

The sky was large.

❧ She was pushing her cart down the produce aisle, looking for mustard greens, when to her right she heard someone say indignantly —What in God's name is this?

She turned in the direction of the voice and there he stood, dressed this time in a gray suit and his porkpie hat and holding up a bunch of arugula.

She had let her cart roll to a stop and stared at them openly but they did not notice, intent on the arugula. She was wracking her brain for what to say when Oppenheimer finally put down the arugula and picked up a Daikon radish.

With this she stepped awkwardly toward him. Her shyness rose around her in walls but she felt pressed forward anyway, audacious, an impostor in her own skin.

—Excuse me.

—Yes?

—I'm sorry for intruding, but can you please—I think I know you from somewhere, but I can't remember where. Can you tell me your name?

—I don't think we've met, but certainly. This is Fermi, Enrico Fermi, he said pleasantly. —I am Oppenheimer. Robert.

Ann looked at him slack-jawed, and then at the bulbous Daikon radish. It resembled a club, and she thought *blunt instrument.*

In the first instant of the faint, as her legs wavered, still conscious but not in control, she realized she was falling and fumbled vaguely for Fermi's arm. He reached to help her, but not fast enough. Fortunately it was a straight shot to the floor and she crumpled conveniently against his side, sliding down and into a heap with her head at rest on the toe of Oppenheimer's leather shoe.

The two men exchanged quizzical glances, and then, unhurriedly and somewhat gracefully, stooped to pick her up. Fermi saw her purse sitting in the basket of the cart, and picked that up too.

—We need to lay her down, said Oppenheimer.

An observer would have seen two men, one tall and thin, the other stocky and balding and elfin, both somewhat antiquely dressed, the taller in hat and suit too large for his gaunt frame, the shorter in shirt sleeves. They walked at a leisurely pace toward the back of the store with a young woman propped up between them. Her head lolled onto the shoulder of the taller man, then flopped back, exposing an arched white throat, and rolled onto the shoulder of the shorter man. Her mouth hung open.

❧ Ben felt that every day he lost her, not for always but from sight. He was apart from the small measure of her life as it was spending itself, which seemed wasteful until he remembered it was fine, it was right. It was right not only for practical reasons but because the separation attenuated the hours and sharpened them to a point. Like abstinence or deprivation it spun out time into timelessness, actually *made the day longer,* and by extension the months and the years.

Still, sometimes he almost could not believe that he permitted these flagrant absences, these brutal removals of her person from his sphere of influence and sensation. These removals of her were virtual *robberies,* covert offenses, assaults on him, almost. That was how it looked when, finding himself alone after she left one morning, it occurred to him that with her gone he was solitary in everything, in the bare, cold roads that stretched from coast to coast intersecting only with each other, the monolithic industry that squatted by the roadsides, hunkered down, of infinite strip-mall suburbs where no sympathy could be found for what had evolved instead of being manufactured, what was abstract instead of concrete, where everything was made for the convenience of the barely sensate, the men who followed football and Nascar and Bud Ice, the women who emptied ashtrays out their car windows as they drove through the redwoods.

In such a gray glittering world it would be impossible to find tired relief, much less home. When she was beyond his reach there was always the danger of her permanent disappearance, and what evidence was there anyway, at those times, that she existed at all? He wondered idly if, like some animals—wolves? Birds of prey?— he might one day develop long-distance hearing or sight, be able miraculously to pick her out in a crowd miles away.

But he was used to a routine of separation five days a week, and the hours when he was with her and without complemented each other neatly. He was not naïve, he knew that even the closest of attachments could exhaust themselves and that absence, when it did not extinguish, tended to renew. And every day when the sun was setting, he saw her again: call him a greeting card but there it was, the light cast on the leaves was red and the branches might be warmed and rounded with gold and on the eastern rim of the sky there might be, from time to time, the earth's purple shadow, a dusky haze over the hills.

These were the shades of the end of day, when he saw her again. After the final colors of twilight in the trees as he walked or drove back up the hill of his street, after the descent of the sun, he had the deliberate routine of dinner, the softness of food in his mouth, the slowness and measured well-being of time in the house.

Then there was the prospect of sleep and a whole night of hours side by side. That was good.

❧ "The trouble with Oppenheimer," said Albert Einstein once, "is that he loves a woman who doesn't love him: the U.S. government."

❧ When Ann came out of her faint she was lying on a striped orange-and-brown couch, apparently alone. She sat up dizzily, looked around and saw she had company after all: in the corner was a dumpy, pale teenager playing a videogame.

She was in a dingy lounge paneled in fake wood, graced with a hulking television whose screen was a jagged green and pink zigzag of snowy images, playing mute and unwatched, and a bulletin board with homemade signs advertising *For Sale Cheap: ATV* and *Free Pit Bull Puppies*. There was also an ancient, faded poster in primary colors advertising the Heimlich maneuver.

Her head ached and she was so parched that she could feel her throat crack. There was a sink against the wall, a row of mugs in bright colors with logos and birthday wishes. She got up shakily and went toward it, but a water cooler loomed before she got there and she bent to fill a paper cone, and then drained it again and again.

—Aspirin over the sink if you wannit, lady, said the dumpy teenager.

—Thank you, said Ann.

She opened the cupboard and moved boxes of tea out of the way to find the bottle, popped a pill into her mouth, washed it down and sat back heavily on the couch.

—Excuse me, she said to the teenager, —Can you tell me something?

—What.

—Who brought me in here?

He shrugged. —These two guys.

—What did they look like to you?

—Whaddaya mean?

—Just describe them. Please.

—Uh, OK. There was a tall skinny guy in a hat that looked, like, old-fashioned or something. Then there was this shorter guy that had a foreign accent.

—Did they say anything to you?

—Nah, they just dumped you there and looked at their watches. Then they took off. Said they hadda go meet someone.

—Thank you.

So she still saw what was widely seen, at least. It might be filtered through a psychosis, but at least the men hadn't been built from the ground up on nothing but neural pathways. Probably the Oppenheimer lookalike had said a name like *Augsburger, Alzheimer's*. The power of suggestion.

Alternatively, he knew he was a dead ringer for Oppenheimer, the most iconic of the atom bomb men, and he cherished the resemblance. Living in a barely visible subculture, trading anecdotes by email and in chat rooms, was no doubt a legion of wannabe Oppenheimers, a host of Oppenheimer pretenders, like Elvises or James Deans or Marilyn Monroes.

Bastard. Preying on her weakness.

Or maybe, like that woman who underwent cosmetic surgery tens—or was it hundreds?—of times to force her face and body into the shape of Barbie's, he sought to actually *be* Oppenheimer and was remaking himself in the image of his private hero.

Fermi was just a sidekick.

—Did they say anything? she persevered.

—Just like to give you an aspirin when you woke up and it was nice to meet you. That was, like, a joke though.

❧ It occurred to Oppenheimer, looking at a piece of angular, metallic public art with no redeeming features, that bad art was infinitely sad.

If both science and art are forms of *unrequited love,* he thought, bad science and bad art are *pining away.*

❧ Szilard stepped off the bus from Chicago on a Saturday after a long trip that would have exhausted a lesser man. He made a bee-line for the public library, where he spoke in his thick accent— Hungarian-German, in fact—to Jeff the vegan. Jeff the vegan, in turn, told Ann about him when she went back to work after the weekend, describing him as "a fat foreign guy."

He had spent hours hunched over the microfiche readers vora-ciously scanning old newspapers, Jeff reported, and nibbling on chocolate bars as he peered at the screen. Intermittently he left and came back with pastries from a store down the street, which he gobbled surreptitiously as he scrolled. Jeff disclosed this with a shake of the head, himself masticating, with superior air, a peanut-buttered celery stick.

Finally Jeff caught him smearing jelly filling on the machine's knobs, eyes fixed on the fine print, oblivious to his transgression. Jeff asked him firmly, even punitively to be so kind as to take his "food" outside, please.

When he finished his donuts the "fat foreign guy" came up to Reference and fired off a battery of questions. (Jeff compared him to Mr. Hofstadt.) He wanted to know everything, Jeff said. He asked

about Presidents: Ford, Nixon, Carter, Reagan, Clinton, the two
Bushes; he asked about Gorbachev, the Berlin Wall, Vietnam, the
Gulf War, the World Trade Center. He asked about credit cards, cell
phones, satellites, GIS mapping, global warming, the disappearing
ozone, the moonwalk, the exploration of Mars, *Star Wars,* Chernobyl,
Madonna, Microsoft, electric cars, commercial aviation, the burning rain forests, the rising tides, the mass extinction of frogs and
birds.

He spent the evening at one of the computer terminals, fasci-
nated by the Internet. Jeff had to kick him out at the end of the day
by turning out the lights, but he was back the next morning waiting
for the library to open, sitting on the front steps, eating a cruller,
and when he saw Jeff, smiling broadly.

By the time Ann got to work, however, he had left, after re-
questing a library card for which Jeff turned him down, since he
had no proof of residency, in fact no fixed address, and no ID save
a worn and sixty-years-outdated University of Chicago faculty card.
On his way out he asked Jeff for the location of the nearest television station.

❧ Recently she had the urge to be immersed in water as soon as
she could when she got up in the morning. She wanted to stroke her
arms through the soft chemical blue and float when she was exhausted, float and think of white minarets, tropical forests, places
lush and quiet where, undisturbed by hunters, vast and gentle animals moved.

Swimming regulated her mind, kept the cogs turning, she felt,
surely and predictably, making her into a mill whose paddles
churned the water to good use, steady, determined, workmanlike.

One Tuesday morning after swimming, her face bleached dry
and pleasantly sterile from the chlorine, she bought an orange juice
and a bagel at a café on the way to work and sat down to read the
newspaper at an outside table, white metal and flimsy. Doves flut-

tered down to the pavement near her feet, dim-witted and dun-colored, barely noticeable in the shade.

On one of the back pages there was a human interest story: a corpulent man claiming to be a European scientist named Leo Szilard had burst onto the set of a local live news show, demanding air time.

He wanted to announce his return from the dead, and claimed to have proof of it in the form of fingerprints. He also claimed, under questioning by the police psychologist, to have once given a razor to Nikita Khrushchev.

Despite a Harvard education the psychologist had never heard of Nikita Khrushchev. For this reason the boast was wasted on him.

The police declined to fingerprint the fat man.

༄ Leo Szilard is believed by many to have been the man who first conceived of nuclear fission. He is also believed to have been the first to conceive of the cyclotron—parent machine of the "particle accelerator"—and the electron microscope. He was a pioneer in information theory, shared a patent for nuclear reactors with Fermi, and designed a liquid-metal refrigerator pump with Einstein. (The pump was impractical and failed to make them millionaires because, though it worked quite effectively, it also regularly emitted an ear-splitting screech.) When, after the war, he switched from physics to molecular biology, he invented the chemostat, which is still used today in microbiology, and was the first to theorize what is now known as "negative feedback regulation of enzyme activity," for which someone else later received the Nobel Prize. He studied sperm preservation and promoted research that would eventually lead to the discovery of the birth-control pill.

And it was Szilard who first suggested—to Nikita Khrushchev, in fact—a nuclear telephone hotline between the president of the United States and the premier of the Soviet Union.

He took out numerous patents including one for low-fat cheese, an early "lite" food product.

Szilard was perennially broke and perennially alone until quite late in life. After two decades of friendship, in 1951 he finally married his longtime penpal and confidante Trude Weiss. He was secretive about this and when belatedly told of the marriage, a colleague at Columbia inquired with genuine curiosity, —Who would marry Szilard? It must have something to do with taxes.

❧ Excited, grasping the newspaper tightly, she left the doves clucking and walking in circles. When she got to her desk at work she clipped the story and called the police department to find out whether the fat man claiming to be Leo Szilard was still in custody. They told her no charges had been pressed and the man had been released, only to turn his attention to the FBI field office in Albuquerque, where he had also demanded to be fingerprinted.

The FBI had refused to accede to his request and had released him on his own recognizance.

For the first time, hanging up the phone, she felt practical, hard-nosed, not adrift but detail-bound and equal to difficult tasks. Recalling that she had found Ben in the phonebook she looked up Detectives, *see Investigations,* which yielded a listing billing itself as *Complete Investigative Services, Professional Expedient Confidential, Criminal Defense Personal Injury Child Custody Missing Persons Pre-Marital & Background Checks.*

She called to set up an appointment and then made several photocopies from a book.

The office of the so-called *Investigative Services* was not dark and strewn with ashtrays but brightly, blankly lit. There were posters of Hawaii on the walls and yellow and orange paper flowers in ceramic vases on the coffee table in the waiting room.

The receptionist noticed her looking at these.

—Vic one of the owners? He just like has a thing for Hawaii, it's like a Magnum PI fixation or something.

On her way back to the library she drove to the mansion, where she parked her car beside Ben's truck and walked down into the garden. He was planting passion flower vines at the base of the bronze horse statue, not without reluctance. He told her the pale tendrils of the vines, thin as threads with curling ends, would grow around the hooves and fetlocks and up the muscular legs. Quickly they would produce complex, delicate flowers of purple and white and hairy green fruits the size of pecans.

When he stood and pulled off his gloves by the fingertips, slapping off the dirt across the thigh of his workpants, she told him she felt lighter, loftier having suspended her disbelief. She told him she had been afraid of collapsing inward, but now she felt she was expanding outward, growing lighter, shedding weight.

—Your first thought will be that I'm psychotic, she said.

—I can't wait.

They sat down on a rock ledge and she went on, with effort,

—There are these scientists that are supposed to be dead.

—What? said Ben.

Before she answered she glanced up at the street, where a Volvo passed and a young blond girl with a smooth and perfect face looked out the window at her, bored.

—I saw them once in a bar, and now I'm looking for them.

❧ In a greeting card store Ann browsed for a card for her older brother. It was his birthday. All over the cards was written *I love you*.

Ann did not select any of those cards. Her brother did not want a card that said *I love you*. People forget, thought Ann looking at the furry animals, the flowery flowers, that even love is only an idea. And the people that believe they hate ideas, the ones that claim no interest in the abstract, buy greeting cards and songs that say *I love you* by the billions. At once brimming with and devoid of meaning, *I love you* is a sacred cliché.

It cannot be assailed.

෨ He liked being alone in the garden. He had long, warm stretches of solitude, broken only by the times when Lynn came and talked to him for too long, when he had to tell his assistants what to do or meet with Yoshi to go over designs. The assistants were mostly self-sufficient and Yoshi rarely needed him, so it was chiefly Lynn who was responsible for interrupting. Luckily she usually kept busy. When she was at loose ends his days could be burdensome.

And even though he resented the removal of Ann he also savored the fact that his daytime separation from her was complete and seamless. There was a neatness in the division between work and play, one he had to admit he did not mind. So it jarred him when her coworker Jeff from the library called him on the cell phone, intruding.

He barely knew Jeff. Jeff tended to wear a pinky ring, he recalled, of a small coiled snake with forked tongue protruding. It was this snake he remembered when he pushed the TALK button and heard the man's voice. Vaguely he also saw carrot sticks in a freezer bag that Jeff had been carrying the first time they met, in the library's parking lot. And he recalled Jeff's checked shirt, which featured fake mother-of-pearl snaps, and the flaky dryness of Jeff's lips.

—The thing is, said Jeff, —I was wondering if there was anything going on that I should know about. At, you know, home. I don't mean it's my business, obviously it's not, I just mean in case that would help explain things, or help me in terms of dealing with any changes in, you know, work habits that I might be observing? At all?

Ben was rendered speechless. He walked across the yard and leaned against a crab apple tree with the phone to his ear.

—Just in terms, Jeff went on, —of any irregularities that might, you know, eventually cause problems in terms of work performance? I mean I'm not her supervisor, you know, I mean actually she's mine, technically. This is more from a, you know, wanting to help her out kind of situation. That I'm asking.

—I'm sorry, said Ben. He was surprised, even shocked at the suggestion that Ann had begun to be remiss in the work that she had always done impeccably. She had always been a good librarian, neat, organized, accessible, kind, at least the way he saw it.

And then there was the claim she had just made to him, that resurrected A-bomb scientists from World War Two were lurking in the bushes.

Possibly she was suffering from post-traumatic stress. It would not be surprising, given the violence of the schizophrenic man's death.

But he put that aside, as he had trained himself to do when protocol demanded an impersonal response.

—What are you asking me? Whether my wife and I are having *marital* difficulties?

—No! said Jeff, —no, I didn't mean that, totally. Just if there's anything going on, like maybe illness in the family.

—I don't quite understand, sorry. Are you calling because you have something to ask me? Or tell me?

—Oh, said Jeff, —Well I guess both. Just that she hasn't been keeping her normal, the work hours she's normally committed to, is the thing. Which as you know, she's always been real prompt, I barely even saw her take a sick day before now. So I was wondering if there was a, say, mitigating circumstance.

—May I ask why you're speaking to me about this instead of to her?

There was a brief silence, during which Ben thought he could hear a carrot being bitten into and ruminated. Or possibly celery.

—I kind of did but it didn't seem to be getting results.

—I see, said Ben. The guy was an asshole. And now Lynn was approaching across the back patio, a deliveryman pushing a hand-cart behind her with what appeared to be—yes.

A stone cherub. It held aloft a large cluster of grapes.

—So I just thought I would make sure, you know, before I bring it up with anyone or whatever, I mean if that comes up. I mean the absenteeism issue.

—I'm sorry, said Ben, —I appreciate your concern but I can't help you. I don't discuss my wife's personal life with her coworkers without her knowledge. I will say no, there have been no deaths or illnesses in the family since her parents died. Beyond that you'll have to take up this question with her. And let me just say for the record that calling me was completely inappropriate.

—Huh, said Jeff.

—OK? So I'll have to go now, I'm at work, said Ben.

Lynn, standing on the edge of the patio in high heels, was waving at him frantically, as though she was marooned on a desert island and he was flying overhead, her sole chance of rescue.

—If you, could you at least do me a favor, though, too?

Ben suppressed a sigh. —Doubt it, he said.

—If maybe you could give me a couple days' lead before you let her know that I called? Just because then I could bring it up with her again, like, myself. It's that I've, like, been having—

—No, said Ben. —Weren't you listening to me? I don't keep things from her. Again, I think it was wrong for you to call me about this.

—That's hardcore, said Jeff. —But whatever I guess.

—Good luck, said Ben. —I hope you work it out.

He pressed END as Lynn, impatient, actually stepped off the patio and into the deep earth of the south rock garden, freshly turned and aerated. Her stiletto heel sank deep instantly and she stumbled, shrieking.

Behind her the deliveryman stepped up and grabbed a windmilling arm.

—Are you all right? asked Ben, drawing near, pocketing the cell phone.

—That's my bad ankle! I've had physical therapy on this ankle *six times*! raged Lynn, and flapped angrily at the deliveryman with her free hand as she sat down hard on the flagstones.

—Are you going to need an ambulance? asked Ben.

She looked up at him sharply, but seeing only polite concern had no recourse.

—No, no, no, she grumbled. —I just need to not fucking step in fucking mud.

She pulled a shoe off to reveal gold toenails and a heel broken, dangling.

—Uh, so where do you want this? asked the deliveryman.

—Damn it! That was a Badgley Mischka!

She hurled the shoe into the soil again.

—That, uh, the statue is for the back—? inquired Ben.

—In with the—somewhere back there! Near the hummingbird garden! she said angrily, massaging the ankle, and he nodded at the deliveryman.

—Past that acacia, go along the path there to the right, he said. —You can leave it beside the birdbath. Can I get you some ice?

—Help me inside, said Lynn. —I'll put it up first.

She hopped beside him, steadied on his arm, lurching into his side with every hop. At the back doors he hesitated to slip off his work boots and Lynn leaned insistently on his shoulder, as though he was furniture.

—Just take me to the chaise over there, she said.

He deposited her on a pink chaise lounge and headed to the kitchen. Crescent-shaped ice rained out of the refrigerator into a glass, and he wrapped the crescents in a dishcloth.

Back in the cavernous living room she had draped herself artfully on the chaise, tasseled cushions behind her head, one leg over the back, her skirt hiked up to mid-thigh.

—I don't know that you'll be able to balance these on the ankle like that, said Ben. —Maybe we should move you to the chair and pile the cushions on the footstool?

Grudgingly she dropped her leg from the back of the chaise and handed him a cushion from behind her head.

—I'm fine here, she said.

He leaned down and lifted the ankle onto the cushion, then put the ice on it, adjusting for stability.

—Just get me the phone, would you?

He brought her the portable from its silver cradle.

—And could I have some water?

Water, like the crescents, rained.

—Oh, you know what I need? We have some like soothing lotion, like menthol rub? It's in the vanity in the master bath.

—I should probably make sure he's all right back there, said Ben, gesturing out the back door, thinking of the deliveryman stomping through cosmos. —Would you like me to ask Marcia to help you?

—It's Marcia's day off. She's in Gallup. And Roger's in La Jolla, he won't be back until Tuesday.

—OK. I'll get you the lotion, and then I should get back to work.

In the master bath he was deluged by scents. The floor was strewn with Lynn's lacy underwear, tangled nylons, bikini segments, padded bras, the counter with cleansers, moisturizers, atomizers, even an almost-whole cucumber with slices cut off one end, paper-thin slices now wet and clinging to the bowl of the sink. There was a curling iron, a blow dryer, sunscreen, self-tanning gel, under-eye cream, cuticle cream, cellulite cream.

Roger's modest shaving kit huddled in the corner, apparently frightened.

Ben opened the vanity determined to notice nothing private, but the lotion, unfortunately, was nowhere to be seen, necessitating increasingly close scrutiny. Past a package of condoms, batteries, dental floss, past antidepressants, tranquilizers, razorblades, organic alcohol-free deodorant, lip gloss, eye shadow, he finally found a small brown-glass container.

When he got back to Lynn she was lying with her head back and her eyes closed.

—Could you just smooth some on for me? she murmured, without opening them.

He noticed that somehow, from her prone position, she had brushed her hair to fan out over her shoulders and applied fresh lipstick.

—Sorry, I'll just put it down here for now, said Ben gently. —I have to go see about the delivery guy. I think he may be trampling your nasturtiums.

❧ "I love you" is everywhere, reflected Ann when she saw two teenagers making out against a wall as she walked down Alameda. The popularity of love in general and "I love you" in particular might be ascribed to their deceptive humility. "I love you" seems to privilege "you" over "I" and by this small deception, she thought, becomes sacrosanct. Because what could be wrong with offering to be subsumed?

❧ Saturday morning art buyers and gawkers milled around on the sidewalks looking for more to buy, coffees and shopping bags in hand. Oppenheimer stood in a gallery, looking at a piece of ancient pottery held out from the wall on delicate plexiglass brackets. He was alone.

Ann hovered outside staring in, struck and held. She had caught sight of him from the street when she turned suddenly, hearing her name called behind her. But it was someone else with her name, a woman in a red cowboy hat and a black leather jacket, running in heels to greet someone, smiling a shiny smile and opening her arms.

When she looked away she saw Oppenheimer through the window of the gallery.

After a minute he moved toward the back and disappeared in the white glare on the windowpane. She waited until he came out and donned his hat, her heart beating a panicked beat, and watched him turn to trudge down the driveway beside the gallery building toward the yard behind. As he turned the corner of the building she followed him, slowly gaining. He walked out between two houses, dipped down into a small arroyo, crossed the sandy bed and walked up the slight rise to the street behind, which he turned off into a dirt road behind. Striding up the alley he lit a cigarette, waved out the match and threw it away. She thought how slight he was, despite his height, how slight and delicate a figure he cut.

He stopped and swiveled on his heels to look at a house off the alley, a dusty backyard through which children's toys were strewn, a yellow plastic car, a battered, zebra-striped kite, an orange frisbee gnawed by a dog and a plywood doghouse, water-stained and leaning.

She stopped too, *chicken*, and then started up again, forcing herself, drawing close, looking at the brown leather of her shoes, lightened by dust, and then up at his hunched shoulders.

—Dr. Oppenheimer? she called, feeling it come out of her mouth awkward, almost pathetically eager.

He turned.

—The—young lady from the grocery store?

—Yes. But did you—is that really your name?

—Oppenheimer. Yes.

—The one—Robert. The physicist.

—The only one I know, said Oppenheimer, inhaling swiftly on his cigarette and beginning to walk again.

She found herself walking fast to keep up, in fact scurrying to keep up. Rats scurry, she thought. Rats and other rodents, small furtive animals.

—Who invented the atom bomb.

—Hardly, said Oppenheimer, chuckling. —I was one among many. And I would say *developed,* not invented.

—But you're dead.

—So they say.

—So—what? How do you—how can you be what you say? Are you a liar, or am I having a breakdown?

—Please! said Oppenheimer, surprised, turning to raise an eyebrow in her general direction and stopping. —I have no idea who you are, or what the current state of your psychological health may be!

—I, no, said Ann. —But I mean, how can you—

He started walking again, moving quickly.

—We've considered various scenarios. One proposition, which we've discussed in the vaguest terms only of course, is that this— and he gestured around him at the garages off the alley with their blistering paint, a tire swing hanging from a dead tree, a filthy silver car with a suction-foot Garfield in the rear window—is *our* delusion. Including you. Some kind of postmortem experience of cognition, sounds like an oxymoron I know, maybe based on an energy transfer—

He tossed his cigarette onto the dirt beside a garbage can and ground it in with a heel.

—that occurred at the time of the test, or a massive release of stored chemicals, say neurotransmitters . . . ?

Ann looked from the rotating heel to a mailbox beside them, on the side of the alley. It was a freestanding mailbox painted in camouflage, balanced solitary on a wooden stake in a clump of dried grass beside the hard, rutted dirt of the road. It had been caved in on one side, probably by a euphoric youth with a baseball bat. She was only half-listening to Oppenheimer, at the same time bored and captivated. The mailbox had tried to camouflage itself, but had been blindsided anyway.

—he was suggesting there was some form of surplus energy that remained after the moment of death, which had the capacity to, as it were, ideate—

His fingers were long and thin, forefinger and middle finger stained yellow. It occurred to her that Szilard was right: they should be fingerprinted. Their fingerprints might still be on record; they had worked for the Army.

—use the term loosely to mean "simulate the experience of consciousness"—produce a pseudo-sensory perception. I'm thinking of Einstein's discussion of Leucippus, for example. Early atomism. Death, for the purposes of this discussion, would be construed not as a change in the essence of an individual but as a rearrangement of particles in space—

—Listen, interrupted Ann in a tentative voice, thinking his head was too large for his body, his body like a stringy puppet with a pumpkin on top—this is—

—united by some cohesive force under a specific set of conditions. Since our final memories immediately coincide with the Trinity test, it's been surmised that there was something in the event, something anomalous and unprecedented, that managed to duplicate us over time, essentially move a copy of us, as it were, while the originals remained, forward through—

—Time travel? This is like science fiction?

—I make no claims as to genre. My point is, there have been a number of suggestions, but none of them make much sense. And believe me, none of them have anything to do with you.

He paused

—Incidentally, you would be—?

—I work at the library downtown. A man who said he was Dr. Szilard came in a few days ago—

—Leo! I see.

—He asked my—another librarian a number of—

—Leo is the opposite of discreet. Always was. He's a one-man assault on good taste.

—But I have to ask you, I mean—if you are who you claim to be—how did you—?

—One minute we were down in the desert near Socorro counting down to the test. I was very tense, there had been forecasts of inclement weather and I was worried about what you now call "fall-out," and worse, what if after everything we'd been through we had a complete bust on our hands anyway—I wasn't sure it would work, I really wasn't—and we were under T-30 seconds, under T-10, and I was holding on to a post, so nervous I could barely stand. Then it went off. And it was . . .

—What?

—. . . It was something no one should ever see. But seeing it, we were transformed instantly. Like the matter itself. I don't expect you to understand that. My colleague has suggested that possibly we too became energy. But then again, here we are. We seem to be animals as always. We still have the same old bodies, and we sleep. And we breathe.

—When I passed out you carried me, she said vaguely, thinking of their real legs as she fell, their real feet.

—And then I was here. In a motel.

—A motel?

—Sadly yes. I recollect waking up in a bed with a lumpy mattress. There was a print on the wall of a naked child holding a nosegay. Crass.

—You're saying you went from—

—First it was '45—the early hours of July 16th, around 5:30 to be precise, and then here I was in the next millennium. Purportedly.

—So you just materialized in a motel, you're telling me.

—Actually I was lucky it was a motel. Fermi fetched up in the pouring rain on a street just off the Plaza, lying in a gutter. He was almost run over.

—You understand it's not—I mean it's obviously not believable, you being who you say you are.

She tripped: a blunt, burnished tongue of metal sticking out of the packed dirt of the road. Recovered but felt itchy on her skin, the swell and tingle of awkward humiliation. It was not good to trip during a first meeting. She had already been nervous.

—I hope you won't take offense, but as far as what you may or may not believe, I'm indifferent, frankly, said Oppenheimer, amused.

—You claim the world is unreal, you're real but the whole world is unreal.

—There *is* a real world, of course. This just isn't it.

—Right.

—Clearly the vision, presentation, landscape—whatever it is—is dystopic. I mean you don't expect me to believe . . .

He gestured at a house they were passing, whose backyard, grass still brown from beneath winter ice, was full of rusted motorcycles and bright red and yellow-painted totem poles bearing the caricatured faces of movie stars. An old man with a gray beard sat on a stained toilet in the middle of them, watching a talk show on a small television on a stump.

—. . . You don't propose that *this* is the world, I hope.

Then they emerged from the alley onto a bright, wide street, and Oppenheimer waved at a short man on the other side. She recognized him: Fermi.

—Anyway, a pleasure, said Oppenheimer lightly, and shook her hand in dismissal. —Excuse me.

She pulled up short and watched him walk away.

❧ —She says Szilard is here too, Oppenheimer told Fermi, whom he was trying, as usual, to extract from a trance.

—Insult to injury, murmured Fermi.

❧ It was early afternoon when they emerged. She had gone into the coffeehouse once for a glass of ice water and watched them with mugs at their elbows, bent toward each other in conversation. Above them hung a spider plant, brown at the points of its leaves. They were sitting at a window. She had gone outside again and perched on the curb for a while, her feet in the gutter. She could see Fermi's shoulder and arm if she looked in from the right place.

She had paced an arc around the side of the building, leaving a wide berth, waiting. And finally they came out, and she walked behind them, keeping her distance.

Behind them as they moved along the sidewalk, Oppenheimer lighting up as usual, tossing a burnt match into a jojoba bush, Fermi shaking his head, she skulked at a fair distance, too far to hear them, too close to lose sight. There was an aimlessness to their walk, it was brisk but going nowhere, somehow, and she was drifting too.

Then in the turn of an instant Oppenheimer leapt off the curb into the street to flag a passing taxi. Of course there was no other taxi near. She noted the name on the door and squinted to make out the number as they stepped in and the car pulled away; then she raised her cell phone to her ear and dialed 411.

But the dispatcher would not tell her where the cab was going and she watched as the car crested a hill and disappeared.

She had lost them, but at least she had talked to Oppenheimer and the salient details had been established. If he was a pretender he was immaculate in the pretense, down to the yellowed fingertips and the frail, pompous gentility. And she had been neat and quiet behind them, unassuming and respectful.

Leo Szilard, it turned out, was none of these things.

❧ It was two days later that Investigative Services delivered the goods. He had not been difficult to locate. He was urgently attempting to transact business all over northern New Mexico. He had spoken without success to several newspaper reporters, an assistant at KUNM who would not let him past the front desk and whom he accused of being narrow-minded, and finally, apparently desperate, a reviewer of modern dance from Taos, who was very open-minded indeed.

He was checked into a cheap motel on Cerrillos Road, and was taking most of his meals, which exceeded three per day, in nearby ice-cream and pizza joints.

Ann drove to the motel during her lunch hour and knocked on

his room door. When he answered Szilard was wearing a white terrycloth robe. Drops of water stood out on his pink face and the bathtub gurgled and sucked behind him, draining. A talk show droned along at low volume on the television.

—Sorry for the intrusion, but—are you Leo Szilard?

—Yes! said Szilard, and smiled. —Yes I am!

—I read your book, said Ann, —*The Voice of the Dolphins.*

—Indeed! beamed Szilard. —I have not yet had the pleasure! I did read a synopsis, however. On the Internet.

He opened the door, stepped back and padded across the indoor-outdoor carpeting in his bare feet, to root around in a suitcase and pull out a pair of balled socks. She stepped in and stood beside the veneer-top table, littered with papers marked PRESS RELEASE in large letters and stapled lists of addresses.

—I work at the library, said Ann. —You were there the other day and I heard about it. And I—I saw Robert Oppenheimer. I talked to him.

Szilard, sitting on the edge of his bed and pulling on a sock, looked up quickly.

—He's here too?

—And Fermi.

—Enrico!

—I should say, men claiming to be Oppenheimer and Fermi, and now you, claiming to be Szilard.

—Claiming correctly, said Szilard. —I *am* Szilard. This is good! I was expecting them, I knew they would come. I had no concrete indication, however. Until now.

—But you—Szilard is dead.

—You shouldn't presume, said Szilard, struggling with the second sock. —It's irrational. We know next to nothing about death. It is an undiscovered country.

—Where did you come from then?

—Anyway I can prove it. They would have to pull my files, this is the problem. Somewhere the armed forces may have my finger-prints. Could be the Army, the Air Force, the Department of Defense—they definitely had Oppie's and Fermi's, everyone who worked on the project. It was under military jurisdiction, as you may know. If you know about us. Do you know?

—I've been doing homework. But that was a long time ago.

—Don't be fooled. The military has a long institutional memory. So where is Oppenheimer? And where's Enrico?

—I don't know, said Ann, —do you mind? and pulled out one of the chairs to sit down. —I've tried to follow them but I always lose them. They haven't been, uh, making public appearances like you. So I can't trace them as easily.

—Call expensive hotels, said Szilard. —Guarantee you, that's where Oppenheimer will be. Only the finer things for that guy. He's a snob. I need to talk to them. There's a directory in the nightstand there, see?

It was in a black plastic binder dangling a broken chain, clearly stolen from a payphone.

—You're asking me to call?

—Yes please, said Szilard. —I'll go get dressed. You call please.

He plucked pants and a shirt off a rack and trundled into the bathroom, slamming the door behind him. She heard something crash, a rattle as it fell, and then the toilet flushing.

She had called in sick to work and made it through seven hotels when he emerged, unkempt-looking, his hair toweled into a short frizz, his shirt wrinkled and buttoned wrong and too tight around the midsection.

—Nothing yet, she told him. —Could he be registered under another name?

—I don't think so, no need, said Szilard. —He has nothing to hide. Hand it over, I'll do a few.

❧ They met Oppenheimer in the lobby of the La Posada. —Step outside, shall we? he said, tapping a cigarette out of his pack. —They don't allow smoking in the lobby. In other respects I'm quite satisfied here.

—Nice place, nodded Szilard.

—Also, they claim to have a ghost, a female ghost who wears a hood. I myself have not, uh, seen her, needless to say. Probably only comes out for the tourists. In any case, I enjoy the courtyard, and the casitas are nice.

He paused to light the cigarette.

—Where's my old friend Fermi? asked Szilard eagerly.

—Just around the corner, at La Fonda, said Oppenheimer, and exhaled a plume of smoke. —He prefers it. And where are you, Leo?

—A motel on Cerrillos. I *was* in Chicago, on the campus. But then—

—You came here.

—I had to come. This is why, you and Fermi. I knew I wouldn't be the only one. I've always had good timing. Got me away from the Nazis. Also, there was nothing for me to do in Chicago. And it was cold.

He turned to Ann.

—But what's your interest?

—Just, said Ann, —that I found you.

Oppenheimer glanced at her sidelong.

—Lunch please? asked Szilard. —I'm hungry.

❧ Oppenheimer's old summerhouse in the tropics, on the Virgin Island of St. John, is a decaying yellow bungalow in a well-hidden cove. Unlike most other houses on the island it is built directly on the sands of the beach instead of up on a hill. At the top of the drive-way down to this small beach is a decrepit wrought-iron gate on top of which only the letters P HEIMER BEACH remain.

After Oppenheimer died, his ashes were scattered off a rock by his wife Kitty. Five years later Kitty herself died; another five years later their daughter killed herself. Eventually the house passed into the hands of a nearby village, which, being poor and having no convenient use for the house, neglected it. In the decades following, the ocean slowly encroached upon the house and waves began to lap against the wooden deck.

Children played on the beach. One or two of them treasured the house and the salty palm fronds that brushed across its dust-covered planks in the gentle trade winds. They assumed that the house, in all its dereliction, was a permanent fixture. One or two of them would remember the house fondly when they were grown up as *that old house on the beach,* never having noticed the letters on the grail gate, never knowing it had also once been known as *the Oppenheimer house.*

But as they played their parents knew that the house was on its last legs. Their parents knew that one day soon the house would be eaten up by the sea.

❧ Szilard hinted at fried chicken but Oppenheimer turned him down demurely. He did not like modern fast food. It was bland. The grease did not bother him, the probability of Bovine Growth Hormone, the potential for E. coli. He had read about these but he was not particularly unnerved by them. The world had never been sterile, he said. Why should it?

No: it was the lack of seasoning that was unacceptable to him. Flavor, he rebuked Szilard in gentle tones, as though talking to a baby.

For lunch he often patronized a restaurant across town. They would be his guests, he said generously.

Ann explained her situation to them as they walked to her car to drive to the restaurant, Oppenheimer striding with his jacket flapping loosely, Szilard bustling. She felt out of place but oddly secure, more solid herself between figments.

Unlocking her car doors and ushering them in, she said to Szilard, who stood beside her apparently waiting to have the car door opened for him, —You say *I'm* a figment of *your* delusional system but that could be a part of *my* mental illness. All your complicated theories? Just my mind. Refusing to recognize its insanity.

—Hmm, said Oppenheimer, trying to fold his long legs into the passenger seat of her Toyota, —but haven't you already recognized the insanity? Frankly you seem quite eager to accept it. This car was made for a midget, I think.

—You can push the seat back, said Ann, and Szilard leaned around from the back seat and raised the lever on Oppenheimer's right.

—They don't say "midget" anymore, said Szilard. —I saw it on the Internet. They say "little person."

—Oh for Chrissake, said Oppenheimer. —Perfectly good word, wasn't it? What's wrong with "midget?"

—The midgets don't like it.

At first she'd been panicked, she told them. —On the brink of hysteria, actually, if you want to know, she said, —which you probably don't.

But now she was caught up in the proposition that they were real—a miracle, or a revolution. It fell to her to move with the fluid currents, observing, paying close attention. She would pretend she was in gentle waters to stay afloat, retaining her buoyancy.

But she was choking.

—Could you at least roll down the window, please? she asked Oppenheimer, who had not discarded his cigarette.

—Of course.

—Can I ask how you're living? asked Ann. —I mean did you show up from the afterworld with a credit card?

—Personal checks, though if you'll permit me it's hardly your business, said Oppenheimer. —My checkbook was in the suitcase. And I can do without the sardonic inflection.

—Stop the car! yelled Szilard. —I think I see Dick Feynman!

Oppenheimer glanced out the window, mildly bored. Szilard pointed. Ann flicked her blinker on and started to pull over, but the driver of the hulking SUV behind her leaned on the horn insistently.

—I said pull over! urged Szilard. —Pull over!

—I'm doing my best, she snapped, and finally pulled in at the head of a line of parked cars as the SUV surged out from behind her, horn wailing.

Szilard jumped up and got out, moving with surprising agility. The car door stood open as he jogged back along the sidewalk.

—So, said Ann, —where's Fermi today?

—He stayed in, said Oppenheimer. —I think he may be a little down. He was always very rational. A practical man. No time for frivolities like, say, philosophy or religion.

—This is hitting him hard, huh, said Ann.

—He used to talk about taking early retirement and going back to the land, mused Oppenheimer. —He came from peasant stock. Piacenza, in the Po River valley. He said he wanted to be a farmer when he was finished with physics. Personally I had trouble picturing it. But apparently he died before realizing the dream. At the ripe old age of fifty-three, if I'm not mistaken. He's a first-rate mind, Fermi.

Someone rapped on Ann's window: a cop.

—This is a no-parking zone, ma'am, he said, when she rolled down the glass.

—I'm sorry, I was just waiting—

—Fine, but you just want to pull up and around the corner there. You see? Right there, across from the mailbox.

—Sure. OK. I'll pull up.

—And you sir, you been wearing your seatbelt?

—What business—

—He was just relaxing while we waited for—

—Make sure you do.

The cop slapped the roof of the car and she pulled around the corner.

—I thought we beat the fascists, said Oppenheimer.

—Well, it's all for—we know some things about public health we didn't know then, said Ann. —Statistics—

—It wasn't him, burst out Szilard, sliding into his seat again. —It looked like him but it wasn't. I had a feeling it was just the three of us here, but I wanted to make sure. Why'd you move the car? I thought I'd lost you.

—We were fugitives on the lam, said Oppenheimer. —The law was after us.

—It was a no-stopping zone, said Ann. —Can we go now?

—Dick Feynman, bright young man, mused Oppenheimer, as Ann pulled away from the curb. —But sadly, deranged. I just read it yesterday: he once locked himself up in Bob Serber's basement. He was trying to teach the dog to speak English.

❧ The restaurant had a full bar and apparently, in Oppenheimer's opinion, it was never too early for bourbon. Ann left the two scientists at the table and called Ben, standing outside the front door with the phone hot against her ear, in the shade of a honey locust.

—I'm with Oppenheimer and Szilard, she said. —I'm trying to find out if I'm dreaming them or they're dreaming me.

—I hope you're dreaming them, said Ben calmly.

❧ But after he hung up he told the guys he would be back in half an hour. He exchanged his workboots for soft-soled shoes on the back patio and padded through the house, passing the vast cathedral space of the dining room, where Yoshi was nodding patiently as Lynn said, —I mean it's just not the way I pictured it. So OK. So I'm the client and I'm not happy. I'm paying. Get it? So then make them rip it out!

He stopped in the laundry room to bend over the faucets of the industrial sink. He scrubbed his nails and washed his hands as usual, looking out the small, deeply set window at a bushy young box elder slated for destruction. He would not allow this; he would remove it with roots intact and replant it elsewhere, in his own yard if need be.

He and Yoshi and the other workers were under orders to use only this bathroom. The guest bathrooms were barred from what Roger liked to call "work traffic," since the perfection of their delicate floors of tropical hardwood and slate could easily be marred by heavy boots.

Ben was glad, personally, because he had ventured into the front bathroom on his first day, ignorant of the rules, and found it chock full of angels. China angels and glass angels holding potpourri were massed on the surfaces, counters, window sills, even the edge of the bathtub, along with stuffed, fabric angels, beanbag angels, stone angels, painted angels, plastic angels, even angels made of twigs and dried flowers. On the wall there were black-and-white photographs of babies with angel wings affixed, sprouting from their baby backs. Cherubs were crowded on the toilet tank, staring at him as he stood over the bowl.

They appeared to take a prurient interest.

❧ *Love of knowledge* can draw on its credit indefinitely, Ann was thinking as she pocketed her cell phone and turned away from the shade of the tree. In love and knowledge there are two ostensibly virtuous quantities, so love of knowledge is ironclad.

Reaching for its heavy iron handle of the restaurant door she looked at the gleaming glass and the dark wood, felt drawn to them, these strong and beautiful surfaces. She saw the scientists inside and felt the momentum of returning to them, returning to the anomaly, the spectacle of them sitting and eating and saying they were people they could not possibly be, not, at least, if everything she had ever learned in her life was still true.

Feeling the air-conditioning rush up to meet her, goose bumps rise on her arms, she thought: *Love of knowledge* is still and always sacred, no matter what damage it inflicts.

❧ Driving he wondered if it was wrong that he was tracking her down, if his appearance would irritate her or strike her as intrusive. He hated to make her uncomfortable: her discomfort, even slight, made their separateness heavy. He was happiest when he could interpret the tacit understandings between them as evidence that they were the same.

On the other hand there was something in her demeanor that warned him to pay close attention, that signaled to him the presence of novelty. Where she was concerned he did not want novelty. He wanted everything to continue.

Parking the truck in a dirt lot across the street, mimicking Ann unawares, stalker after stalker, he walked around the side of the building gazing into windows. He wanted to know that she was in the company of others, safe where she'd said she would be. She was not at a window table and finally he had to put his face up close to the glass, stucco window edge against his cheek, dotting it with points of almost-puncture, to see inside without being seen. He did see her then, at a table in the bar area, talking to a portly man who resembled a lawyer, an insurance salesman, someone in a workaday profession. A few feet away, standing with his elbow on the bar, smoking, a third man—gaunt, elegant, and somewhat effete— watched them with an aspect of listening.

Ben stayed motionless, his eyes fixed on them, until the thin man finished his cigarette and ambled over to rejoin the others.

❧ —What we need, said Szilard, —is to get a meeting with someone who can pull strings in the Department of Defense.

—He wants to get you both fingerprinted, to prove who you are, explained Ann to Oppenheimer.

—Why you are so eager to establish our identity is a mystery to me, said Oppenheimer, shaking his head at Szilard. —What is it exactly that you think it's going to accomplish? We have no assumptions to work from here.

—There are always assumptions, said Szilard, forking up a morsel of shrimp cocktail. —We need leverage. A foothold. Before anything we need authority, we need a purview, legitimacy, for lack of a better word. We're invisible now. We can't do anything living out of hotel rooms. We need positions, affiliations, the machinery. You should know that better than anyone, Oppie. Don't you want to be useful?

—So you're assuming that what we do has significance of some kind, said Oppenheimer.

—Would either of you gentlemen care for another drink? interrupted a waiter. His blond hair fell over one eye in an extravagant flip, and it reminded Ann of high school for a second before he turned away.

—Thank you, yes, said Oppenheimer.

Szilard shook his head impatiently.

—Should I make the opposite assumption? Ridiculous. Also, my funds are nearly depleted. I had cash only. I will be out on the street. Unlike you I have an economic incentive.

—I can help you, said Ann. —You need a guide, right? I can help you.

—I know one way you can help, said Szilard. —If I run out of money, can I stay in your home? Until I have resources?

Ann was stopped short.

—*Here* you are, said Ben, and there he was beside her, a hand on her shoulder, glancing across the table at Oppenheimer. —Do you mind if I join you?

—Oh! This is my husband, said Ann, and made the introductions.

❧ The man calling himself Oppenheimer delicately spooned at his soup while Ben, a chair pulled up, gnawing at a buttered roll, gazed over Ann's shoulder at some library books she had eagerly pulled out of her bag.

—Just a minute, I'll show you, she said, flipping through pages as Szilard slurped loudly on his iced tea. —Here.

She propped the book against the table edge and pointed to a portrait of Oppenheimer.

—There, that's him.

Ben looked at it, and then up at Oppenheimer, who was certainly identical. No argument there. —J. R. Oppenheimer, he read, from the caption.

—It was taken in 1940, said Ann. —The picture.

Ben looked down at the page again.

—I'm supposed to have died since then, said Oppenheimer apologetically. —I know. Believe me.

He went back to eating his soup, and Ben abandoned his half-eaten roll and leaned over the book again. Although Oppenheimer was ignoring him, Ann was observing him closely and he could feel her eyes on him. He strove to keep his expression neutral.

—And here, she said, fumbling with a paperback. —Leo Szilard. That one was taken in '45.

Ben took the second book, looked at it and looked at Szilard, and then gave the book back. Also a dead ringer.

—I died in '64, said Szilard. —We're both dead. Technically. But we don't recall that. Last thing we remember it was summer of '45. And then here we were.

—They're both dead, said Ann. —See?

She flipped to an index, where a line read Oppenheimer, Julius R., 1904-1967.

Ben flipped back to the portrait in the first book and then to the front cover, which featured a mushroom cloud.

—He's definitely a lookalike, he said slowly.

—There's another one around too, said Ann. —I mean, dead physicist. Enrico Fermi.

—He died in '54, said Szilard.

—So, said Ben, —you say your name is Oppenheimer, Robert?

—I do say it, said Oppenheimer, putting down his spoon and patting at his mouth with a napkin. —In fact I maintain it stead-fastly. My name is Oppenheimer.

—I see. I don't mean to be rude, but would you happen to have, like, identification?

—I believe I can oblige, actually, said Oppenheimer mildly, and pulled a billfold from his pocket. —I don't have much, but we all came with wallets. It was part of the package, apparently. Here you go.

He passed Ben a folded piece of paper.

—There's no picture on this.

—We didn't have photos on licenses then. Let's see, this is an ID badge for Site Y. Security clearance. This one does have a photo. There. Also a gasoline ration card, a commissary card—

—"War Department, U.S. Engineer Office." You're Oppen-heimer the famous atom bomb scientist, then.

—I like to think so.

— Uh huh. Who died in 1967.

—That is my understanding.

—The one who was discredited during the McCarthy era.

—So I hear. There's also a photograph of my wife Kitty—

—I have ID too, said Szilard. —From the Met Lab. Basically, we showed up here the way we were in July '45, July 16th, right from the time of the Trinity test. The explosion. We came here from that moment.

—We were watching the blast. The explosion of the first gadget. I was, anyway.

—Not me, said Szilard. —I was in Chicago. But I was aware. I knew it was happening. The hour of the test had got leaked to me, actually.

—Who? asked Oppenheimer.

—Forget it.

—And then I was in a motel room. On a cheap bed.

Ben sat back and watched the waiter remove Oppenheimer's soup bowl.

—How was your soup? he inquired politely.

—Mediocre at best, said Oppenheimer.

—So how did you first—meet my wife?

—At the grocery store, said Ann. —I didn't tell you that?

—So many different vegetables you people eat! said Szilard.

—I was shopping, said Ann, glancing at Oppenheimer, —and I saw him and I recognized him from some research I'd been doing at the library. I went up to them and asked them their names. He said he was Oppenheimer.

—Then she fell onto my foot, said Oppenheimer.

—They carried me to the employee lounge, put me down on the couch and took off, said Ann.

—We were late for an appointment Szilard had made at the university, said Oppenheimer.

Ben put down his water glass and sat back, thinking *assholes*. He crossed his legs and folded his hands on his lap.

—So you're claiming to be dead physicists who worked on the bomb project at Los Alamos in the '40s. You have no memories of any other, uh, identities.

—None at all, said Szilard.

—You, uh, woke up in these old suits with old ID documents in your pockets.

—Hardly old, asked Oppenheimer. —This was tailored for me in '43.

—Fine, said Szilard. —We woke up, fine. Put it any way you want.

—And how did you know where to find each other?

—I found Dr. Szilard, said Ann. —And he knew where to find Dr. Oppenheimer.

—I actually ran into Fermi weeks before that, in a so-called Mexican restaurant that makes a very weak chili, said Oppenheimer.

—How about the logistics? asked Ben. —I mean how do you, uh, support yourselves as dead physicists?

—I have means, said Oppenheimer. —My old bank has been honoring my checks. The account dates from the '40s of course but it does contain funds. It took some doing to track it down, of course. The bank has changed names several times.

—You're living off "Oppenheimer's" savings?

—For the present, yes I am, said Oppenheimer. —I had apparently left funds in a minor account from my days at the ranch, before the war. On the site we were not permitted offsite bank accounts. Postal orders only. But I had a passbook in my wallet and I took it in. The funds were not inconsiderable. They had accrued interest. Believe me, I was amazed to discover it too. But I can hardly be defrauding myself.

—Oppie and Fermi think all this is a delusion, said Szilard. —Personally I have not formed an opinion.

—We're all still recovering from shock, said Oppenheimer. —We speculate about the situation, but we're not on familiar territory. It has been suggested that this is a projection of sorts, I use the term loosely, a psychological product, as it were, not an objective reality. But we don't know. So for the sake of argument, to get through the day, as it were, we're pretending this is the world, and we're in it. We're acting as though this is real. And why not?

—So you admit you're deluded.

—Clearly, said Oppenheimer.

—What else, said Szilard. —Are we supposed to believe in time machines or reincarnation or something? I like H.G. Wells as much as the next guy, but please. We are men of science.

Ben sat without moving. There was quiet around the table, and Ann reached out and slid her hand into his. From across the room the waiter was moving toward them with a tray.

—My rump roast! exclaimed Szilard, with the joy of a child.

4

❧ So an egg hatched in 1945 and out of it, preening, crawled a bird that would never stop flying.

❧ It should have been apparent to him always, Ben told himself when the dead scientists first arrived, that his way of loving her was primitive and simplistic and would serve him only under a clear blue sky, not in adverse weather conditions. He began to understand that she was not a guarantee of herself.

She could slip away without leaving him.

And only a few days into this, only a few days along in her investigation of the alleged dead scientists, her *obsession,* call a spade a spade, with these ostensibly deceased masters of the physical universe, he was working in the mansion's gardens, he was resting for a minute, dizzy from standing suddenly, and aimlessly rubbing a bud off the trunk of a young maple with his thumb when it came to him that this, in fact, *this itself* was going to be his task, his test, the unquestioning and blind leap of faith. This was him waiting in the rocket ship, preparing for zero gravity.

❧ Szilard has been described by some historians as a "happy warrior" and by others as "selfless." "His lack of self-interest," an economist friend once wrote of him, "evokes mistrust."

He was also described variously as "bossy," "a genius," and "an ass," while Oppenheimer has been called a "suffering computer."

But Oppenheimer was also described as a "magnificent" person—a person who, even as he was effectively managing the largest enterprise of physical science the world had ever seen, managed to make himself deeply admired and beloved by many of those who worked for him.

Opinion is sharply divided on Oppenheimer. It was Oppenheimer, after all, who was the celebrity.

As for Fermi, because his pronouncements on science were held to be infallible, as a young man he was known to his fellow physics students in Italy merely as "the Pope."

Ben's first impulse was to rebellion, even derision, but he knew he could only be generous. It was strategic. Anything else would drive a wedge between them. He was hoping that his collusion in the fantasy would set her free to be bored.

And that was how the short, fat man calling himself Leo Szilard first came to live with them.

—Dr. Szilard is homeless at the moment, Ann told him after their first lunch with the scientists.

They were driving home in separate cars and talking on their phones. Ben could see her car ahead of him, the neat oval of her small head over the driver's seat.

—Between apartments? asked Ben.

—Hotel rooms, said Ann. —He's about to be kicked out of his motel. I think he's run out of money, if he had any in the first place. I know this is a lot to ask, I know it seems like a risk, but it's important to me: can he stay with us for a while?

For a second as he drove he was conscious of the other cars on the road being far away. He felt his arms reaching for the wheel spiderlike, segmented and nearly detached from the main bulk of his body.

❧ Faced with the end of history people tend to ignore it. But Szilard was not one of these.

From the first he led the physicists' opposition to using the bomb. While he was working for the Met Lab in Chicago in 1945, Szilard tried to arrange to see Truman to convince him not to drop the bomb on Japan. Despite the high regard in which physicists were held by the White House, Szilard was blocked by Truman's new secretary of state.

An overheard conversation—possibly apocryphal—between

Szilard and a security guard at Oak Ridge, where plutonium nitrate was being manufactured, is said to have gone like this:

SECURITY GUARD: Why can't you be a good American?
SZILARD: Like who?
SECURITY GUARD: Well, like me.
SZILARD: Ugh.

Fermi, by contrast, wanted very much to be a good American. After he emigrated to the U.S. he chose to register Republican because he had the impression that Republicans were more American than Democrats. After the war, he moved forward almost unbroken in his stride except for something he told Oppenheimer: I have lost confidence in the validity of my judgment.

Fermi was an honest man who walked the straight and narrow no matter how treacherous the path. Yet he was not without insight into his own foibles. —With science, he said, —one can explain everything except oneself.

Until he gave up hope completely, Oppenheimer too had great faith in the intelligence and resourcefulness of his fellow men.

❧ The following Friday Ben got home from work to find Szilard established comfortably at his kitchen table, a granola bar in his right hand and a can of Coke in his left. There were books open on the formica tabletop in front of him, and Ann hovered at his shoulder.

When Ben set his water bottle on a chair she came over and put her arms around him. He held them and kissed her lips and they were pliable and firm, local as home. She was so known, the sweet smell of cheeks and the nubs of elbows, rough skin over the smooth and nosy bone. Between them was a real border, yes, but he could barely believe it. He knew exactly the span of her wrists, the angle of her chest and shoulders leaning in to him, how her weight felt different from others and no other weight could ever feel like hers by mistake.

The same as ever, except for her insistence on the impossible, everything as ever except what screamed *never before*.

—When I died I was older, said Szilard. —You see?

He leaned over in his chair, tugged at Ben's shirtsleeve and beckoned him over to tap impatiently at a frayed-looking black-and-white picture in one of the books. In it an older, grayer, fatter Szilard was beside a woman in thick glasses, white flowers on her lapel.

—He's with Eleanor Roosevelt! said Ann eagerly.

—It was taken in 1961, said Szilard, reading off the page.

—And there's one from '64, with Jonas Salk.

—Right before I died, said Szilard. —I was practically dead!

❧ One day, when Oppenheimer was on a boat full of world-renowned physicists, he was asked what would happen if the boat were to sink.

"It wouldn't do any permanent good," he said.

❧ Over dinner Ben subjected Szilard to a battery of informal tests. It would have been easier had he remembered more from Advanced Physics and less from Intro, but he had to give it a shot. If the man was, for instance, a vagrant with a mental disorder, the façade of erudition would crumble instantly.

Over the salad, as Szilard dropped a large dollop of dressing onto a two-inch piece of lettuce, Ben forced himself to ask: —So how did you first get into, uh, chain reactions?

—I was already interested in the '30s, but I refrained from working on fission myself. I knew what the repercussions of fission would be. In '39 I wrote a letter with Einstein to President Roosevelt. You've probably seen it in a museum?

—Not per se, no.

—Teller picked me up in his Plymouth. He drove me to see Einstein in his cottage on Long Island and that was where I got him to sign off on the letter. In it we warned Roosevelt the Germans might be getting close to a self-sustaining reaction.

Ben was distracted by a smear of dressing on Szilard's chin. It did not please him.

—You know, because here are the Nazis, and we all knew what bad news they were.

—Sure. But uh, you've got a—

—And they had Heisenberg, a very bright guy, working with a friend of mine in Berlin, von Weizsäcker. We couldn't let those goose-stepping morons get a weapon like that. That was the politics. We were alarmed. I knew what those people were capable of. We needed funding for the work. The government was the only place we could go. It was the last gasp of pure science in this country, uncorrupted by commerce. You know, before the corporations owned the universities.

—Sorry, said Ben. —Did I miss something?

—Then there was the research itself. In a nutshell, I had my work cut out for me convincing Fermi uranium fission was serious business, but he came around after a while. We started for real in 1940. It was January 1940 when I made the first design for what they call nuclear reactors. The first specific design, that is. It was rudimentary, of course, but quite detailed. We called them piles then, uranium piles. What's the whitefish?

—Halibut, said Ann.

—They grow halibut in the desert these days?

—They flash-freeze it and fly it in, said Ben. —Cargo freight.

—Anyway. Mailed the design to myself so I had proof of the date. After that I went to work with Fermi at Columbia. Started off with a paper on graphite-uranium systems. The Germans were stuck on heavy water, using heavy water in their piles as a moderator, you know, to slow down the neutrons. But heavy water was in short supply, plus all the Nazis' heavy water was lost when Claus Helberg and some other commandos blew up a plant in Norway. Whereas we, here in the States, we got the idea to use graphite, which meant we didn't need heavy water. Graphite without impurities such as boron, which eats up neutrons. I saw to that. What's in the sauce?

—Lemon, said Ann. —Butter. Garlic. Simple.

—It's not bad. We were getting our graphite from an outfit called the National Carbon Company, and out with these guys for lunch one day, thinking of the worst possible elements that could have been contaminating our graphite, I said "You wouldn't put boron in your graphite, would you?" Purely as a joke. But it turned out they were letting traces of boron get into their samples!

—I see, lied Ben. Szilard shook his head ruefully as he dipped it to his raised fork, never raising his eyes from his food.

Men of Szilard's generation, thought Ben, avoided eye contact. No one had taught them to look into the faces of others.

—Obviously the boron was corrupting. My point is . . . and he trailed off, distracted. —What are those, green beans?

—Snow peas, said Ann.

—Snow—?

—What do you mean, asked Ben, —slow down the neutrons?

—For uranium 238 to split, said Szilard, —it has to be bombarded with slow-moving neutrons, not fast ones. Right before the invasion of Czechoslovakia I did this experiment with Walter Zinn, using radium and beryllium blocks, that showed a large neutron emission. We—uh oh. Spilled.

He looked down at his shirtfront sulkily.

—I'll get that, said Ann.

—But can you explain to me, asked Ben doggedly, resolved to urge him into a telltale stumble, —what makes a neutron slow?

—I'm not a high-school teacher, said Szilard, irritated. —But I'll try. You know a neutron has no charge, right? Which is how it can enter a nucleus.

—I do remember that, said Ben, nodding.

—What's in the salad dressing? It's good.

—Ben made it, I didn't, said Ann, swabbing at the butter sauce on the table.

—Cilantro, said Ben. —Cilantro is the key.

—What was I saying? Oh. A nucleus has an electrical barrier around it. Heavier elements have a more powerful barrier, so charged particles like protons can't get close enough to interact with the nucleus. Since the neutron has no charge, it can hit the nucleus. A fast neutron actually tends to bounce off the nucleus, especially if it's stable, and so it doesn't lose momentum . . .

Ben found himself nodding mechanically, wishing he was doing something else. One thing was clear: the vagrant had tenacity. And there was no way for Ben, lacking in expertise, to tell whether he was full of shit.

—. . . what gives us beta decay, and how we make plutonium, by bombarding U238 until it turns into a heavier isotope of itself, and then a transuranic element with atomic number 93. Is there any more bread?

—Uh, sure, said Ann, just sitting down, and rose from the table again.

The testing methodology should be changed. In fact it would have to be developed from scratch. Ben did not currently have a plan of action.

—Well thanks, Leo. That's cleared up. More salad?

—I'm not finished.

—That's OK. Don't worry about it. I mean thanks. But I'm not keeping abreast. I should probably read a book or something and save you the trouble.

—You don't want me to finish explaining?

—I'll pass for now, said Ben. —I've got this headache starting.

—Honey, asked Ann, —do you want me to get you some aspirin?

—No, said Ben. —Thanks.

—We were reading a biography, said Ann, putting down the bread and slicing. —Leo met luminaries all over the world in the years after the war. He really got around.

—It was news to me, said Szilard.

—How about Winston Churchill, did you ever meet him? asked Ben.

—Not personally, it would seem, said Szilard. —But, you know, I did once meet an advisor of his. Lindemann, also known as Lord Cherwell. Talked to him in Oxford in '43. Tried to get him to convince Churchill we needed strong international arms controls. Did no good. Turned a deaf ear. The British are stubborn as mules. Is there any dessert?

He was an effective impostor. Good to know they were being conned by a professional, at least. It took the sting off.

Later that night, before settling down to his lengthy bath—in the course of which, Ben did not fail to notice, he monopolized the only bathroom for no fewer than ninety minutes, emerging pink, perspiring, and puffy as a blowfish—he put in a request to Ann for no fewer than twenty yellow legal pads. —I'm always having ideas, he said, grinning. —Have to jot 'em down when I have 'em. Could be lost if I didn't!

Washing the dishes, Ann said she would pick some up for him at the drugstore in the morning. Then he pressed his luck by putting in a further request for a dinner of veal on the following evening.

Ben was relieved to hear Ann turn him down.

❧ Fermi once had the idea that chimpanzees could be trained as servants. This idea was not among his finest.

Oppenheimer, when he was first hired to head the Manhattan Project, decided that all the scientists who worked on the Project— many of them newly emigrated from Europe—should have to join the United States Army as part of their service agreement. (The scientists almost uniformly demurred.) Later he explained his impulse guilelessly. He said that he himself would have been honored to be inducted, and had not, at the time, understood that the others might not.

But Szilard was the master of bad ideas. He generated ideas by the thousands and took out patents on almost anything that came into his head. This arrogant gesture, repeated endlessly, worked in his favor; he sold valuable patents to, among other entities, the Army. Most of the ideas were bad, but on occasion an idea was of uncommon strength, and also new to the world.

In the shower together they could hear the blare of CNN through the wall. Szilard had been glued to it the minute he exited his bath, taking copious notes. He watched the anchors with his head cocked pensively to one side, as though deciphering a code.

Drawing the bar of soap up and down Ann's back and then in circles over her shoulder blades, Ben bent and kissed the top of her head, wet but still unshampooed. He wondered how it was that she could *smell warm*.

—You really think this guy is a dead physicist.

—Not right now.

She turned toward him and took the soap from his hand, pushing him to turn so that she could scrub his back.

—I mean obviously, he's not dead at the moment.

❧ In bed with the lights out she rested her damp head in Ben's armpit as he lay quiet staring at the ceiling.

She said, —Dr. Szilard. He's so *smart*, I mean, clearly, but also so, I don't know . . .

Ben exhaled gently into the darkness, rolling his eyes, wondering if the exasperation traveled through the air.

—He's a guy with a lot of drive, he said. —He's very energetic. But you don't have to be quite so— and as she turned her face up to him he chose a new word, —gracious. He can be overbearing, don't you think?

—Oh, said Ann. —I guess so. I mean, I don't think he means it.

When he finally fell asleep he dreamed he was standing in a box with a crowd of hot dog-bananas. It was not clear which they were, hot dogs or bananas: although yellow they were also tubes of gristle and intestine. They were ungainly and had gigantic feet. They smelled like barbecue and were hemming him in, jostling like so many broad-shouldered businessmen in an elevator.

But in the morning, when he awoke disoriented and warm to find a stripe of sun over his eyes, Ann was already awake and was climbing softly on top. She whispered, —I didn't tell you before, I stopped taking the pill.

He remembered how the wide scope of the world could be jogged out of view by the smooth bend of an elbow. He remembered how, for an animal like him, all things could be forgotten for the sake of one.

෨ Ann was distracted. Her mind was not in the bed but above it, in the mosquito net that hung there as she gazed at it, knotted white gauze and nothingness. It reminded her of something she had once longed for and lost.

—Is that good? whispered Ben. —Do you like that?

—Yes, she whispered back, though it felt like an interruption and she barely heard what he was asking.

෨ Fermi had come over for a cocktail but was not interested in drinking. He did not want to be alone. Oppenheimer could tell. Eventually he dozed on one of the hotel room's double beds.

There have always been alarmists, mused Oppenheimer with his library books spread out in front of him on the hotel room table, those Chicken Littles who believe the end times are upon us, the apocalypse is nigh, the world is coming to an end.

But that does not mean that it won't.

Still people believe in this superstition, which says awareness of a possible disaster serves to avert it. *Just because he's paranoid doesn't mean no one's out to get him.*

Because they fear without reason, the superstition goes, there is no reason to fear.

—But the reassurance people offer that *life will always go on* hangs on a condescension, he said to Fermi, who had stirred and turned over on his bed. —It implies that those who call attention to what is in fact the *constant emergency* of life are merely seeking to dramatize their own parts in the action.

—Can you turn off the light? asked Fermi, blinking in disgruntlement.

—The insult of *being an alarmist* is dealt by those who wish not to be alarmed, he went on as he stood up to reach the light switch. —And these people are most people. Most people do not wish to be alarmed because, understandably, they would rather exist in denial than in horror.

—Thank you, said Fermi, and turned away from him again, plumping his pillow.

So the quick reassurance of most people, he thought, effectively silences the others, those who have glimpsed in a flash the terrible instability at the root of being.

❧ When she got out of bed and went to the bathroom, and then into the kitchen, she found Szilard on the phone berating a civil servant. —It's Health and Human Services, he said grumpily when she asked, but did not elaborate.

Over breakfast he announced he would be conducting personal business for the remainder of the day, and would Ann bring back a book on DNA testing from the library, please. Also, he added as an afterthought, scrawling a list of names on the back of a receipt, all books by these authors—many of them his late lamented colleagues!—plus a dozen donuts, including plain glazed and double chocolate.

❧ Still in bed after she was gone, Ben stretched out his limbs under the sheets and thought he felt young. But a few seconds later he curled up again and tiredness covered him, and he felt old again.

❧ Such people are remarkable, thought Oppenheimer, turning on the hotel coffeemaker, not because of this glimpse, which in fact almost everyone has, but because they are willing to live trembling in the memory of the sight. They're strong enough to be afraid.

In affluent countries and families, he thought, reassurance is the dominant form of censorship.

❧ Ben took Szilard aside before he left for work.

—Listen, he said. —We've welcomed you into our home but I'd really appreciate it if you stopped making so many demands on my wife. She's not your personal servant.

—You realize, said Szilard, —she offered to be my guide. It was an offer. No one forced her, you know.

—I know, said Ben. —I know she offered, and she has good intentions. So what I'm saying is don't take advantage of her. She thinks you're a burning bush, but I think you're a guy off the street who wanted somewhere to flop and can talk a good game. And if anything happens that makes me uncomfortable I won't hesitate to ask you to leave.

—I assure you, said Szilard earnestly, —I am not a confidence man.

—We don't really say "confidence man" these days, said Ben, relenting slightly as he pulled on his boots. —Just "con man" works.

—People don't like syllables anymore, mused Szilard.

—See you later.

He made his way down the steps.

—Wait! called Szilard. —I know how to drive!

—Congratulations, said Ben.

—Chance of using your truck today?

—You've got to be kidding, said Ben.

—No, I really need it. I'm an excellent driver, said Szilard. —Though I normally prefer to walk. A brisk constitutional is good for my digestive system.

—I'm supposed to let you drive my truck around? A man who believes he invented the atom bomb and on top of that has been dead for more than twenty-five years? More to the point, a man without a valid driver's license?

—Details, smiled Szilard. —Would you rather I asked your wife? I believe she has a vehicle too.

—So it's blackmail now?

—I prefer to call it a friendly negotiation. The bus doesn't go where I need to go and I can't afford a taxi, I really can't. I have twenty-three dollars that has to last me forever. In change.

Ben raised an eyebrow.

—It was a parking meter. It was already broken, I just—you know. Made an appropriation.

—How do I know you won't make an appropriation of my truck?

—Please, said Szilard. —Do I look like a Grand Theft Auto?

Ben sized him up, a frumpy, rumpled man in striped pajamas, blinking in the sunlight on the top step.

—OK, I admit, said Ben. —Not so much.

—There are things I have to deal with, said Szilard. —Look at it this way: the sooner I get myself established, the sooner I'll be out of your hair.

—A compelling argument, said Ben. —OK. You'll have to drop me off and pick me up at work though. Get your clothes on quickly. I'm already late.

❧ Ann was excited to have Szilard in the house, his unkempt busy presence intrusive, bombastic, but with a vector, a flurry of moving purpose. Up until now, she realized, before this time, there had been a lack: there had been a good life, a pleasant life, what she recognized and acknowledged was relatively speaking an outright gift of a life, but always without a slope.

Now she was running uphill, felt herself accelerating to the top, her soles angry against the ground and her knees jarred by the shocks.

❧ —Stop! said Ben, as Szilard began to reverse out of the driveway and a cement truck rumbled past.

Szilard braked so hard that Ben felt his neck strain.

—Jesus Christ!

—There's something wrong here! cried Szilard, and sat shaken and dumbfounded at the wheel. —I barely touched it!

—Power brakes, said Ben, running his hand through his hair and clicking the seatbelt into place. —Power steering. You're not familiar with that.

—Certainly not!

—Right, I forgot. Being from the 1940s and all.

Szilard shook his head at the dashboard, perplexed, and leaned in close to squint at the digital readout on the odometer.

—OK, said Ben. No point in quibbling. —It'll take some getting used to. Think of it this way: a hair trigger.

—But it's dangerous! protested Szilard. —It's a death trap!

—Just ease up on the clutch and touch the gas gently. Barely any pressure there. Easy does it.

—How people aren't careening all over the road, grumbled Szilard, as they jerked backward out the driveway, seizing and shivering.

—I gotta tell you, said Ben. —So far your skills do not impress.

❧ Einstein believed that Szilard overestimated the role of reason in human affairs. Admittedly Szilard felt, with Plato, that the world should be ruled by scientists, philosophers and other men of intellect—men, in fact, who closely resembled himself. If only human beings could marshal their rationality, policy changes could be made; structures and systems could be adjusted; a new social compact could be agreed upon and signed by all interested parties.

In life, Fermi was irritated and annoyed by Szilard. Chiefly an experimental physicist, he came to dislike working with Szilard because of the latter's exceptional laziness when it came to the nitty-gritty of the experiments. But he had to concede Szilard's genius, and made at least one speech in which he referred to Szilard as "extremely brilliant."

Szilard liked Fermi but did not like Oppenheimer, finding his politics acceptable but his character unpleasant. Even those who worshipped Oppenheimer—and they were many—admitted he was impatient and sometimes sharp-tongued; Szilard's bad manners took a more languorous form. He routinely slept through colleagues' lectures sitting in the front row, snoring loudly and waking up only to confront them with painful and often unanswerable questions.

Oppenheimer and Fermi liked each other, Oppenheimer remembering Fermi after his death with fondness.

About Szilard, it is difficult to say exactly what Oppenheimer thought. During the war, Szilard's insistent petitioning against the use of the bomb was certainly an irritation.

❧ Jeff took her aside when she got in and cleared his throat several times. Then he confessed that on his Coworker Feedback Form he had mentioned her recent lateness problem.

—I wouldn't have except you didn't seem to like want to have a meaningful dialogue on the issue, he said.

—OK, she said. —Don't worry about it.

—I just don't want it to be awkward or whatever, so I hadda let you know.

—OK. Thanks Jeff.

—But it's totally not personal.

—I understand.

—But so are you—

—Yes? What?

—Are you like gonna be keeping the more, like regular hours again? See it's that I just get tied up and then there's like people waiting, and the phones. So then I get totally stressed, which besides the whole, you know, like spiritual drain is harmful to my GI tract, because you know I had all that stuff with my colon, the bad high colonic and the whole thing with the litigation? Plus it gives me these headaches that are almost like migraines. Borderline migraines actually.

—I'm so sorry to hear that.

—Stress can also cause thinning hair. My brother, you know, who's the commodities broker? He's got like not a single hair on his head. And here's a guy that practically had a Jewfro when he got out of college.

—OK Jeff.

Not long ago she would have been horrified at the evidence of her laxity, the self-indulgence it laid bare. For the first time she was not toeing the line, was not upholding her end of a bargain. She had always been a good soldier.

And there was a nice flight in it, it turned out, a light swoop of clenching, smug and giddy joy. Things were moving upward, over and over.

❧ He knew there was a place for reassurance: but what was that place? On the one hand there is loyalty and faith, on the other skepticism, rigor, even common sense. In choosing to stand beside his wife in what looked like a grand delusion he was opting for the former.

Finally, though he was not without powers of reason and not without rigor at times, he believed that the world outside them, with its judgments and categories, could do its worst. Let it exclude them both, let it bother and nag and harass them with its definitions and prohibitions. He would keep her close to him all the time, enclosing, a human shield.

But that didn't mean he had to let himself get creamed by an oncoming tour bus. Szilard was idling the truck in the middle of an intersection, craning his neck to look past Ben to the right, and there, bearing down on them from the left, was a purple leviathan with tinted windows.

—Gas! screamed Ben like a six-year-old girl, and the truck lurched forward at the eleventh hour, the grinding whine of the tour bus's horn Dopplering behind them.

He turned his head to watch it pass and saw a flash of yellow and purple and the ghostly faces of a legion of seniors peering vaguely through the darkness.

—OK, that's it, he told Szilard when he had his breath back. —No way are you driving this thing without me. You're completely incompetent.

—A learning curve! protested Szilard weakly.

He was sweating at the temples.

—Whatever. I'll get out and walk around. You scoot over.

—There are too many vehicles, OK? said Szilard as Ben slid into the driver's seat. —It's crowded everywhere!

—Welcome to the twenty-first century.

—You may not know this, said Szilard, —but I was always a strong advocate of birth control.

ᘒ The Navajo basket display in its solemn glass case had become a small Bermuda Triangle that Ann steered past warily. Sometimes it occurred to her that there was something there that pressed outward, a force field of warning. When she had to walk past the display case she allowed it a wide berth.

Finally she decided to take action. First of all, the baskets themselves had to go. Their hour had come round at last.

She had always found them incongruous anyway. She had nothing against a basket, certainly nothing against a Navajo basket-weaver, but the idea that here, in this neat box on the sterilized carpet, tribute could be politely paid via six cute decorative handmade reed containers to a people ruthlessly exterminated, robbed, enslaved, driven into the hot dust of their homeland and then roped off on a dry piece of ground slowly to agonize through generation after dirt-poor generation at the decay and death of all their parents and grandparents and ancestors had ever held dear did not please her.

The baskets had been put in the case by a docent at the Historical Society, a coral-lipsticked, bumbling Bettina whose gentle hands shook with palsy as she painstakingly placed the baskets on the glass shelves. It was impossible to refuse Bettina anything. Therein lay her power.

Resolute, turning back to the dangerous space, Ann opened the case and began to remove the baskets. Turning away with basket-heaped arms, she came face to face with Oppenheimer.

—I'm in an embarrassing spot, he said.

Yet she was the one laden chin-high.

—Follow me to the back, she said, and cocked her head. A basket threatened to topple, but she caught it with a well-timed shrug.

❧ —There should be a licensing process, said Szilard eagerly as Ben drove. —To own and operate a vehicle you have to take a test. There are fees you pay, rules you have to observe. But to create and harbor life? Exploit it, subvert it, neglect it? No! To *own and operate* a human vehicle for at least sixteen years, do you need a permit for that? Reproduction: a sacred so-called human right. Why?

—You just can't stop people from having children, said Ben.

—There are ways, said Szilard. —The Chinese!

—I don't know that they've been a hundred percent successful, said Ben. —Plus there's the personal freedom thing.

—In this country freedom's just a euphemism for selfishness, said Szilard, bending forward and twisting around in his seat, struggling vainly with the seatbelt. —But listen: I really need to get where I'm going today.

—What can I say, said Ben. —You're not qualified to operate this vehicle. You failed the test. You're a danger to yourself and to others. My wife wouldn't forgive me if her favorite dead scientist got himself killed his first day out.

—Don't be ridiculous, said Szilard. —I'm not dead.

—I know that, said Ben. —Believe me. If you were you'd shut up.

—What if you went with me?

—I have to go to work, said Ben. —I have a job. Those of us who are not dead scientists have to have livelihoods.

—But after that.

—I'll consider it, OK? Here, this is me. You got something to do until five?

—Can I use the bathroom before I go?

❧ Oppenheimer had underestimated the cost of living. His hotel bill was far more substantial than he had anticipated and as a result he had exhausted his savings at the bank.

He had never, he explained to Ann, found himself in this position before. It was not, he assured her, habitual for him.

Not only were there financial problems of an urgent nature, but he was concerned about his colleague Fermi, who in his withdrawal and passivity appeared to Oppenheimer—merely a layman, of course, when it came to psychiatric diagnoses—to be exhibiting telltale signs of clinical depression. He slept almost all day, he spoke little, he did not have an appetite, and his responses to questions about his well-being were almost inaudible. Although Oppenheimer was no psychiatrist, needless to say, he admitted to Ann that he himself had suffered from depression for a brief time in his youth. Call it depression or call it existential anxiety: fortunately, a vacation in Italy had helped to alleviate the discomfort.

He and Fermi needed time to gather themselves; they were at loose ends. They wanted the leisure to consider their new lives without the pressure of hotel bills.

In short they were both, he confessed, seeking lodging.

❧ Ben was planting lamb's ear, touching a furred and silver leaf, when he remembered his mother. When she came back to him he felt a piercing sadness, and then he felt his limbs soften, under the flesh and the forgiving organ of the skin he felt the frame that held him up dissolving. She had been a first-generation Irish immigrant who had grown up in a farmhouse with a thatched roof in County Cork. He remembered her expressions, Cat got your tongue? and Jeeee-sus-Mary-and-Joseph, her busy movements in the kitchenette, a yellow-and-white checked dishtowel with a red embroidered apple and green leaf. The dishtowel had hung from the door of their small refrigerator and sometimes over her shoulder while she was cooking.

Then there were the shades later, stale smell of the sickness at the end that always made him think of her even though it shouldn't, it had been something that was *done* to her, not what she was. But that was sickness, it turned the person into itself, memories of a mother into memories of a disease.

He had sat beside the bed and from the bedside table her colorful pictures of weeping saints held out their arms to him. Gone bald, face pasty as a doll's, puttylike, she stopped moving once and for all, alive but motionless. To ease her pain they were told to put sleeping pills under her tongue. Later that night his father had been sitting and rocking in the chair, listening to the radio. Usually he listened to Golden Oldies but that time he had put in a cassette. No talking, she had said weeks before; at the end just play me the music to help me on my way. She liked the old folksongs sung by tenors of the first half of the century, "Believe Me, If All Those Endearing Young Charms" and "Down by the Sally Gardens." Now whenever he heard the strains of these songs he remembered her death. He remembered home had vanished one afternoon, turned alien suddenly because she was gone.

She had been all that was warm, all the comfort known in the world, and then dead. Never die, he murmured to Ann sometimes, as though it was a decision to be made. Even in his sleep he would say it.

Then his father, fading: good man of few words, as the fathers often were, bound up and speechless. Their bodies were taut with instinctive defenses that kept them from opening their mouths.

And other than his father he had no one. Looking for evidence of an extended family, before he met Ann, he once attended a reunion in Aspen where second and third cousins milled around in a conference room. The formica-topped tables were decorated with dried flowers and the distant cousins wore nametags on their lapels, ate vanilla cake and drank watery nonalcoholic punch. Strangely the family had hardly reproduced at all in his generation so there were no children running through legs. Instead the family was simply aging, cousins and aunts and uncles dying off and the ones left alive growing more and more decrepit and sedentary until finally they could be gathered in this hotel room and displayed in all their infirmity, a sprawling and crippled gray horde.

But his father, trapped in himself, was even now alive, a good and kind man though always so silent as to vanish in plain sight. He should call him: it had been over a month. In fact *now*, he thought: this was the time. What if something had happened to him?

Heading in the back door to get his cell phone out of his bag he met Lynn. She was in a caftan, gold and green, and tottering on the usual four-inch heels. Her fingernails, which picked up the gold in the robe, were drying and she agitated her hands in the air as she walked.

—I showed your uncle where you leave your car keys, she said.

—Excuse me?

—Your uncle Leo? He said you were letting him use your little truck?

—Are you kidding?

—What I would advise is, he should go in the Zone. I had a fat decorator and it really helped her.

—He already drove off?

—Now she's a skinny mini. Men, you know, can find it hard to commit to weight loss. But once they do the results are often very rewarding.

☙ Ben's cell phone answered after one ring, which meant he was probably talking on it. She couldn't leave a message, so she waited to redial. In the meantime she set some ground rules for Oppenheimer.

—You can't smoke in the house.

—I will be happy to step outside.

—And someone's going to have to sleep on the sofa, in an area that doesn't really have a door that closes, this room that's between the study and the kitchen. We just call it the extra room, we haven't done anything with it. Because there's a futon in the study but other than that—you know, Dr. Szilard's already set up in the guest room.

—I'm sure we can make do. I hope it won't be too long.

—And we only have the one bathroom. So we're going to have to set, I don't know, schedules with that. I don't want to irritate my husband.

—No. I do understand.

—It's me, honey, she said to Ben, when he picked up. —How are you?

෴ So reassurance is aimed at protection, thought Oppenheimer, but often it protects only the speaker, hiding behind itself.

෴ In life Szilard was once approached by someone he had not seen for a very long time. This person exclaimed over the fact that Szilard had *become a great man.*

"I was always a great man," said Szilard.

෴ Ann waited outside La Fonda in her car while Oppenheimer went in to roust Fermi. She had detected some reluctance in Ben but all in all he was as patient as always, patient and open to a certain looseness of events, a shifting ground.

It occurred to her as she tapped her fingers on the wheel that she was missing a brown-bag lunch discussion of New Tools for a World Wide Web Research Etiquette.

෴ Ben was holding himself in check. He had not revealed Szilard as the car thief he was to his credulous fan when she called; he had given an alleged fat dead physicist the benefit of the doubt. The grace period was not indefinite, but he would wait to see what cataclysms were wrought by the joyride. Szilard was the worst driver he had ever personally observed.

And his father was the same as he had been for decades now. Yes, he picked up the phone; he went that far, but no further. The telephone was an instrument, he seemed to believe, seldom employed in the service of good.

Only monosyllables had emerged.

Finally there had been the announcement that the doors of his home were being flung wide open. To be precise it had come in the form of a question, but her wish was his command. He was stubbornly maintaining his laissez-faire policy. Possibly the situation would grow worse, exacerbated by the crowds, and she would give up the project sooner. But he wasn't sure. She could be tenacious.

Still, there was a silver lining. Lynn, now sporting a turquoise visor above the glittering beetle hues of the caftan, stood in front of her tomahawk-wielding warrior for the first time and frowned.

—Do you think he gives off, like, a hostile vibe?

❧ Fermi shuffled wherever he went like a sleepwalker but Oppenheimer was the one whose body was skeletal, whose eyes shone in a drawn, bony-cheeked face. He subsisted on cigarettes and cocktails. To Ann he seemed ethereal, on the brink of nothingness, which was also how he had been described by some who worked with him on the Manhattan Project: a skeleton animated by nicotine, a frail and fatless martyr to work and the war.

—Someone can sleep in here, she said. —It's my study, but this chair here is actually a single futon—see? It folds out like this.

—*Fu*-tong, enunciated Fermi slowly.

—Why don't you take this one, Enrico, said Oppenheimer. —I'll bring in your bag.

—Fine, said Fermi, nodding.

He spoke from a point so far away that despite the solidity of his barrel chest and his arms and his legs the character that inhabited them seemed absent. He had assigned a clerical worker to walk around in his body for him; he had delegated authority.

—I'll just leave the keys under the mat, and remember to put them back there when you go out, said Ann, smiling. —Do you have any plans?

—We're still learning, said Oppenheimer. —I read all the time. There's catching up. You don't know. I have more books in my bag than clothing. And then there are the newspapers. I use them as cues: I take notes when I don't understand an assumption. Then I look it up. The volume of information gives me headaches. And the concentration. There are passages I have to read ten times to separate what I understand from what I don't. You have no idea how difficult it is to assimilate a world.

—It's just lucky you're geniuses, said Ann.

This fell flat. Oppenheimer nodded curtly.

—Do you have an aspirin or two?

—In the medicine cabinet. I'll get you the bottle.

—And Enrico, said Oppenheimer, —you wanted to sleep?

—I want to sleep, mumbled Fermi, and turned away from them.

When she brought the pills and a glass of water Oppenheimer was sitting alone on the sofa staring into midair. She tipped the pills into his hand.

—Do you want to come to the library with me?

—It's walking distance, correct?

—About ten minutes.

—Thanks, but I'll come in later.

She left them in the house and walked out down the path, the sun warm on her shoulders. Parry's penstemon were starting to bloom, pink. They stretched out skyward. And behind her she felt the scientists in the house, bees in a hive. They were living among her possessions, the objects of her own life. She liked having them there; she was invigorated by her new devotion. Latent beneath her satisfaction, her tendency always to shrink away, had evidently been a longing to have something to offer up. It might be seen as desperate from the outside, viewed coldly, she suspected. But from the inside it was ripe with the promise of transport.

People have a habit of seeking answers, she thought. They want to believe there are always answers: all problems have solutions, all wrongs a right. Everything works in twos. Some instincts of thought can never be suppressed, and so people refuse to give up on the reversibility of what has gone wrong.

There must be something they can do, a person may say.

She was no different, she saw this.

Because she was convinced there was a clue here, the key to a solution. So what if it was naïve of her. There had to be hope, and hope needed an object. And if she was wrong about the scientists nothing would have been lost or disrupted but routine.

Leaving the house she felt more than ever that she had something hidden there, a secret that glowed.

❧ Three men, one tall, tubby and sagging, the other two short and musclebound, removed the bronze horse and Indian rider on an industrial dolly. Small mercies.

The afternoon wore on, Ben told himself as it did, hacking away at rocks, dislodging them from the soil.

Szilard did not return.

❧ Ann came home again to find the house empty and quiet and the setting sun casting long doors of light across the clay tiles. She sat down on the sofa and smelled lavender. Through the window she watched the inching movement of cars along the street beyond the trees as they rounded a curve that led up the hill, and the sky above them was violet. The cars were the only intrusions and without them the repose was complete. She felt more rested than she had felt in weeks.

Wandering into her study she found Fermi's jackets hung neatly on an old coat stand she never used. Papers were stacked on the desk in neat, symmetrical piles, and several library books on quantum physics and cosmology had been added to her bookcase. A small travel alarm clock sat on the edge of the desk, along with a copy of the *Wall Street Journal.* She picked up the clock and turned it over: it was old, with no battery compartment.

Oppenheimer's suitcase was opened at the end of the sofa in the extra room and his suits were laid over an arm. Without contemplating the act she picked one up, lifted it to her face and inhaled: cigarettes and something she could not identify, musty and sweet.

೫ —If you can drop me off on your way out, said Ben to Roger. At 6:30 p.m. he had still not seen his truck again.

—Sure. I'm heading to the club to play some squash, said Roger. —You play?

—Racquetball, used to, said Ben.

—Racquetball's a fag's game, said Roger. —Just kidding. Wanna join me?

—Thanks for the invitation, said Ben, —I appreciate that. But I have to be getting home to my wife.

—What I'm offering you, said Roger, —is a superior product. C'mon, wife versus squash and single malt after? No contest. I mean who's shittin' who here.

೫ The call came while they were outside after dinner, leaning against each other. Ben had been talking about the child they would have while Ann listened and smiled faintly, her fingers brushing along his arm also light, skimming over the skin, not holding it. The night was warm and Ben had the sense of a boundary between them, renewed. She was with him only the way someone else would be, casual, not herself but a distant acquaintance. Her distraction was distracting him: he did not follow it. It nagged at him like a mistake that was only half-forgotten. Was she there or not?

If he were coloring it in, the crayon would stray outside the lines, leaving ragged loops of green and blue and hazy brown to confuse the blank space. The boxes were not aligned, the fields were not in place. Things were disorderly.

They let it ring three times and then Ann relented, thinking it might be Oppenheimer. —Would you? and Ben stepped inside to pick up. It was Szilard, who reported that he was in police custody.

Ben hung up and went outside again.

—Excuse me? said Ann when he told her.

—They'll release him if we post bail and pick him up.

—But what's the charge?

—Breaking and entering.

❧ There are men and women who have neat and benign visions about how to improve the world and others who have dramatic and urgent visions about how to save it from catastrophe. Many of these men and women are passionate and gather followers behind them.

Szilard should be counted among both groups, though he had few followers during his lifetime.

Frequently these men and women with grandiose visions do not believe the laws that apply to common people should apply to them. Because they have a mission, unlike the scurrying nine-to-fivers, the billions of performers of mundane tasks, they believe themselves to be exempted from obligations and niceties. Besides being so-called *great men,* for example, they may be shoplifters or kleptomaniacs, reckless or absent-minded drivers, habitually late or chronically unwashed.

The truth is, they know they can get away with it.

Also they know that many of the customs and rituals with which we fill our time are just that. So many routine acts seem invented to use up the day.

For those who are not invested with a sacred sense of purpose, organization may become important. A small landscape, say a kitchen, a closet, or a drawer, takes the place of a kingdom.

It is transparent, but that does not mean it is obvious.

❧ To be fair Szilard, though he saw himself as exceptional, did not see himself as superhuman. In fact he identified with the masses. "I am a worker, not a drone," he once said while attempting to shrug off the affections of a young woman named Alice.

It was not Szilard's job, he was saying, to service the Queen.

❧ When they got to the jail the clerk told Ann they were releasing Szilard only because a police shrink had deemed him mentally unstable.

—So they're not pressing charges, they said, said the clerk. —The Army, you never know. Sometimes they're hardcore, like with radicals or whatever, other times, if it's just a crazy, they shrug it off.

—The Army?

—Yeah, didn't they tell you? When they picked him up he was trying to break into some Air Force facility. He got stuck on a fence or something. Razor wire.

—And my truck? He must have had it with him then?

—Impound lot.

❧ Ann waited for Szilard while Ben went to reclaim the truck. When he emerged from a door at the back, unattended by cops, she almost ran to get to him. There were scratches on his white arms, and his hair was tousled, but otherwise he looked the same as always.

—Are you OK?

—Hungry, he said cheerfully.

He did not seem remorseful.

—What happened?

—There was a young man in the holding cell who'd never heard of World War Two, he said. —Fact he'd never heard of Europe.

—I meant, before.

—A very interesting case.

—Why did they arrest you?

—I was in the wrong place.

—You tried to break in, they told me.

—I did break in. They caught me on the way out.

—You did? What did you—

—Forget it. It was a waste of time. The new systems are computerized but the archives barely go back. No use to me.

—What is going *on*? asked Ann. —Would you clue me in, please?

—Records, said Szilard. —Fingerprints.

—You were looking for them?

—But no luck.

In the car driving home he stared out the window, tapping his fingers on the door panel.

—Wait! he said, jerking forward. —What if I gave up my body to science?

—I don't see how that would help, said Ann. —Frankly.

—No, I mean then! In '64! Maybe it's still around somewhere, or part of it. DNA! Right? They can do that. Compare!

—I doubt it, said Ann. —I don't think they keep the corpses for that long. Unless cryogenics existed then.

He was quiet for a moment.

—Also, a small matter. There was a—I had a traffic incident.

—Incident?

—There's a dent now. In the side door where a lady hit it. Just a little caved in. It still drives though.

—You had an accident in his truck?

—It was a woman driver. They are less competent.

—Uh *huh,* she said.

—Present company excluded of course. You are a credit to your sex.

Suppressing annoyance was hard work, and draining.

—Unlike you.

—What?

—Forget it.

They drove on in silence, Szilard oblivious, she was sure. He was opaque as well as irritating. He never told her anything.

After a while he turned to her and spoke again.

—Did you get the donuts?

❧ Fermi had gone to sleep by the time they got home but Oppenheimer was still awake.

—Put yourself in our shoes, he said, when she and Szilard came into the kitchen. She flicked the light on as Szilard, donut box in hand, trudged to the refrigerator and extracted a Coke.

Oppenheimer had been sitting in the dark. There was a tumbler of whiskey on the table in front of him and the kitchen was full of cigarette smoke.

—OK, said Ann. —Just let me get myself a beer.

She moved around him to open the window.

—It's a world you recognize in pieces. It's worse than a different world, it's the same world turned alien.

—I can imagine, said Ann gently.

He was far from sober.

—I doubt it, said Oppenheimer, shaking his head. —You can't imagine something you've never known. It's beyond you.

—I believe you, said Ann. —I do.

The phone rang, but she ignored it.

—Like finding limbs from your own body strewn across the landscape. Do you know what this desert used to look like? Of course you don't. You never saw what I saw. It's not there anymore. It's all gone.

—What are you talking about? asked Szilard.

—A man who's blind from birth can't know color. He doesn't know there *is* color. He hears "the sky is blue" and it's a foreign language to him. It means nothing. Not only *blue* but *the sky*.

—Actually, that's not strictly—

—It's a metaphor, Leo.

—Windbag, said Szilard mildly.

—Please, said Ann.

Szilard shrugged, turned away, fished around in the donut box and extracted a double chocolate, which he gobbled with zeal.

—Well, I can't speak for him, said Oppenheimer doggedly, —but for Fermi and me. The two of us have spoken and for us I can speak. I can speak—

—Then speak already, said Szilard as he chewed.

—In the dream, here's the thing, went on Oppenheimer, slurring his words. —You're walking along, you see something—under a bush, under a hedge—you can't tell what it is until the last second. Leaning down close. And then: it's your leg. Your own leg. Long-lost leg! Lying under a bush!

He raised his glass as though for a toast.

Ann was glad she was seeing him drunk. Usually he spoke with a formality that sounded scripted, though this habit had been disintegrating since his arrival under a constant barrage of new slang. When a teen spoke obscenities in his earshot he would often say: What a surprising expostulation!

Then Ben was at the kitchen door. There was trajectory to him, like a thrown ball. —I need to talk to you *now,* he said to Szilard through gritted teeth.

—It was not my fault, I assure you, said Szilard, his mouth smeared with sticky brown. —It was an accident caused by another driver!

—Right. And did you get his insurance information?

—She left the scene in a hurry, said Szilard. —She was upset.

—*She* was upset? Come to the garage, Szilard. Come let me show you what you did to my truck. You could have killed somebody! Do you realize that?

—That's ridiculous, protested Szilard. —I'm a very good driver.

—What I mean is, just a disembodied leg lying under the bush, mumbled Oppenheimer, staring at the ceiling light fixture. —And it's not that you're even *missing* a leg. The leg is a reminder.

—So what does it remind you of? asked Ann.

—Oh, said Oppenheimer, and paused for a long moment, apparently lost. —. . . I guess . . . legs?

—Father of the A-bomb, said Szilard. —Witness the genius.

—Come on, Szilard, said Ben. —Garage, now. I mean it.

—I regret the accident, certainly, said Szilard, shuffling off toward Ben, who shunted him out the door ahead of him. His voice was plaintive, trailing off. —But the damage is minor, and it had nothing to do with me.

—I remember having dreams like that in the other life, went on Oppenheimer softly. —The first life, I mean.

Ann twisted the cap off her beer and sat down across from him.

—You're walking in a dark forest where you've never been before, said Oppenheimer, —I mean you've never seen these trees, a type of tree you've never seen before with leaves like moths, fans or moths . . . how they hardly move at all, just with their wings trembling. . . .

He seemed to be drifting off.

—Are you with me, Dr. Oppenheimer?

—And the monarch butterflies on the coast, clusters of them on the branches, by the thousands. Have you ever seen that? I saw them in California, when I was living there. We would drive up the coast. It was in Santa Cruz, I think. They look brown then, not orange, brown like paper bags. All hanging there waiting for, I don't know. The end of winter.

—You were saying you were walking? In the forest?

—The world I knew was beautiful, Ann.

—I'm sure it was.

—I've heard people say there *was* no golden age. But that's just an excuse. It relieves them of responsibility. The fact is: things fall apart. Yeats! Newton! Entropy increases. The world was more golden when it was young. Poor sad world.

She got up for another beer.

—We drive past parking lots and fast-food joints and then I see an old house, say an old adobe that's always been there. Back when I knew it there was a grove of trees there. I remember cottonwoods and willows. There were other adobes on the lot back then, in the shade of the trees with stone pathways between them. All the casitas were built by the same family, the Reynosos. They had beautiful girls. Girls with deep brown eyes were the children of that family. They used to ride horses.

He nodded, staring into the distance.

She took a bottle from the refrigerator and as she turned back to him he leaned forward eagerly.

—Cars have conquered this country, he went on. —I did not foresee that.

—They're everywhere, anyway, said Ann, feeling helpful.

—The places in the world that I loved were like my children. The mesa, the pine forests. Now those places are an ancient withered child. The skull is showing through the gray hair and the face is a wrinkled bag of skin. Do you see? The world was my baby once. This was my smooth and beautiful infant that I held in my arms.

She tipped up her second beer—she was drinking them right from the bottle on an almost empty stomach, quickly to keep him company—and looked at him closely, the crows' feet at the corners of his eyes, the nose that was austere. Roman, she thought, almost. But then what was Roman? She had never been to Rome.

Rome, Babylon, the Planet of the Apes.

He was a Roman emperor in a plaid workshirt. Ben had lent him the shirt, a faded flannel like all his others. She knew the shirt well. She had handled it both warm from the skin beneath it and warm from the dryer. The lines were dim on the cloth, the cloth was soft to the touch. The shirt was ancient with wear.

And yet the cloth held fast.

She was suddenly overwhelmed by affection for the shirt and the bones and flesh that filled it, beneath the breast pockets the breathing lungs. She wanted to reach over and stroke the fabric but did not move. He would have been an old man, older than her grandfather would be now if her grandfather were not dead. Had she met the first Oppenheimer, the one who went down in history, she would have been a little girl and he would have been an old, old man.

Her grandfather had worn plaid shirts too. She felt a fondness for all men who wore plaid shirts, plaid shirts of faded cotton or rayon whose labels bore a name in flowing stitched script. Her grandfather's pants were pleated and he had called them "trousers." Like Oppenheimer he had said "trousers" and "fellow," but unlike Oppenheimer he had also said "I'll be golldurned" and, for a curse, "Dang nab it!" He had owned a shoehorn and collected silver quarters. What had happened to shoehorns since then? Who ever had a shoehorn now? He had a tortoiseshell shoehorn and brown shoe polish.

These things disappeared, you could barely recall them except when you thought about childhood. Or as time went on you remembered *remembering* childhood, one step removed if not more. You went back not to the first memory but the ones that followed it, the many references to the memory you'd made over the years and subsequently added to the bank of even older memories. Like what Oppenheimer was describing, though less tragic and sweeping in scope: small objects rendered obsolete by custom, and the constant manufacturing of new things, the constant discarding. In her grandfather's youth—at least this was the impression she had—things had been made to be kept, and repaired many times by men with highly specialized skills, men who took care.

For example: the men who had the shoeshine chairs in airports now, weren't they a vestige of a bygone age, anachronistic and out of place? Those men, if truth be told, were not for shining shoes but for sitting above. A businessman liked to have another man kneeling in front of him and scrubbing at his feet. That was why they still existed. Their sales technique and their product was subservience.

Oppenheimer was not her grandfather. He should be a century old now but here he was, only a couple of years older than Ben but far, far more tired. Tired: yes.

For her Oppenheimer had risen over the horizon, startling in suddenness, but for him this was just an extension of the routine exhaustion he had known before, the exhaustion of work in an institution. For him there was no wonder in being here, only confusion and the degradation of an accelerated, busy future choked with chemicals, cars and ugly buildings. It was void of loved ones and packed with indifferent strangers, a future of anonymity and isolation, a half-life.

He was injured.

Oppenheimer leaned back in his chair, arms crossed on his chest above the table edge, and closed his eyes.

—More than any of it, he murmured, —what astounds me is the blindness of you people now. A civilization that is blind to itself. I mean *blind*. In my day there was ignorance too: ignorance is timeless. But at least we were ashamed of it.

❧ —You see this? How the door's hard to open? That's going to cost me hundreds of dollars to fix, Leo. And I don't really have the money.

Ben had almost no investment in the appearance of his truck; the door would function well enough and the damage didn't reach the wheel well. But he was angry at Szilard anyway. The guy had deceived him on purpose, in premeditated fashion, and then on top of it, after he wrecked the truck and made an incursion on a stronghold of the U.S. military, had the cojones to call *them* to bail him out. They should have left him in jail. One night might have done him some good.

Also, after all that, not a word of thanks had passed Szilard's lips. Szilard stuck in his craw.

Ben watched him standing beside the dent, gazing down at it without evidence of interest. That was what needled him with Szilard: the man was impenetrable. The truck might be dented but Szilard was untouched. Szilard was so convinced he was right that no competing opinions could even be entertained.

—I mean for all intents and purposes you're a freeloader, said

Ben, in a gambit to get his attention. Admittedly he didn't know what he'd do with it once he had it.

Szilard nodded slowly, meditative.

—And if that's not bad enough you're a freeloader who steals and then wrecks my truck.

—Why now? asked Szilard. —Have you asked yourself that?

—Why you wrecked my truck *now*? Why you stole it and wrecked it *today*?

—Why we're here, said Szilard impatiently, and came around the hood to stand uncomfortably close. Ben could see donut sugar lining his upper lip. —The three of us.

—Because my wife had a dream, said Ben. —And you are a freeloader.

—What I'm telling you, said Szilard, —is that it's coming to a head. History does have an end: ask the dinosaurs and the Carolina parakeet and the giant sloths. The drums of the very last wars are beating.

❧ Oppenheimer sat beside Ann on the side of the fountain, where she always sat at night. He crossed his legs and she noticed his bony knees, and the knees brought her own dream back to her again. He had been bent then, with grains of sand on his skin. The skin was scraped. When the mushroom cloud rose he had skinned his knees.

She had always known there was something disturbing in a skinned knee, something wrong, like chalk screeching on a blackboard. Where that enormous thing had been, that blossoming and roiling pillar and cloud in the sky, also nearby there was something as minor as a skinned knee. Too near each other were the pinprick and the vast desecration. They were not separate enough.

She recalled that Oppenheimer, in life, had been concerned that the scientists working on the Manhattan Project should not be *compartmentalized*. He had been opposed to compartmentalization. Groves tried to insist upon it, to some degree at least. Groves did not want the right hand to know what the left hand was doing, unless the hands in question were both his own. Groves got his way in many things, but in this he had not been completely successful. Compartmentalization meant that some of the scientists, technicians, and engineers knew what the project was doing overall, and some knew very little.

She herself wanted things to be separate, she wanted categories, she wanted some spaces reserved for particular things and other spaces prohibited to them. She did not like how the scraped knee, the texture of the torn pants that had opened up to show her the knee in her dream, and the mushroom cloud could be so close. They were of different orders.

But this was a weakness of hers. She should be comforted instead of displaced: because if small things were vast, then vast were also small, and ceased to be fearsome.

—Of course, said Oppenheimer, —we may have been the beginning of that. It doesn't escape me. The beginning of the end. When I accuse you, I'm accusing myself too. It doesn't escape me, what we left to all of you.

—What are you—?

—Forget it.

They were quiet. She took one of his cigarettes.

—It's a nice garden, said Oppenheimer, lighting the cigarette for her.

—Thank you.

Dreams, she thought, both of us. Why we talk about dreams, think of them as anchors: because everything in a dream must be true. That it cannot be explained only makes it *more* true. More not less. How it vibrates near the edge of the mind, or forever buried.

—I saw a picture of my son today.

—Peter?

—Peter. Yes. He's alive. He's older than I am now. I tell you what . . .

He leaned back, holding the cigarette up to his lips and closing his eyes, face upturned. The light of the moon made his face metallic: if skin could be made of metal, his was. It was silver, and his eyes hollows there.

—What.

—My children were never happy.

—Oh, now . . .

—They grew old and one of them has already died. My daughter killed herself. She was unhappy and she took her own life.

—I read that. I'm sorry.

She could not see his face anymore. Behind him in the dark of the garden crickets chirped and made the darkness larger.

—When I last saw my son he was an infant, did you know that? He was born during the war. In 1941, in Berkeley.

—It must be—

—But we discussed it, Fermi and I. We can't be in touch with our families, the ones who are here now but who we left behind when we died. We wanted to. Believe me. It was the first thing we thought of when we understood where we were. But clearly, it would be a disaster.

—That's probably very—

—How does a man have happy children? Is there a way to be sure?

—I don't know. I don't think so.

He nodded slowly. She noticed his Adam's apple.

—Because I did love them, even if I was preoccupied. So that's not it. It wasn't the absence of love.

—I'm sure it wasn't.

—And I hardly saw Kitty at all those last weeks. We didn't have time. I'm supposed to believe she's dead now? Overnight?

—But she had a happy life with you. It went on for decades. After the war it went on for twenty-two years, until the day you died.

—She might not have been robbed, but I was.

—I know.

—That wasn't me. *I* am Oppenheimer.

—But it might have been.

—It was not! I am *here.*

—I know that. But maybe you were there then, and you're here now. Maybe you were both.

—Sometimes I think the books are just books, the films and the microfiche are nothing but objects. It might as well be a stage. It's just props, all of it, everything around us. Around me. Even you. It's elaborate, certainly, well-articulated, but in the end the facts are just documents. They're not the people of my life. How am I supposed to believe them? It's a production. It's not real. All the history you put in front of me—it could be a joke!

—I know.

—But then I feel it. I smell things, the sage, the creosote in the rain, and I remember. And I can no longer deny that this is the world I knew. The world I knew grown old.

The light from the open garage made the driveway visible, the cactus along its adobe wall and the weeds growing through cracks in the stubbly gray pavement. From the garage itself she could hear the faint drone of Ben's voice.

—It happened so quickly, whispered Oppenheimer.

She let the silence sit until he ground out the cigarette under the toe of his shoe and a tired calm settled on both of them. He sighed and hunched over, his chin tucked in toward his breastbone, arms straight, fingers curled around the rim of the fountain, rocking forward and lifting himself slightly on the heels of his hands. Again she thought of a bird: his eyes were always so large in the bony face. She recalled a passage Mr. Hofstadt had read to her: *The ocular caverns of a bird can occupy most of the space in its skull.*

—So you're starting to know this is real, she said finally.

—It's wearing me down.

The night was tranquil. There was no breeze, only the burble of the water in the fountain and behind it the soft regular chirp of the invisible crickets. She felt tender toward the garden, how it seemed to want so little. The wind chime hung steady in the air and she thought: at such a moment I myself could believe this is all an unreal life. I myself could believe what he said.

If he told me all the world was a river of unconsciousness, that all of us here are nothing more or less than the dream of the universe, I could almost believe it.

❧ Escape is the most common impulse, thought Oppenheimer as they went inside to the warmth and left the night outside them. He stubbed out a cigarette in the usual place and then stepped over the piles of newspapers Leo always left on the floor along the hallway. Governments offer solutions that assume only the worst about human nature: they fight back in anger, a flying outward, a panic of blame, as if the problems are always outside the subject. Sometimes crimes are perpetrated by others, yes, he thought, but more often crimes are perpetrated at home. Only those who live at home cannot see them. The crimes have become part of the wallpaper, a pattern no longer noticed.

Not knowing better, observers may even find them attractive.

The crimes of others bring terror but our own are almost quaint, he thought. To discuss them is in bad taste: it smacks of desperation. It smacks of needing someone to blame, of a whining attachment to the right to complain.

It is so out of style that its substance is irrelevant.

❧ —Not just any war, but the last war. Remember the last time they said that? How hopeful it was? The War to End All Wars? But this is the real McCoy.

Ben walked around to the back of the truck and began to unload gear from the bed. He would need it in the morning, for work here before he went back to Lynn's. Trowels, pruning shears, hoe. Szilard followed him, shaking his head, huffing as he began to pace.

—Did you hear what I said? We're here for the last war. Because we started it. We're needed.

—You think quite highly of yourself, don't you, said Ben.

—You think this is arbitrary? You think we're here because we chose to be?

—I think you're here because my wife and I are the only fools that would have you, said Ben.

—It's going critical, said Szilard. —It'll reach critical mass.

—What, said Ben.

—For the first time since '45 they're planning to use nuclear weapons in war. They want to throw out deterrent strategy. Mutually Assured Destruction. It was a so-called gentlemen's agreement. It worked during the Cold War, as well as could be expected. But when that was over all bets were off. You can never trust a gentleman. Believe me.

—What are you talking about.

—They want to be able to use nuclear arms like any other weapons. Just another tool in the toolbox. They're chomping at the bit. Did you even know that? Do you even *notice* the government? You people have so many games to play you have no time for what's real. It's coming to a head. Next thing you know they'll be building mini-nukes and lobbing them across battlefields. Battlefields like cities and farms. They've even mentioned the neutron bomb. The neutron bomb is being planned for battlefield employment. Do you know what a neutron bomb is? It's an enhanced radiation warhead. Designed to kill the maximum number of people but keep buildings safe. How's that for materialism? They've already decided. The clock is ticking.

—Who are *they*, Leo? You're a conspiracy theorist, aren't you. Add that to your resume. Schizoid delusions, conspiracy theories.

—The public either buys it wholesale or just isn't watching, you tell me. When I see what you people have done to democracy it disgusts me.

—You can fix it all though, can't you Leo. But not the dent in my truck.

He ran his hand over it again.

—I predicted it, of course, all of this. I always do. But I had hoped my predictions were wrong.

—Perish the thought, Leo. You're never wrong.

—Afghanistan maybe wasn't quite the right target for them. People too poor, country already a garbage heap. Neither was Iraq. They used uranium-tipped shells over there during the first Persian Gulf War, remember? In a few years we'll find out what they did the second time. Last time they left *hundreds of tons* of DU in the desert when they left. Depleted uranium. Hundreds of tons. You people don't bother to know the basic facts about what your government does to other countries. You really couldn't care less, could you?

—Stop haranguing me, Leo. I'm not your whipping boy.

He turned to go inside and Szilard followed him up the driveway toward the door, badgering.

—I'm telling you, they've started. I don't know who the ultimate enemy's going to be. I can't tell yet. It doesn't matter right now. What matters is they want it. They *want it.*

—Nuclear war? Get real. No one wants it. Come on.

He opened the door to the kitchen, now empty. But once inside Szilard would still not leave him alone.

—Look at the evidence! Read the posture papers! I can give you the documents. Any exchange could mean escalation. You know that, right? You only need a thousand hundred-kiloton warheads. That's the threshold for nuclear winter. I've been trying to convince Oppie, tell him we have to act. He won't listen. He never listened, and where did it get him? It got him blacklisted, basically. In life I mean. He wouldn't take my advice because he was too busy being a bureaucrat, cozying up to the powers that be. And what good did it do him? They threw him out with the bathwater as soon as it suited them. At the end of the day all his kissing up to the establishment brought him nothing but tears. And now he has a second chance and he still doesn't listen to me.

—Leo. You're starting to sound hysterical, said Ben. —Tone it down. Take it slow.

He cleared cigarette butts and an empty bottle off the table as Szilard hovered over his shoulder.

—I'm not kidding. We're on the brink. I've come up against this before. Remember? They have tools they've spent money on and they have to use them. Inertia. They have to and they want to. Do you get it? It's not reason. It's not strategy. It's a fantasy of power. It's what they *want*.

❧ That a man, a group, or an institution should want to employ a nuclear weapon, should *desire* its employment is difficult for a thoughtful person to credit, thought Oppenheimer.

And yet weapons are full of desire, shaking with it. They are instruments for the expression of longing.

He said goodnight to Ann and left her drinking a glass of water at the bathroom sink, staggering into his bedroom.

At the window he thought of missiles streaking across the sky streamlined and ardent with purpose. He lit the evening's last cigarette and studied its ember. In an instrument of mass destruction is distilled great artistry, a gorgeous swiftness and a fierce will.

What was it Leo had said, lecturing him on current events? *The four largest defense contractors in America have spent forty million dollars lobbying over the past three years,* he had said. In one year alone, he claimed, these businesses received $35 billion in Pentagon contracts.

Therefore weapons of mass destruction are big business, yes, thought Oppenheimer, and turned to look out his door to where

Ann was padding along the corridor in sock feet, carrying her toothbrush and stumbling into her bedroom.

In fact, in monetary terms, *the biggest business there is,* Leo had said. Was that possible?

Leo made it seem like it was all about profit, greed and expansion. But it could not be.

The cynics are wrong, always wrong, thought Oppenheimer as he ground the cigarette into the outside wall beneath the window.

Because finally all the most obsessive work in the world is done not for profit but for pure devotion.

❧ After extracting various promises from Szilard—no more illicit driving, no more auto theft, no more felony B&E—Ben went down the hall to the bedroom to find her standing on their bed, a chaos of clothes erupted over the bedroom floor.

—You're drunk! he said with great insight.

It was rare. To drink enough to get drunk she had to be goaded like a teenager. Left to her own devices she had little interest in alcohol.

She was indifferent to the observation. Naked, wearing a mint-green facial mask, hair sticking out, she was making piles. Briefly he saw her as a child, forlorn and reckless. He thought: a child will look like her, a child will stamp like this on the mattress, teeter there overlooking the room as though the room, and only the room, is her kingdom.

—Szilard seems to think he's here to stop the apocalypse, he told her, sitting on the edge of the mattress and picking up a black feather boa. He recognized it: it was left over from some old Halloween, but it had never been worn. He threaded it through his fingers and ran it over his bare forearms, felt the soft and tickling strands.

—Getting rid of the extra, she said. —Look at it! Give it to the Goodwill. Or the Big Brothers. I mean the Boys Club. You know.

—Yes, he said. —Good. Did you hear me?

—I wish I had some water! she said, jumping off the bed and stumbling over a tangle of shoes.

—Let me get you some water. You'll feel better as soon as you drink it.

⟳ Head already throbbing despite the fact that she had dutifully drunk the water and swallowed three aspirin, her eyes aching and dry, she tiptoed into Oppenheimer's room later, unable to sleep, to find him reading in a pair of Ben's pajamas and smoking a cigarette, far soberer than before.

—Sorry, he said smoothly as she came in, and held the cigarette out the window.

—Dr. Szilard says you're here to stop the apocalypse, she told him.

—Goodness gracious.

—He says World War Three is looming.

—Leo has always been a pain in the ass, said Oppenheimer. —He's a professional panic artist. It's a gift. Don't let him upset you.

⟳ After she left the room Oppenheimer turned to the window to flick his cigarette butt outside. He followed the arc of its spark as it hit the ground in the darkness, and kept watching until the spark died.

Past the black pool of the garden he saw the stubbled gleam of the road, a single streetlight bathing its asphalt surface in texture. He was about to turn away from the window again when his eye caught a slight movement across the street. A man stood near a telephone pole, shapeless away from the light. Oppenheimer had the distinct sensation the man was watching the house. Possibly the man could even see him.

Quickly he reached over and flicked off the floor lamp. He stood motionless at the window in his dim room, waiting.

Finally the man turned and walked behind a screen of trees. Looking into the mass of branches with his hands braced on the window sill, where the fingers lightly trembled, Oppenheimer heard the faint slam of a car door and an engine firing.

Slowly disrobing after the car drove away, he could not shake the conviction that the man intended to come back.

The man was looking for him.

❧ Our parents, thought Ann, tossing and turning, still with alcohol in her blood, dizzy. She sat up.

Our parents and their governments: they yearned to roam the universe.

She remembered footage of the moon landing. When the first men got to the moon they planted an American flag there, doing their duty, leaving it stiff and unmoving in the cratered earth of the moon with the black sky behind it. Then they danced in the different gravity, carefree, bobbing up and down in their giant suits, bouncing and singing songs without words, da-da-da, dum-dum-dum.

II

WHY TALL PEOPLE
FEAR DWARVES

1

❧ What do we seek to feel?
Happy, they say, frequently.

❧ Hiroshima was selected as a target for the atom bomb in the late spring of 1945, when trees were budding in Washington.

Outside several of the buildings where the decision was made grew Yoshino and weeping cherry trees. They had been planted by the thousands some thirty years before, a gift from the empire of Japan. They bore thick clusters of white flowers that were reflected in the glass of the windows as men talked to each other inside. The blossoms grew so close together that their stems were invisible.

❧ At first Oppenheimer was consumed by the need to read about his own life. Ann brought him biographies and he would skim them with an amused expression, shaking his head now and then at an incorrect detail. —It's not what they say that's wrong, he told her, —it's how they say it.

He would never forget how hard he had worked on the Project, how it had began to turn his hair gray and stretched the skin so taut on his bones that even *he* noticed that he was shedding his body. He remembered how for three years he had taken no vacation.

And still there was the cold fact that he had personally recommended, along with Fermi and other scientific luminaries, that the bomb be used on the Japanese. When he read that he was filled with a dread of himself. He let the dread lie dormant inside him and moved around it fluidly: but it was always there.

❧ When Jeff the vegan heard that Ann was taking a leave of absence from work his jaw dropped, quick as a cartoon. Ann relished the moment: it was almost a gift.

—He's just *letting* you *do* that? For how long?

—I don't know yet, she said. —At this point it's indefinite.

—And when you come back then bingo, there's your job waiting for you?

—No.

At this Jeff patted his ruffled hair down, turned away and sorted paperclips. Clearly he wished to conceal his delight.

—Listen, he said after a minute, —this isn't about the Coworker Feedback Form, is it?

—No Jeff. It isn't.

—Good, OK good.

Later he revealed his own big news: he was giving up veganism due to protein deficiency and creeping anemia. He would now take up the far lesser task of lacto-ovo-vegetarianism.

—The world is just too hard a place to be perfect in, know what I mean? I mean it's the *world* that's wrong, not me.

❧ Leaving work at the end of the afternoon Ann strolled across the plaza to a restaurant with a wide balcony on the second floor. It was Friday and groups were laughing raucously at tables. She felt pleasantly untethered, drifting up the stairs and onto the balcony, nodding at the hostess, sitting in the shade beside a cool deep adobe wall and sipping lemon water from a frosted glass. A mariachi band was playing in the depths of the restaurant. It was the music of nostalgia, she thought, pure sentiment with words only for placeholders—as though that was the only function of music, to convey either nostalgia or longing, the same emotion in different tenses.

Inside, over the bar, a television blared. On CNN a newscaster told of news from space: a planet had been discovered, the oldest ever known. Far beyond the solar system, it was three times the age of earth.

Looking out across the street, over treetops, she studied the sky and felt she was studying what was possible: wide, empty and spectacular.

The ground is where history has happened, she thought, and when the future is mentioned many eyes are cast upward. Far above in space there are numerous phantom worlds, millions of light-years away. Their high meadows lie untouched, the white peaks of their green mountains blinding in the sun. Blowing grasses weave the shapes of wind across the wide plains and rivers run clear as glass.

The planets there are home again, she thought: the land before we came. What we have done wrong can be forgiven, for there is the earth reborn, again and again forever.

❧ When he was in a good mood Ben convinced himself the scientists were growing on him. Even if they were patients escaped from a psych ward, the fact that they had extensive training in physics was clear. Either that or they had extensive training as actors, because their language was convincing.

Szilard was annoying but offered comic relief to compensate for his homeliness, like a flat-faced dog. To himself he constituted the final authority on all matters. But despite this there was an unflagging courage in his persistence. He neither wished for nor had a private life: the human race was his family.

Oppenheimer was a distant and austere presence except when caught up in oratory, and then he was borderline pretentious. Ann did not seem to notice.

And poor Fermi was vestigial, barely there, generously polite, neat, soft-spoken, retiring quickly to the room where he slept after mealtimes and lying there unmoving. At intervals he would take a book to bed with him but for the most part he lay silent. He asked for little.

Oppenheimer also asked for little: he followed a precise and orderly routine and with his cigarettes, coffee, and drinks at cocktail hour seemed to have all that he required. He borrowed clothes from Ben and cigarette money from Ann, keeping careful accounts in the form of a running IOU in a small notebook.

It was Szilard who did all the asking.

❧ The sky has always been home to paradise, always the light and vacant kingdom, holding out a promise. This is why no one is surprised when promise finally descends, silver and purple, a fiery dragon of the air, rising, swelling and falling again, and the ground and the sky are together at last.

This was what Oppenheimer thought when he looked into the emptiness above Santa Fe.

No one is surprised as dirt disperses in the sky and what descended from the sky spreads all across the ground below, the past turning into the future, the future vanishing in the past.

❧ Szilard knew exactly what he was called upon to do. His clear duty was to change the world. This was not the Pollyanna sentiment of a do-gooder or an idealist: rather it stood to reason. The world was a problem that needed to be solved. He would tackle the problem stoutly.

❧ On the sidewalk outside the restaurant they were waylaid by one of Ben's former clients, a woman wearing tight riding pants on her lean thighs. She insisted on grilling him about a gardening problem as Ann waited beside them, shivering and hugging herself against the chill. A young girl crossed the street clutching a child's hand and further along the block two soldiers were getting out of a jeep.

—It sounds like root rot, Ben was saying to the woman in jodhpurs.

The soldiers strode together down the sidewalk toward her. There was nothing exceptional about this save for the fact that they were both looking at her, looking directly at her as they grew near and saying nothing to each other. She began to feel nervous and interrupted: —I'm sorry, I'm cold. Can we go?

—Of course, said Ben, —sorry, and the woman in jodhpurs stared briefly at Ann and then turned back to him.

—You provide such an *awesome* service, she said, and flashed a smile that showed bright lipstick against white teeth.

The soldiers were almost on them as they got into the car. Ben, in the driver's seat, was noticing nothing, but she kept her eyes on their faces and never looked away. Both of them stopped short as the car pulled off the curb and turned their heads calmly, in unison, to watch it leave.

❧ Ben came into the living room with his morning coffee and found Ann with the war books, which she read when Oppenheimer was not reading them to keep up with him. She did not want to be caught out in ignorance of the world they had lived in, she had told him, and was constantly studying.

—A short walk, maybe?

—Sorry honey I can't, she said, and smiled briefly before going back to the books.

❧ Hiroshima was chosen partly because it had remained unharmed throughout the war till 1945 and partly because it contained a small number of military installations. Its innocence made it an ideal target, unlike Tokyo or Kobe where firestorms caused by air raids had already destroyed thousands of buildings. The new injuries to the land, buildings and people of the city could not be confused with the ravages of previous assaults.

In Alamogordo there had been only cattle and scrub, but in Hiroshima, for the first time, there would be human subjects.

The ancient capital city of Kyoto had also made it onto the shortlist, but was not selected for bombing because Secretary of

War Henry Stimson, a lover of antiquity, decided it was too attractive to be destroyed. This was lucky for Kyoto's people, as well as its thousands of Shinto shrines and Buddhist temples, gardens of moss, and blood-red maples.

The leaflets that were dropped on Hiroshima before the bombing were few in number and similar in content to leaflets that had been dropped before, in other parts of Japan, warning of so-called "conventional" air strikes. The government of Japan should surrender, they said, lest the force of American arms be further loosed upon her citizens.

They did not mention a powerful new weapon, different from any that had come before. They did not mention an atomic bomb; it would have ruined the surprise.

❧ This trying to feel something is a strange ambition, she thought as she put aside her book and picked up the newspaper.

She was preoccupied with feelings since Eugene had died, when she saw how easily she could be their victim.

Oppenheimer had put in a request to see *something new, out of Hollywood.* He said it as though Hollywood was a quaint boutique. As she flipped through the pages looking for movie reviews she thought: I like feeling because it seems like the opposite of reason. Reason is boring even if it does make us human, where feeling is the breath of life and stands apart from reason, all transmogrified.

Then she remembered the soldiers turning their faces in perfect synchronicity to watch Ben drive her away, and what she felt was fear.

❧ The last few times he'd left the house she had barely noticed him leaving, barely felt, as far as he could tell, his arms going around her before he left, his mouth on her cheek, barely heard what he said. As far as he could tell she must hardly be noticing his absence in the house when he was gone; he was a shifting element in her eyes but no longer a central one.

His wife had new enthusiasms.

❧ Szilard and Oppenheimer began to take what Oppenheimer called "constitutionals" after breakfast, walking down upper Canyon Road toward the galleries and cafes. Breakfast for Oppenheimer was a piece of dry toast; for Szilard it was eggs and bacon and buttered scones or English muffins or chocolate chip cookies with pecans or walnuts, of which he had become very fond. (He also liked a banana, and could be seen with his cheeks full, munching, at intervals throughout the day.)

During their walks Szilard kept up a constant patter as Oppenheimer smoked. She would see Oppenheimer nodding slowly at what Szilard said as they made their way back into the house, or occasionally shaking his head.

Oppenheimer adopted a clay pot on an exterior windowsill as a repository for his cigarette butts. They built up daily, a grave full of bones rising. Whenever she passed the pot on the windowsill she worried that there were too many dead cigarettes in the soil. They were vandals, dirty and derelict.

She shrugged off a suspicion that he was going to die for the second time soon.

❧ Ben decided to wait it out, open his arms and persist. He would not pass judgment, or at least not be raucous in his disbelief; he would let her believe what she wanted and meanwhile prosecute his life as he had before, seemingly impartial, waiting for a revelation that was not even his.

❧ In *Make Way for Ducklings* the mother duck walked through the city followed by the winding line of her young. She was aided in this enterprise by kindly policemen, who stopped the cars to let the ducklings cross the street. Ann herself, though, had seen few policemen come to the assistance of ducks, and often observed drivers swerve on purpose not to avoid a snake or rabbit but to run over it.

She worried about Oppenheimer and Szilard when they were out of her sight.

Thinking of *Make Way for Ducklings,* on the table near Eugene's body, she also reminded herself that she did not believe in signs or portents, inherent purpose behind coincidences. A friend of hers who owned a card shop believed the world had, for reasons of its own, special business with her. If gift wrap in a tulip motif arrived at the store on the same day she happened to dab her neck with perfume bearing a tulip logo, she viewed the simultaneity as a miraculous gesture of goodwill, pregnant with significance, from the hovering divine. The simultaneous presence of the tulip-related items, despite the fact that both had been directly and purposefully acquired, reinforced in her the conviction that she herself was blessed; at these moments she became righteous with the certainty of her own transcendent grace and sure of the complicity in this grace of the great goddess Gaia, the cycles of the moon and tides, and her menstrual blood. This blood contained, she had told Ann, molecules from the bodies of ancient cavewoman ancestors, ancestors Ann pictured as breast-beating, hair-tearing, and possibly employing hardy reeds as dental floss.

Ann did not wish to see meaning latent everywhere. If she let herself feel that the world was laying omens in her path she might soon believe she was receiving marital advice from stray pigeons, strutting on the pavement like bug-eyed morons. She might soon see a secret intelligence in the eyes of a passing Standard Poodle, and pin it down spread-eagled to force it to confess.

Now that she had an actual contestable belief, a preposterous, irrational belief—namely the conviction that something that seemed impossible was real—she would have to discipline herself. She would have to keep herself temperate and measured so she did not spin off wheeling into the night, an object of derision.

❧ Szilard had argued with Oppie, as he called him now, near the end of the war in the Pacific. The argument concerned the bombing of Hiroshima and Nagasaki. Oppenheimer knew the bomb would be used; he knew three years of his life had now been consecrated to the machine of its eventual use. But Szilard did not think the bombing was defensible under any circumstances. He did not fully understand that he was beating his head against the sturdy wall of an edifice that later would come to be called the "military-industrial complex."

But then Szilard could be oblivious on many levels to the exigencies of politics. He believed reason could conquer all, could talk a man down from the perilous heights of compulsion. He steadfastly refused to admit that the feral urges of man, his bloodlust and his will to power, most often trump his capacity for logic and empathy.

In fact Szilard was oblivious in the physical world, in matters of the body. It has been documented that on one occasion, as a guest in someone's house, he slept poorly for three nights, complaining every morning about his uncomfortable mattress. It was finally discovered, in an investigation that followed his third complaint, that before his arrival, after the mattress had been lifted off the bed to be turned and aired out, it had never been replaced.

He had been sleeping on the bare springs.

❧ Ben was exhausted now and then with an exhaustion he had barely known since his childhood. He stopped driving Szilard anywhere except when taxis were the only alternative and Szilard threatened to get the cash for the taxis from Ann.

For his part Szilard restrained himself. He made the threat only when he was serious about getting somewhere, and it became shorthand for "You will drive me."

☙ For Oppenheimer reading had turned into a fierce and ugly act. He was afraid of it, but he had to persist.

☙ At the time it was bombed Hiroshima also had a prisoner-of-war camp full of Allied soldiers. One of them, from a gentle town surrounded by cornfields in the American midwest, was a thin man grown far thinner on his prisoner-of-war diet. He was given to picking at his cuticles and had worked unsuccessfully to conquer a stutter.

Only a few short years before he had been a strapping baby. When he was seven months old and twenty-six inches long by the measuring tape his mother had hurt her back lifting him, and in the ensuing years her back had never fully recovered; but she loved him so much, his small beaming face, that she quickly forgot how her back had been injured and never thought of it again.

Still, after her back was injured she had switched to a carriage instead of carrying him everywhere. When she pushed him down the street in his carriage he had lain in the carriage and beamed, watching the treetops pass overhead like weather.

☙ Ann had a savings account and a small package of funds from her parents' life insurance company. In the last days, after they fell from middle-class comfort into the tight and watchful penury of a small pension plan, she and Ben had helped to support them. Her father had been mildly disgraced: an employee under his supervision had embezzled hundreds of thousands of dollars over the years, siphoning it slowly, and because he did not notice the accounting discrepancies he was held responsible in the end and forced into early retirement.

He tended not to stand straight after that, even though it was commonly known that lack of vigilance, not criminality, had been responsible for his downfall. There were sad testimonials from his coworkers and even cards from a corporate vice president or two, signaling the appropriate level of patronizing regret. Her mother had actually been sent a funeral wreath by her father's secretary, no doubt a mistake at the florist's.

Ann had the modest life insurance payment that had come to her after the accident and a few thousand dollars in her old savings account from before her marriage. There was a lawsuit pending against the trucking company, but she seldom thought about it and had no hopes of a return.

She brought the subject up with him when they were in bed, when he was happy and drowsy and curled around her, his warm breath on the back of her neck. She had not planned it, but the word came and she saw no reason to hold it back. —Hiroshima, she said quietly as people will, evoking in one word, one place name, the unspeakable, a vague but jarring memory of guilt, something like an original sin.

❧ Why is this happening to me, was what ran through Ben's mind after she told him where she wanted to spend her long-earned vacation. But he suppressed the complaint.

❧ Oppenheimer confided in Ben that he had considered taking Fermi to a psychologist. But as long as he was destitute and unsure of himself he did not wish to approach any authority or institution. Authorities would do nothing but judge them, exactly as the police, he said, had briefly—though apparently with supreme indifference—judged Szilard.

They were watching television because Szilard had developed an interest in reality shows, which he claimed reminded him of the circus freak shows of yesteryear. They took the place, said Szilard, of the Siamese twins and deformed fetuses in pickle jars that had long been outlawed.

Oppenheimer watched distractedly, smoking out the window, drinking bourbon and making conversation with Ben. He and Ben had agreed to disagree on the subject of identity. Oppenheimer did not blame him at all for his skepticism. It was exactly, he said, how he would have felt if their positions were reversed.

—The one thing a shrink could do, said Ben, —would be to convince you you're not who you claim to be. Your delusions of grandeur are pretty common. I mean in hospitals where they treat psychiatric problems there are literally hundreds of Napoleons, Kennedys, Pope John Pauls, and Mahatma Gandhis.

—Believe me, said Oppenheimer, —I'd rather be one of them.

❧ Ann slipped into the car and slung her plastic bag of groceries into the passenger seat. In an overpriced gourmet food store she had run into a woman named Melanie who had once been a friend and was now an awkward acquaintance. The friendship had always been uncertain and finally Melanie stopped calling and Ann did not call her either. They had little to say to each other.

Beside the deli counter Melanie had smiled palely at her, clearly bored even as she asked with forced interest: —Hey Ann, so how have you been?

Ann had wanted to answer: —You don't have to fake it for me. Just grab your pasta salad and run.

But instead she had answered with equal politeness. It occurred to her that Melanie's life was sealed off from her now, but she did not care. She felt she should regret this, but did not.

—Is she happy? she wondered, flicking her signal for the turn into her driveway, and then conjugated. —Am I happy? Are they happy?

She thought: when people ask these questions they mean the

reverse. Is it a happy marriage? means: Is it *unhappy*? Is he a happy man means: is he *unhappy*?

People do not *mean* happy. Happy is never meant. On the subject of happy the mind actually draws a blank.

When she got home, grocery bags in her arms, and pushed the front door open with her hip, her foot slid as she stepped over the threshold and looking down she saw a scuffed envelope. It was unmarked so she put down her bags, picked it up and ripped it open. Inside was a photograph: a shadowy figure seen through a white window curtain. It had been taken at night, from outside the window looking in.

She put the picture down on an end table and was in the kitchen pouring herself a glass of water when she realized it was her bedroom window, and the figure was her.

Glass in one hand, picture in the other, heart beating quickly, she went to find Oppenheimer, who was reading in the garden. Her hand shook as she held it out to him.

—I think, he said slowly, —someone is watching us.

A few minutes later she picked up the ringing telephone to hear, at the other end, a man's voice she did not recognize. It said only: *Get them out of your house. They are not good for you.*

She told Oppenheimer about this but she did not tell Ben.

❧ When it came to money Ben could dig in his heels. He was cautious about spending it, always in the certainty that men of any age could easily become poor, cast out onto the street to shake cups for pennies and fall to drinking malt liquor. When he heard the words *old man* this was the first image that entered his mind; when he heard the word *poor* he thought of *father.*

The first time he'd heard The Lord's Prayer he had thought the words went *Poor father, who art in heaven, hallowed be thy name. Thy kingdom come, thy will be done, on earth as it is in heaven.*

And if he had to be frail-boned and brittle, if he lived that long, at least he would be sure not to be yellow-haired, brown-toothed, at the mercy of young passersby in slick garments, with clean faces, shining eyes and confident shoulders. He would not be abject.

He had opened a retirement account when he was nineteen.

But Ann had always associated those who planned too carefully for their advancing age with a denial of life, an eagerness to be done with it. She had an uncle and aunt who had lived in a small house with a dry brown lawn in Anaheim, California, for forty years. She had visited them as a freshman in college and again in her late twenties. The aunt and uncle rarely went outside; their groceries were delivered once a week. When she saw them in her twenties they sat her down and brought her a glass of iced tea, the same flavor of iced tea they had offered her when she was eighteen. She sat in the same beige armchair and placed her tea on a round, straw coaster that, though she could not be perfectly sure, also looked familiar after more than a decade.

Her aunt liked to do large sailboat and nature-scene jigsaw puzzles, which she later laminated and hung on the wall. Her uncle watched sports and collected small bottles of tequila from all over Mexico, though, being in AA, he did not drink them. But chiefly, she had seen from their reticence and rigid bodies and their obvious reluctance to hear new information, they wished that all the rush was over. They wished the job of living was already resolved and perfect in completion. If they could be statues they would, but failing that they would float forever on the surface of their lives.

Ben feared cataclysmic events but more and more she feared the lack of them. So his resistance to Hiroshima did not surprise her. It was like rope, long, quiet and strong. How were they going to get passports for the scientists, for instance? Szilard was handling the details, she told him. Szilard had investigated. Szilard was determined not to be obstructed by what he called "the logistics of being dead." Ben said the bills would add up. He said it made no sense to spend thousands of dollars on a whim. Weren't they giving the scientists enough already? The scientists were *living off them*. They, Ann and Ben, had become a charity, but far from being rich they were an unemployed librarian and a gardener.

—A charity, finished Ben, —without the tax benefits.

Ann stood behind him, arms folded, on the opposite side of the kitchen, the edge of the sink lodged sharply against the small of her back as she watched him chop vegetables with a sure hand. It was difficult to persuade from this position, looking at his shoulder blades. She felt weak.

—I can afford it, she said. —I want to use my parents' insurance policy for the trip. They would have wanted it.

Her parents had wanted her to *see the world* and she had always resisted. During their lives she had never gone far afield. She had always thought travel was beside the point, an escape from what was real instead of a search for it as most travelers claimed. Even now she did not want to travel. She had no interest in Japan before other countries; she did not speak the language and she did not know the country's history except for the single blot, the event. Because of this she would only coast along outside of the culture looking in as she suspected tourists always did, feet leaden, eyes dazzled, spending.

But she could not let the scientists go alone.

—They would have wanted you to give your money away? To hand over your meager savings to men you just met?

—No, you know what I—

—Men who seem to be in the throes of a grandiose schizoid delusion? That's what your parents would have wanted for you?

—They would have wanted me to do something . . .

She stopped, throat constricting, and swallowed so she could go on.

—. . . something I wanted to do.

The scientists were hers, the only cause she had ever held dear. Causes had always kept her at a distance: they cried out for attention but left her numb. There were just too many of them, mostly hopeless.

But now there was only one.

❧ As for Nagasaki, bombed three days after Hiroshima, leaflets were certainly dropped warning of an atomic bomb and exhorting those below to flee the city.

The timing of this is occasionally debated, however. Some Japanese survivors of the bomb maintain that the leaflets were dropped by American planes only *after* the attack, for the sake of posterity.

But there is no debate as to whether the leaflets were helpful to the citizens of Nagasaki. Japan was a poor country then; the war had seen strict rationing, and toilet paper was scarce.

❧ He felt guilty, pulled toward her and pushed away at once, worry nagging. But it was true: her parents would have approved. She had always been too retiring for them. They had raised her with high hopes of social status and she had turned out to be a librarian.

To them it was almost, she had said to him once, as though she had become a nun. A librarian was a nun without God. A librarian could have God, of course, she might or might not have God, but God was not mandatory.

—I'm sorry, said Ben, putting his arms around her. —I didn't mean to upset you.

—I know, she said.

—It's just, I thought you were putting that money away for the kid, he said softly. —Remember? College tuition.

—But there's still time for that, she said, —right? We don't have to live like we're already middle-aged. We're still young. And for some reason I know, for some reason I'm sure about this. I have to stay with them.

❧ Japan was the first destination on Szilard's list but only the second on Oppenheimer's. Oppenheimer had an even more pressing appointment.

With Szilard's collusion he prepared quietly, buying fake driver's licenses and University of New Mexico faculty IDs and arranging to join a chartered bus tour. The bus would be full of civil servants from a federal agency that regulated the nuclear power industry. They had scheduled a private tour of a national historical site.

Because of their status as civil servants in the industry these bureaucrats had special privileges. They would be attending a conference in Albuquerque, and on the side, in their spare time, wished to be educated in history.

He wanted to go back to the place from which he and Fermi had first disappeared. It was not easy because the Trinity Site, on the White Sands Missile Range near the strip-mall, fast-food town of Socorro, was open to the general public for only two days a year.

After all the primary function of a missile range is not, it has to be admitted, the entertainment of tourists.

❧ —No, I don't need to go, Ben told her when she asked if he wanted to go with them. —From what I hear there's not a lot to see, just some bare earth and busloads of fat people snapping their cameras. I have to work.

❧ It was Oppenheimer who chose the code name Trinity for the first-ever atomic blast. When he was asked about this baptism, according to the history books, he said: "This code name didn't mean anything. It was just something suggested to me by John Donne's sonnets, which I happened to be reading at the time."

Apparently there were two poems he had in mind by Donne, one of which went *As West and East are one, So death doth touch the Resurrection.*

The other, a devotional poem, went *Batter my heart, three person'd God.*

❧ At the White Sands Missile Range they parked the car near a guarded entrance called Stallion Gate. It was here that they would meet the Army personnel who would lead them on their tour.

—It had a different name back then, said Oppenheimer as he got out of the passenger seat and ground his cigarette out on the roadbed with the toe of his shoe. —Alamogordo Bombing and Gunnery Range. Back then we called things by their names. Remember, Enrico? Stimson was the secretary of war; now they have a secretary of defense.

—Apparently these days the government likes to pretend that all war is defense, said Szilard.

Fermi nodded vaguely.

—It's what I said would happen, said Oppenheimer. —I read it just yesterday in one of my lectures. The government has to lie because it's afraid of the people.

—Doublespeak, said Szilard. —You can't believe a word they say.

—Democracy has become very crude, said Fermi prissily. —Have you seen the magazines for women?

—And the popular music, said Oppenheimer.

—Eminem, said Szilard. —He's good. But I got an old album by Ice Cube that I like better.

—Ice Cube? asked Oppenheimer.

—"Your daughter was a nice girl, now she's a slut," said Szilard.

—Excuse me? said Fermi.

—Ice Cube. The rapper. It's a song. "A queen treatin' niggaz just like King Tut. Gobblin' up nuts, sorta like a hummingbird."

Fermi was confused. —A hummingbird is not a seedeater.

—People are very crude when they want to sell things, said Oppenheimer. —But the government is as evasive as the Japs.

—Japa*nese*! said Szilard. —You racist.

—I'm sorry. The Japanese. I bear them no ill will. Old habits die hard, you know that. Not everyone picks up the jargon as quickly as you do, Leo. My point is, the government talks in words that make horror trivial. But the people talk in words that make the trivial horrible.

—Well, said Ann. —Here comes the government now.

⌁ Government turned out to be a friendly woman with a nametag that read *Hi I'm Keri*. She took a quick look at their fake IDs and ushered them into her U.S. Army minivan, where, with the looming tour bus following them, a debonair swish of orange along its massive body, they set out south on the long dirt road to the Trinity Site.

Plains of sagebrush and dirt stretched out on both sides, interrupted only by spiky clumps of yucca. The scientists sat at the back of the minivan while Ann sat near the front and talked to Keri. Keri's perky assistant, in the passenger seat, was wearing strong perfume that smelled like a chemical version of peaches. It brought tears to Ann's eyes.

—You ladies in the Army? Szilard called up to Peaches curiously.

—Civilian employees.

A herd of black and white animals with extravagant horns ran across the road in front of them, kicking up clouds of dust as they disappeared into the scrub.

—They're from Africa, explained Peaches, pleased to inform. —They're African oryx! Way back in the '50s they shipped them here across the ocean for the hunters to shoot. You know, the ones that come in from L.A. and Santa Fe on the weekends? They just let 'em loose! They done real good. You know, breeding.

—They compete with the native pronghorn for forage, said Fermi stiffly. It was a rare moment of speech.

Fermi was developing an interest in endangered species.

—Oh goodness, said Peaches. —There's plenty to go around. I *can* tell you we don't allow cows on the Missile Range anymore. They're bad for nature. Right, Keri?

—There was a study done, said Keri. —Cows do more damage to vegetation than the A-bomb did. Course they're not quite as speedy.

—But we still do lots of ordnance testing, said Peaches. —See over there, in the distance? That building is just for blowing up.

—The pilots swoop in all the time in their planes and blow it up, said Keri. —Then later they rebuild it.

—Taxpayer dollars, said Szilard.

Keri and Peaches drove them first to the cabin where, in the weeks before the Trinity test, the gadget had been assembled. Peaches slid back the minivan door and Szilard jumped out eagerly. Standing beside Ann he gazed up at the tour bus as it rumbled and screeched to a stop across the dirt road. Behind him Peaches waited politely for Oppenheimer and Fermi to disembark.

But they stayed where they were, staring out the window toward the cabin, ignoring the open door.

Over the van's silver roof Ann could see what looked like the skeleton of an ancient wooden windmill. She glanced at the cabin beyond it and then back at the scientists, anxious. Fermi sat looking at his lap, scrutinizing his fingernails as Oppenheimer gazed steadily through the tinted glass at the cabin, his face impossible to read.

Finally Szilard, impatient, barked up at them —What are you waiting for?

When the two of them stepped tentatively onto the ground, Szilard, trotting behind Keri toward the cabin, turned to Ann and whispered: —I think they were hoping it would change everything to come back.

But there they were in the flat light of the cloudless desert sky, in the flat light that turned the landscape gray and indistinct and at the same time dazed the eyes like a slap. Still behind them was the shining bulk of the minivan, and still with them were all the people they should never have known had they remained in the *real life*, where they were supposed to be.

Shoulders slumping, Oppenheimer and Fermi picked their way slowly between the creosote bushes, eyes on the ground. Their tailored suits were starkly out of place against the crowd of civil servants descending from the bus behind them, who seemed to be wearing Western vacation garb. The civil servants were all dressed for leisure in newly minted cowboy hats and stiff pointy-toed cowboy boots.

❧ —You know, said Peaches to Ann, catching up, —you want to know what just occurred to me? One of the researchers in your group here looks exactly like Dr. Oppenheimer, who was in charge of the program to build the bomb back in the 1940s!

—You're kidding, said Ann. —Really?

—At least from the pictures I've seen. Is he related?

—Beats me, said Ann.

—I used to archive photos sometimes so I went through a bunch of them. He really is, he's a dead ringer! And he seems so sweet too. So *Old World*.

—OK, folks, said Keri, stopping in front of the cabin. —This is a self-guided tour, you're welcome to go through at your own pace. I'll just give you a real short intro.

The cabin had been renovated, she told them, cleaned up and repaired for Army use, but then it was designated a so-called National Historic Landmark. So in the interest of authenticity, and at some expense, the Army promptly undid the renovations, returning the cabin to its original state of disrepair. They even repainted the old graffiti onto the walls and door frames.

Leaving the lecture behind her, droning, Ann went through a green door, on which was painted, in white, PLEASE WIPE FEET and PLEASE USE OTHER DOORS—KEEP THIS ROOM CLEAN.

Down the door jamb was painted, in a more panicked tone, the words No!!! No.

This, she heard Keri tell the crowd outside, was the door to the room where the Trinity device had been assembled. —In those days, said Keri, —the protocol on handling radioactive materials was kind of, uh, *relaxed.*

—You were barbarians, Ann whispered to Oppenheimer.

—And we paid for it, said Szilard. —Didn't we.

ॐ In the dusty interior, shabby black-and-white photos of the scientists and workers of the Manhattan Project were propped carelessly along the floor, along with snapshots of the bomb before it was dropped, being hauled to the top of the tower. The display had an amateur feel, as though a six-year-old was charging grownups a dime to look at a pile of favorite junk in his bedroom.

Oppenheimer was captivated. Except for the soldiers he knew everyone in the pictures, and to look at their faces again on the ancient photographic paper, now yellowed and brittle, was to see them through a long lens of time. It brought tears to his eyes and often he would stand in front of a photograph for many minutes, not speaking to his companions, to allow the tears to be quietly reabsorbed.

Civil servants milled through the dim wooden rooms behind him in an apparent trance of disinterest.

—Look, there's you, whispered Ann once, close beside him. She pointed to a discolored photo of him with Groves. —That's a famous one. It's in all the history books.

—I have seen it there, he said slowly, nodding.

—So for you that was taken just, what? Five, six weeks ago now?

—You're telling me this is where we made history? asked Fermi, on her other side. He was incredulous. —*This* is what they call a National Historic Landmark? This is a *monument*?

—The Army doesn't have a huge curatorial staff, if I remember correctly, said Oppenheimer drily.

—In Italy we know how to do monuments, said Fermi.

—And dictators, said Szilard.

When they finally emerged from the dark into the bright blankness of the desert Oppenheimer could see the gray-striped Oscura mountains low on the horizon, beyond a low stone wall and a huddle of derelict stone buildings. A civil servant beside them on the porch, wearing a nametag that said DARYL and eating a chocolate bar, cocked an eyebrow at him.

He was wearing a Hawaiian shirt, clearly bucking the trend toward cowboy attire.

—Don't see a nametag, he said to Oppenheimer out of the side of his mouth. You with the group?

—No, said Oppenheimer. —We came independently.

—He looks just like Robert Oppenheimer! Don't you think? squeaked Peaches, emerging from the cabin behind them.

—Huh, said the civil servant, squinting at him and then turning to her with a grin. —Really? I dunno. I wasn't really paying attention to the history lesson. Sorry, teach.

This was said in a flirtatious and puerile jeer that Oppenheimer found highly repulsive. Peaches giggled.

On his other side another civil servant confided in a colleague: —The DOD has already approved the use of tactical nukes in the War on Terrorism. You hear that?

—Excuse me? said Szilard, moving in close.

—Sorry, have we met? asked the civil servant.

—No. Did you say "approved the use of tactical nukes"? urged Szilard.

—Oh, just a formality, he said.

—You see? whispered Szilard insistently into Oppenheimer's ear. —You see? From the horse's mouth. Am I crying wolf now?

—OK gang! said Keri brightly, and clapped her hands. —We're off to see the original Ground Zero!

❧ The original Ground Zero was nothing but a low, level field on which grasses and wildflowers grew. Once the Trinity bomb had been dropped there from its hundred-foot tower and exploded. But now nothing remained of the tower or the bomb, only dirt and weeds.

There were no yucca plants and this alone distinguished Trinity from the fields nearby, the fields beyond the so-called crater and its chain-link fence. In the center of the field towered a plain, dark obelisk with a date printed on it and the phrase TRINITY SITE: WHERE THE WORLD'S FIRST NUCLEAR DEVICE WAS EXPLODED. Around its base flowers sprouted, the pale orange bells of globe mallow and some small yellow and purple blooms, common but so nondescript that Ann had never bothered to learn their names. Ben would know.

The dent of the crater the bomb had made was barely perceptible. It was less a crater than the outline of a circle, so faint it bordered on the imaginary.

—After all, you have to remember, said Keri. —This bomb was really just a baby at twenty kilotons.

Peaches was carrying a handheld Geiger counter and showing the civil servants how little radiation remained as the counter clicked above dry clumps of grass.

Oppenheimer peered over her shoulder, intrigued.

—Follow me, said Keri to the group, —if you'd like to see the Trinitite.

Under an odd, padlocked shelter at the end of the fenced-in field there was soil, and in the soil—which Keri showed them by unlocking and opening a hatch—there were clumps of Trinitite, the fused, greenish substance the bomb's explosion had left crusting the ground. She picked it up and held it in the palm of her hand, crumbling it with her thumb. Most of the Trinitite had been cleaned up decades before when it was still radioactive, trucked out by the Army and deposited in what Keri told them was *an unknown location.*

—Look at the field of the blast, said Fermi a little sadly, as they were shepherded past the chain-link fence toward the dirt parking lot again. —It's hardly changed a bit.

We say we're looking for happiness but in fact we're just waiting to be found by it, thought Ann as they walked away, found by chance as the blast found the field. She wondered if she was a kid hiding behind a tree exhilarated, preparing to leap out with an expression of glee, who never realizes no one is looking for her.

∽ Driving back toward Stallion Gate Keri popped a tape into the minivan's stereo and Kenny Rogers sang "Ruby, don't take your love to town."

—And before you leave the area, said Peaches, —you should stop in the diner right up the road and sample their green chili burgers. I mean those things are amazing.

—We saw the sign for them on our way in, said Ann.

—You won't get a better green chili burger anywhere in the world, said Keri. —That's a promise.

She dropped them off at the entrance, where they stretched their legs, waited for Oppenheimer to smoke a cigarette and then got into the Toyota and drove north. Oppenheimer and Fermi lapsed into silence again while Szilard talked, and turning out onto the main road again Ann did not see the black Hum-V draw in behind them till it rammed into their rear bumper.

—Dio! said Fermi, as the car jolted.

—What the hell! said Szilard.

Ann flicked on her turn signal and began to pull onto the shoulder, but as she slowed down the Hum-V rammed them again.

—He's doing it on purpose! cried Szilard. —Speed up! Speed up!

Ann veered off the shoulder again, heat rushing to her face, her hands shaking on the wheel.

—Can you see who it is? she asked.

—The windows are too dark, said Szilard. —Drive fast!

—Here, she said, and rummaged in her purse as she floored the gas. —Call 911!

—Give it to me! said Szilard, and grabbed the phone from the purse just as the Hum-V rammed them a third time and stayed with them, pushing their car in front of it. Ann smelled burning rubber and screamed, and as she lost control of the steering vaguely heard the hoarse sound of the others screaming too. They were veering, pushed, veering off the road again, the right half of the car in a ditch, undercarriage grating against the road, more burning, and the car was up on its right wheels, up, up, and they came off the ground and flipped sideways, rolling.

❧ Kneeling to fix a spigot on the irrigation system Ben knew suddenly that he could not let Ann go to Japan without him. They had never been apart for more than three days, and the scientists, unpredictable as any unknown quantities, could not be entrusted with her welfare. Also, there was enough new distance between them already.

He got up, brushed the dirt off his knees and went to find Lynn, who was stretching on a mat in the living room in a purple leotard.

But Lynn was not used to breaches of contract.

—No fucking way! she said. —I mean we have a timeline here. We're having the Fourth of July party and what if it's not finished by then? You can't just go away for two weeks. It's ridiculous. I mean

Yoshi can't tell the workers what to do, the guy doesn't even know how to speak English! Are you fucking kidding me?

—I realize his English is still improving, said Ben quietly. —He's not up to speed yet. So I thought I'd hire a temporary foreman for you. He's very reliable. I'll bring him in tomorrow and if you don't like him for any reason I have a great second alternate. They both have excellent credentials.

—I didn't hire them, I hired you!

—I know, said Ben. —Of course I understand your position, and these weeks will represent a financial loss for me. But you'd actually be getting someone who's out of my league professionally, who's a lot better known than I am, Joe Kessler, his work has been in magazines, *Connoisseur* maybe? Or *Architectural Digest*? I can have him send over a portfolio. He's actually taking a two-week break from working on a place in Malibu. Joni Mitchell, I think he said. I mean this is a guy we'd be lucky to—

—Joni Mitchell?

❧ She woke to the car door being jerked open. She was upside down and they were pulling her out. Her head was heavy, throbbing with blood.

—Incredibly lucky, said the emergency worker, and led her over to the ambulance, where she sat down on a stretcher as they moved around her, touching her hair and temples, dabbing her with something wet, asking questions as they prodded at her torso. The scientists stood nearby, apparently unhurt. Oppenheimer was smoking in rapid puffs as he met her eyes, Fermi sat on the hood of a police car with his head in his hands, and Szilard paced on the dead grass jabbering into her cell phone. —All of you.

❧ When they got home Ben was beyond relief to have her back whole and safe. Szilard had called and thrown him into a panic.

It never occurred to him that the crash had been anything more significant than a road rage incident.

♥ Oppenheimer read steadily, informing himself through the books Ann brought him from the library.

In his memoirs, Truman had described the factors that influenced his decision to drop the bomb and his *emotions at the time.* He wrote: "Let there be no mistake about it. I regarded the bomb as a military weapon and never had any doubt it should be used."

When the bomb fell on Hiroshima, Truman was aboard ship. Said a reporter of his expression as he announced the attack to crewmen: "He was not actually laughing, but there was a broad smile on his face."

Without reading the mind of Truman or his military advisors, however, it is nonetheless possible to make some stipulations, reflected Oppenheimer as he read. First, though the line taken officially was different, some commentators suggested that the bomb was dropped not primarily to defeat the Japanese but to demonstrate American military superiority over the Soviet Union, erstwhile ally, and thus indemnify American hegemony against the burgeoning power and imperialist designs of Stalin, whatever those might be.

Second, it was a fact that the Japanese were definitively losing the war in August 1945, and despite their militaristic and nationalistic will to victory they had already begun to make attempts to surrender, via these same Soviet allies. But the U.S. chose to discredit their overtures and insist that it would accept only *unconditional* surrender. Under the terms of such a surrender the emperor could be compelled to forfeit his throne, and perhaps more importantly the Japanese would not be permitted to save face. This was the public rationale for dropping the bomb.

Since unconditional surrender would be required, the fight must continue until the Japanese were forced to their knees. And *given* that the fight was to continue there was, to be sure, a need to minimize the loss of American and yes, suddenly, even Japanese lives. The bomb would save lives by taking them; by killing hundreds of thousands of Japanese civilians instantly the bomb would save the lives of American soldiers.

The elegance of this argument, he felt, was that its validity could never be determined. Certainly many lives would also have been lost if, in order to effect the all-important *unconditional* surrender, conventional warfare continued.

In the early summer of 1945 U.S. military planners estimated a ground invasion of Japan would cost twenty to sixty thousand American lives; George Marshall set the figure at forty-six thousand. Yet curiously, after the war, Truman would make claims ranging from a quarter-million to more than a million American lives—a claim that was still being upheld almost fifty years later by bestselling Truman biographers and news sources such as *Nightline* and *USA Today*.

These numbers, as far as Oppenheimer could tell, had no basis in fact.

❧ They were sitting reading after dinner when Fermi appeared in the living room doorway and cleared his throat.

Surprised at this uncharacteristic boldness all four of them turned to look at him.

—This incident was the last straw, he said. —I do not want to go to Japan. I do not think my presence will be a benefit.

—You're coming with us anyway, said Oppenheimer, who brooked no dissent. Szilard pretended to be immersed in an issue of *Scientific American*.

Fermi stood there for a while and then turned and shuffled back to his room.

❧ In life Fermi had been an avid hiker, climbing quickly and energetically through the Jemez and the Sangre de Cristo and before that the Italian Alps, always at the head of the column, liking to be first and liking to be fast, wielding a walking stick.

The afternoon after the accident Ben came home for lunch and Fermi was perched on a stool at the kitchen's wooden bar nibbling quiet and rabbitlike at an egg-salad sandwich. Then, following his daily custom, he retired to his room to lie on his side and close his eyes without sleeping.

Ben followed him and knocked on his door. Fermi sat up on the sofabed and waited politely.

—I was thinking, maybe you'd feel like taking a walk in the mountains when I get off work. There should be color in the high meadows now, Indian paintbrush blooming. Back in your time a big fire went through there, and now the hills are covered in aspen.

It took Fermi some time to answer.

—I'm tired, he said finally.

—You don't have to go far, said Ben. —You don't have to go fast. Do you good to get out.

Later they drove upward, winding, almost in silence except for once when Fermi asked if he could open the window. He rolled it down carefully, as though the handle might break in his fingers. Then he leaned. He reminded Ben of a dog, listing toward the opening to catch the force of the wind in his face. His hands rested neatly, almost formally on his knees, but his torso leaned away toward the breeze, which rifled what remained of his hair.

When they got out Ben handed him a full water bottle, which he accepted wordlessly. Along the wide disused Forest Service road, hard-packed dirt, dried grass, tire treads and small-headed yellow flowers bending along the edges, Fermi followed him uphill, trudging the gradual but wearing slope. When Ben said something and turned to look at him he would nod or shake his head, but he was distant.

Where the trail narrowed a hawk swooped suddenly over

them, the white of its underwings so close Ben thought he could touch the feathers. He wondered what had drawn it so low, what prey it had dipped to catch. Fermi stopped in his tracks and stared up at it, arms hanging at his sides, head tipped back, as it lifted on a swell and rose away from them again.

After that he began to walk faster. He passed Ben and strode ahead more and more quickly until finally Ben didn't feel like keeping up.

—Turn back, he called, —at four thirty! OK?

He thought he saw the back of Fermi's head move vertically in a nod, but he wasn't sure.

At five he got tired and turned back, hoping that Fermi, ahead of him, further up and in colder air, was doing the same. One knee was hurting where he'd had surgery. He waited for him at the car, until the sun set and the dark dropped. There was silence around him except for the wind in the trees now and then, and every few minutes a car passed behind, headlights swinging as it rounded the near curve.

After a while he was too irritated to do nothing. He hummed and swung his arms, walked in circles and stretched his legs, counted branches, trees, stars and constellations. He cleaned the car's interior, wiping the dash with wet wipes from the glove compartment, collecting bubble gum wrappers and paper cups and the wrinkled stiff white balls of wax paper that Szilard invariably tucked under the passenger seat after eating his daily donut. He thought of Szilard's fleshy face, his sloped shoulders. Normally Szilard was the butt of his private jokes but the longer Ben waited for Fermi the better Szilard looked by contrast: the reliable homebody, the good dog on the hearth.

It was almost ten when Fermi came trotting briskly down the path again, water bottle in one hand. He was smiling, and when he got into the car his apologies were so profuse and heavily accented that Ben smiled and forgot to be angry anymore, and they drove back down the mountain in a warm exhaustion that was almost contented.

❧ —Goodnight, said Oppenheimer, stepping into the living room where she sat and waving to her after his last cigarette of the evening. Szilard was in bed and Ben and Fermi were still in the mountains.

She turned a page in the book of photographs she was looking at, beautiful photographs of foreign landscapes. She felt a surge of joy looking down at them and decided it would be wise never to go there. This was best, sitting here, looking at them like this, flat, fully captured, perfect.

Joy rises unexpectedly, she thought, now in peace, now in crisis. The feeling of it escapes design, surging only at the far end of endurance, on the lip of despair. It trills a faint pulse beyond the normal in the tiredness of limbs, a lifted grief, the flash and glitter of the sea.

❧ When they came in the door they smelled of the cold. Ben could tell, smelling the cold that was on his own face.

He and Fermi smiled at each other quickly when they saw Ann curled on the couch. She had fallen asleep with a coffee table book on her lap, in the dim glow of a lamp.

Fermi slipped off his shoes and went quietly down the hall to his room while Ben lifted the book off her lap and picked her up gently to carry her to bed.

❧ In actual fact so-called conventional warfare had already devolved into total war, that is to say, war waged against civilians on a sweeping scale. Both the Allies and the Axis military had been guilty of this. The American firebombings of Tokyo, for instance, killed one hundred thousand citizens in two days, who died mostly by burning alive. The Japanese rape of Nanking left more than two hundred thousand civilians dead and involved the rape and mutilation of tens of thousands of women and girls. The English bombing of Dresden killed one hundred and thirty thousand. All in all, the Soviet Union saw seventeen million civilians killed in the war, China nine million, Poland six million, Germany four million. England suffered only sixty-two thousand, and the United States almost none.

❧ The sheets needed to be washed. Even the coverlet, the down comforter, all of them smelled faintly of skin and sweat instead of detergent because she had forgotten routine in the past weeks, forgotten the care she always took and how it had both framed the day and hung itself on the day's frame. Herself she liked these smells of sleeping but her mother had lectured her often on the hygiene of linens, how they should bear the fragrance of soap instead of humans.

—So listen, said Ben.

This was where most of their negotiations were conducted now, where most new information was disclosed since the advent of the scientists, which had made public space of the rest of the house.

—Yes? she murmured, though she had actually departed already, even as she decided the sheets were dirty and she didn't mind. She had emerged into an airport, onto a long automatic sidewalk, where blocking the sidewalk ahead of her was a kangaroo in an overstuffed chair, reminding her of Szilard.

Then she remembered: he and Fermi had been out late. She had waited for them. She was jarred awake.

—What took you so long? she asked plaintively.

—Listen, whispered Ben. —I'm going with you to Japan.

She lifted herself up, alert, noticing now his crow's feet, the bags under his eyes. He seemed older to her in the half-light, lying down, the back of his hand against his forehead, palm up and fingers curled, a gesture he made only when he was very tired.

—*Really*? she asked. —You can leave work for two weeks?

She settled against his cool naked side, adjusting herself so that her cheek did not lie against the sharp lines of the ribs. Once a lung had collapsed, and there was a scar beneath his arm, across the side of the ribcage. When a lung collapsed, he had told her, air continued to be inhaled into the body but could not be exhaled again, and so the body swelled and rounded, ballooning till finally the heart stopped. He had warned her the lung could easily collapse again. If they were alone in a place with no telephones or ambulances she would have to make the incision herself. She would have to remove the ink cartridge from a ballpoint pen, he said, and stick the hollow pen into the hole to let out the air.

—Lynn wasn't happy about it, he said. —But I convinced her. I told her the sub was taking a break from doing Joni Mitchell.

❧ Oppenheimer and Szilard had begun to discuss their colleagues of an evening, their *former colleagues from life*. Szilard had tracked down various biographies and for light reading after dinner he and Oppenheimer would read from these. They read about themselves privately, with advance psychological preparation, but they were always jarred when they found references to themselves in books they were reading about others.

Ann liked to listen to them and Ben liked to sit with his arm around her shoulders. Two nights after his walk on the mountain, Fermi even joined them.

—Uh, Bob Serber—, said Szilard, putting down the book from which he was reading aloud. It was one of several autobiographical tomes by the physicist Richard Feynman, rich in frolicsome anecdotes and reports of clever practical jokes Feynman had played on his fellow academics.

—What about him? asked Oppenheimer from the open window where he was standing, arm and cigarette outside. His mind had been wandering, Ann could tell.

Szilard appeared to reconsider speaking further. He fumbled with the Feynman a bit nervously, flipping through it as though searching.

But now Oppenheimer was interested.

—Biographers seem to believe he had an, um, special relationship with Kitty, is what Dr. Szilard was probably going to say, said Ann. —He's going to learn it sooner or later, she went on, turning to Szilard. —He might as well hear it now.

—They may have been just friends, said Szilard quickly. —Like me and Trude.

—You married Trude, said Ann.

—The other guy did that, not me, said Szilard. —She probably begged him to. I wouldn't have done it personally. But it wasn't his fault anyway. He put up a good fight. It took her twenty years to convince him.

—Bob Serber, said Oppenheimer slowly. —With my wife?

—You were already dead, said Szilard. —Don't worry.

—I hadn't read that, said Oppenheimer. —I wonder how I missed it.

—They were mourning you, put in Ann, anxious to mitigate. —They spent a lot of time together after your death. Kitty was lonely.

—Kitty never liked to be on her own, said Oppenheimer. —I wouldn't expect her to.

—Anyway, Oppie, said Szilard, —you were dead.

—No one acted out of turn, said Ann.

—But how about Bob's wife? Charlotte?

—She died too, said Szilard. —She died young.

—Dear Charlotte. That poor girl. She was our librarian! Just like you, said Oppenheimer with sudden tenderness, turning to Ann.

Ann felt flustered and went on talking to cover her confusion. Oppenheimer was rarely affectionate.

—Serber remarried after Kitty died, said Ann.

She had researched the subject because she felt an obligation to know about the scientists' personal lives. It seldom occurred to them to explain themselves, so to follow their conversations she needed a complete background. Oppenheimer in life had been close to Serber and so she had read about him: born and raised in West Philadelphia, the grandson of immigrants from Russia and Poland, he had been thirteen when his mother died of a nervous system disease, having spent her last years in dim rooms, shielded from noise and light. Scarlet fever had left Serber himself near-sighted and all his life he wore bottle-thick glasses. Yet women had tended to find him attractive. He had lived longer than any of the atom bomb scientists save Teller, finally dying of cancer in 1997.

—A younger woman.

—Bob was a good physicist. A great help. I was quite fond of him, said Oppenheimer with a studied mildness.

Both he and Szilard liked to pore over pictures of the young scientists they had known in 1945, images of these men that had been made long after they had known them. Even Fermi could be roused by this, occasionally moved to laughter by the sight of his boyhood friends transformed—somewhat gruesomely, it had to be admitted, in one fell swoop—into doddering old men.

—There's Segré! he said, crowing and pointing. —My God! Emilio! We used to call him the Basilisk when we were at school in Rome. He turned a fiery eye when displeased. So much taller than me. And then look at him! He liked to fish for trout. Now he looks like one.

—Not *now,* said Oppenheimer. —Now he's deceased.

—You know what I mean, said Fermi.

—His son wrote a book about him, said Ann. —He said he was emotionally unreachable.

—Is that bad? asked Fermi.

—I think you, on the other hand, said Oppenheimer to Szilard, —aged quite well.

—Oh, Leo was always the same, said Fermi. —Fat. Fat people retain a youthful appearance.

—What? said Szilard.

—The fat puffs out the wrinkles.

—*What?* repeated Szilard, indignant but willing to ham it up if his performance would help draw out Fermi. He turned the book toward him to scrutinize himself posing for a group photo. —That's the other guy. Maybe he got fat, sure. But not me. You're saying I was big like *he* got to be, even when I was young? That's bullshit! I'm young now! Look at me!

—You're going native, said Oppenheimer, smiling. —Since when did you use such offensive language?

—When in Rome, said Szilard. —I don't know about you, but I don't want to be a fossil. Not when I already have being dead to deal with. I go by the school, talk to the kids between classes. It's quite an education. Haven't you talked to the kids?

—I can't understand a damn thing they say, murmured Oppenheimer.

—I'm learning the language. Bullshit dopeass gay-ass mother-*fucker,* said Szilard carefully. —Girlfriend, you a stanky *ho.*

❧ One morning after Ben had left for work she was heading down the hall in her nightgown and gnawing on a piece of toast when she heard Szilard singing tunelessly in the shower. He sang a song he had apparently learned from the radio or in the CD store, where he sometimes spent an afternoon *conducting research on our nation's vibrant youth culture.* —You and me baby ain't nothing but mammals, so let's do it like they do on the Discovery Channel.

It made her laugh abruptly, alone in the hallway. She stopped and stood there and ate the last crust; then she opened a door at random and stared inside at the dusty photo albums standing on a shelf beside a stack of linens. They were not hers but her parents', part of her inheritance when they died. She had taken them out of their apartment when she was going through their belongings but since then she avoided looking at them. It had hung over her since.

She picked up the album on top of the pile and opened it to a black-and-white picture of her mother as a child, standing with a blond boy in swimsuits on a beach, holding sandcastle shovels. Their faces were young and perfect, large soft dark eyes and unlined skin.

Joy, she thought: maybe when you don't have it yourself, when you don't have the grace, you look for it to shine out of someone nearby.

She felt her smile fading and thought: Watch yourself. It wasn't the answer to look elsewhere just because she couldn't make her own light.

—Can you give me a towel? interjected Szilard loudly, sticking his wet head out the bathroom door.

She reached into the closet again and pulled one out, crossed the hall and handed it to him. He shut the door without further comment.

We're so many, we're so hard to distinguish from each other, but we long to be distinguished, she thought, putting the album away without looking at it any more, shutting the closet door and walking away from Szilard and his ingratitude.

Because of that we feel compelled, beyond being happy, also to feel chosen. We want to feel anointed and brought in, to know we have been spoken to, she thought, and went alone into the yard, shutting the door behind her softly to watch the neighbors' solid, square-faced tabby cat stare up into a tree without moving. She walked over to pet it and then retreated to her front steps to sit down again. The cat resumed its observation of the tree and she followed its gaze: in the high branches was movement, a small animal.

But then when she looked back at the cat it had fallen onto its paws. Its chin was resting there, and slowly it rolled sideways onto the ground. There was something wrong with the movement and she got up suddenly and ran over to it. It was breathing shallowly, and its eyes rolled toward her slowly though it did not turn its head. She felt its side, the warm roundness of the stomach, the sleek back, and there was nothing: but then she shifted on her feet and craned her neck she saw blood on its neck, a small bloody hole. And then a larger hole at the shoulder.

There was black on her eyelids as she squatted beside it, swaying, a hot prickle in her cheeks. Blood seeped from the hole in its throat to disappear in the grass and the cat closed its eyes with her beside it, touching it in panicky small pats and pleading —No! No no no! in a whisper.

Finally she rose on quaking legs and ran out of the yard, onto the street. No one was around. She saw nothing.

But the cat had clearly been shot. And the shot had been silent.

—Help! she said weakly. Her voice was almost gone.

There was no one visible.

Dazed she walked back into her yard and sat down beside the cat. She put a hand on its still, warm flank, looked at its quiet face and felt a searing pity. Soon she turned her face up and her eyes stung with the light of sky through the tree branches, which she was staring at without blinking.

Even on a gray day, it occurred to her, you could not stare at the sky. I should go in, she thought: what if I get shot too?

But she sat with the dead cat. She thought quickly that she was having a nervous breakdown, but then she forgot this thought and lost herself staring up at the sky, tears dripping down her cheeks because she refused to blink.

She picked up the cat, which was limp and heavy, and held it in her lap, her cheeks wet, her throat aching. I am all it has, she thought, now, in its last moments: and I too am small and don't go far. How narrowly contained is all the knowledge of a life.

We want to feel infused, she thought, her arms around the cat, holding tight. We want to be dear to the leaves and the sky. I know what it is to long, we say across the air of time, I know what feeling is. We want to think we will be there, always with the others that were and will be. We want to glow in the dark.

2

◦ After the bomb was dropped ostensibly to ensure that the emperor was removed from his throne, the emperor was not in fact removed from his throne. Far from ousting Hirohito, whose stubborn refusal to surrender *unconditionally* had allegedly provoked them so far that only the atom bomb could spell peace, American authorities kept him on the throne for decades.

For some, this appears to reinforce the notion that the bomb was dropped not out of wartime desperation but as a combination political maneuver–field test. It insinuates that the hundreds of thousands of Japanese men, women and children who died, either through instant vaporization or through long months or years of suffering, were the first American sacrifice to the care and feeding of the infant Cold War.

After the war the Allies did, however, force Hirohito to reject his claim to divinity. Japanese emperors could no longer be descendants of the sun goddess.

◦ Ann told Oppenheimer about the cat and together they carried the body to the neighbors' house, wrapped tenderly in one of Ann's mother's old scarves. Later they told Szilard, who dismissed it as the work of a child with a BB gun.

When he came home from work she also told Ben, but only that the neighbors' cat had died and she had found it. She did not tell him how.

She felt a pang of guilt at this but reassured herself that it was for his own good: he would only worry.

She also told herself that if the shooter had wanted to aim for her he would have: it was a campaign of intimidation. And it was working; often she was afraid, now, when she was by herself. But it did not deter her when it came to the scientists: they were still her charges. And because she was fearful when she was alone, she tried to stay with one of them at all times, with one of them or with Ben. When she was not with the scientists in the course of a day she dwelled on them, admitting her need for them, to feel chosen by them. The desire to feel chosen was sad to her, in part for being a child's longing that stretched out over a lifetime. But even though it was sad she could not dismiss it. It was never to be outgrown, sad in its futility, sad in its solitude.

Still it is there, she thought, no matter how clearly you see it. And it persists past anything.

❧ Fermi had acquired the habit of following Ben around the vegetable garden when he got home from work, asking questions about native chili and squash and new varieties of tomato. He became familiar with the drip irrigation system and began to study xeriscape gardening, something he had not learned in New Jersey in the 1930s.

He still did not want to go to Japan. He was sick of movement in general and did not wish to be moved. He felt he had already been forced to travel more than he had ever wished to, already had to adjust where adjustment was next to impossible. He had been shunted from Rome to Pisa to Leiden and Göttingen to Florence and back to Rome and through Stockholm to New Jersey to Chicago to Los Alamos, and then, final insult, from 1945 all the way to 2004.

It was the last leg of the journey that left him embittered.

❧ Little Boy, the uranium bomb that was dropped on Hiroshima, killed between seventy thousand and one hundred and forty thousand people instantly. It is often estimated that over the next five years the death toll reached two hundred thousand, though U.S. government estimates tend to be lower.

Fat Man, the plutonium bomb that was dropped on Nagasaki three days later, killed fewer though it was a more powerful device. The mountains served as barriers.

In Nagasaki estimates of the dead range up to one hundred thousand.

❧ There were instances in which Ann and Ben felt euphoric with each other, hysterical and giddy as children. It was a wave that rose and swept them up, catapulting them forward and beaching them on the sand.

The euphoria came when they escaped their houseguests. They would steal out of the house together to a bar or a restaurant or to walk down the street in the dark, quietly, as they had always walked in the days when there were no scientists. Ben remembered this ebullience from the months when they first met, in the excitement of novelty. He had not felt it since then. And it went far: on the basis of a few occasions of abandon, he could survive for weeks.

Because they had this privacy in snatches and the strange elation that covered them when they escaped, he could almost believe at times that he was learning to overlook his wife's new faith, though he continued to anticipate a lifting of the scales from her eyes. After all it was only one ripple on the surface where there could be far more.

And in the long days between their privacies he reassured himself: She is still who she was.

❧ Szilard spent hours every day lobbying Oppenheimer and Fermi to join him in a campaign. It was not clear to Ann what Szilard was proposing: she knew only that Fermi ignored him and Oppenheimer was opposed, that despite the evidence Szilard apparently marshaled and brought to him he only waved his hand and shook his head.

❧ Yoshi told Ben that there was still a Japanese emperor, in name only, but virtually no politics since one party had ruled for decades and there was no significant opposition. In Japan, he said, little remained but industry: the whole country had been given over to corporations and was now skyscrapers and concrete, interspersed with rice paddies.

It was what America was planning to be in the future, he said.

He told Ben that the spaces were small in Japan. He had never noticed when he lived there, he said, but now, when he went back, even outside he felt claustrophobic.

His own brother's apartment in Tokyo was so narrow that you could not open an umbrella.

—I think there is no air, he said.

They would be staying with his wealthy art-school friend in Tokyo: he had set it up for them. He told Ben how to bow and say "Thank you very politely." He also said Ben should tell the others not to eat or drink while walking. It was considered rude. There was much, he said apologetically, that was considered rude.

But Ben did not need to worry, he said: Ben would be fine. Ben was American.

❧ The scientists had never seen mass commercial air travel. From the moment they got to the airport in Albuquerque they had to be herded like sheep. Fermi walked at a measured pace, looking around cautiously; Oppenheimer plowed along with businesslike focus but was privately elsewhere; and Szilard rubbernecked. He was drawn to the other passengers and speculated on their mode of dress, marveling at the sheer number of gates and airlines, at what he thought were obscure destinations on the digital boards and at the swollen newsstands with their critical last-minute dental flosses and tampons and hundreds of magazines. He strayed over to the rack and picked up a copy of *Cat Fancy*, holding it up to Ann with a quizzical look.

Ben had barely slept the night before and in a daze he bought an expensive pack of nicotine gum. The flight would exceed ten hours and none of them told Oppenheimer he would not be allowed to smoke. Ann had a prescription for sleeping pills from her doctor chiefly so that Oppenheimer, if he succumbed to the symptoms of nicotine withdrawal, could be decommissioned. Or she could tranquilize him with blue tablets her friend Sheila bought by the hundreds in Mexico and had given her when her parents died. She was retaining her options.

As they approached security Szilard proclaimed in stentorian tones *X-ray scanning machines! Do those show hidden explosives?*

—Shut up, hissed Ann. —Just don't say *anything*! OK?

—They can't arrest me for talking, can they?

—In a second, said Ben. —So shut up.

—And with the fake ID, forget it, said Ann. —They'll send you to Guantánamo and you'll never be seen again.

—I think we should gag him until we get to Tokyo, said Oppenheimer. —What can it harm?

—Great idea, said Ben.

—They gang up on me, said Szilard. —They impugn me. Enrico! Don't listen.

❧ Ben held her hand and said nothing as they waited, as the fingers of her other hand drummed on the arm of her plastic chair. But when they boarded the tired woman at the gate barely glanced at the scientists' fake passports, and then they were in the airplane and settled in their seats. Beside him Ann walked more lightly, actually smiled and flicked her hair back carelessly as they sat down.

All the scientists paid close attention to the speech on safety precautions, listening with solemn faces as though great wisdom was being imparted. Szilard was so intent on the flight attendant's instructions about what to do in the unlikely event of a water landing that he spun in his seat and hissed out an angry *Shh!* to two Japanese girls chattering excitedly behind him.

Ann heard them begin to giggle hysterically as Szilard turned smugly to face forward again, pleased with himself for a job well done.

—You can barely feel it move! he crowed as the plane rose off the runway.

—We are inside a building that flies, said Fermi quietly.

—What? asked Oppenheimer a minute later. —Did they just say you can't *smoke* in here?

❧ —We could go into one of the bathrooms, whispered Ben as the aircraft began to level off. —While everyone is sleeping.

—I don't think those bathrooms would put me in the mood, she whispered back. —They smell bad.

Reflecting on her reluctance she wrote in the margin of her book: *In the end, saying that happiness is superior to pleasure is an insult to the body.* It was a book about the war in the Pacific and she was finding it difficult to concentrate on. *Also, it assumes the mind and body are separate.*

They are not, she thought. They are not.

And she realized she was relieved to be airborne, leaving the country. She was relieved to be flying away from whoever was watching them.

❧ One moment everything was as usual in the city. It was a sunny morning and people rode their bicycles to work, hung laundry, pruned bushes, ate breakfast. Schoolchildren, called to work duty instead of class to do their part for the war effort, assembled by the hundreds in open fields where they waited to be assigned to their tasks for the day.

Only a few seconds later the city was leveled and black. Over the scorched earth where streets had been just seconds before, where buildings and tall trees had been and now only their twisted skeletons remained, husbands, wives, small children walked in a daze. Some of them appeared to be intact, though confused. Others moved forward with their arms held up in front of them, zombie-like, and the skin hanging off their arms and faces in strips. Some dropped to all fours and groped blindly along because their eyes had been liquefied and were dripping down their cheeks.

Around Ground Zero, everything and everyone was vaporized except a European-style building that later came to be called the Atomic Bomb Dome. Further out the occasional structure remained and a few people lay in the dirt maimed but still breathing; here and there a dead horse or dog was visible, splay-legged on its side on the ground.

In the hours and days that followed the blinding flash many thousands of people wandered around the devastated city, which was almost nothing but rubble, as animated corpses. Some of their body parts were already dead while others, such as the brain, were stubbornly functioning. A few people who had been instantly incinerated left their images like shadows on the concrete, shadows cut into stone by the blinding flash of the blast.

All who were left alive but wounded to the brink of death, flesh melting, disfigured, shirts forever fused to their chests, shoes fused with their toes, were overcome by a terrible thirst. Many wanted nothing but a drink of water before they collapsed, and wandered or crawled through the ruins begging for it. Some threw themselves gratefully into rivers, and drowned in such numbers that the log-jams of bloated bodies had to be skimmed from the water and burned in piles.

But such is the power of culture that the residents of Hiroshima, walking melted or burned through a scene of black and red and orange that many would describe later as *hell on earth*, watching a mother or father burn to death pinned underneath a house or stumbling over the charred skull of a three-year-old child that on further examination proved to be their own, would often greet each other as politely and formally as ever. They offered humble apologies to those they encountered along the way. In some cases they apologized for the offensiveness of their mutilated appearance, in other cases for their inability to offer help.

In some cases, when those they were addressing had suffered an obvious great loss—say, were carrying a dead baby or pulling themselves along the ground dragging two stumps of legs—they even apologized for being spared.

❧ Szilard exclaimed at the monitors built into the backs of the seats in front of them. —You can choose from ten channels including four different movies! he crowed. —Just by touching the screen!

He ripped the clear plastic bag off his headphones with greedy haste.

—My God, said Oppenheimer under his breath. —Look at this. A chicken in every pot, and in every airplane seat a television.

—It's the American dream, said Ben.

Szilard shook his head.

—Modern man can't bear to be left alone with his thoughts for a second, can he?

—What thoughts, answered Oppenheimer, and pulled out a book.

❧ He read about Hiroshima as they flew. Most of what he read was a list: timelines, decisions, destroyed buildings, the dead. They were litanies, chants with the solemnity of a judgment.

The bad acts of which people were capable seemed to him to have grown and swelled in magnitude through history. Of course, he did not have the figures in front of him. It might be an illusion, this conviction of a trail of dead widening as time passed. It might be an illusion that everything was collapsing as the culture dreamt itself forward in time, on over the long fields to the burning gate.

As soon as we saw history as a line we also saw its end, he thought: because then it was not merely our deaths that we had to contend with but our extinction.

But it also seems to be the case, he thought, that what goes on and on has to be going *somewhere*, finally. And litanies were well-suited to the expression of an outrageous grievance. In litanies there was a repetitiousness that bordered on maniacal, and with it the growing weight of the deaths that came not instantly but in the unfolding time of the aftermath. In litanies there was both the longevity of the bomb's effects and the tedium of hopelessness.

He had seen a movie with Ann that was set in Washington, D.C. It featured a scene near the Vietnam War Memorial, a dark, sleek and impersonal thing at first glance, with a very long list of the names of the dead. Modern memorials no longer featured the faces of men, he thought. Instead they were often abstract. Statues of human forms had all but disappeared as public art, he thought.

Now they looked old-fashioned, absurd. Even he could see that.

❧ A survivor of Hiroshima said, "I just could not understand why our surroundings had changed so greatly in one instant."

❧ Minor turbulence over the ocean caused Fermi to clutch the arms of his seat nervously, and even when it subsided he remained wary for some time, staring out the window.

Two seats away from Ann Szilard watched a movie and lectured loudly about its shortcomings. The movie promised to be about Albert Einstein yet featured almost exclusively the perky grin and yellow tresses of Meg Ryan. He declaimed loudly at the movie's flaws in the realm of factual accuracy, poking first Fermi, then Ben on the shoulder to call their attention to this. Apparently Meg Ryan, whose character in the movie purported to be of great intelligence, did not appear to Szilard to give a credible imitation of being intelligent.

This irked him. Not only were the moviemakers and their audience apparently stupid, he complained in a droning voice, they were incapable of even *pretending* to be smart. Furthermore Walter Matthau, playing a particularly spry and fun-loving Einstein egged on by mischievous friends who, like the famous relativity theorist himself, sported ludicrously thick crypto-European accents and zany mad-scientist hairdos, was an insult to the great man. It might as well be a minstrel show, said Szilard.

Meanwhile Oppenheimer, growing increasingly agitated as nicotine withdrawal set in, lost his customary polished calm and became desperate to use all means at his disposal to sleep through the ordeal: first a tranquilizer, which put him out for two hours, then three sleeping pills, and finally a fourth and fifth sleeping pill. After that he consumed Ben's entire pack of nicotine chewing gum voraciously, pacing up and down the aisles as he chewed.

—You know what, he confessed to Ben, —I've actually never been deprived of these things.

It left him disgruntled, drawn, mint-smelling and tense with exhaustion. There were not enough newspapers and in-flight magazines to keep him occupied, and he had packed and checked all his scientific literature, so he finished the flight standing at the back amid flight attendants busy shelving food items and passengers waiting in line for the bathroom, chewing the final piece of gum— long ago drained of chemical merit—and jiggling one leg as he leaned against the wall, distractedly flipping through a well-thumbed paperback called *Are You There, God? It's Me, Margaret.*

This last had been donated to him selflessly by a twelve-year-old girl who noticed his hands shaking and took pity on him.

On their arrival in Tokyo he shifted from one foot to the other while he was waiting to file off the plane and then bolted up the walkway. But inside the terminal he slowed between Ann and Ben, shoulders crumpling: he was getting no glimpse of the outside and continued to be denied any such glimpse as, among tired, slow-moving crowds, all of them gave in to the current and slogged their way to customs.

Finally he excused himself and stepped away out of the crowd to light up in the men's rest room where, even if someone objected, he was unlikely to be arrested for the offense. The others waited for him on the shining white linoleum outside the rest room in silence, except for Szilard who, seated on his duffel bag, energy seemingly unflagging, continued his indignant exegesis of the documentary failures of the Meg Ryan Einstein movie. It reflected, he said, *a rampant disregard for intellectualism itself* and in fact *entirely repudiated the life of the mind as a cultural value.*

Fermi yawned.

❧ Oppenheimer struggled to remember the last time he had been deprived of cigarettes or a pipe, and could not. It must have been years.

He thought of the non-smoking rule on the airplane and what punishment a minor regulation could bring. The law, he thought, and everyone. Ridiculous. Damn it, he thought, America did not sacrifice the few to the many very often—far too seldom, in fact, as the communists had rightly argued before they were driven out of the culture squealing—but here was an instance.

—Crowds aren't bodies, are they, said Ann as they waited at baggage claim, watching suitcases pass. —I mean individual bodies.

—It depends on the crowd, he said.

—What?

—Whether the crowd is familiar or not. Crowds of Americans, you know—those are considered human, I think. At least by their own government.

The bodies of those in other states actually had no rights at all, he guessed. The bodies of absent masses cannot be known and so their minds cannot be imagined; a mindless body can be hurt with impunity, hardly more complex than a side of beef.

This is the irony of the dualist, he thought, watching one of Leo's legs stick out and get caught on a passing field-hockey stick. As Szilard tripped, falling higgledy-piggledy onto the small child beside him and loudly blaming the child, he thought: The mind can be fondly imagined, but only the body can be known. The mind is revered but unproven. So the dualist pretends to elevate the mind, but in a sense he is an unbeliever.

❧ Some of the citizens of Hiroshima felt fine immediately after the bombing and were relieved at the lack of physical harm, but in the weeks that followed developed strange symptoms.

These were not pleasant, of course. Weakening, they lost their teeth and their hair, were infested by maggots as their flesh turned necrotic, and finally threw up the dark, fluid remains of their internal organs. Some bled out through the skin, their blood, unable to coagulate, leaking out through the pores. Many died of this new disease they called "radiation sickness" with no medical care and no painkillers or shelter or comfort, their children or parents sitting near them, watching.

❧ As soon as they got out of the airport and into the train for Shibuya station they were overwhelmed.

Standing surrounded by the close-packed throng of fellow passengers she watched Fermi begin to sweat, Oppenheimer press his lips together, and Szilard start to complain. She found herself hoping no one else in the train spoke English but knowing she hoped in vain.

—My God! squeaked Szilard as a short businessman reading a comic book jostled him against a door. The strap of the duffel bag he was lugging, which was full of books and papers, had worn a red rut into his plump, white shoulder and he was irritable. Over the businessman's shoulder Ann could see a cartoon picture of a large-breasted, naked woman with flowing hair. —Look how many there are! How can they live like this?

—Please, Leo, said Fermi. —Shut your mouth just for once.

❧ Distant bodies are excluded from the world of the mind, Oppenheimer was thinking as a small woman in a gray suit beside him ground her elbow into his lower ribcage, because they are both abstractions and matter, a sheerly living whole and an insensate mass but also a pure idea of flesh, hopeless in their plurality. Each man or woman alone we can love, but a carpet of them teems like ants.

As they bustled out the doors, all of them tall between short, slim strangers, he looked back and saw Fermi staring slack-jawed at a poster for a movie about a transvestite.

—Enrico! Hey! Move! We're getting out! called Ben.

❧ It was even worse when they changed from the train to the subway system, not knowing where they were supposed to be. Ben was laden with suitcases and bags, Ann grasped an open phrasebook as she walked, and people surged rapidly around them as they gathered with their clutter of luggage at a ticket vending machine. Ann and Szilard stared together at the hundreds of colored buttons bearing characters they were powerless to interpret.

And when they emerged from the subway station at their final destination in Tokyo Fermi gasped audibly. The throng was infinite, infinite and intimidating, and the navigational proficiency of all of its parts was far superior to their own. Around them blocky gray and white skyscrapers loomed close, the streets were almost treeless and neon glared and flashed in oppressive profusion. Ben felt grateful he was not epileptic. The pavement of the street, a vast intersection, could not even be seen beneath the crowd, so dense and wide, a drifting continent of heads and limbs.

—I don't like it here, said Fermi, and stopped walking, dropping his bags heavily on the pavement.

Commuters surged around him.

—I want to go home, he said. —Now.

—Yeah right, said Ben, in his first-ever expression of impatience with Fermi.

—Come on, Enrico, said Oppenheimer paternally. —You'll be all right. It won't be like this everywhere.

—I don't like it, said Fermi stubbornly. —I don't want to be here. It's already too full!

—Listen, said Ann. —Let's get out of the crowds. We're going to get a taxi. We're going to Yoshi's friend's apartment. You can rest there, you'll have peace and quiet, OK? You can't stay here, anyway, can you? Here, on the sidewalk? Where it's the worst?

Fermi stood stock-still until finally, reluctantly, he stooped to pick up his bag again and followed them to the curb, looking down at the ground as he shuffled.

❧ And so a crowd does not receive our love, but only individuals, alone.

Staring out the taxi window Oppenheimer saw a man walking by himself along the sidewalk and thought he was magnetic: and behind him the crowds were dull.

❧ Some of the survivors of Hiroshima, known in Japanese as hibakusha, carried deforming keloid scars from radiation burns on their faces and bodies for the rest of their lives. A few would later say to psychologists that they felt that they had in fact actually died on the day of the bombing, that subsequently, for the rest of their days, they felt they were living what they called a "death in life."

Many spoke of the quality of their lives after the bomb as *muga-muchu:* without self, in a trance.

❧ Yoshi's friend Larry's apartment was palatial and almost empty, with large, light rooms floored in tatami mats, tall, long-leafed plants casting soft shadows from corners and wide windows overlooking the squat gray clusters of buildings around them.

When the maid ushered them through the front door into the living room Larry, who wore a T-shirt and faded blue jeans generously ripped at the knees, stubbed out his long black-and-gold cigarette in an egg-shaped glass ashtray and rose slowly to greet them.

Oppenheimer saw the cigarette and instantly asked if he could light up.

—Sure, man, said Larry.

And the Coordinator of Rapid Rupture was finally released.

❧ Ann excused herself and went to wash her face. The bathroom was lined in black marble, cold and slick, but there was space all around them in the apartment and that was what mattered. They were not hedged in by the millions.

When she got back to the living room Larry was explaining that in Tokyo smoking was allowed everywhere. Oppenheimer told him that Santa Fe was a virtual prison for smokers, or rather for what seemed these days to be called "nicotine addicts" by a culture that pathologized, said Oppenheimer, each and every single human behavior.

—In fact, Oppenheimer went on, after a long and satisfied exhalation, —the tendency of the culture to pathologize is so compulsive and so chronic that it might itself be described as a pathology. In other words, the culture is pathologically prone to pathologize, that is, as it were, *pathologically pathological.*

—Whatever, man, said Larry, and smiled. —But no worries, you can smoke anywhere. It's the nonsmokers that suffer here.

Nothing could go wrong for Oppenheimer after that, and where Fermi was sour and quiet, his demeanor oppressively sullen as he brooded at the corner of the table, Oppenheimer was effusive.

—Surfing! he exclaimed, fixing his eyes on a photo on the wall. It was Larry on a surfboard, riding a wave. —Is it a profession these days?

—More like a religion, said Larry.

❧ A Japanese photographer assigned to Nagasaki after the bombing said this of the scene he surveyed: "I tried climbing up onto a small hill to look. All around the city burned with little elf-fires, and the sky was blue and full of stars."

❧ Later they sat around a low enamel table cross-legged on cushions on the floor, drinking beer from overlarge Asahi bottles and waiting for their sushi. Except for the fact that his long legs were tucked uncomfortably beneath him, the knees jutting upward at acute angles, Oppenheimer was the model of leisure. He savored one of Larry's expensive black-and-gold cigarettes with his beer and watched with a gratified smile as the drift of smoke was sucked without a trace into a filtering device near the ceiling vent on the wide, bare wall.

—My father likes Cuban cigars, said Larry, following his gaze, —but his wife has asthma.

Neither the cigars nor the asthma was negotiable, Larry told them, so the ventilation system in the apartment was state-of-the-art. Oppenheimer was highly appreciative.

—Here it is, said Larry.

The maid bent over them with trays of sushi.

—Excuse me, said Fermi, after staring down at a piece of tuna for some time, unmoving. —This fish has not been cooked!

—Never had sushi before? asked Larry. —You kidding? Where you guys from, anyway?

—Another world, said Ben, and picked up his chopsticks.

Ann had introduced the scientists by their real names, hoping Larry would notice nothing amiss. In fact he had noticed only the strangeness of the names and asked where Szilard came from. He had asked one of his father's assistants to prepare a train schedule for them, with stopping points at Hiroshima and Nagasaki. Tickets had been purchased and seats reserved for them on the bullet train, green car.

—The green car's first class, he said. —Don't worry about it. It's on me.

—You're kidding! said Ann. —But that must be, I mean, hundreds of . . .

He waved his hand dismissively and pushed the schedule toward her as he picked up a piece of sashimi.

—Thank you so much, she said, casting her eyes over the columns of times and seat numbers. —But isn't that too much—a gift that's—I mean—for us to accept?

—My dad's footing the bill, said Larry. —He doesn't know it and he never will, but don't worry about it. He's got more money than God. Worse personality, though.

—I don't know what to say, said Ann. —That's very nice of you.

—Thank you kindly, said Oppenheimer.

—And you wanted to talk to bomb survivors, right?

—Survivors, said Oppenheimer. —Yes we do.

—If possible, survivors with a science background, put in Szilard. —They'll be able to tell us more. We haven't read the first-person accounts, except for Oppenheimer. We want to hear it from the horse's mouth.

—You guys are, what? You doing a movie or something?

—They're researching the Second World War, put in Ann. —They'd like to know about the bombings from the biological and physical standpoint. Eyewitness accounts, personal stories.

Larry nodded and said he had asked the assistant to set up appointments for them. He himself had little interest in the subject.

—Ancient history, he said. —No one cares about that anymore. They barely even teach it in school.

—Really? said Szilard brightly.

—So do you guys smoke?

—Just Oppie, said Szilard.

—Foul habit, said Fermi.

—No, I mean *smoke,* said Larry. —You know. Pot.

He opened a drawer in the table, removed a packet and started to roll a joint.

—Pot? asked Szilard.

—Marijuana, said Ben.

—Reefer, said Fermi sagely, nodding. —Reefer madness!

—Not for me, thank you, said Oppenheimer, gesturing with a cigarette. —I have everything I need right here. One vice at a time.

—It just puts me to sleep, said Ann. —But thanks anyway.

—Sure, said Ben, who rarely indulged.

—It was popular with the Negroes, in my day, said Oppenheimer. —Tea pads. I remember when New York City was full of them. You ever go to one, Leo?

—*Negroes?* said Larry. —Dude, not too PC. Where you been? And whaddaya mean in your day? You're like barely, what? Five years older than I am?

—For Chrissake, Oppie, they don't say "Negroes" anymore, said Szilard. —How many times do I have to tell you?

—African-Americans, said Oppenheimer. —Jazz musicians in particular. They were very fond of marijuana before it was made illegal.

—It used to be legal? asked Larry curiously.

—Till they passed a law in the late '30s, said Oppenheimer. —'37, if I'm not mistaken.

—That's rad, said Larry, and lit up. —What comes around goes around, know what I mean? So, Robert. Are you like a history teacher?

—Not history, said Oppenheimer. —Physics. Though I've always been interested in the humanities. As a young man I studied Sanskrit.

—Physics, cool, said Larry. —I tried to take a physics class once. It was astrophysics or whatever, the whole Stephen Hawking thing? Because I saw that trailer for the documentary about him where he's in the wheelchair looking all blissed out and retarded and shit but we know he's actually this supergenius? And then they show the stars and galaxies and the voiceover goes, in that freaky robot voice he's got, you know, "And we—can—see—the mind—of God." I thought that was pretty cool so I enrolled in this class at the university. But then the guy who was teaching the class is giving this talk the first day and he said there was no life in the rest of the universe. So I bailed.

—Quite a disappointment, nodded Oppenheimer sympathetically.

—What do you think, man? Are there aliens? Extraterrestrial life and all that? Are there, like, bizarre alien fish swimming around deep down under the ice on Europa? I read that somewhere. You know Europa, one of the Jupiter moons? They think there's these weird alien fish there, swimming around and shit. But what I want to know is, have the aliens already landed here on Planet Earth?

—It's not my area of expertise, said Oppenheimer, amused.

Ben exhaled for a second time, leaned in close to Larry and whispered, —Put it this way. He's not at liberty to say.

—No thank you, said Fermi, when Ben passed him the joint.

—Really? You ever been to Area 51? Or Roswell?

—Roswell? Yes I have, as a matter of fact, said Oppenheimer. —I've been to Roswell on several occasions. Of course it was some time ago, in your terms. When I was working for the Army.

—He used to work on a secret base in northern New Mexico, whispered Ben. —I'm not kidding.

—Come on, urged Larry. —Spill the beans, Bob!

—Spill what beans?

—*When* were you there, huh? Was it after the alien crash? Were you part of the military coverup? Huh Bob? Did you see the dead alien corpses?

—I'm not familiar with any dead aliens, said Oppenheimer.
—You have my word on that.

—They dissected them! There was a movie of it but it turned out to be fake, said Larry.

Szilard accepted the joint from Ben awkwardly, inhaled, coughed vigorously, and promptly asked Larry if there was anywhere he could get a donut.

—They got Mister Donut, said Larry. —Right around the corner. The donuts kinda suck though.

—He's not picky, said Ben. —Believe me.

—Come with me, said Szilard to Ann.

—How about *asking* her, said Ben.

—Do you want to come with me, said Szilard.

—OK, said Ann, and shrugged at Ben, smiling apologetically.

—Umbrellas near the door, said Larry. —You're gonna need 'em. It's like two blocks over, right out the building, turn the corner, pass the kind of like river thing and then make a left.

—Thanks, said Ann, Szilard already bustling out the door.

Larry turned back to Oppenheimer.

—So seriously Bob. I'm not a security risk, I swear. I won't breathe a word. Were you involved in the coverup?

—Coverup? asked Oppenheimer.

Larry nudged Ben with his elbow.

—Man, you know what I'm talking about. Don't play dumb.

❧ The rain was light but steady, the crowds thinner. Bicycles passed close by them as they walked through the drizzle, careful and distracted, holding their umbrellas far above their heads for visibility. It was soon to get dark.

—Do you think it's heaven, Leo?

—Tokyo? More like hell.

—No, I mean, heaven the idea. It lets us think the world isn't enough. You know, that bodies aren't enough, we have to separate ourselves from them to be happy.

—Did he say turn right after the river?

—Left. I mean, if we didn't have heaven, or if some of us didn't, would we behave ourselves better? If this was the only world?

—The munchies, they call it. I saw it in a video.

—I'm serious, Leo. Why won't you ever talk to me about anything?

They crossed a bridge over a cement canal and peered down to see fat gray carp hovering nearly motionless in the shallow water, only the tails waving in slow precise symmetry. Floating garbage gathered around them and stuck, and above them raindrops pinpricked the surface. Planted at the top of the walls of the canal, level with the street, were azalea bushes with blooms three lurid shades of pink.

—The brain of a carp . . . , started Szilard, and then trailed off, distracted. —Can I get a cup of coffee at the donut shop? I want a coffee with the donut.

They walked past the Mister Donut looking for a coffee shop and found a hole-in-the-wall McDonalds and a fried chicken place that featured, confronting them assertively on the sidewalk, a life-sized cardboard cutout of Colonel Sanders clad in startling Samurai armor.

Finally they caught sight of a Starbucks and Szilard, who had acquired a taste for strong contemporary coffee and now shunned the weak coffee to which he had become accustomed in the war years, announced that he wanted a latte.

Ahead of them, stamping out his wet shoes as he went through the door, a man in a black suit slipped his closed umbrella into a metal stand beside the door and then extracted it quickly.

—Look at that! crowed Szilard.

The wet folds of the umbrella were now sheathed in clear plastic. The metal stand was a machine.

—So it won't drip on the floor! exclaimed Szilard, standing still to marvel.

He ate a filled donut as they walked back to Larry's.

—Whatever's in here, he said, chewing, —this green paste? It's disgusting.

He spat a clump of chewed dough into a garbage can as a thin old woman, passing them with her arms full of folded laundry, spied him in the act of regurgitation and shrieked.

❧ After Fat Man and Little Boy were dropped Oppenheimer received a commendation from the Army for his good work as Director of the Manhattan Project. At the ceremony, however, his mood fell somewhat short of euphoric.

In his moment of glory as the egghead-hero of the war, and with his customary flare for drama, he said solemnly to the assembled company: —If atomic bombs are to be added to the arsenals of a warring world, the time will come when mankind will curse the names of Los Alamos and Hiroshima.

Even as he said this some in the audience were distracted; one man had closed his eyes and was thinking of how his wife smelled, and another probed a loose tooth with his tongue.

❧ The bullet train garnered high approval ratings from Fermi, who set great store by cleanliness and spaciousness in public conveyances. He appreciated the black leather seats and the shining wooden floors, the hygiene of the bathrooms, the shine of the windows. As they sped toward Hiroshima Ann could barely stand to stare out the window: the fastness of the train blurred everything, both far and near, and gave her a headache. She looked long enough to see suburbs and industrial parks spreading out on either side of the train line as far as the eye could see, and in the distance, on occasion, the bald mound of a mountain long since logged clean of trees.

Ben went with Szilard to check out the snack car, where Szilard bought a bento box decorated with a picture of geishas walking beside a pond. Picking at the seafood morsels in the box with his disposable chopsticks, he puckered his mouth in displeasure and shoved away a half-eaten morsel of dry brown mystery fish.

—How about you just throw it away instead of making that face, said Ben. —Because you look like a tourist asshole.

But Szilard ignored him, staring over his neighbor's head at an open book. Suddenly he crowed aloud.

—Mine! That's my equation! he said, and in a flash was tapping the reader's shoulder with an insistent finger.

Szilard operated under the blithe assumption that everyone in Japan spoke perfect English, and so far it had served him well. Dumping the plundered bento box onto the snack counter he grabbed at the open page, nodding eagerly at the startled young man who was holding the book.

—I predicted that effect in 1943! he told him.

—The Szilard complication? asked the young man politely.

—That was my work! I am Szilard! I am Leo Szilard! said Szilard excitedly.

People were staring. Szilard grabbed his wallet out of his pocket and wrestled with it, finally extracting his fake ID.

—See? That's me!

The young man, puzzled at first, looked back and forth from the driver's license to Szilard's face, nodding with increasing confidence. If he was surprised by Szilard's apparent youth he did not show it.

—It is a pleasure, he said finally. —I am Takashi. I am a student at Tokyo University.

Szilard promptly launched into a loud and rapid disquisition on the exothermic release of stored energy by atoms dislocated by radiation damage. It turned out that Takashi, besides displaying familiarity with a number of interesting recent developments in the field of biomedical nanotechnology, by which Szilard was intrigued, also had a smattering of knowledge of the historical development of nuclear reactor design, in which Szilard, of course, had played what he often called "a leading role."

Ben listened to them vaguely until the snack car became over-crowded, and Szilard, brimming with satisfaction ever since the young man had known his name, led Takashi back to the green car with them. He huffed and puffed down the aisle as he negotiated children's protruding arms and legs and simultaneously lectured Takashi on the subject of electroosmosis.

—You know, said Ben to Szilard as they walked, —he probably knows a lot more about physics than you do. I mean, it's come a long way since your day.

—Don't be ridiculous, snapped Szilard.

They sat down across the aisle from Ann, Takashi perching pre-cariously on a seat arm as Ben slid into his seat beside her.

He still failed to understand the conversation, which was less like an exchange than a monologue, and chose to focus instead on Takashi's thin torso and spiky hair. He studied the retro, fifties bowl-ing shirt and tiny, girlish silver-and-pink cell phone protruding from Takashi's front pocket. A gaudy pastel-colored plastic chain dangled from the top of the phone, glittering Mardi Gras beads with a small plastic dog on the end. Or a bear or a mouse. He could not discern identifying features.

Szilard spoke volubly, his voice rising and falling and irritating other passengers, who turned periodically and stared until a pass-ing conductor shook his head at Takashi and barked out an order.

—I have to go back to where I am sitting, Takashi told Szilard. —Worse ticket! See?

—Ridiculous! said Szilard angrily to the conductor. —He's not even taking up a seat here!

But the conductor did not speak English and apparently had little interest in learning.

When Takashi was gone Ben was relieved. His ears were ringing, and Ann, distracted, had given up trying to read her book to gaze dreamily at the seat in front of her.

—Why don't you take a nap, Leo? said Ann. —You didn't sleep at all last night.

But Szilard scoffed, got up and set off after Takashi, bustling pompously down the aisle in the direction of the cheap seats.

—Quite a handful, isn't he, said Oppenheimer as he sat down beside Ben, having lately crossed paths with Szilard on his way back from the smoking car.

ᔑ Hiroshima was a nondescript city. Sitting in the back seat of the taxi with Ben beside her and Szilard in the front, rounding a curve and catching sight of a distant looming tower that Szilard claimed authoritatively was a rebuilt ruin known as Hiroshima castle, Ann was swiftly and decisively disappointed. She found herself in a dawning indifference to the trip, where she was, and *this day;* she felt a sense of waste and detachment, resignation to boredom.

She thought: After all that there is nothing much here.

Or there was plenty, a surfeit of normal shapes. The city was a dull continuum of buildings, roads and trees, in short a city like other cities. Nowhere was there a vast and yawning crater, nowhere a dismal military graveyard stretching out with its army of uniform stones that testified to an enormity of deadness.

In the fifteen minutes it took them to travel from the train station to the hotel she felt the mundane actually oppress her, the sameness of urban geography throb in her temples, on the tired end of an arc that had lifted and dropped her, halfway around the spinning globe, only to gaze dully at billboards and concrete, confronted with the same gray dirt you found in say Albuquerque or any other spreading and bland inhabitation.

She had not wanted to come here, but she realized as they cruised along the busy multilane road, compact cars buzzing behind, around and ahead of them in spurts of efficiency, that she had expected to find the confirmation of an expectation nonetheless. She had thought she would disembark from the plane into impor- tance: a brooding and massive loss, a moment trapped forever in structures. She had thought she would find an architecture of grief, outrage, horror, a place that felt like a cry of shock, husky and shad- owed aftermath, dark broadcast that *this was the place*, the place where the end had begun.

But Hiroshima was businesslike and had buried its past in nor- malcy. Where the bomb had been dropped was now a park with a deep, cement-lined canal that passed for what had once been the Motoyasu River, old trees, green manicured stretches of lawn. Small, grimy crafts advertised as "river pleasure boats" took tourists on rides past the "A-bomb dome" and the banks with their planted shrubs and fading impressions of pink blossoms.

❧ Asked about it later, many of the atom bomb physicists said they did not regret the dropping of the bomb on Hiroshima. Many of them were lucid and thoughtful in defense of the decision, and many were also staunch advocates of nonproliferation after the war. The eminent Manhattan Project physicist Hans Bethe, for instance, believed the decision to drop the first bomb had been the right one but also believed that Nagasaki was a crime and that the decision to use nuclear force should never be made again.

Hiroshima, he believed, should have remained a *singularity*.

Bethe, by all accounts a kind and considerate man, arrived at his belief that Hiroshima had been justified by using reason. He used reason both before the fact and after it, when nothing could be undone.

❧ In the hotel lobby, scientists clustering around them, Ann and Ben studied their guidebook's crude map and picked out a route to Ground Zero, which now housed a Peace Museum. The radioactive debris had been buried in soil, covered in grass and planted with trees, and the area had been renamed the "Peace Park." They left the lobby and walked with the scientists a few paces ahead of them until finally they crossed a bridge, found themselves surrounded by monuments, and stood still.

None of them moved for a minute. Oppenheimer did not even reach for the pack of cigarettes in his inside breast pocket. They were standing on soft grass in a grove of widely spaced trees; over the tops of the trees they could see parking structures and other tall and graceless buildings, skirting the park, looming. Near them was a sculpture that looked like a rocket with a little girl standing on top of it, her arms raised. It was built in the middle of an expanse of pavement, and in front of it sat schoolchildren in dark blue uniforms, in perfectly straight lines, listening to their teacher. A booth near the foot of the statue was full of bright colors.

No one broke the silence, and cars passed until finally, in a quick shuffling movement from Szilard's foot, there was the suggestion of restlessness. Slowly they walked toward the statue and the booth, its green and orange and yellow contents. The air was humid and still.

Ann noticed azaleas blooming here too, light pink and hot pink and white on the same bush.

—It does not look as though a bomb fell here, said Fermi as they walked.

—It was almost sixty years ago, Enrico, said Szilard. —You don't think they've renovated? Get a clue.

She resented the azaleas. They were the ugliest flowers she'd ever seen, she said to herself, possibly the first ugly flowers she had ever seen. No: it was not the flowers that were ugly but the bushes they grew on, bulky and square. It was the bushes that made the flowers ugly.

—Cranes, said Szilard, as they approached, reading a sign. —Paper cranes.

The little girl on the sculpture, they read, had survived the bomb only to fall sick ten years later with radiation-caused leukemia. In the hospital she had folded hundreds of cranes out of colored paper, following a Japanese legend that said that folding a thousand cranes could make her well again. She never made it to a thousand, but now children all over the world made cranes and sent them here in memory of the girl.

—What a sentimental story, said Fermi.

—The crane is a lovely, mythical bird, said Oppenheimer.

—Look at those dirty pigeons, said Szilard.

On the ground pigeons clucked and hustled, fat and greasy as back home. They were pecking at the papery remains of what appeared to be a McDonalds cheeseburger.

Ann recalled that pigeons could be highly intelligent, and then looked at Szilard.

—We all died of cancer too, said Fermi. —All of us.

—Except me, said Szilard.

—You died of being fat.

Walking over the lawns of the Peace Park toward the Peace Museum they passed monuments and fountains, large, stylized stone hands open wide to release water that flowed along a white trough toward a cenotaph whose plaque was covered in cut flowers. Its stone chest contained all the names of the dead.

—More than three hundred thousand, announced a Japanese tour guide to a group of tanned and camera-clicking Germans. —Every year on the anniversary they open it, add more names to the list, of those people who just died that year from long-term effects of the atom bomb. And then they lock it away again. But there is a controversy. Some people say not all of them have died of radiation sickness or cancers from the bomb. Some of them just died from regular cancers, some people say. Some people say they just want their dead parents' name in the cenotaph.

❧ In the lobby of the Peace Museum they introduced themselves awkwardly to Keiko, a neatly dressed housewife who worked as a volunteer while her children were in school. She met tourists at the museum and took them on tours of the exhibits and the monuments. She bowed repeatedly, shaking each of their hands in turn.

—I will be your interpreter today, she said, nodding and smiling, in case they had not yet fully understood the arrangement.

She pointed out a tall digital clock looming beside the door. It said PEACE WATCH. It was counting the days and hours and seconds since the bomb was dropped on Hiroshima, and beneath that, said Keiko, since the most recent nuclear test, which had taken place at the Nevada Test Site a few weeks before.

It had been a subterranean, subcritical test that had not made the papers in the United States. None of the new tests ever did, said Keiko.

—I thought testing was banned, said Oppenheimer.

—Not *subcritical* tests, said Szilard.

—This peace clock is a hopeful clock, said Keiko, continuing to smile pleasantly.

—Hopeful? asked Oppenheimer.

—When all nuclear weapons are abolished from the earth, then it will stop ticking forever. But until then, it will just keep on ticking.

Fermi shifted impatiently from one foot to another. He had no patience for melodrama.

—Hope the thing is built to last, said Ben.

—Well then, said Oppenheimer, —why don't we buy our tickets and go in?

—They are very cheap, said Keiko, and smiled again. —A bargain!

☙ Reason, like bombs, can be deployed from far away. Closer up there is nothing but feeling.

☙ When Ann and Ben emerged from the museum at the end of the day the skies had lowered. It looked as though it might rain and Ann welcomed this.

They sat on a bench beside a tree that had been scorched by the bomb, burned black up one side of its narrow trunk, and was still leafing out more than half a century later. It had been moved from its original site, further out from the hypocenter, to a carefully maintained plot on the lawn beside the museum. Visitors could inspect the damage and marvel at the tree's longevity.

The scientists, who had been behind them in the museum, finally exited the lobby and came walking slowly across the concrete, Oppenheimer limping. He and Fermi wore tight leather shoes with leather soles and no rubber components. Szilard, by contrast, had made Ann buy him new shoes, and as a result now had a spring in his step. She had driven him to a mall in Albuquerque, where he had purchased some bulky cross-trainers. Only the women's model had been on sale and Szilard, impatiently waving off a protesting salesman, had selected a pair with garish purple and turquoise trim.

Oppenheimer, wearier than ever, sat down heavily on the bench beside them. As he was fumbling in his jacket pocket for his cigarettes Fermi, still a few feet away, stopped walking abruptly, turned, and began to run away from them, pell-mell toward the parking lot, his arms windmilling.

—Stop him, said Oppenheimer, and then more urgently, to Ben, —Stop him! I can't run!

Ben dropped his camera on her lap and dashed off, and Szilard, moving at a slow jog that resembled race-walking, reluctantly took up the rear.

—Sorry, said Oppenheimer to Ann. —But I have blisters. I never had one before. In my real life I would ride for days in leather boots and never have a problem. Now both heels are torn. I could barely walk by the end of the tour.

—What's going on with him? asked Ann.

Oppenheimer shook his head, as if too tired to speak, and slipped off a shoe to reveal a gray sock-heel caked in brown blood.

—There are Band-Aids in my suitcase, offered Ann softly as she gazed at it, thinking nothing.

❧ A few minutes later Ann had nowhere to go and Oppenheimer slumped beside her, silent and smoking. All he said before he fell silent was that he had not expected the weight of the evidence.

❧ In the years after the war, survivors of Hiroshima and Nagasaki were often shunned for their disfigurements and illnesses. Many became pariahs, their scars a great source of shame.

❧ Szilard and Ben came back exhausted and dragging, without Fermi.

—I couldn't catch him, said Ben. —He was surprisingly fast. He just kept on going. He pulled ahead and ran around that Starbucks on the corner and when I got there and looked down the street he was gone.

—Quite fast, nodded Szilard, whose empurpled cheeks shone with sweat. —Must be all those Alpine hikes.

—We'll probably see him back at the hotel, said Ann, and turned to Oppenheimer. —Do you think he was—did he run because he was upset by what he saw?

—Upset? asked Oppenheimer. —*Upset?*

He pulled on his cigarette and did not elaborate.

—By what he saw, said Ann finally.

—*Upset,* mused Oppenheimer, exhaling two plumes from the nostrils, dragonlike. —Yes. You could probably call him upset.

—He hadn't read anything before, said Ann. —About the bomb effects. Had he.

—Are you upset, Robert? asked Szilard.

—Upset, repeated Oppenheimer flatly, and nodded.

He sat with his bare feet touching the ground, bloody socks

balled neatly on the bench beside him. The blisters on his heels had burst, his shoes had rubbed off the skin, and the bony, naked heels were raw meat, glistening wet near the cement beneath them. Ann looked at him, waiting for him to say more. His profile was that of an aristocrat but his feet were torn like a beggar's.

After he inhaled he tapped his cigarette carelessly and Ann watched the flakes of ash fall down. One settled on an exposed heel and stuck to it.

She winced.

—You have an ash— she began, but he was ignoring her, staring off at the museum's elevated walkway.

—*Upset,* he said again.

❧ Eventually they got up and walked toward their hotel, only four of them now, Oppenheimer carrying his shoes on two crooked fingers, smoking with the other hand, none of them saying anything.

As the sun set they passed beneath overhanging branches and saw a large red billboard for Coca-Cola looming over the museum, dominating the parking lot, the peace monuments, and the trees that grew over Ground Zero.

3

❧ Ben woke up damp from the weight of a heavy floral coverlet in the weakly cooled room, tossing off the bedspread, the furry blanket beneath it and the sheets. He got up to find Ann already in the bathroom, brushing her teeth, face drawn with worry. They had stayed in their room the night before, drinking beers Ben bought at a convenience store on the corner while Szilard ate on the bed in the next room, Oppenheimer drank overpriced mini-bar whiskey in an armchair, and all of them separately were silent. Ben and Ann had blearily watched Japanese television until they fell asleep, staring half-comprehending at a dreary sequence of greasy cooking shows shot on video in fluorescent kitchens, pastel-colored dating shows, and the best of the lot, shows that featured dogs and cats, sometimes dragged by their owners, struggling bravely through obstacle courses.

—Fermi hasn't come back, she said, and already as he reached out to stroke her shoulder in consolation his strength was sinking at the prospect of a dull and thankless day.

When he went next door to talk to Oppenheimer he found only Szilard in the room, reading an English-language newspaper and drinking off-white coffee.

—Where's Oppenheimer? he asked.

—He went out, said Szilard, not turning.

—I can see that, said Ben, and through gritted teeth: —*Where? When?*

—Said he'd be back for breakfast, said Szilard. —Actually, I'll join you. Should be ready to eat again by about ten. I just had a little chocolate croissant from Starbucks.

—Uh huh, said Ben, and retreated.

❧ But Oppenheimer did not come back for breakfast.

Ann and Ben walked idly through the city, along the riverbanks and over the sandy walkways of the Peace Park, between the poorly sculpted death monuments, muddy perimeters trodden and flattened by tourist shoeprints in intricate geometric patterns. *Beneath this grassy mound lie the ashes of a hundred thousand soldiers.*

—If this is the form public memory has to take, said Ben once in the Peace Park, —I would rather be publicly forgotten.

They left the sculpture gardens finally, worn out by the cold shapes, and went to a shopping district where they wandered into stores distracted, barely looking at the English-language T-shirts, sweatshirts and glossy jackets that bore such enigmatic slogans as BABY COOL FLIES and HIGHWAY 66 RED SHERIFF NOW. They ended up at a noodle shop for lunch, where they ate miso soup laden with tan-brown fish flakes.

Ann became agitated as the day got old, insisting one of them should go back to the hotel just in case, but Ben would not agree to this and stuck to her side, and presently she gave up.

By night Oppenheimer had still not returned. Fermi did not come back either.

The next morning there was a note for Ann at the lobby desk. It was from Oppenheimer. It said he was on his way to a retreat at a Buddhist monastery.

—Jesus Christ, said Ben.

☙ Through her annoyance she wondered: At what point did the pain of others become too much? It was overwhelming to Oppenheimer because of his nearness to the cause: and the farther you were from the cause, the freer you were to forget.

☙ Oppenheimer's close friend Robert Serber had written of his tour of Hiroshima in his autobiography, which Oppenheimer read just before they left New Mexico. Shortly after the bombing Serber had been sent to the city to make scientific observations of the bomb's aftermath, to measure and describe its destructive capabilities. He wrote his account completely without color or detail, as clinically and remotely as possible, barely mentioning the dead or the suffering or his own emotions. It was a report written by a robot.

To read his description of the devastated city without knowing Serber, thought Oppenheimer, was to be inspired to dislike him; yet Oppenheimer had been fond of Serber and could not shake the old fondness, even after he was told about Serber and Kitty. And watching a videotape of Serber made in his dotage in the 1990s, Oppenheimer had thought his old friend a kindly, humorous man, almost a caricature, with a creaky voice and a grating, infectious laugh. Apparently, sometime in the postwar years, he had developed a penchant for wearing comical glasses and blindingly bright-colored jackets and ties.

❧ —They're *sensitive*, said Szilard, perched on the side of the bed in Ann and Ben's room the third night in Hiroshima.

He had come in bearing a tattered copy of the *New York Times*, New York metro edition, cajoled off a businessman in the lobby. He was eager to discuss global diplomacy as it pertained to the American government, against whom he always inveighed in moments of conversational lull. But Ann was quiet and deflated and could barely nod at Szilard's opening sally, which consisted of the assertion that *The birth of the limited liability corporation was the death of freedom.*

—Sensitive, repeated Ben, with an edge to his voice.

—They're in shock. Sure. And I'm not. You understand: my position is different. It's not as painful for me.

—How's that, Leo, said Ben.

—His opposition, said Ann. —He wasn't behind it like them. He isn't directly responsible.

—I *am* responsible, said Szilard. —Of course I am. All of us were implicated. But I was not, you know, I was just not *in power.* I was not institutional. Not part of the *team* like them. Groves tried to have me thrown in jail, for Chrissake! Just for disagreeing with him!

—So you're telling me, Leo, said Ben, —that these guys are having nervous breakdowns or something?

—I mean what do *you* think happened? asked Szilard. —You saw how Enrico took off.

—But you don't suffer breakdowns.

—No I don't.

—Just grandiose delusions.

—What*ever,* said Szilard.

Distracted, Ben was thinking this might be the break that would end it. Severe shock could sever the delusional from their delusions—hadn't that been the idea behind electroshock therapy, something like that?—and if it could, then maybe the trauma of this upsetting experience would liberate the so-called "Oppenheimer" and "Fermi" from their assumed identities. Realizing with nauseous certainty that their *heroes of genius* had been chiefly civil service cogs in a vast war machine, tools like any other, less martyrs to science than weak-chinned gunsmiths with hungry women and thin-armed children in their crosshairs, Oppenheimer and Fermi would admit their real names were, say, Runsen and Hodges, Al and Fred, and sheepishly return to their jobs teaching physics and chemistry at an underfunded high school for gifted students in Omaha, a drab Canadian university full of future electrical engineers, someplace mundane and familiar from which they had fled.

There would still be the problem of Szilard, of course.

—It's not their fault, said Ann, —they're upset.

—Enrico hasn't gone far, said Szilard. —Ten-block radius maximum. I guarantee it.

❧ After she set the digital alarm clock and Ben turned off the bedside light they lay with their heads close together, not touching but facing. This was a waiting position, one they assumed at times when they were not sure they were ready for sleep but were tired, no more to offer than a warm silence.

He smelled the cheap cotton of the hotel pillow, a cotton like old age in a hospital, antiseptic and musty, and heard the sounds of the street out the window. It was not chaotic noise, like Tokyo, only a faint rush and now and then the whine of a moped. From her slightly open mouth he could smell toothpaste, and her face was eclipsed by the dark round of the pillow between them, no features, only steady breath.

In the second before he said it he was anxious but hopeful. This was his chance to return to the old routine, the worn, gentle routine, the routine that he craved. Here it was, the escape hatch, within reach, inches off.

—Listen, honey. They're gone. Two of them just took off, and here we are with no one but Szilard, who by the way is eating us out of house and home. Food is expensive here. He's impatient now because he's seen what he came to see and he wants to get home, back to where the action is, or as he puts it he can "be effective." Why don't we just do what he wants and cut our losses? We can change the dates on the plane tickets, we can leave tomorrow morning if you want. And go back. The other scientists can find their way home later.

Ann hesitated, a span of restraint that stretched out painfully. Briefly he thought maybe she was asleep. Then he felt the curt, tidy shake of her head on the pillow, the back and forth of her forehead against his own.

—I can't, she said. —You know I can't. I could lose them.

He waited for her to say more, trying to send the message unsaid toward her that her *clinging* to the dead scientists, this devotion, this adherence above and beyond what they asked of her, past common sense and reason and way past entertainment, was not self-explanatory. He knew what her instinct would be but he wanted to know if she would still realize that she *should* explain herself, whether she would still have the benefit of perspective or whether she was too far gone.

—This is just—this is a problem, she said. —It's an obstacle. But leaving is out of the question. I can't leave without them. They could disappear. I might never *see* them again. Then all this would be for nothing. Wouldn't that be the worst?

—But what do you want from it? What do you expect anyway? I mean what's the happy ending?

—I can't abandon them here.

—We would still have Szilard, said Ben, feeling desperate. There could be no weaker boast.

—But I can't leave Robert here. You know that. I mean you knew that before you even *asked* me.

❧ There was an early knock on the door at 7 a.m. and she opened it to Keiko the interpreter, who entered in a flurry of bowing and smiling, as usual, just in time to catch Ben towel-waisted, coming out of the bathroom, and turn away blushing, covering her mouth with a raised hand as she giggled.

—Excuse me, said Ben, and Keiko smiled and bowed again as she retreated to stand as far away from his half-naked body as she could, backed up against the heavy floral drapes of the window, so embarrassed it was almost painful to look at her.

He himself had been given the job of babysitting Szilard—as though anyone could effectively guard Szilard, who in his purple-and-green cross-trainers, powered by processed sugar and adrenaline, could make off anywhere, trundling, turbocharged, at the drop of a hat.

Together they would scour the city for Fermi. Ben did not relish the prospect of picking his way through the humid, narrow streets with Szilard, bickering as they always did. Elsewhere Ann would be moving forward without him, free of the burden of Szilard, her interpreter mincing along beside her, helpful, self-effacing, and unlike Szilard more than willing to just shut up.

He was barely dressed when there was an explosion of hammering on the bathroom door and he opened it into Szilard's bug-eyed face, all too close.

—What are you waiting for? Primping in front of the mirror?

—You give me a headache, Leo.

—Bye sweetie, said Ann as they went past, —I'll leave you a message if I go out.

Before they reached the elevator Szilard was already delivering a sermon on Oppenheimer and Fermi's participation on the Scientific Panel of the Interim Committee on Atomic Energy.

—Stimson, you know, at the War Department, convened it in '45, purportedly to find out whether there were technical alternatives to dropping the bomb on Hiroshima.

The elevators slid open and they stepped in, Ben leaning forward to push the button marked *1*, Szilard curiously scrutinizing his blurred and elongated face in the stainless doors as they closed but not suspending his relentless patter.

—Of course there were alternatives—I was advocating several myself, including a demonstration of the bomb without human victims—but Oppie and Fermi ended up saying "No, there's no alternative." Keep in mind that these guys weren't soldiers, they weren't military planners, they were just basically academics with an analytical job to do, an essentially *qualitative* job, a subjective assignment they'd been given by civilian government, and they could have said anything they wanted to. But the scientific panel—and of course this was after Trinity, this was something *this* Oppie and *this* Fermi didn't formally have time to do before they showed up here with me, it was their other selves that did it—Oppie and Fermi and some other scientists you never met, officially they put their names to a document that said "All we can do is bomb women and children." They said: Go ahead. Use the bomb.

❧ Ann sat across from Keiko on the bed as she made calls from the room phone, a reel of niceties, *Domo arigato gozaimashita*, one of the few Japanese phrases she had learned, repeated over and over. Yoshi had taught it to Ben and Ben taught it to her. Thank you very politely.

But the monasteries would not disclose names over the phone, Keiko said, this was not something they would do; if Ann went in person and showed a picture, and if Oppenheimer was actually in residence, they would at least ask him if he cared to receive her.

Keiko could not come along, she had to get back to her duties at home, but the inquiries themselves would be simple. Ann had a picture of Oppenheimer in one of the books she had brought with her, and she could show it wherever she went.

❧ After the bombing of Hiroshima and Nagasaki U.S. occupying forces ordered a moratorium on photographs and films of the destruction and the victims. As American interests rebuilt the country with the help of many of the Japanese industrialists who profited from the war, the Japanese government was complicit in this suppression.

❧ —I've been working on them, you wouldn't believe how hard, all the time I've been talking to them, trying to motivate them, said Szilard urgently, just as they stepped into a pachinko parlor.

Happily for Ben his voice was instantly drowned out by the overwhelming racket, clinking and jangling of tens upon thousands of coins, bells ringing, metal balls dropping and colliding, infinity of slots paying out constantly, nothing but clamor, chaos, hysteria of noise, screaming machines. Players sat slumped at their stations, baskets of silver balls between their feet, staring forward, oblivious, cigarettes dangling from their dry lips or growing long ashes on the sides of flimsy ashtrays.

Szilard, however, continued to talk. Ben ignored him.

Walking down the widest of the crowded rows, Szilard shoving and tripping behind him, he checked briefly from side to side like a cop on patrol, head right and left, everywhere, seeking a hunched-down, shivering, destitute Fermi, choking as he tried to breathe through the heavy, stale smoke. The air was so thick it almost closed his throat.

❧ The word *suffering* is full and whole and perfect as a pierced heart, sweet, rushing and tender, thought Oppenheimer. *Suffering* is the joy of someone about to be martyred, illumination of something given up as an offer. When *suffering* is invoked only its magnitude remains to be specified, he thought, and turned to stare across the lawn at a blurry monument.

Nothing is nearer or more sympathetic than the one who suffers.

In the museum there had been an exhibit all about radiation sickness, and now the suffering of victims of radiation sickness seemed to him to have a tinge aside from other sufferings. It was as though the poisons that emanate from a divided nucleus infected the body more insidiously than all the sickness of the past, as though a death from invisible rays was indecent, dirty and dishonest.

Only cancer approaches the stigma of radiation, he thought, the disease that in life had supposedly killed him. Cancer has come to seem a symbol of insidious decay, a sign of something gone fatally wrong deep beneath consciousness, rotting in stealth behind the curtain of the flesh, where spectators cannot presume.

❧ Ann sat on the train by herself, not a bullet train now but a local train, dingy and old with worn, frayed upholstery and faded linoleum floors. She watched the passing of the flatlands as they rose into the hills, the drab lots, warehouses, apartment buildings fanning out on both sides, signs on buildings she still could not read, was now and always would be blocked from reading but also in fact had no interest in reading, finally.

Keiko had written sounds for her in a lined notebook, sounded out the Japanese for "Hello, please excuse me, I am searching for my friend," after which she was to present Oppenheimer's photo. She repeated them again and again under her breath, —*Sumimasen, tomodachi o sagashiteiru n desu ga,* and then, when the car briefly emptied, out loud. When the hills began she was relieved to be in the shade of cedar and fir, on the gentle slope upward, out of the floodplain.

❧ Some say that when they walk at night near Hiroshima Ground Zero and there is wind in the trees they can hear the *genbaku obake,* the ghosts of the atomic dead, weeping for their children.

❧ Beyond aspects of pain that are physical, thought Oppenheimer, sickness or injury or privation, beyond the so-called *obvious,* suffering can be a work of art. It can be made of buried and rising things, helpless and undiscovered, song of frustrated want, silence after desire. It can be the test of the self falling short, constrained, distorted, disturbed or rebuffed, the vacuum left by longing, call without an answer.

In a face-off with happiness suffering often wins, he reflected, not by being a necessary hardship but by being chosen. Suffering is *chosen* over happiness by almost everyone. It is designed, coddled, caressed and persuaded; it is worked over by the brain so that it informs the limits of our freedoms and the shape of our fulfillment. It ties us to other people where happiness does not.

Suffering is embraced.

❧ The men approached Fermi when he was sitting on a park bench, staring ahead of him dazedly. On his lap he had an American newspaper, freshly purchased but not opened.

One was older, the other was younger, but neither was of an age to be noticed. They wore suits and had faces and voices that were difficult to remember. Later, thinking back, he would ask himself whether one of them had a Dutch accent: had it been Dutch or had it been German?

They sat down on either side of him, too close.

—We are given to understand, said the first one quietly, —that you are a reasonable person with no ax to grind.

—I'm sorry? asked Fermi politely. His fingers curled on the front page of the *New York Times* so that the edges of his fingernails scratched into the fiber.

—He must confide in you, said the second one.

—Who? asked Fermi.

—The man who calls himself Leo Szilard.

—Who are you? asked Fermi.

The men shot each other glances of amusement over his head.

—We have been watching him ever since his arrest at Kirtland, said the second man.

—What is Kirtland? asked Fermi.

—You don't know?

Fermi looked at him blankly.

—Kirtland Air Force Base, said the first man.

—Albuquerque, said the second. —He tried to break in. It was laughable but it drew our attention. And then we stopped laughing.

—I was not told about this before it happened, said Fermi quietly. —Are you the police?

The first man only smiled again.

—We had secret police in Italy, said Fermi. —You cannot intimidate me.

—We do not intend to, said the first man.

—Do you know what Szilard wants to do? asked the second man.

—No, said Fermi.

—Would you tell us if you did?

—Not necessarily.

—You have heard nothing? He hasn't told you what he's planning?

—He talks to Robert, said Fermi. —The two of them have conversations. I have not paid attention.

—I find that very difficult to believe, said the second man.

—Well, said the first one briskly, and got up, —thank you for your time, Dr. Fermi.

The second man rose too, a little reluctantly.

Fermi did not like him.

The first man leaned forward, clapped Fermi firmly on the shoulder and smiled without opening his mouth. Then they both turned and Fermi watched their backs recede as they walked away. Finally they turned a corner and were lost to sight.

Several minutes later he got up himself.

❧ —We're not going to find him like this, said Szilard as they left the pachinko place. —He was a betting man but not exactly a gambler, you know what I mean? And he hated smoking. He and Laura would have parties and people couldn't even smoke in the house. And this was in the '30s. Everybody smoked then. He would never be in a place like this.

—You could have said so before, couldn't you, snapped Ben.

—I think we should look for Italian restaurants, said Szilard. —Let's look there. They have Italian restaurants in Hiroshima, don't they?

—I really don't know, Leo, said Ben. —Have you seen any?

—Plus then we can get lunch, said Szilard. —It's already past three. We can order pasta. Those spiral ones.

❧ Oppenheimer had been thrown by the shock of the effects of the bomb, laid out there in the museum in panoramic display, in black-and-white photographs and videos on wall monitors that showed the torments of the dying. He had been struck by all the names and faces of these victims, girls and boys, the five-year-olds and the six-year-olds, the seven-year-olds, the eight-year-olds, the nine-year-olds and the ten. A child should not die. There was death, and death in the natural order was a simple grace; it gave life over to those who were newly made. He had no quarrel with it then. But surely, in violence and in sickness too, the infants should be spared.

He had been silenced by the frail old men talking humbly to rooms of schoolchildren, telling them in soft voices all about the bomb and what it had done, how it had made a world vanish in plain sight and whisked away their mothers, mothers barely remembered.

❧ Fermi had simply wanted to be alone until the weight that oppressed him lifted to give some slight relief. Not only was there the evidence of the bomb, what it had done to innocent children, but there was the cloying thickness of the world around him, from which nature had been removed. Cities were built and built and over time converted into prisons. Apparently the Japanese did not demand trees on their streets: beyond the park the city was all gray blocks, unrelieved by green.

But now there were the questions, and the attitude of the men who asked them.

❧ At the second monastery she was ushered in by a monk wearing a robe of pale orange, his bearing serene. He could not understand her question, *Sumimasen, tomodachi o sagashiteiru n desu ga,* so she sat waiting in a high-ceilinged anteroom while he went to find someone who spoke English. She was shy, embarrassed at the ungainliness of what she had probably said to him. She told herself she should have had Keiko write down the characters for her so that she could show her paper to the men at the monasteries when her tongue failed, like the deaf-mute she was, wandering door to door. She turned her face up to a skylight, through which the sky was a bland and senseless white. What was Oppenheimer doing? Was he near or far, alone or in company, still or speaking? Was he still the same? He should not have left without telling her first.

She wondered whether she should plan on saying something sharp to him when she found him or sacrifice her anger in the name of finding him, whether anger would stop her from finding him, finally, because angry she did not deserve to.

❧ There was a small Italian restaurant right near the Peace Park, near the Starbucks, near the Coca-Cola sign. Everything was convenient.

—So what I need is a favor from you, said Szilard, forking up tiramisu. —Can I count on that?

—My wife wants to find them, said Ben, staring into his espresso. —That's all that matters to her. And you owe her, Leo. Don't try to bargain with me. Just lead me to Fermi. You're smart and you know him well. You can do it.

—It won't be a problem, said Szilard. —This isn't quid pro quo or anything. Of course I'll help you find him. I want to find him too. It's separate, the favor I'm asking for. It's for when we get back. I'm asking you as a friend.

Setting down his espresso cup on the glass table Ben glanced over Szilard's shoulder and could almost not believe what he was seeing. Beneath a gay painted bower of entwined grape leaves that stretched across an arched doorway at the back of the restaurant, beside a gaudy mural featuring an antique-style portrait of some classical Italianate person in a jaunty yet foolish cap—possibly Dante Alighieri—was Fermi, neither destitute nor shivering, emerging from the men's rest room.

—Enrico! exclaimed Szilard, turning from his plate with dessert fork dangling, a morsel of tiramisu straying onto his pantleg as he rose. —Where the hell have you been?

Fermi walked over unsurprised, placidly, as though he had fully expected to find them.

—I'd like to order some food, he said to Ben. —I'm hungry.

—Go ahead, said Ben. He was actually relieved to see Fermi. Of all of them Fermi was least offensive to him: there was an element of dignity in the man's self-contained demeanor, his reticence, his unwillingness to play the game. But then right away he was thinking of Ann, how she was off somewhere, and it was Fermi's and Oppenheimer's behavior that had put her there. Here was one of the culprits, and far from being beside himself with agitation and therefore not responsible for his actions he seemed calm, unmoved, business as usual, and as far as Ben could see impervious to her distress.

—The pesto fusilli is good, said Szilard. —But spill it. Where were you?

—Nearby, said Fermi, and shrugged.

—My wife's very upset, said Ben. —Do you realize how much anxiety you caused her?

—I apologize, said Fermi simply and sincerely, and then Ben was distracted by the messy spectacle of Szilard rising from his seat to flag down a waitress by waving a dirty napkin and shouting —Hey!

—That's rude, Leo, said Ben, but the waitress was already upon them, smiling nervously. Fermi ordered spaghetti carbonara.

—I have to tell you, said Fermi when the waitress had left, turning to Szilard. —Two men came to talk to me. They asked me about you and Robert.

—You're kidding, said Szilard. —Why didn't they come straight to me?

—They asked me what you were planning.

—What *are* you planning, Leo? asked Ben.

—They were not good men, said Fermi.

—They know we have something, said Szilard. —They know we are a threat to them.

—Who's they?

—The government, said Szilard.

—What government? Ours? asked Ben. —You've got to be kidding me.

❧ Fatigue set in almost as soon as Ann got her answer from the third monastery, a cheaply built compound on the swampy outskirts of a national park, gray grassy hills receding behind the low buildings. On her way back to the bus stop, where she hoped to catch the last bus of the night before they stopped running, she walked slowly, her shoulders heavy. Once, when she looked up at the pavement ahead from the pavement beneath her feet, she was frozen in her paces by the sight of a large brown monkey loping across the road, his knuckles touching the ground.

Her feet hurt from walking so much but she felt glad as soon as she saw him.

The monkey was not Oppenheimer.

❧ Walking dumbly, thinking of the dead children in the museum of the atom bomb, Oppenheimer knew suddenly that suffering was what gave onto love. Suffering itself is beloved: love and suffering are far closer to each other than love and pleasure.

❧ Ben went back to the hotel room to sleep hoping she would be there, having extracted a promise from Fermi not to run again. Far from rebuking Fermi he found himself promising that when they got home Fermi could help him with summer plantings in the garden. With Szilard rebuke was second nature and he often felt like a high school principal, an absurd father figure doling out warnings and slaps on the wrist—without, admittedly, wielding any threat of real punishment.

But with Fermi he felt more like a nursemaid. Fermi was a rigid man with something vital broken.

Instead of Ann in the room there were two messages waiting for him. One was from her, telling him she hadn't found Oppenheimer, of course. She was staying in a small bed-and-breakfast about two hours distant by train, and here was the number if he needed it. The second was from Oppenheimer, calling not from an isolated monastery high up on a hill, where Ben had imagined him, but from a slick apartment in Shibuya, Tokyo.

4

❧ —It was a total, like, revelation, said Larry. —I'm not even kidding.

She stared at him and then at Oppenheimer, who sat smoking in an armchair holding a tumbler of whiskey. He was wearing a well-tailored new suit and new leather shoes. Cross-legged on the floor at the low black enamel table in his living room, a few feet away, Larry cradled a large bong.

Fermi had retired to a bedroom as soon as they arrived and Szilard, who stood across the room talking on Larry's cell phone, was not bothering to listen.

—He calls me to ask about places to go meditate, right? Like retreats and all that. Meanwhile since you guys were here I've been reading up on shit, like the alien autopsy, abductions, Roswell, and then all this stuff about cattle mutilations and the military and Alamogordo and the A-bomb and all that. And then I'm looking at this old Time-Life book my father's got back there. He's got a whole set of them, right? So I find Oppie's picture. I can't believe you guys didn't tell me!

—It's hard to explain, said Ann with a note of apology.

—Some people tend to be skeptical, said Ben drily.

—I was blown away. I mean blown away. Totally. So when he calls I'm like, just come here, man. You're welcome. I go, If you want a like spiritual retreat or whatever I'll just clear out for a few days, I'll leave you in peace, know what I mean? I mean he's the Father of the A-Bomb! And he's supposed to be dead.

—That's when Larry called me and told me about it, said Larry's girlfriend, sitting next to him on the floor. Her bellbottoms were so wide and long she had to hold them up when she walked. Ann had visibly marveled at this sacrifice to fashion—Ben had watched her watching—but also at her hair, so long she could sit on it, dyed blond interspersed with red and green, and artfully dread-locked.

Larry took a bong hit and nodded, his face pink from held breath, as his girlfriend leaned across the table and took Ann's hand in both of her own, charm bracelets dangling onto the table's surface, squeezing the fingers warmly.

—Tamika really admires you, said Larry, on the sighing end of a long exhalation.

—Me? asked Ann.

—I think it is *so great* that you believed in him and supported him, said Tamika. —That is *so great.* And oh yeah, the other guys too.

—Oak Woods Cemetery, said Szilard to the cell phone. —Chicago.

— I mean it's amazing, said Larry. —Robert's basically been reincarnated as himself. That's like *completely* unheard of. It, like, *never* happens.

—Never, agreed Tamika solemnly.

—You don't say, said Ben.

—He came back to tell us something. He has a mission here. This guy is like a messenger. I'm serious. I mean it. You know what he is? He's basically *a prophet.*

In the hush that followed Larry and Tamika turned their gaze up to Oppenheimer, who in his large, straight-backed chair presided regally over all of them. Ben waited for Oppenheimer to say something, make a self-deprecating gesture, a witty, light dismissal in his usual style. But Oppenheimer was distracted, smoking and gazing past them, paying little attention to anyone but Szilard, who chose that moment to yell angrily into the innocent cell phone —Damn it! I want the body exhumed!

—Leo, said Oppenheimer, when Szilard had stabbed at the END CALL button several times and handed the cell phone back to Larry, —we need to discuss your manners.

☙ The guest bedrooms in Larry's father's apartment were well-appointed. Each had its own bathroom and jacuzzi with electronic controls, and Ann and Ben sat in one of these, water jetting around them, before they went to bed. On the wall hung a print of a painted scroll depicting a fat, angry demon with bulging eyes.

—So Larry's a fan, I guess, said Ben.

—He is, said Ann, and she sounded distracted and confused, almost puzzled by the evidence that people other than she could be convinced of the scientists' legitimacy.

Ben thought: She's lost her monopoly.

—Almost an acolyte, you might say, said Ben, pressing home his advantage.

—I don't know how deep it goes, though, said Ann uncertainly. —I mean I like him and he's been good to us, he's a really nice guy, but I wonder if he's—I think maybe the scientists are just his Movie of the Week, you know?

—You mean because he's a stoner he doesn't really have opinions, said Ben, smiling.

—Of course I didn't mean that, said Ann, and lapsed into silence, staring at the foaming water.

Ben put his hand on her knee, worried he had been callous, staring at the damp hair clinging to her wet cheeks, the flush of heat in the skin beneath her eyes.

—You may be right, he said, —this may be just entertainment for him. He probably doesn't take it as seriously as you do. I mean who does, right?

Faint smile at that but he was still feeling she needed more, reassurance or comfort, he wasn't sure which.

—Tomorrow we'll ask them if they still want to go to Nagasaki, he said, since planning could sometimes distract her from current events.

—OK, she said, but she was still baffled.

—Listen, he said softly, —it's going to be OK. It'll be fine. We can always use a friend. Right?

—Of course, she said, and let him squeeze her hand. —But how about the men who threatened Fermi?

—I don't know, he said.

He had been thinking about this and had come up with nothing.

—What if they really do something?

—What I'm hoping, he said, wiping a soap sud gently from the curve of her ear, —is that they were people Szilard pissed off just by being himself.

—Here in Japan?

—Szilard can piss people off anywhere.

She was not mollified by this, staring straight past him and nodding distantly.

—Who knows what he's been doing while our backs were turned? You know Leo. He's annoying.

She kept nodding, but he knew she was not listening to him.

❧ She got up when it was still dark and early enough to feel like night and crept through the apartment to knock on Oppenheimer's door.

Larry had put him in the master bedroom, where he usually slept himself, which featured a four-poster canopy bed, a gilt-edged mirror, and a massive wood cabinet containing a big-screen television. The door was cracked a few inches and after she knocked lightly and got no answer she went in. She found the sheets and blanket rumpled on the bed, the shallow depression left by Oppenheimer's long, thin body, and the room empty of all but the new suit Larry had bought him, hanging in the open closet. On the floor of the closet were his old shoes, and picking one up, hooking a finger on the worn leather where it had blistered his heel, she remembered a time before she knew him, in her own bedroom, looking at shoes, looking at clotheshangers: what was it? Ben in the next room, shaving, and the world about to turn liquid.

It was before she and Fermi had met Oppenheimer, before she talked to him, but after she saw him in the bar and heard them speak, faces reflected in the warped mirror where she stared at them, the air almost *lit* around her, before she knew.

The days after Eugene shot himself had been delicate with perception of minute things. Details had been gilded, brought out from their backgrounds, each of them like an adoration of the whole thing. She had forgotten but even walking down the street those mornings, walking in a straight line, she had stopped and hesitated, waiting, infused with sensation and willingness. The parts of the world had been arresting. Something had stopped her and made her look at them.

She left the room, stepping carefully, not to wake the others, not to be heard by Ben, through the living room where Larry and Tamika slept on a wafer-thin futon on the floor, Larry snoring with his arms flung wide, Tamika nestled into his side in the fetal position. Her multicolored hair trailed onto the tatami. There was a silk sheet pulled over both of them, which Larry held up to his chin, and beside the futon their clothes were crumpled, an orange and black sarong covered in primitive shapes of fish, olive-green army pants with multiple pockets.

Ann thought how young they looked as they slept, how despite the fact that Larry was probably pushing forty he had the aspect of a man in his twenties, not because he surfed and smoked pot but because he was innocent, there was something innocent about him, guileless, as though he was trying to impress no one.

She felt old by comparison just because she was more reserved. Reservation was an element of adulthood, embarrassment with forethought.

Larry had offered up all four of his private bedrooms to his guests and volunteered to sleep on the floor. She couldn't suspect him of having an ulterior motive: what motive could there be? There was no profit to be had by believing in ghosts and as far as the health of the ghosts themselves went, Oppenheimer, Szilard and arguably Fermi all needed to be seen and acknowledged by more people than her, alone she was not sufficient, alone she was a crazy woman, in fact she should be grateful to Larry for making her look sane. Sleeping with his mouth open he was an overgrown child with childish enthusiasms, and she should be fond of him, as she was fond of them all.

He could not be behind the warning. No: it was simple.

All the way from New Mexico they had been followed.

She went back to bed then, Ben murmuring in his sleep and rolling over toward her.

❧ Far away, as though it had never happened, was his past before this, unchanging, a silver place. It gleamed like pavement after rain.

He had been dreaming again of his everyday life.

❧ When she got up in the morning, mouth and eyes dry, it was because there was a haze of pot smoke in the air. She came out of her room to see Larry fishing around in a drawer and then handing a wad of bills to Szilard. Tamika sat up naked on the futon, sheets bunched around her waist, apparently unaware of the resulting discomfort. Oppenheimer stood near the door, behind Szilard, consciously turning his glance away from her breasts, and Ann thought of Keiko doing the same when Ben came out of the bathroom, of the aversion of eyes everywhere. Between people ran lines of eagerness and furtiveness that were clear and strong and sprung with tension.

Only Szilard didn't seem to notice anything out of the ordinary. He never seemed to pay attention to nudity. Szilard seemed completely asexual, as though he actually possessed no sexual urges.

Szilard was like a prepubescent boy who never reached reproductive maturity. It was impossible to envision him in sexual ecstasy. No wonder he had warned a girlfriend once that he was not breeding stock. She remembered it clearly from his biography. "I am a worker bee, not a drone."

—What are you up to? she asked Oppenheimer, as Ben came into the room behind her in boxer shorts, rubbing his eyes.

—We're just in and out, we came to get funding for breakfast, he said. —We're trying to decide what comes next.

—Engaged in high-level talks, said Szilard, and shoved Larry's money into his pocket.

The term referred to any talks involving him.

—Just tell me, before you go out, I mean should I be making train reservations again? Do you still want to go to Nagasaki?

—Nagasaki? said Szilard distractedly. —No need for that. Right Oppie?

—No need for Nagasaki, no, said Oppenheimer, and smiled at Ann, almost in apology. —Hiroshima was enough.

—So —what? Are we going to fly home, then?

—We're discussing it, said Szilard brusquely. —We'll get back to you soon.

After he shut the door behind them, Larry rolled a joint. Tamika yawned widely and Ben put his arms around Ann and whispered into her ear, —Leo's got a new attitude, doesn't he.

She heard Szilard's patronizing tone for seconds after he had left the room, and felt like an unpaid servant.

๛ A girl who was eight years old when Hiroshima was bombed later said: "I escaped from the city by walking over many dead bodies. There were people with severe burns or people grabbing my legs asking for water, and I escaped by deserting these people just because I wanted to live. I ran away from those people who were held under some objects and were asking for my assistance but I deserted them without giving even a lift to help them out. My life has been miserable since then. I have been ill and unable to succeed in anything I try."

☙ —You won't believe what day it is today, said Larry.

—It's someone's special day, said Tamika coyly.

—Let us in on it, said Ben. —Please, I'm begging you.

His resentment was making him bitter. The bitter skin alone, he knew, the sour rind of his impatience could reduce him before his wife, but he could not help it. It had snuck up on him. Before this kindness had come easily to him and now he tried and failed to be generous, and even external generosity, that is the *appearance* of generosity, was hard to pull off sometimes, more and more often.

He did not want to be outside her belief, her fundamental opinion, but he could not help it and at the same time he could not stand to be excluded. He wanted to be in the believers' club, a member in good standing. He wished her credulousness was open to him, that he did not think, finally, that this was all just a load of bullshit.

—Guess! urged Tamika.

—No thanks, said Ben, struggling to be gentle. —Just tell me, OK?

—Oppie! she squealed. —It's his birthday!

—April 22nd, said Larry solemnly. —1904.

—So that would make him, what, a century old if he's a day, said Ben. —And he looks so young!

—I don't know that he actually *celebrates* his birthday, said Ann to Larry. —It's not really his style.

—What kind of cake should I bake? asked Tamika.

—Oppenheimer doesn't eat cake, said Ben. —But don't worry. Szilard will eat the whole thing.

—Who doesn't eat *cake*?

—He hardly eats at all, said Ann.

—We're getting a whole bunch of friends to come over, too, said

Larry. —Make it more of a party. You know? Mostly surfing buddies, plus some folks I used to follow the Dead with and Tamika's friends from the yoga studio. It's a historic occasion. This guy's come back from the dead and it's his birthday. How often does that happen, right?

—You're kidding, right? said Ben.

—He needs joy, said Tamika. —Joy and light.

❧ Ann went out with Oppenheimer that afternoon, walking down a gravel road in a park of towering trees.

—So what have you been talking about, you and Szilard? asked Ann. —I know he's been working on you but he doesn't talk to me about what he wants. I want to listen to him and Ben just wants him to shut up, but still he talks to Ben instead of me.

—Leo has some old-fashioned ideas about women, said Oppenheimer, sliding a cigarette from a silver case. Since he'd come back to Tokyo he was immaculately fitted out in expensive accessories, as though Larry had appointed himself personal shopper. He used the new accessories easily, a man accustomed to fine goods who had sorely missed them in the brief period of his dependency on lesser resources.

—Yes. He does.

—I had time to think after the visit to Hiroshima. I had time to think on the train, and I had time to think when I came back to Larry's apartment. I had time to think after Fermi told me about the men who threatened him. I thought about all the warnings we've had, the incidents at the house and the men who followed us here. I listened to my instincts.

—And what did your instincts tell you?

—They told me Leo's on the right path. What he wants to do is what we have to do. It's what we came here for. If it wasn't no one would be hunting us. So I've made a decision: I'm going to join him.

—Join him how?

—Let's sit down a minute, said Oppenheimer. —Wait: not here. It's disrespectful to sit down inside the grounds of the temple. The wooden bench there, out through the gate.

Sitting down, putting out his cigarette, he leaned forward and leaned his chin against the steepled fingers of his hands. Nearby some teenagers sported careful pink mohawks and expensive leather jackets. One of them performed an awkward break dance.

—So what does Szilard want?

—The United Nations.

❧ —Surprise!

—Happy Birthday to you, Happy Birthday to you, Happy Birthday dear Robert . . .

—Happy Birthday to you!

A crowd converged on them as they came in the door, a pot-smoking crowd beneath a floating island of balloons, white and silver helium balloons clinging to the ceiling, bumping against it as the people moved beneath them, densely packed. It was dark and hot and full, lampshades draped with red and purple cloth giving off a sultry light, music warbling beneath the hum of talk, an old song Ann could not identify.

—I can't believe this, said Oppenheimer under his breath.

—I promise, whispered Ann, —I told him not to do it.

—OK, everyone, said Larry, clapping his hands and jumping onto the coffee table as Oppenheimer slipped off his shoes, embarrassed, to step onto the tatami. Oppenheimer had his head down, was almost *hunkering* down, Ann thought, as though he could slip through the throng and melt from sight. Tamika was busy ushering people out of the kitchen, shushing them as she gestured, to hear what was clearly an impending speech.

Larry's guests looked like transients, she thought, grateful to have a place to be, she thought, a comfortable apartment, anywhere, roof over their heads, free food and drink. Possibly some of them were rich and aimless, too rich to care how poor they looked, heroin chic, spending their money on drugs and sleeping wherever they fell. The room grew fuller, and she felt claustrophobic despite the size of the place, which had always seemed bland and vacant. There was goodwill in the crowd, warm and boneless. All was well as long as the deep smell of marijuana pervaded the air.

❧ A man who survived the bombing of Nagasaki said later: "I walked around my ruined house looking for my daughter. After two days I found her at last. I dug the gutter and found her pants that had partly escaped the fire. So I picked up her bones in a small burnt bucket.

"After my wife's death I carried some dead trees into the hollow of the emergency crematory, put on some petroleum and cremated her by myself. I picked up her bones in the evening."

❧ —I have some introductions to make! cried Larry. —Today is the birthday of our new friend Robert, my new friend Robert that I want to be your new friend too!

—Happy Birthday, Robert! echoed the crowd.

Larry consulted a wrinkled piece of paper.

—And his full name is Dr. Julius Robert Oppenheimer, Father of the A-Bomb, Director of the Manhattan Project—

—Whoo-hoo!

—Born in 1904 and risen from the dead!

—Go Robert!

—The Dead?

—What I want to say is this. Seriously. Robert came to me without, like, advertising who he was, right? He didn't claim to be anyone. He didn't claim to be, like, who he is. I did some research and found out. This was totally by chance, I mean it. I just got curious one day after I met him—he actually wasn't even here, he had already left—and I did my homework. Otherwise I never would have known. Which to me is proof he's not a scammer. Right?

—Go for it Larry!

—So I found out who he was from the history books. And when he called me up I go, Are you *the* Robert Oppenheimer? Are you the famous scientist who invented the nuclear bomb and died in the '60s? And he goes—this is all he said—*I am Oppenheimer.*

—Oppie!

An arm pumped somewhere nearby and Ann thought she noticed a slight shift in the crowd, a movement from festive jeer toward idle speculation.

—And you know what? I believe it. This guy *is* Robert Oppenheimer. I like to call him Oppie.

—Go Oppie! . . .

—Can you believe this? asked Ben audibly, coming up with a glass of beer in hand. —He's sincere. He actually wrote a *speech*. Where is he getting this stuff?

—And what I wanna say to all of you, my good friends and those of you I've just known a little while —

—And my friends from Yoga Zone! put in Tamika. —I'm so glad you guys came!

—. . . all of you guys, check the pictures, look at the books over there on the sideboard. These guys are the real McCoys. I'm not kidding. They're not ringers. These guys are *authentic*. It's something you feel in your gut when you talk to these guys. There's nothing like authenticity, you know?

—It's so real, said a woman next to Ben, nodding pensively.

Someone sucked audibly on a large bong, bubbling the water, and it passed in front of Ann's face, hand to hand.

—Where's my chocolate chip cookie, man? urged a thin man in camouflage pants with a stringy pigtail.

—I think these guys are here for a reason. And I wanted to give you guys the chance to meet them and decide for yourself.

—I choose to believe! cried Tamika to a chorus of applause, and Ben, incredulous, shaking his head, turned and made for the bathroom, through the crowd, abandoning his empty beer glass on a tabletop as he went. Ann followed him partway, pushing past shoulders and greasy ponytails until she got to Fermi, leaning over to say into his ear, over the hubbub, —Are you OK?

—Eyes of the world! said the man in camouflage, swaying until he almost stumbled. There was beer froth on his handlebar mustache. —Thighs of a squirrel!

Fermi gazed down into his glass, blinking rapidly. She was afraid he would cry.

☙ Ben watched Oppenheimer step onto the coffee table to loud whistles and claps, half-pulled by Larry, half-pushed by Tamika.

—We are grateful for your good faith, he began. —I can't tell you how we came to be here—only that we are. And we find ourselves in a bankrupt society—

—Hear hear! said the man with the pigtail, and nodded as he reached for a tray of champagne glasses.

—He pulled these people off the street and paid them to come in, didn't he, said Ben to Szilard.

—a society, went on Oppenheimer, —that has done nothing since we left it, nothing since the split-second after the flash of the Trinity device but die a long death.

—I can't believe this, groaned Ben. —He's a preacher now? He's going to deliver a sermon on modern morality?

—Oppie can be a little sanctimonious at times, said Szilard. —But of course he's entirely correct.

—What shocked us most, said Oppenheimer, and raised his cigarette to his lips, —was that it does not shock *you*, that it does not *stun* you all and send you reeling with horror, this long death of civilization unrolling before your eyes. Not only does our own civilization fall, it falls heavily, taking all of creation with it.

—Trees! said a woman beside them. —Trees only *give* to this world. What crime has a tree committed?

—We're only men of science. None of us are politicians. We can only speak from the heart, as people who entered into this dese- crated landscape from another time and who may be able—I make no boast, but this is what we feel—who may be able, for that rea- son, to see the state of things with greater clarity than those who have lived within this prison all their lives.

—We're all prisoners of the man! someone yelled.

—Because all around us we see signs of imminent catastrophe. We see commerce run rampant. We see the rich devouring the poor . . .

—This from a man with a brand-new platinum cigarette case, said Ben.

—. . . devouring the land and the waters and the life they give us. We also see greed building to a fever pitch . . .

—Fever pitch, repeated a fat man in a greasy wifebeater.

Ben made his way to the apartment door, then stopped in his tracks: a contortionist was sitting on the carpet in front of him. He was twisted up like a pretzel. Ben stood there gaping, barely listen- ing to the speech behind him.

—. . . propose that all the countries of the world, both rich and poor, abandon their nationalistic fervor, said Oppenheimer, and stubbed out his cigarette while fishing in his breast pocket for a new one with his free hand. —In short we want to propose that the United Nations, that much-maligned body, that body that has ap- parently been so undervalued and so underused—

—United Nations? asked the man with the pigtail, confused.

—Go Oppie! shouted someone unseen, and clapping started at the back of the crowd and moved forward.

—for the sake of a glorious future . . .

—This a party or not? asked the wifebeater.

—world government. We propose a unity, not of corporations

across the globe, not the exploitative union of the World Trade Organization, the General Agreement on Tariffs and Trade—

—Tariffs? asked the wifebeater. —What the hell is he talking about?

—of the so-called North American Free Trade Agreement, but of people, of people and their directly elected representatives, a democratic global union that controls the spread of weapons and the distribution of wealth with the goal of establishing—eventually, that is, for the struggle will be long—

—Long! I can dig it, said the camo man.

—the goal of establishing—at long last—universal world peace.

—Peace, man, peace! crowed Larry, making the two-fingered sign to a terminal spatter of applause.

—Thank you, said Oppenheimer weakly. He took a gulp from his glass and stepped down onto the tatami, where he was instantly engulfed.

❧ Five percent of people killed in wars at the end of the nineteenth century were civilians. In World War One this percentage rose to fifteen, and by World War Two it was sixty-five.

This was nothing compared to the wars of the 1990s. By that time the percentage would grow to ninety.

❧ When she emerged from the bathroom Ben took her arm and Larry and Tamika converged on them, camouflage man in tow. He smelled like an armpit.

—Hey, guys. You meet Clint? asked Larry.

—Pleasure, said Ann, but Ben was impatient.

—What is this all *about*? he asked Larry. —You're telling me you really believe these guys are risen from the dead?

—I'm with Larry, said Tamika. —I definitely think it was reincarnation.

—Karma, said Clint, head bobbing, and then turned to grab

Larry's arm. —They did bad shit. Where'd you get the Humboldt, man? That stuff's been scarce around here for months.

—It's not Humboldt, said Larry, —it's Mendocino.

—My point though, said Ben, —is you actually think these people are physicists from World War Two?

—Shit yeah, said Larry.

—Don't you? put in Tamika.

—*I* do, said Ann, —but Ben, you know, sometimes he can be a little suspicious of them. He's just very protective. He doesn't want me to be taken in.

—Negative energy, said the bald woman, and shook her head in warning.

—That's me, said Ben.

—Hi, said the woman to Ann, —I'm Leslie. I'm a survivor.

—You're kidding, said Szilard. —Hiroshima or Nagasaki? You don't look a day over fifty.

—Cancer, said Leslie, frowning. —And I'm forty-two.

A Grateful Dead song was playing, Ann didn't know the Grateful Dead from a hole in the wall but people in the room were twirling and dancing. *There comes a redeemer and he, too, fades away.*

She felt exhausted, seeing Tamika lean on Larry's arm and smile, watching Szilard, bored and restless, looking around the room for someone new to talk to, Fermi slumped against the wall, paging through a book. She was tired enough to disengage from Ben's hand on her waist and walk away from them all, wishing herself away, wishing herself into another place, where she had been before, before Eugene fired the shot that bounced off the wall, before she found any of them, before this had happened, when things were easy. She thought of the leisure she used to have, the nice slow movement from one hour to the next, the space around her then, around her arms, her own house and its peacefulness, the comfort of passiveness that now, later, she relished.

—I'm over it, but the memories, right? Like I was sitting on

Phil's side, this was Berkeley I think? said a man who stood over the punch bowl talking to Clint as Ann made her way past them to the kitchen. —And this space invader chick with this frizzy red hair sits down and asks me if she can score a dose. And that redheaded chick was the woman I married.

—I know he's dead, but I don't feel like he's gone. I mean, do you think Jerry's God? asked a blond woman on the other side of the punchbowl.

—Course she left me six weeks after the ceremony.

—Believe me, said Oppenheimer, coming in from the kitchen and forced up against her by the crowd behind him, —I didn't want to be up there. They grabbed me and pulled me up. You think I don't know how simplistic it sounds? I wasn't ready to make a public statement. But Leo says I have to practice.

—I think there *is* a God, said Clint, nodding slowly as they passed him on their way out. —But I don't think it's Jerry.

❧ —I'm tired, she said.

—I am too.

❧ Ben had his fill of alcohol and marijuana. He circled the rooms in the apartment listening to conversations, suspending judgment because for once he could. It was a relief. As he had become bitter lately he had also become more judgmental, had noticed himself in the transition, meaner than he had ever been before, sharp-toothed. He regretted this but there were bands of steel around him, squeezing.

Now comfort eased him and the bands loosened. Maybe this was the answer, he thought, maybe it's as simple as this. Get stoned.

—The thing is, said a tall blond woman, —if Robert Oppenheimer can be reincarnated, and that guy Fermi and the fat one too, then why can't Jerry?

—But like they were a negative force, know what I mean? And Jerry was a positive force, said a middle-aged man who spat when he talked. —It's a whole different thing. Maybe they were brought back to atone for their sins or whatever. That's what Leslie was saying. Jerry was totally positive.

Making the rounds Ben interrupted Szilard in an earnest conversation about Osama Bin Laden with a broad-faced, ruddy Australian rugby player named Frank and a jewelry maker from Santa Barbara hung liberally with her own wares. She liked to show them off and tell the history of each one.

Szilard tried to make a point about reactor by-products and treaty verification protocols but was repeatedly frustrated by the Australian's single-minded obsession with a pyramid scheme to spread world peace. Beside him the jewelry maker showed Ben her pièce-de-resistance, a necklace-and-earring set made out of a goat femur.

What could it harm? he thought, as she told him the femur had healing properties. It was charged with positive ions, she said, which caused healing.

All of this, he thought, everything he had first ridiculed was benign.

Sunk deep into a leather sofa he also listened, swayed into empathy by the pot and a piece of chocolate cake, to a dialogue about crop circles and cattle mutilations between Clint, Larry, and a Belgian food activist whose claim to fame was that he had once helped burn down a McDonald's in France.

When he finally went back to his room he found Oppenheimer and Ann in the bed, fully clothed on top of the coverlet, one behind the other and fast asleep. He lay down on the floor beside them. They were chaste and fraternal as a priest and a nun, unless it was only an illusion of innocence; but still he did not like to be the one on the floor.

He tried to count sheep but was troubled by the resistance of his mind to sleep, how it dwelled on a hazy vision of the young Szilard trotting into an Old West town with pistols on his hips, holding a rose and riding on a rat.

❧ —Fermi's family won't let me dig up his body for a DNA test, announced Szilard petulantly at dinner.

A cleanup crew had come and gone and Larry and Tamika had taken Fermi out to see an Italian movie. Szilard and Oppenheimer had politely declined.

—You actually called up one of Enrico Fermi's descendants and asked him if you could dig up the poor guy's body? asked Ben, astonished.

—Several, said Szilard.

—You're so obnoxious, said Ben.

—I didn't tell them who I was, of course, said Szilard. —I said I was a researcher at U. Chicago doing a longitudinal study of rates of cancer death among nuclear industry professionals.

—You're kidding me. And they believed you had to dig up their grandfather's body for that, said Ben flatly.

—They certainly appeared to, said Szilard.

—I have to insist, Leo, said Oppenheimer. —You should steer clear of relatives even under a pretense. I thought we decided that.

—This was important, said Szilard. —I made an exception. Anyway the effort failed. Since you and I were both cremated there is literally no other way to establish our identity through forensic pathology.

—That's rough, said Ben.

—Unless, of course, we break the law, said Szilard. —We could dig up the body ourselves. I found out where it is.

—You kill me, said Ben.

—If the point is to establish credibility, Leo, said Oppenheimer, —we can't do it by grave-robbing, can we.

—I have it all worked it, said Szilard. —We can establish our legal authority post facto, through the court system if necessary. After all, no one has a clearer right to dispose of a corpse than the dead man himself. When we prove Fermi is the dead man, we'll also prove he had the right to perform his own exhumation.

—Not much of a lawyer, are you, said Ben.

—That's far-fetched, said Oppenheimer. —As far as my own involvement goes, at this time, Leo, I'd have to give you a firm no.

Szilard, irritated, scooped a second helping of scalloped potatoes out of the serving bowl.

—I'll put it on the back burner for now, he said grudgingly, —but I think you'll want to reconsider in time.

—No doubt, said Oppenheimer.

❧ —Anyway, said Szilard to Ann a few minutes later, trapping her as she made her way into the bathroom for a jacuzzi, clad only in a towel, —I forgot to tell you: we talked about it and we're ready to go back. We have several appointments in the United States. I have to meet with my attorneys.

—Your attorneys?

—Your attorneys? echoed Ben, pulling up as he passed them in the hallway. —What, has the government decided to prosecute you on that B&E charge?

—The government is not suing me, said Szilard haughtily. I'm suing them.

—You're what?

—If they refuse to release our records under the Freedom of Information Act.

—Your records? asked Ann.

—Our personnel files and fingerprints. They will establish our identities.

—You're telling me you hired a lawyer to get your fingerprints? asked Ben.

—Initially I hired him to file a Freedom of Information Act request. The DOD had a deadline. But it's coming up. If they fail to meet it, that's when we'll sue. I say *we* because Oppie and Fermi are now working with me.

—I see, said Ann.

—Once we have the prints, of course, we will be able to go public.

—Go public? asked Ann.

—With the campaign, said Szilard impatiently, and turned around to head toward his room.

—What campaign?

—Global disarmament.

They stared at his retreating back.

—Excuse me, Leo, said Ben. —Where'd you get the money for a lawyer?

—At first I wrote a bad check, confessed Szilard over his shoulder. —Before we left, when I originally hired him. His retainer. But just when it bounced and he was going to quit I was able to get money from Larry. We wired it. No problem.

—No problem, huh, repeated Ben.

—Here I thought you were flat broke this whole time! said Ann. —I didn't know you even *had* a checkbook!

—Strictly speaking, of course, I don't have one per se.

He opened the door to his bedroom.

—Then whose, uh—checkbook—?

—We'll talk later! called Szilard, with a hasty, furtive glance at Ben, and closed his bedroom door.

—I'm going to kill him.

—This is what they were talking about, said Ann. —The men who tried to interrogate Fermi. Doesn't he care?

—Are you joking? Szilard loved being stalked. It made him feel important.

❧ Ben changed their ticket dates in a hurry, eager to put them on the first flight out. They took the Narita Express early in the morning. Larry had left them a note on the table: See you later!

Making her way down the aisle of the airplane with her shoulder bag held in front of her, almost tripping over a scissor-legged Barbie doll on the floor, Ann thought she recognized a man from the birthday party as she passed him seated: the food activist from Belgium. He had helped burn down a McDonald's in France, it was said. She wondered whether she should say hello, but did not remember his name.

—Ben! she hissed as they went past. —A guy from the party was sitting back there, did you see him? The one who threw the Molotov cocktail at the Ronald McDonald statue. What's his name again?

—Adalbert, or something. He only eats what he grows.

And then she heard a familiar voice ring out from the middle row of seats in front of them, and found her eyes drawn to a cascade of green dreadlocks over a seatback.

—Tamika?

—Surprise! said Tamika, turning.

Other heads turned to her right and left and she realized they were surrounded by guests from the party: Ashlee the jewelry maker, Boogie the surfer, Leslie the cancer survivor, and Clint the heckler who'd worn camouflage but now seemed to be garbed in a suede cowboy jacket with a long, swinging fringe. There were other faces she recognized without knowing names.

—She's all surprises, that girl, said Ben under his breath.

—We're coming with! called Larry, smiling broadly as ever from his seat beside Tamika.

Ann took a breath and smiled back at him shakily, and as she sat down she turned to Oppenheimer, who was assigned to the seat behind them.

—I didn't know, he said, and lifted two fingers to his brow. —Scout's honor.

Leslie had a seat directly in front. She turned to prop herself up on the headrest.

—Larry paid for our tickets, she confessed in a hushed voice. —Fourteen of us! Besides them.

—I don't understand, said Ann. —Are you just coming for—?

—Larry offered, and some of us believe in him, you know?

—You believe in Larry?

—Oppie!

—Be*lieve* in him? asked Ben.

—Like Clint for example. He saw Oppie's head in a vision and it was surrounded by this halo of pink sparks but on Arnold Schwarzenegger's body.

—That would have been the LSD, I'm thinking, said Ben.

—Don't be so negative. Some of us choose to believe, you know? No offense, but try not to poison us with your cynical attitude, OK Ben?

—Please take your seats, said a flight attendant, pushing past. —We have passengers behind you here who need to get through. OK?

—Sorry, said Ben, and closed the overhead compartment.

—I don't follow, said Oppenheimer. —He saw me with pink sparks coming out of my head? And now he's coming with us to New Mexico?

—He had a vision, said Leslie. —Clint! Oppie wants to talk to you!

—Quite all right, said Oppenheimer, sinking down into his seat and stretching a long leg out into the aisle. —Maybe later.

It was too late: Clint the camo man, stringy-haired and leathery-faced with his drooping mustache and fringed cowboy jacket, bore down on them from his seat a few rows behind. He blocked the aisle to talk to them as the last stragglers onto the plane stowed their gear.

—Yeah, man, he said, —it was yesterday, the day after the party, you know? I was sober by then. Or at least I was hung over. I wasn't tripping.

—Sir, I'm going to need you to sit down, said the flight attendant, passing again. —You can feel free to continue this conversation once we take off, OK?

Clint moved into an empty seat.

—I left Larry's place and I got on the subway, right? I was looking at this ad, it was for some movie I think, and then where the guy's head was—

—Didn't you say it was Arnold Schwarzenegger? broke in Leslie. —That's what you said.

—But I'm not so sure it was him anymore, OK? I don't go to movies that much. It could have been some other buff guy with a bodybuilder thing going on. Like Stallone.

—But you said—

—Just shut up, would you Leslie? Anyway he had a big gun and so the train's going along, right? I was standing up and it was one of those ads that hangs down right onto people's heads, right? So I'm tired, I'm kind of falling asleep as I'm standing there, holding on, you know? And I look up and here's Oppie on this movie poster instead of the other guy. Now *he's* holding the gun. But his head is surrounded in this sort of—

—Pink light! said Leslie eagerly.

—Would you shut your piehole? It wasn't a pink light, it was more of a—what do they call them, a scarf? No wait. Like the old Spanish ladies wear, you know, wrapped around their heads.

—A shawl? said Ann.

—A shawl? asked Oppenheimer. —I was wearing a shawl?

—I don't think you were seeing Oppenheimer in the subway there, Clint, said Ben. —I think what you saw was a transvestite.

—Ha ha, man. It was Oppie. I'm telling you. This shawl, it wasn't a normal shawl, OK? It was like a shawl of awareness.

—What? said Ben.

—Don't knock it, OK? said Clint. —I'm just telling you what I saw. And his face—your face, sir—it like had this saintly look. Like it does. I mean look at him! This guy looks like a stained glass window!

Ann almost remembered something, but failed. She studied Oppenheimer: he was pale and his eyes stood out. It was true that he looked, as he had always looked, paper-thin and absorbed, hunger shining.

—But the deal is, like, the shawl made me understand, it was this like feeling coming off the shawl. The shawl was like, I don't know. Holy.

—Congratulations, said Ben to Oppenheimer. —You can let the whole Robert Oppenheimer identity go, finally. Now you're the Virgin Mary.

—I don't want you to be disappointed, said Oppenheimer earnestly to Clint. —I mean this isn't a circus. We're not going to perform. What exactly do you plan to do in Santa Fe?

—Just go with the flow, said Clint. —Keep the eyes open, you know? Eyes of the world, man. Don't sweat it.

—Santa Fe is a powerful healing place, said Leslie. —I've always wanted to go there. I've never been to New Mexico.

—If you're thinking of finding a vortex, said Ben, —I should warn you that's Sedona.

—Sir, the seatbelt, please, said the flight attendant to Clint, making a sweep past Leslie before she turned. —Ma'am? Can you sit down for me please? You need to have your seatbelt on for us to pull away from the gate.

❧ —We'll need your help, said Szilard to Clint, leaning around from the row behind Clint as the plane began to pull back from the gate. —We need manpower. We're launching a major PR and legal campaign as soon as we get back. You'll be a highly valuable member of the team, Clint. Believe me.

Ben considered how quickly Szilard had picked up the business language to add to his canon of slang. Whatever you can say about Szilard, he thought, he's sharp as a tack. He assimilates information at a rapid rate. He *never stops learning*.

—Where are they going to *stay*? whispered Ann to Oppenheimer, turning in her seat once Clint had been distracted.

Ben shot him a look of warning, or tried to. *Don't impose.*

—Don't worry, said Oppenheimer.

He had understood.

—They're not staying with us, Ann, said Ben. —Robert wouldn't ask that of you.

—Of course not, said Oppenheimer smoothly. —I'm sure Larry will take care of it. From what I understand his father is one of the richest men in the world. Larry is his only son so his funds are virtually unlimited. The trust fund alone is worth hundreds of millions. And he told me he's never known what to do with all that money, other than buy marijuana and go surfing. Now he feels as though he has a mission, for the first time in his life. How did he put it? He wants to be a *warrior for peace.*

—That's nice, said Ben. —Catchy, yet stupid.

—So when it comes to money, don't worry, Annie.

—Larry can help them much more than we ever could, said Ben to Ann, trying to be comforting.

❧ Ann smiled at Ben as the plane began to taxi, thinking it was the first time Oppenheimer had called her Annie. It was the first time anyone had called her that since she was very young.

As they leveled after the steady climb she watched Oppenheimer undo his seatbelt, struggle to cross his long legs in his seat and then give up and reach for his packaged headphones. He tore them out of their plastic, put them on his head and adjusted them to sit right. He played with the channel buttons on the arm of his seat and listened intently to each channel before he changed to the next. It was astounding how quickly he had adjusted, she thought, to modern commercial flight, to technology, to all the routines that were new to him. It was the same with Szilard. Only Fermi was slow, and the slowness was due to disinterest, she thought.

We can adapt to anything, she thought looking out the window, *homo sapiens.*

At first the trait seemed praiseworthy, evidence of a lively and supple intelligence.

But then a long shadow was cast across the wing and she remembered the crowds in Tokyo, the infinite crowds spread across the concrete and the streets bare of trees.

❧ One of the walls of the Peace Museum at Hiroshima is covered in letters, carefully typed on official stationery. The letters are arranged neatly in chronological sequence. Each letter was written by a mayor of Hiroshima, each successive mayor in his time, on a long series of dates after World War Two.

They are not form letters. Each is carefully written from scratch, in English. Some are addressed to a president, others to a prime minister or a premier, and all are written on the day of a nuclear test.

Each letter, one after another down through the years, makes its request politely. "Dear Sir: Please be kind enough to cease building nuclear weapons, for the good of all nations of peace."

❧ To feel sympathy for people outside ourselves we need to know each soul can be alone, thought Oppenheimer. We need to be sure that each body can feel the separation of itself from other bodies, to know desire lives there, in every one separately. We have to feel how longing surges from the hearts of others.

More than that, without longing the other is not a self, and beyond longing, even, it is the pain of others that is the source of our sympathy. A being that does not know pain cannot be the object of pity, and so a being that does not suffer also does not receive our love.

There is nothing to fasten to there, in who does not feel pain.

III

THE DEAD MAINTAIN
THEIR GOOD LOOKS

1

❧ We were not made to fly, thought Ann like many fearful passengers before and after her, but here we are aloft.

It was precarious. When she flew she was on the edge of air, between air and nothing.

They were moving steadily at thirty-seven thousand feet above a thin layer of cloud that gaped open over the Sierra Nevada and then dispersed into clarity. Colors showed beneath.

She stared down at the colors with her forehead against the cool windowpane, looking out over the clean white wing. She saw the Grand Canyon yawning purple and gray and brown and then the dust-red nation of the Navajo. The lines of its orange cliffs spread like floods of sand beneath them and towering stone monuments cast dark, blunt shadows. The government had given the Navajo a very large piece of barren land, thinking this a clever swindle; and the dry soil would never make them rich, that much was true. But the land was so beautiful the joke was on the government.

When the plane began its descent into her own high desert, gentle brown mountains in the distance with their dark green skirts of pine, Ann felt homesick. Only from here could she know her own country best, far above with no way to touch it.

❧ Larry had booked the scientists a lavish suite at La Posada, the establishment Oppenheimer preferred.

—Let me take the burden off you, OK? Money is no object, like the man said. I couldn't spend it all if I had six lifetimes. I'm serious. I mean you have already been *so great* to these guys.

They were in a flight lounge in Albuquerque, she and Ben walking fast with Larry beside them as the others trailed behind. She was moving out of relevance, she thought, away from the center. There was nothing to object to, because of *course* they would stay in a hotel. It was better for them. No one would turn down that offer.

—So you just feel free to take a break from playing hostess, OK?

She nodded and felt them slipping out of her hands, leaving in her a defeated, flat calm.

Larry leaned closer as they walked and whispered, in an understanding tone, —I know it's been hard on you. Robert told me you guys have been a little strapped for cash recently. No worries, he told me in confidence.

Oppenheimer discussed her finances with Larry, Larry with his Tall Grays at Roswell, his autopsies and abductions and extraterrestrial squid swimming ceaselessly in the orbit of Jupiter.

—I mean I'd be happy to reimburse you for everything you've spent on them. I'm serious.

—Larry's our sugar daddy, said Ben to Ann.

—Oh, no, said Ann. —Thank you, but—

—Are you kidding? It was our entire savings. We say yes, said Ben. —Reimburse us. Feel free! It's been at least ten thousand.

—No problem, man, said Larry. —I'll get the accountant to cut you a check. You need something, you just come to Larry.

—So you're staying at the La Posada too? asked Ann quickly to cover her embarrassment.

—Nah, Oppie wanted his space. We got rooms at La Fonda.

—Lar! called Tamika from behind them. —They're boarding!

—I gotta go, said Larry. —You're driving from here, right? We're flying. Oppie and Szilard too.

—Oh, said Ann.

He patted her on the shoulder. —You can see them whenever you want, right? It's all good.

Then he went to rejoin Tamika and the rest of his group, who were milling around a water fountain between the rest room doors. Szilard was holding forth to Leslie, who listened to him nodding slightly but constantly, as though her head was bouncing on a rubber stalk. Straightening up from the water fountain, wiping stray water off his chin, Oppenheimer waved at her jauntily and tipped his hat.

❧ Fermi had declined Larry's invitation to stay in the hotel room with the other scientists. He did not wish to be indebted to Larry and his friends, who he claimed reminded him of gypsies, as he insisted they had been called in his day. They were insufficiently washed, it was possible they would steal, and they had loose ways of living.

He would be just fine where he was, as stationary as possible. He was looking forward to working in the garden again.

—I hope it's not an inconvenience? he said to Ben, leaning up from the backseat to put his head between them. —If it is, I can go with them of course. But I wish to stay with you for a little longer if it is not a problem. I will be happy to work in return for my room and board. I am not lazy.

—We know you're not, Enrico.

—I just don't want to be around all those people all the time. They make me nervous.

—Of course you can stay with us, said Ann. —It's what we were planning. Right, honey?

—Right, said Ben.

There was no edge to it, and she realized he was fond of Fermi. When it came to Fermi he still did not believe, but he also did not suspect.

❧ It was soon after the end of the Second World War that the American government began exploding atom bombs in the air. Now that the bomb existed it had to be improved and refined.

When the Soviet Union made its own bomb, a little later, it too would begin exploding the bombs in the air. Both countries would reach thermonuclear fingers into the most remote and unsullied parts of the globe. They would look for places where they could explode their gadgets without obvious and immediate fatalities and quietly measure the gadgets' effectiveness. These tended to be places where only poor people lived, sparsely distributed and ill educated, unable or disinclined to speak up in their own defense. Even if there was an outcry in such far-flung places, it would likely go unheard. And even if by some fluke it was heard, it would not be heeded.

Such places could be found both far away and close to home.

∾ With her cheek and eyelid against the cool pillowcase of her own bed she felt she could rest the true rest, which she could never find anywhere but at home.

∾ Ben talked to no one and was glad. Behind him a fire burned in the fireplace despite the warmth of the evening and Larry's friends lounged beside the hearth, some of them sitting around the large, deep wood table, others standing up with their drinks, clustered near Szilard. In the warm flickering light he was almost content. It was probably the wine.

He liked the curve of the goblet against his fingers. Since the arrival of the scientists he rarely felt the fullness of life, rarely ended the day as he used to in a globe of comfort. The closest he came anymore was alcohol and Larry's pot.

He should probably be worried.

Beside him Fermi was trying hard to avoid conversation, affecting a shyness that bordered on the rude. He stood behind Ben's right elbow, his head down, listening and saying nothing.

Outside Leslie and Clint stood on the sidewalk with Oppenheimer, talking to him eagerly as he smoked. Their conversation was inaudible but Ben suspected they were boring him. His expression was disinterested and his head moved in slight, bobbing nods, chickenlike, between cigarette puffs.

Near Ben, a tray of appetizers passed and was grabbed at by a tall, clean-cut Gomer with a braying laugh who looked to be straight out of college.

—This is Ted, said Szilard. —He's going to be suing the Department of Defense for me. Suit gets filed tomorrow.

—Pleased to meetcha! said Ted, and grabbed eagerly for Ben's hand.

—I'm Larry, said Larry, skirting the table and clapping Ted on the shoulder. —The guy who pays the bills around here. Sometimes anyway!

They brayed together, ha ha ha. Ben thought *families that bray together* and sipped his wine to hide his face. He was humiliated by the pun.

—So what's the outlook, hombre? Are we gonna beat the pants off the Feds?

—Ha-ha-ha.

—Larry! called the Belgian food activist from across the table in what sounded to Ben like a caricature of a French accent. That was typical of French accents: they always sounded like caricatures of French accents. —How we know where the vegetables here on the menu is come from? Maybe they modified! Everything in this country GM or GE!

—Get the chef for us, would you please? said Larry to a flustered passing waitress.

—I think we have a decent chance! said Ted, trying to get Larry's attention. —The problem is this whole War on Terrorism thing.

—But the records he wants are from World War Two! What, that's going to be classified still? interjected Ben.

—Just in general, they don't have to get to things like this right now, it's low priority, said Ted. —They got paperwork backlogs with FOIA requests already. And now the terrorist wars and all that.

—The wars are why we're doing this, Ted, said Szilard.

—Course Leo. I get it. Other thing is, they may not actually have the records anymore. Can't produce what they don't have. Even if they do, it's been twenty-one working days since he put in the request, they don't return his phone calls, but that doesn't mean they can't give him a No Records response or claim national security.

—They can claim national security even if all they're doing is looking in some naked chick's window, said Larry.

—Ha-ha-ha, brayed Ted.

—They have the records, said Szilard firmly, paying no attention. —Are you kidding? The Manhattan Project's historic.

—Do you have to take this antagonistic approach? asked Ben. —They have nothing to gain by guarding your precious fingerprints, do they?

—What a stupid question, said Szilard. —It's the Army.

—Leo? Don't be an asshole.

—Larry! Larry! yelled the Belgian food activist past the back of a sous-chef, who stood at the table talking to him. —It is terrible! I can't eat here! There is nothing for me! This so-called food is agribusiness byproduct!

—He ran out of the whole grains he brought with him, said Szilard.

Ann came out of the bathroom finally. She had washed her face and looked fresh, but her eyes were still tired. She stood next to Ben, leaned against his shoulder and fluttered a hand over to take a sip from his glass.

—Everybody! said Szilard, clapping his hands. —I've got press releases that have to go out in the morning about the lawsuit! Who's going to get on the phone and do media with me?

Hands raised around the table. Even over the babble of conversation Szilard was being heard. It struck Ben as surprising: they were listening to him. Szilard was actually being taken seriously.

—What's the count? One, two, three—eight of you. Great. OK, phone banking starting at nine a.m., said Szilard. —Copies of the press release will be in Larry's room along with a list of newspapers to call. There's a package of information for each of you, with a script for you to read from. I'll divide up the call list between the eight of you plus me. We're going national with this one so everyone's going to be making about forty, fifty calls.

—You've got to be kidding, said Ben under his breath. —You think newspapers are going to cover some wacko suit against the Army?

—We'll see, won't we, said Szilard smugly.

Ben noticed one of Szilard's shirt buttons was undone, just over the belt. It gave a view of poking flab.

He kept it to himself, gratified.

—Ann, said Oppenheimer, taking her arm gently as he came in from the front, the smell of nicotine wafting from his mouth as he spoke, —Can I talk to you briefly?

—Of course, said Ann, and as they moved away Ben saw their heads go together in confidence, and wondered what it was Oppenheimer had to say to his wife that he could not say in front of him.

—What can I eat? asked the Belgian food activist angrily, in Larry's general direction. —What do they have for those people who do not wish to eat a grotesque mutation?

—I wish he would shut up, said Frank the rugby player.

—I will tell you! One single chili!

❧ On the back patio there was an artificial waterfall on a rock wall and house-shaped birdfeeders hanging from aspens and mesquites. Candles in paper bags glowed on the ledges of low adobe walls.

—I just want you to know, said Oppenheimer to Ann as they walked out onto the stones, —that much as I appreciate everything Larry has done for us, I—

He hesitated, and she looked up at him.

—I consider you my dear friend.

She stood without moving. Her eyes were filling. She was embarrassed.

—Thank you, she said finally, and kept staring down at the ground at their two pairs of feet on the flagstones, his in leather shoes, hers in sandals. She thought how exposed her toes were, yielding and tender. Toes were naked things.

—I mean it, he said quietly. —I'm grateful to Larry. He's been exceptionally generous.

—I know, she said, shaking her head.

—But from you I had something more important. I still do.

—Thanks, she said again, trying to hold the shake in her voice.

—You were kind to me when I had nothing. I won't forget it.

—I'm just—, she said, and stopped. —I'm afraid of being left out.

—You can go with us wherever we go, said Oppenheimer. —I promise. As long as you want to.

Stiffly, almost formally, he leaned toward her and put his long, thin arms around her, formal but protective. It was an awkward embrace, and she thought a firm hold would alarm him so she let her arms rest lightly.

Even when he tried to be close Oppenheimer stayed distant. He was always himself bracketed, at least one step away. But still he had consoled her.

❧ Ben was sitting at the breakfast table before work, his plate dirty and coffee mug emptied, about to fold the newspaper closed when he saw it, buried at the bottom of the sixth page. He jerked back in his chair, startled.

Ann was sitting across from him and a few feet away stood Fermi at the counter, pouring tea.

—I can't believe this! he said. —*Scientists Sue Defense Department!* They ran Szilard's story.

—Read it to me, said Ann.

—Yes please, read it, said Fermi anxiously, walking over in his sock feet with teacup raised.

—*A consortium of nuclear physicists has filed suit against the Department of Defense, the Department of Energy, and the Los Alamos National Laboratory,* read Ben.

—Does it say our names? asked Fermi nervously. —Oppenheimer's, Szilard's and mine?

—I don't think so, said Ben, scanning. —*Along with the Coalition for Global Disarmament, a student organization at the University of New Mexico, the scientists, including John Ramager and Rajiv Sarathy*—who the hell are they?

—Szilard convinced them to be on the suit, said Ann.

—. . . *have alleged that the Department of Defense is withholding both personal and medical records they requested under the Freedom of Information Act. The scientists say they're entitled to the documents, which they claim contain information they need for medical care. Says Sarathy, a research fellow at UNM, "This is also information that may prove the eligibility of some of the people we represent for federal funds under the Radiation Exposure Compensation Act. It's an underused law that lets victims of nuclear research and testing programs conducted between the 1940s and 1960s—"*

—Let me read it, OK? asked Ann, and he held out the paper to her. —*"This is a classic case of the Department of Defense violating the law to avoid transparency," said Ramager, an associate professor of physics. "There's nothing in these papers that poses a risk to national security. These are personal medical records we're talking about. This is a perfect example of the Army showing it doesn't have to abide by the law, that it's not responsible to the average American citizen."*

—Yeah. Szilard's John Q. Public.

—His name isn't here anywhere.

—Good, he's invisible, said Ben. —Just the way I like him.

—They're leaving on a trip, said Fermi. —I talked to them this morning. They called when you were in the shower. Did you know?

—Another trip? Already?

—Where to? asked Ann.

—Somewhere out past Hawaii, said Fermi.

Ben looked at Ann over the newspaper and saw her face fall, surprised by disappointment. He reached out to touch her wrist, against the edge of the table.

—Damn it, he said. —He promised he would keep you in the loop, didn't he?

—You can go if you want, said Fermi to Ann. —Robert told me to tell you. They're leaving tonight.

—I see, said Ann slowly.

❧ The two-piece swimsuit known as the bikini is named after Bikini Atoll, destroyed by a bomb in a televised test. The garment was christened by a French designer, who put his product on the market soon after the first atomic tests in 1946.

The Bikini natives, who were relocated from their coral reef home while the U.S. prepared to blow up the island with Shots Able and Baker, lived out their lives on a string of other nearby islands. They were shuttled between them over the decades that followed, from island to island, avoiding the bombs.

After the first series of tests, the leader of the Islanders, known to Americans as King Juda, was told by U.S. representatives: "You have made a true contribution to the progress of mankind."

❧ When she called Oppenheimer she got Szilard.

—I wish you'd given us some warning, she told him.

—We just decided yesterday. Larry and Tamika were already going there to see giant clams. *Tridacna gigas.* Four feet long. They're an endangered species, ask Fermi.

—You're going to see clams?

—Of course not. They are. I will be busy. I have no time for mollusks.

—When are you coming back?

—We're not flying into Santa Fe. We have an appointment at the Nevada Test Site first. Oppie wants to see the craters. Wait, here he is.

—Ann? said Oppenheimer, getting on the phone. —You're not going to come with us?

—To the Pacific Islands? I don't *think* so, she said stiffly. —I'm tired of long flights. I wish you could have waited.

—I apologize for the scheduling, said Oppenheimer after a pause.

—Will you call me at least? Keep me up to date?

—Of course I will, said Oppenheimer heartily.

She nodded tightly to herself, saying nothing. He spoke into the silence.

—Come to Nevada at least. Meet us there. Won't you? You can drive. It won't be expensive. And if you want to fly I'm sure Larry will foot the bill.

With money everything was possible, she thought. There were no bounds to life except for the end of it.

—I'll think about it.

꒰ The atolls of the Marshall Islands, which had once been a paradise for the small number of natives who lived on them, fishing and swimming in the turquoise shallows, diving among coral, eating breadfruit, coconut and crab, were thus re-christened by the American military. The new name was "Pacific Proving Grounds."

Here numerous test series were carried out. Shot Mike, with a yield equivalent to ten million tons of TNT, or ten megatons, was detonated two days before the presidential election, on Halloween day in 1952. The Mike device itself, and the housing that contained it, weighed sixty-five tons.

It vaporized the island of Elugelab.

In 1954 Shot Bravo, with a yield of fifteen megatons—about a thousand times the destructive force of Little Boy—spread lethal radiation over seven thousand square miles of the Pacific Ocean. Fully one-hundred and twenty miles away from Ground Zero, on an atoll called Rongelap, radiation was so intense that the people there doubled over to vomit.

Later, when burns were rising on their skin, the Atomic Energy Commission announced breezily to the press that "All were reported well."

❧ —I thought we were trying, said Ben a couple of nights later.
—We are, said Ann.

She was turned away from him on her side, reading an article about the Marshall Islands testing program. Several of the bomb tests had sunk old warships, incinerating pigs and rabbits that had been placed on the decks in cages.

Reading was a distraction from worry. It had been nagging at her that she was missing what was essential, that her exhaustion was an excuse, a capitulation to life as usual, flat and dry with all the new suspense relinquished.

She had to be there herself, she thought, she had to be among them, near what was happening. But it was too late now: she had missed it. She had actually said *no.* And there was no way of reaching them when they got there: they had not left an itinerary or the name of a hotel. Szilard's new cell phone, bought for him by Larry, would not receive thousands of miles into the Pacific Ocean, would not ring in Micronesia, among the palm fronds and coral reefs in the middle of seemingly infinite water, when she dialed the number.

They were the ones standing on piles of sand in the middle of the world's vastest ocean but it was she who felt the panic of isolation.

—I mean trying the usual way, said Ben, and rested his hand

on her hip where it jutted up, covered in sheet. —Not by praying for an immaculate conception.

—I'm not even close to ovulating, she said, and read *perforating the reef with gigantic blast craters.*

❧ Are you even there anymore? Ben was thinking, but refused to turn away from her and give up. This was the sole job of the male of many species, he told himself wryly: disseminate his semen often and broadly. The biological imperative broadly he had forsworn for the social imperative narrowly.

But he knew he was cheating. Jocular humor would save the day but not the marriage.

She resists, but single-mindedly I go forward. It is not that she has forgotten me.

❧ Of course, she thought in resignation, give in. It was kinder, it was easier and it would be fine by the end.

She let the pages slide to the floor and turned. Strokes of the limbs, the usual bent head, the ministering, and she felt tended and passive as a plant, and then guilty for the passivity. Trying to infuse herself with momentum and will she moved, smiled, bent down herself in an awkward spiral of repositioning arms and legs. She would not neglect him, she would not be disappointing, since what if this was all there was, and after this there was no more of either of them?

She knew it with her stomach suddenly, a weight of guilt and certainty caving her in. In the past months, with herself in other things, she had left him behind and forlorn in a corner. She had betrayed him gradually, not all at once like infidelity but here and then, more and more. Now, left out and discarded herself, she was getting a taste of her own medicine.

She felt it with a twinge, how mean it was. Nothing was as lonely as abandoning.

—I'm sorry, she whispered, and he looked down at her face and he knew what she meant, she could tell. But it was too sad to dwell on; it was not conducive. So she applied herself as though for a job. Usually it was not like this between them but now she felt it was necessary because she had too much to atone for to seem half-hearted. For once in recent memory she wanted to have *given, furnished,* even *satisfied,* as though she was being paid. Adequate was inadequate; she wanted him to go to sleep without doubt, if that was still possible. He should feel safe again.

Even if, she realized as she set herself to the task, expression everywhere welling out of her, body stirring and full of gesture, he was *not safe,* even if he was not he should be unaware, for who was safe now, ever? Who was perfectly safe forever?

❧ Scientists at the Atomic Energy Commission took advantage of the testing in the Marshall Islands to study the effects of radiation on people.

In 1956, at an AEC meeting, one official admitted that Ronge-lap was the most contaminated place on earth. He said of the Marshall Islanders, reportedly without irony, "While it is true that these people do not live, I would say, the way Westerners do—*civilized* people—it is nevertheless true that they are more like us than mice."

❧ Sad, he thought, sad, collapsing himself into concave places and rounding himself over convex ones, fawning on the surfaces. Sad, without knowing why he was thinking it.

❧ It was her desperation to be in the fray that had led her to leave her husband behind, forgetting him while he was in plain sight. She was ashamed but could not help herself even now. She was pulled by a desire to be central to them, to Oppenheimer and Szilard and even Fermi, that solid, self-effacing Republican. The strength of her desire made her worry even when she was covered by her husband's body. It made her strain toward the tropics far to the west, float dreamily in the white-and-blue elsewhere, the sand and the islands, because that was where they were, the others. And she was not. She only here, and it was not enough.

What was *crucial for her to see* could be happening right now, all because she was here, lamely here.

She was not proud of her desperation but that did not change it. It was the child in her, not the innocent child but the one that screamed for attention, face a fat red fury.

She forced herself to let the anxieties subside, press them down. Just for a short time: the end was in sight. In the meantime he knew her well enough to feel her distraction if she felt it, he would know she was going through the motions. She had to absorb herself in the skin, the arms and the legs, push and pull, the movement, drive the rest all away.

❧ It was almost right, it was almost the same, he thought, but finally it was not the same. Something was wrong with it. He tried to forget the feeling, this unfamiliar difference, he tried to reject it, and going away from it, thinking of other times, he was able to come.

❧ At 4 a.m. a week after the scientists had left, the telephone rang. She leaned over Ben, who was waking up in irritation, to pick up the receiver.

She heard static, and brief surges of voice.

—Robert? Is that you? she asked after a few seconds, and Ben sat up and turned the nightstand light on beside her.

—. . . tried to . . . ould be . . . ocked . . . appened—

—I can't hear you, you're breaking up, she said loudly, deliberately. —Can you call me back? Or give me your number?

—. . . ropical—orm . . . arning . . .

—I can't hear you, she repeated. —Robert? You need to call me back, OK?

There was only static.

She hung up reluctantly.

A minute later Ben had just settled back into his pillows when the telephone rang again.

—Where are you? she asked when she picked up. —Why don't you give me your number? I'll call back.

—We're on Majuro, said Oppenheimer. —It's near—

—Just the number, she said. —Before we get interference again.

—There's a storm coming in. We haven't been—

—Robert, give me the number first.

—I think you dial—Leo! Is it 011?

—Just the local number, she said. —I can track down the rest.

—8—4 . . . .sk for—bin number—

—I can't hear you! The static's back! Robert?

—. . . yphoon—lanes fly—n or out. There may be . . . lay—

—Try me again when the storm's passed, will you?

—ant . . . ou—

—Try me in the morning, I can't understand you, she said, enunciating clearly, and hung up for the second time. —They're on an island called Majuro now, she told Ben. —Szilard told me about it when I picked them up for the airport. I think it's near Kwajalein. Where the government still tests ICBMs.

—So how's the surfing, he said groggily, and flicked the lamp off again.

❧ Oppenheimer was interested in the islands from an anthropological standpoint, but Szilard was not. He had no time for anything that might distract from the mission.

While Oppenheimer enjoyed a cocktail on a hotel balcony, overlooking the shimmering ocean, Szilard was often downstairs in the hotel office, huddled over a fax machine. While Oppenheimer heard about the history of violence in the islands, the traders and whalers who had come there in the nineteenth century and the massacres that had occurred in retaliation for the kidnapping of island women, how first the Germans and then the Japanese colonized the islands, exporting coconut and copra, Szilard was scheduling a series of conference calls with New York.

❧ In 1956, to make up for the disruption of their lives and the radioactivity of their ancestral seat, the U.S. gave Bikini and Enewetak Islanders the kingly sum of twenty-five thousand dollars.

Curiously, the money was handed over in one-dollar bills.

Congress set up trust funds in larger amounts later on to compensate the natives, making *ex gratia*—that is, *admitting no guilt*—payments for high radiation exposures.

In the 1980s, a class-action lawsuit by the Bikini Islanders would be dismissed, but at the same time the U.S. government would quietly set up a seventy-five-million-dollar trust fund for them. In 2001, a body called the Nuclear Claims Tribunal would award the Marshall Islanders five hundred and sixty-three million, but lack any funds to pay out on the judgment.

In the meantime, from the 1940s to the 1950s the U.S. would conduct sixty-seven aboveground nuclear tests in the Marshall Islands—the largest explosions the world had ever seen.

❧ Fermi had planted squash, chili, tomatoes, peas, and various lettuces. In the morning after Ben left for work he was watering these with a watering can, bending over each plant to inspect the undersides of the leaves, when Ann shuffled out onto the patio with her coffee. She had barely slept.

He looked like someone's country uncle, she thought, a humble and stooped old man tending his garden.

—Hey, she said, —Robert called last night.

—Yes?

—We're supposed to meet them in Las Vegas in a week, right?

—You have the information, said Fermi. —I don't.

—But I'm worried there's something wrong. The call didn't work. There was too much static.

—I'm sure they're fine, said Fermi, and went on watering. —And if they're dead, good for them.

It was not what she wanted to hear. She swallowed her tepid coffee and went inside again.

On the Internet she searched for Marshall Islands, weather, and watched as a satellite picture loaded: the eye of a storm. *Upgraded to hurricane warning.*

∽ —How's your little wife doing? asked Lynn, coming up behind him while he was burying a light fixture.

—Little?

He waited for her to rephrase. It took a long time.

—You know, uh, she's so delicate!

—She's fine, thank you.

—I went to the library the other day for a book-on-tape, you know? To drive to Taos for my weekly regression. I just thought I'd say hi to her? But the guy at the desk told me she doesn't work there anymore.

—No, said Ben. —She's taking some time off.

—Probably traumatized. I mean that schizo shot himself right in front of her, right? I heard there was actually *brain matter* on the bookshelf. The crime scene unit missed it or whatever and a TV camera caught it? And they even aired it before they noticed. So people actually ended up seeing a shot of the dead guy's actual brain.

—Really.

—A friend of mine plays softball with one of the cops that was there. He said it looked kind of like wet oatmeal. And it was stuck on a copy of *Moby Dick*. I mean why did he do it at the library? That is so selfish. To blow your head open right in front of someone.

—He had some problems, said Ben evenly, projecting what he hoped was polite neutrality.

—This friend of mine in New York was married to a bipolar guy once? He used to have delusions and think parts of her body were planning to attack him. Like just a single finger or her elbow? And one time a breast. The left one. She'd just gotten implants.

—Uh huh?

—Finally he attacked her savagely with a pair of scissors.

—Huh, murmured Ben.

—But they were nose hair scissors.

—Nose hair—?

—So they weren't sharp on the end. They were curved, you know? So they didn't hurt her.

He smiled into his chin, face hidden from her as he tightened a screw.

—I can give you the name of my therapist if she wants to see him, she went on. —He's amazing. He's an MD from Harvard? But he also does past-life regressions.

—You've been regressed? asked Ben, raising an eyebrow as he grabbed a second fixture and sank it. —I never would have guessed.

—When we lived back East I *never* would have done something like that, said Lynn. —It was just work work work in those days. But now I try to know myself a little better. Metaphysics has really helped me.

—Does Roger do past-life regressions too?

—Are you kidding? He won't even see an analyst. He wouldn't even see a therapist back when we lived in Tribeca. His idea of therapy is slamming a ball against a wall until he's bored into a stupor and then throwing back a stiff drink. Or six.

—He swears by his squash, said Ben, wishing she would leave so that he could dig his holes in peace.

—He gets back tomorrow, said Lynn wistfully.

—Well, said Ben, rising, —it looks like we're almost done here. Another few days. Are you happy with it?

—Actually I was going to talk to you and Yoshi about that, said Lynn, and lifted a foot to inspect the bottom of her shoe, upon which she found a thumbtack. —Oh my God! Do you see this? It almost went right into my foot! I could have caught tetanus!

—Close call.

—Which reminds me! Did you get that mouse shit cleaned up? In the shed? Because someone could catch the Hanta virus! And like sue us.

—Yes, I did. You were saying about the design of the garden?

—There's this one part of the yard where I have a completely new vision.

—Oh, said Ben, and nodded.

—Here it is, said Lynn. —Can we get a big rock?

—A rock?

—Like, a boulder.

—How big?

—I don't know, maybe about as tall as you are?

—You'll need to talk to Yoshi.

—It's not *your* fault, said Lynn. —I've been reading this book? And I think how it is now isn't good feng shui. I mean Yoshi should have known. He's Japanese, isn't he?

❧ Later he was sitting in the foyer putting on his street shoes when Lynn, passing him on her way upstairs, trailed her fingers suggestively along his upper arm.

He did not like her, he did not find her attractive, in fact he found her unattractive, in fact he disliked her actively, truth be told. At the same time he felt faintly reassured, almost pleased. He saw her for a second as a type moving past at high speed, fake and bronze and pampered, but a type that wanted him.

When he registered this he disgusted himself.

❧ She could find no specific bulletins on the passage of the hurricane through the Marshall Islands, but once it was gone the weather in the islands returned to sunshine.

Sometimes it all seemed subdued to her, feeling. She watched television news and read a lot while Oppenheimer and Szilard were away, and it was clear to her once or twice that what was missing was vast, what was missing from public life was anguish. None of it was expressed.

If there were only something that rose out of crowds, more than a compulsion, more than a roar, if people would only cry or something, she thought lying in bed with cramps one day while Ben was at work, the television in front of her playing *Oprah* with the mute button on. If they could even speak honestly, forget the sentiment, about anything more grandiose than themselves; if they could be brought together for some purpose beyond sport or personal gain. There would have to be unity about it but no victims, not the fever of dominion but some will that went through time instead of trying to be a shield against it, some will that knew it stood for the passing and the small.

But then all unity and resolve seemed to come for vengeance: seizing and getting. For the cause of others it was weak and piddling, never massive, never a well-oiled machine. People only built big machines to speak up for the self.

❧ It was not until 1963 that Marshall Islanders exposed to Shot Bravo began to develop thyroid tumors.

❧ The night before she left for Las Vegas Ben told her she would have to go without him, —If, he said, —you're still insisting on going.

His clients were unwilling to let him leave again.

—Lynn has this feud going with Yoshi and I have to run interference, he said. —She feels she's an expert on feng shui. But will you be OK without me?

—I'll be OK, she said. —It's only a couple of days I'll be gone. I'll miss you.

—Will you? asked Ben, and she tried to put his doubt to rest.

Fermi did not want to go either.

—They didn't call, did they? he asked her.

—No, but the tour's already set up. If they don't make it, it could be months till they can get on another one. So I'm hoping they'll show. I called the people in the Alameda house, but they haven't heard either.

—I'll pass.

At first she was reluctant to go by herself but later, on the way down the long hill toward Albuquerque, she rolled down the car windows and the air whipped in.

2

❧ The storm had passed. Oppenheimer sat with Szilard at an open-air restaurant on a thin spit of beach, brown palm fronds and long mounds of dead seaweed littering the sand. He drank beer and poked at a slab of greasy fish with disinterest as Szilard pushed away his plate and complained about the service.

They had been there an hour with only the cook for company, waiting for a small plane to land on a nearby airstrip and pick them up, when a man in an officer's uniform appeared out of the straggly grove of palms beside the café, walked over to the building at a leisurely pace and sat down at the next table. He was tall and gray-haired, and if his insignia were authentic—and Oppenheimer had no reason to suspect otherwise—he was an Air Force Major General. Oppenheimer recognized the double star and the Air Force Cross.

He spoke softly.

—It would be a good idea for you to drop your lawsuit, Dr. Szilard.

It took Szilard only a few seconds to recover.

—Who are you? Are you one of the ones that questioned Enrico?

The major general raised a hand to the cook, hovering nearby in his smeared apron, and gave a curt nod. It was not clear to whom.

The cook bowed.

—Why do the armed forces care, asked Oppenheimer, —about our activities? Assuming the armed forces is who you represent.

—I'm afraid I did not come here to have a conversation, said the major general.

—What impact could our activities possibly have on the Air Force? asked Oppenheimer, and pointed at his empty beer bottle as the cook waited politely. —Another, please.

—It would be very embarrassing for you, said the major general, and smiled with an air of apology, —wouldn't it? If the prints didn't match.

—But they will, said Szilard. —They do.

—Really, said the major general, as the cook brought him a bottle of mineral water and broke the seal.

—If we're such a threat to you, said Szilard, —why haven't you already shut us up?

—You are still marginal, said the major general, and smiled again. —You have done nothing. We have time.

Oppenheimer looked at his face closely. He was a handsome man, with a straight nose and thick, arched eyebrows. A small scar, like a checkmark, bisected his earlobe. There was something of the patrician in his bearing.

But as he was gazing at the man's face he heard the sound of the Cessna approaching and looked up. It was bearing down from the east, a red and white plane emerging from a low bank of clouds over the rolling surf.

—Excuse me, said the major general, and slipped a worn bill smoothly onto the tabletop as he rose. Then he turned and smiled at them and waved a hand over the waves curling onto the beach. —Both of you have worked hard in your lives. Why don't you retire? The surf is lovely.

And he rounded the corner of the restaurant and vanished.

—He didn't even touch his water, said Szilard.

He reached for the bottle and drank.

❧ The Pacific Proving Grounds were selected as the preferred location for explosions so massive they could not be conducted on the American mainland due to the risk to life and property.

But for the many smaller tests that were desired, the U.S. military felt it needed a site closer to home—somewhere near enough to put troops and equipment cheaply, but far enough from human settlement that it would not attract undue negative attention.

For this purpose they selected the Nevada Test Site.

Chosen for its "remote" location in the desert, the test site is about sixty-five miles from the city of Las Vegas.

Before the worldwide ban on aboveground tests was imposed in 1963, one hundred and twenty-six aboveground tests were conducted in Nevada.

❧ They were slated to stay at the Luxor, which Ann had never seen. Oppenheimer had professed a fondness for things ancient-Egyptian, including hieroglyphs, mummies, and pyramids. It was with great interest, he had told her before he left for the Pacific Proving Grounds, that he had once, in days long past, perused *The Book of the Dead*.

The airport shuttle left her at a side entrance and she wandered along a sidewalk to the front, passing weeping willows and clean, plastic-looking palm trees. Over the main entrance a massive sphinx guarded the door, and stretching up behind the sphinx's haunches was the vast black pyramid of the hotel, its peak shooting a vertical white beam into the sky.

She walked past the taxi stands and twin black statues of what looked like dogs lying down. Anubis, she thought suddenly, remembering a book she had located for Mr. Hofstadt in the old days, when he still came into the library. *Jackal god. God of the deceased.*

In the cavernous lobby there were pools of blue water lit from beneath. She wished she could wade in them. Kneeling rams presided over the pools, and above the rams, on either side of the tall doorway that led to the casino, massive female-looking figures with jugs on their heads were standing guard.

When she walked through them she found herself facing a maze of slot machines.

—Do you have some guests staying here under the name Szilard?

—Can you spell that for me, please?

—S-Z-I—

—Nothing, I'm sorry. Is there another name it might be under?

—Oppenheimer? Or Larry. Uh, Pickering.

—I do have a reservation under Pickering. Those guests have not checked in yet.

—I'm the first in that party, said Ann, relieved.

—The credit card that was used for the reservation, please?

—Oh! I don't have it, it was a friend's.

—I'm afraid we can't let you into the suite until we have the credit card that was used to make the reservation, said the clerk. Ann gazed at his mouth as though it was a foreign object that had settled on his face. —Hotel policy.

Finally she rented a room of her own and took the elevator up. Signs referred to it as an "inclinator" because it traveled at a forty-degree angle up to the top of the pyramid. When she got out on the fifteenth floor she stumbled sideways.

❧ One of the soldiers who witnessed Shot Hood, a seventy-four kiloton test in Nevada in 1957, told a story at the hospital where he was taken for radiation sickness. After the test, he told his doctor, he had seen the burnt corpses not only of animals in cages but of men shackled to a chain link fence.

"I was happy, full of life before I saw that bomb," he told a photographer years afterward, "but then I understood evil and was never the same."

He had been a thin young boy from Utah. Later he grew fat and paranoid and claimed he had been held at a psychiatric facility where *they were doing something with the top of my head*. There they had told him to forget what he had seen.

He was clinically paranoid, but other troops had told the same story.

❧ Above the Pacific in a 747 Oppenheimer laid his head back on the headrest and waxed nostalgic. He daydreamed of the remote islands of the tropics.

He did not think fondly of the Marshalls, for they were sad ghettos created by the military and it had made his throat close to see what the people had endured and how, even still, his countrymen treated them like slaves. Also, the seas were rising as the planet's atmosphere warmed, according to his colleagues in the earth sciences; and the poor Marshall Islands, seven feet above sea level, were sure to be among the first submerged.

He thought of the Virgin Islands of his first life and then also Hawaii, where they had recently stopped. Islands with mountains: there a man could retreat, to look out on the sea. He remembered sailing in his twenty-eight-foot sloop the Trimethy, the first boat he ever owned, out around Fire Island in the roaring twenties. Lately he had begun to miss islands with a thirst he did not recall feeling before. He would find himself lost in thought and realize he wanted nothing more than to be back in his old beach house in St. John with Kitty and the children, the house that was now, he had read, empty and slowly collapsing, scoured with salt and nearer the waterline every year. He recalled the large, waxy-leafed bushes that shaded the porch, the steep incline of the hillside path down to the cottage where it was nestled in its bower of palms on the sand.

But if he left all this now, looking for that subtle peace in the scent of red-blooming flamboyant trees and trade winds, he would only get there and find himself alone. He had no one to share it with since all the people he had ever held dear had suddenly become dead.

Without them there was no refuge anywhere.

He was a man with no future, a man who might as well sit forever facing forward in this same airplane seat, hands on his sharp-boned knees as they were now, eyes glazed over, and outside his white metal capsule the neverending clear cold blue that was too thin to breathe.

⊷ By the time she had played a few hands of video poker and decided to go to bed, the scientists and their followers had still not arrived. Their tour of the test site was supposed to leave from an industrial park in North Las Vegas at seven in the morning.

The bed in her room was comfortable, hieroglyphs crawling all over it, the covers printed with them, the headboard engraved with them. But even in comfort willing herself to fall asleep failed, as all acts of will seemed to fail recently, despite the soothing influence of the cobras, storks, vultures, and dogs marching across polyester. She tried to suppress her irritation. It was how she spent her time these days: she suppressed herself. She waited on the lip of time, always anticipating a moment that never came, a change that never occurred, a surprise unveiling.

❧ In reference to the possibility of radiation from bomb tests hurting those who lived near the Nevada Test Site, one of the commissioners of the Atomic Energy Commission said to another in 1955: "People have got to learn to live with the facts of life. And part of the facts of life are fallout."

The same year, the public was invited into slot trenches to watch the Shot Apple-2 at a distance of two miles from Ground Zero. Shot Apple-2 was a twenty-nine-kiloton shot, larger than Little Boy.

A *New York Times* article called "Watching the Bombs Go Off" supplied a list of upcoming test dates to its readers, encouraging tourists to visit Nevada on the test dates to watch the splendid mushroom clouds rise from vantage points along the highways and in the nearby mountains.

Along with the series of test dates, the article provided the reassurance that *"there is virtually no danger from radioactive fallout."*

❧ —I like first class, said Szilard. —The food is better.

—Hey, Oppie. That longhair over there's been staring at you, said Larry, and pointed.

Oppenheimer turned and followed his finger. A hollow-cheeked man with a beard gazed at them from his seat in coach, eyes glassy.

—He looks like he really needs a shower, said Tamika.

—Oh, him. I met him when I was in line for the bathroom, said Szilard. —He's crazy. All he does is talk about God.

❧ She had paid for her meal and was headed outside to take the *Free Tram! To Excalibur!* when a disturbance in front of the long reception desk to her left caught her and spun her around.

—Call security! someone yelled.

In relief she recognized the voice: it was Larry.

At the very long desk, the clerk raised the phone to his ear and she saw all of them there, Szilard and Larry leaning over the counter, demanding, a pile of suitcases on carts behind them, some of the others standing watching Oppenheimer in the background, Oppenheimer who was backing up, cringing slightly with his hands raised in front of him as a weeping man knelt on the slick, shining floor at his feet.

❧ He had heard the phone ring and known it had to be her but resisted getting up. Their bedroom window was open and he could hear Fermi walking past, out into the garden, the soft soles of his shoes on the stones. The wind chimes moved in the morning breeze and early light dappled the wall, a pattern of shadow leaves dipping and fluttering.

Nothing was like the light dance of leaves.

He would just give her time, he thought, and wait for relief. Time returned things to themselves.

It was good to lie watching the silhouettes of thin branches shivering, good to breathe the moist air the breeze carried in through the window, filling the curtains.

He moved a hand under the blanket.

—Leo! What's going on? she asked as she came up behind them.

Szilard was wearing a tropical shirt with palm trees on it. It made her uncomfortable.

—A religious fanatic, he said.

Larry was bent down in front of Oppenheimer trying to pull off the kneeling man. With one hand he patted the weeping man's back as though to console him, and with the other he tugged stubbornly at the man's stringy arm, which was grasping at Oppenheimer's Italian-leather-shod foot.

A Japanese family stood staring.

—Let me kiss it! cried the weeping man, but then hotel security converged, tanned well-dressed men with thick faces.

—He's crazy! said Szilard.

—Wait. He's not *violent*, cried Oppenheimer, as the security men hauled the weeping man off him by the back of his shirt. —Don't hurt him! Be careful!

—What *is* this? asked Ann, but none of them noticed her. Oppenheimer's nose was sunburnt, his cheeks tanned.

—Why don't you come with us, sir, said one of the security guards to Oppenheimer as the others hustled away the weeping man. —We'll sit you down and get you a glass of water.

—He's been following us, said Szilard to Ann, and then turned. —We'll meet you in the room, OK Larry? Yours? I can take care of this.

And they followed as the guards walked Oppenheimer through a staff door.

Ann turned and looked behind them, at the weeping man twisting and kicking as they marched him outside.

෴ Children playing, thought Ben, lying in the bed with his right hand motionless. The wet fingers were irritating, but he did not want to get up to wash them. He was considering going back to sleep, but in the meantime he was thinking of the child they were failing to conceive; in particular he imagined the childhood this nonexistent infant would never have.

See Spot Run and a world of picket fences, a suburban dream world: that had been the world Oppenheimer and his colleagues had left to people in the fifties, to their *fellow Americans*. When Ben's parents were teenagers it was the world they grew up in, *See Spot Run,* civil defense, fallout shelters, Atomic Fire Ball candies you could buy at the corner store and pop in your mouth. School drills where they taught children how to get under the desks when the nuclear bombs began to fall. *Duck and cover.*

What is there so idyllic in that fifties vision, he thought, that pastel-colored propaganda of a simple life. It was a wishful return to Eden after the Fall.

He held in his mind the quaint picture of a tarry black road surface melting in the warm sun, the green grass, the mother in her cotton dress lying on a white hammock under broad weeping willows, teasing a foot through the dandelions, *watching the children play.* And while they laughed under the sky with its wispy white clouds she reached for a tall yellow glass and drank the cool lemonade.

But the memory was not his. Where he grew up there had been no hammock, no grass and no lemonade. The fences had been mesh festooned with razor wire and he had been content with that, wandering in the empty lots, among the piñon and juniper bushes fringing the trailer park outside Albuquerque, the dry arroyos and the pale sunsets over the dereliction. Still he had known no other place, so where did the gardens of weeping willow come from?

Suddenly it seemed to him that his memories were plucked from the air, mere impressions that rested on him.

Of course, he realized, of course. Nothing came from inside: you were born with no soul. The world gave it to you.

He sat up then, bolt upright in bed, instantly convinced. A soul was made of love, and love was made of time.

We are born without souls. The world gives them to us.

It is the world with its animals, its washed-out cold pink sunsets and dry arroyos, its lakes and rivers, rocks and swamps and forests, its moon, tides and seasons, he thought: it is the world that gives us such a soul as we have.

It gives us its life and we call it our own.

❧ —I want to make sure the other guards didn't hurt him, said Oppenheimer stubbornly, waving away a cup of water.

—He wasn't hurt, sir, said the security guard with the water. —I assure you.

—You should have let them call the police, said Szilard. —You could have pressed charges. *Now* how are we going to get rid of him?

—Who *was* he? asked Ann impatiently.

—Just some guy, said Szilard. —He was on the plane beside me coming back from Hawaii.

—He was an enlisted man once, said Oppenheimer.

—The Army kicked him out because he's mental, said Szilard. —He said they called it "excessive religiosity." The guy prayed all the time. Anyhow when I told him who Oppie was he fixated on him. He thought he was holy.

—I told him I was a Jew, said Oppenheimer to Ann, with a wry smile. —But he said so was Jesus.

—Nut job, said Szilard. —Wacked.

—He was clearly so devout that it interfered with the discharge of his duties, said Oppenheimer, and cocked his head. There was a wistful quality to him, Ann thought, as though he envied the man.

—I had an uncle like that, said the guard, nodding and popping the tab on his Coke. —He got fired for talking too much about Jesus. But he wasn't in the Army or anything. He worked at a Jiffy Lube.

❧ —I'll reschedule at the Test Site, said Szilard when they got to the suite. It had a jacuzzi underneath the slanted glass wall facing the skyline. —They'll fit us in.

—You can use your cell phone in the bathroom, said Larry, —if you want peace and quiet. There's reception there.

—Annie! said Tamika, coming out of the bathroom as Szilard went in, wearing a rainbow-striped bikini and tanned nut-brown. —You *so* should have gone with us! It was awesome.

—Leo and I found it disturbing, said Oppenheimer, who sat

cross-legged in armchair with an ashtray on his knee. —Larry. Coffee possibly?

—Coming right up, Oppie, said Larry, and picked up the phone.

—Chocolate croissants! called Szilard, sticking his head out the bathroom door and then retracting it.

—We got a tour of this giant clam breeding facility? said Tamika.

—First there was Kwajalein, said Oppenheimer to Ann. —We chartered a small plane and did a flyover. It's a large military compound with the natives for servants. The soldiers and their families live like kings and the Micronesians who clean their toilets live like beasts of the field. They have practically no medical services.

—The scuba was great though, said Tamika. —We have to be positive, right? Do you want to come to the pool with me, Annie? You can borrow a suit if you didn't bring one.

—Thank you, maybe later though.

With Tamika on her way out Oppenheimer said in a low voice to Ann, —The relentless *positivity*. It's exhausting, frankly.

—Lar? I'm gonna pick up the girls in their room and go for a dip, OK?

—And I did the best wreck diving of my life, said Larry, hanging up on room service. —I took pictures for these guys of the ships sunk off Bikini. By the bomb tests, right? There was the ship from the bombing of Pearl Harbor, right Oppie?

—She was called the Nagato. Commanded by Admiral Yamamoto.

—So I went into this aircraft carrier, the Saratoga? It was a shallow dive just to get there, the deck was like forty feet under or something, but then it's technical after that. Thing's bigger than the Titanic. Eight decks. We're talking major size. It was excellent. Plus there were sharks. Want to smoke out?

—No thanks, said Ann.

—They were circling pretty close, I'm telling you. I wished I had one of those cages you see in the movies. But you know, sharks are basically pussycats.

He began to roll a joint.

—It was strictly business for Leo and me, said Oppenheimer to Ann. —I gave a short speech to some of the islanders. Good people, very warm. Leo wanted to, as he put it, establish contact with them. He got me a speaking engagement at a church. The topic was world peace.

—You shoulda seen it, said Larry to Ann. —He rocked. He did. These people were digging him, I'm telling you.

—What was the point? asked Ann. —They live in the Marshall Islands! What use could they be to Szilard?

—We're an equal opportunity employer, said Szilard, bustling out of the bathroom with his cell phone in hand. —I've got some of them coming over. New recruits.

—Are you kidding? Coming over for what?

—For the campaign, said Szilard, —what else would I be doing?

—They ran the article in the *New Mexican,* said Ann.

—Of course they ran it, said Szilard. —We made fourteen papers nationwide. Including the *Dallas Morning News.*

—I was surprised myself, Oppenheimer told Ann. —Leo's always so confident.

—I've been on hold for forty minutes, said Szilard angrily to the cell phone. —This is unacceptable.

—Forty minutes? said Ann to Oppenheimer. —He just called them a few seconds ago!

He shook his head and ground out his cigarette. She noticed he had changed from Lucky Strikes to Dunhills under Larry's patronage.

—But worse, said Oppenheimer, as Szilard withdrew to the next room with his phone, —we were approached by a man in military dress who warned us to withdraw the lawsuit.

—You're kidding, said Ann, and felt her stomach turn.

—He implied they were willing to harm us if we didn't.

—Harm how? asked Ann, and when he raised an eyebrow she wrapped her arms around herself. The air-conditioning had turned arctic. —What are you going to do?

—We haven't decided. Would you like to take a walk? I wouldn't mind seeing Las Vegas again. When I was here last it was nothing like this. You can imagine. It was just a cowtown.

—You deserve a break, said Larry. —Let's go downstairs and play cards!

—I have to call Ben again, said Ann. —Excuse me.

There was a knock on the door and Larry rose to get it as she dialed.

—Wow! said Larry, and beamed at the room-service guy. —I thought you said forty minutes!

—Did we get the croissants? asked Szilard, re-entering from the balcony. His senses were finely attuned. He hovered over the room-service cart as it was rolled in. —What is this, a Danish? A *Danish*? But there's no chocolate on it! I ordered a chocolate croissant!

—Remain calm, Leo, said Oppenheimer.

❧ America has always been the world's leading designer, producer and tester of nuclear weapons, as it is the world's leading designer of guns. Since 1945, more than two thousand nuclear tests have been conducted worldwide, of which about a thousand were conducted by the U.S.

But the largest single thermonuclear explosion ever produced was a child of the Soviet Union.

This fifty-eight-megaton blast, in October 1961, was set off on the mountainous Arctic islands of Novaya Zemlya, inhabited by northern tribes since the Stone Age. It had about six thousand times the force of Little Boy.

The people living on the islands sustained themselves by fishing and hunting. There was also a large herd of reindeer.

❧ —It's me, said Ann, when Ben picked up the phone. —I wanted to let you know they got to the hotel. The crisis is over.

—Good, sweetheart. But listen. There's someone here who wants to talk to Szilard, said Ben. —He's had some problems reaching him. OK?

—Dr. Szilard? said Ted the lawyer, taking the receiver. —Ted here. I've been trying to reach you for days!

He waited briefly and then shrugged in Ben's direction, shaking his head.

—Anyway. We got a problem. So far the DOD's ignored us, right? Radio silence. But then right after you sent that one fax off to Livermore some spooks in suits came to my office looking for you. They flashed Army Intelligence badges but I think they were full of shit. They could be basically anyone. What? . . . Fort Huachuca, they said.

He waited while the receiver squawked.

—Anyway I told them you were out of the country. I'm pretty sure they've been doing surveillance on me. I think I lost them walking over here, they couldn't follow me in their car because I kinda weaved between houses and took some back streets, but these guys are on the hunt. I'm not kidding. These guys are scaring the shit out of me. I think you need to go underground, Leo. These people were insinuating you're a threat to national security. Next thing we know they'll call you a terrorist and lock you up at Guantanamo . . . what do you mean, you already know . . . ?

He waited a few seconds and then his face changed and he hit the wall with his palm.

—Next it's gonna be death threats. And you didn't bother to tell me this? I got two kids!

❧ —I'm tired of listening to Leo yell into the telephone, said Oppenheimer, and sighed heavily. —Excuse us, Larry. I'm taking this coffee with me. Ann and I are going for a walk.

They went down in the elevator and when she stepped out she

was dizzy, as usual. As they wove their way over the carpet and through the crowded labyrinth of the casino, past roulette wheels and card tables, she felt gratified he had chosen her company, chosen it to the exclusion of others. And realizing she was glad she felt like a child in a contest. Being alone with him was a privilege, though it shouldn't be and to think of it that way was in fact demeaning. She had to shake the conviction that she was in Oppenheimer's debt, because in fact if either of them was in debt it was he.

—King Tut's tomb! cried Oppenheimer. —Is it authentic?

—What do you think, she said.

He looked crestfallen.

—I still want to see it, he said.

In the end she was always the supplicant because she was the one who worried about the imbalance, seeking equality.

—This a replica of the Great Temple of Ramses the Second, said Oppenheimer, as they passed out of the casino into the lobby. —If I'm not mistaken.

—Are those jugs on their heads?

—Jugs? They are crowns!

They emerged onto the sidewalk and she was overwhelmed by the bulk of the commerce on the Strip, the massive casino buildings looming in all their cartoon splendor, shining exaggerations. But the heat oppressed and everywhere there were cars, and the smell of exhaust enveloped them. On the pavement they were surrounded by fat middle-aged people in bright clothing, clothing loudly patterned and stretched over broad stomachs and bulging haunches. In the sweltering heat of the low desert tourists sweated and headed doggedly for the indoors.

You were not supposed to be on foot in this place in summer, thought Ann. It was called a sidewalk but it was only a margin for cars.

—Are you willing to drop it? she asked. —I mean these people are serious.

Oppenheimer nodded.

—I mean they killed that poor cat, she went on dreamily, and remembered the feel of it in her lap, warm and limp.

—Leo thinks politics are pure science, said Oppenheimer, his rolling, flat-footed gait slowing as they pulled up short to wait for a light. A long white limousine skirted the curb and narrowly missed their toes. He raised his coffee cup and sipped, incongruous on the busy street.

—I think he believes everything can be calculated and managed, said Ann.

—He thinks all rational men will automatically agree with him when he confronts them with the facts. Leo's not postmodern. How could he be? He doesn't allow for legitimate differences of opinion. And he doesn't allow for brutality.

—But you're going to do what he wants anyway, she said. —Aren't you.

—Probably. What else is there?

—You could just *live,* she said idly, not knowing exactly what she meant. —Like the rest of us do.

—He wants me to build us a following.

—Why should that be your job?

—He says I'm better at public speaking than he is. I think he just doesn't want to do it himself . . . is this city a joke? It looks like a joke. Isn't that supposed to be a simulacrum of New York? Does New York City now have a giant roller coaster through it?

—Robert Oppenheimer!

The weeping man from the lobby was standing in front of them, feet planted wide on the sidewalk, waving his arms in the air.

—Let's turn back, she said swiftly, under her breath. —The only place you're protected is in the hotel.

—Back to the Nile valley, then, said Oppenheimer, and they swung around. —Let us part the waters.

—Robert Oppenheimer! called the weeping man again, with joy. —I ask nothing more than to walk behind you!

He was gaining on them, loping up to Oppenheimer on his other side.

—So I looked, and behold a pale horse!

—Oh no, said Oppenheimer again.

—And the name of him who sat on it was Death, and Hades followed him!

—Listen, said Oppenheimer, —you have me confused with someone else. I sympathize with your devotion to your faith. It's commendable. But I'm just a scientist. I think you—

—To him was given the key to the bottomless pit—

—If you'll just allow me to—

—and smoke arose out of the pit like the smoke of a great furnace!

—Please! Don't touch me.

—Don't touch him, echoed Ann, and made a motion in the air as though she was pushing the man away.

—But it's you! Don't you understand that? asked the man in a state of great agitation. —You're the one with the key! You unlocked the pit of Hades!

—It's certainly unfortunate.

—You need to just keep your hands to yourself, OK? said Ann, leaning over again to try to intercede. The man was scrabbling at Oppenheimer's arm.

—In those days men will seek Death and will not find it; they will desire to die, and Death will flee from them.

—It must be from the Bible, said Oppenheimer to Ann.

—No kidding.

—Revelation 9:6, said the man. He was wearing torn jeans and rope sandals and had a goatee and long brown hair. It was he who looked like Jesus, she realized, not Oppenheimer. —Listen to me,

Julius Robert! You may not know it yourself, you may refuse to admit it, but I have seen who you are! Why castest thou off my soul? Why hidest thou thy face from me?

—Please, go seek help, said Oppenheimer. —Would you do that for me?

As they pushed through the doors the Jesus man bowed down beside Anubis, touching his toes with his fingers.

—I will lift up my eyes to the hills.

❧ When they got back to the room Szilard was a flurry of activity. He shook a banana in the air as he argued with Larry, who was cringing in his armchair. Leslie sat on the couch, her elbows on her knees, her hands laced together and her chin on her hands, staring rapt.

—This is America. I will not be intimidated!

—But Leo, said Larry, —you could be in danger. And the lawyer dude sounded like he was scared shitless.

—So we'll hire bodyguards, said Szilard. —Come on, Larry! This is a *way of life* we're fighting for! It's freedom!

—Since when were you a demagogue, Leo, said Oppenheimer, amused, and bent over the room-service cart to pour himself a new cup of coffee.

—All I'm saying is if we can't speak freely we're no use.

Ann stepped out the room door onto the walkway and looked over the edge into the yawning chasm of the lobby, with its entire cityscape below, its movie theater, its shops and restaurants. The ceiling stretched high above her. She felt queasy, stepped back from the wall and retreated into the room.

—I wouldn't mind a few bodyguards, said Oppenheimer. —I could use a break from the gentleman downstairs, I confess.

—Lar! You won't believe this! squealed Tamika, bursting into the room with a hulking blond man behind her, so tall the upper half of his head was hidden by the door frame. —It's Big Glen!

—Big Glen! I can't believe it! cried Larry, and got up to run to the door. He was enfolded in a bear hug. —Where was it last time? Tijuana?

—I found him in the pool, said Tamika. —Can you believe it?

—Let's finish this in the other room, said Oppenheimer, —excuse us, and he and Szilard and Ann stepped away from the reunion and closed the door behind them.

Ann sat down on the bed wearily while the men stood by the window.

—We have a chain of events, Leo, said Oppenheimer, —that leads us to believe there are real threats to our health and welfare. And not only to Fermi's and yours and mine, Leo. Others could be hurt too.

—If we let ourselves be intimidated, said Szilard, —we're nothing.

—Let Larry hire security, said Ann. —And then keep doing what you're doing. Right, Robert?

Oppenheimer nodded slowly, staring out the window and sipping.

They sat in silence.

—All right, said Szilard finally.

—Hey guys, said Tamika, head in the door. —Wanna try out the jacuzzi?

They shook their heads and she was gone again.

—I used to swim in the ocean off St. John, mused Oppenheimer. —The water was so warm. There were seagrass beds like underwater prairies, and striped fish swimming in them. At the bottom you'd see these big brown rays with rippling wings, just gliding through the waving seaweed. You wanted to go with them. You wanted to be them.

—I forget to tell you! said Szilard. —Look what the courier brought!

He picked up a mailing tube, pulled out a poster and unrolled it: a red-and-black mushroom cloud looming ominously over a sepia-toned landscape.

—That'll really inspire them, Leo, said Oppenheimer.

—No, wait! It's three-D!

He turned the poster so that the light fell on it from a different angle, revealing his own face larger than life. Beside it was Oppenheimer's and then Fermi's, the three of them fading into perspective where the mushroom cloud had been.

—Oh my God, said Ann.

—It's outrageous, said Oppenheimer.

—Get outta here, said Szilard. —It's great. Are you kidding?

—Must have been expensive, huh? said Oppenheimer.

Szilard shrugged.

—This friend of Larry's designed it. See? It's three-D! And we've got more of them coming!

—What for? asked Oppenheimer, amused. —It's very creative, but why would we need more than one?

—We ordered ten thousand.

—*What?*

—We're going to be selling them.

—Leo. Are you crazy? Larry *bankrolled* this?

—It was his idea!

—How about the souvenir concert T-shirts, said Ann.

—They're coming, said Szilard earnestly.

—I'm speechless, said Oppenheimer.

—So you're going to be putting on shows? asked Ann.

—Speaking engagements. Press conferences. Demonstrations. We're also building a web site.

He rocked back on his heels and unfurled the poster in front of him once again, nodding at the depiction of his own face, which wore a benevolent expression. Behind his back Ann and Oppenheimer looked at each other and smiled.

❧ *We Are the World,* said Ben when she had a chance to call him unobserved. —Next he's going to start shooting videos for MTV. Scientists hugging each other and swaying in front of the mikes.

—And then a friend of Tamika's who's a bouncer from her stripper days showed up, and Larry hired him to head the private security team. He's supposedly nonviolent. He told me he refuses to *raise a hand in anger.* He's such a giant no one ever stands up to him. He's like seven-feet something.

—If I know Leo they'll need more security than that. I don't even work for the government, and *I* want to kill him.

—How's Fermi?

—He's coming to work with me tomorrow.

—Pardon?

—He's my new employee.

❧ There was a stretch limousine pulled up at the curb, and with Big Glen covering Oppenheimer they all surged out the hotel lobby and headed for the limousine's open door. —Lloyd George Federal Building! barked Szilard at the chauffeur as they pulled away from the curb.

—Whatcha gonna do there, man, drawled Clint.

—Recruiting, said Szilard.

Around the federal building there were police cars parked, and cops stood idly talking, arms crossed. On the hot cement hippies lay sprawled.

Ann stared out the limo's rolled-down window.

—It's a die-in, said Szilard.

—Excuse me? asked Oppenheimer.

—You know, like a sit-in? Except the protesters act dead.

—That's so cool! said Tamika, reaching for the door to the minibar.

—What's it for? asked Larry.

—It's an antinuclear protest! exclaimed Szilard. —What did you think? Just a minute. Wait here!

He grabbed a file folder and bounded out the door to run over to a man in a pink shirt and long beard, who lay near them on his back with his arms and legs spread. Szilard crouched over, talking to him.

—I didn't know they even *had* those protests anymore, said Clint. —I thought they went out with Ronald Reagan. But hey man, it's cool.

—It's so great, isn't it? said Leslie.

—They must be *roasting*, said Tamika. —I mean what is it, a hundred and five out there? Leslie. You want some of this Perrier?

Ann watched Szilard distribute fliers among the dead. When he had got rid of all of them he waved at the cops and headed back to the car.

—He's enthusiastic, isn't he, said Oppenheimer to Larry.

—The guy's a whirling dervish! said Clint, sitting behind Larry and Tamika far back in the cavern of the seats.

—He's very energetic, said Big Glen in his deep, ponderous voice, and nodded slowly.

—Why don't we invite the dead people out to dinner when they're done? asked Tamika. —I mean we're all in this together!

—Please, said Oppenheimer, —I'd like an intimate meal for once, if you don't mind. Just the fourteen of us.

❧ They played blackjack at five-dollar tables, calling back and forth to each other as they got drunk on cocktails, caught up in the momentum. Finally she quit when she was two hundred dollars ahead on Larry's dime.

Clint scoffed. —You got no ambition!

—I'm what they call risk-averse.

To her it was a modest but satisfying triumph. It would pay for her room for all three nights if Larry forgot to offer.

Oppenheimer stopped playing and was drinking and smoking at the bar, engrossed in a conversation about waves with Boogie the surfer. It involved the word *quantum*. Boogie had pushed his face up close, listening and nodding rapidly, and Oppenheimer was nursing a martini. She tried to catch his eye as she walked past but did not want to interrupt his disquisition, and anyway she was tired.

She felt more alone than usual in her room, having slunk away and left the crowd with the night still ahead of them. The floor vibrated and hummed beneath her and she found herself wishing they weren't going to the test site in the morning, that they were *never* going to the test site and that, in fact, Szilard would abandon his desperate quest for fame, or whatever it was. She wished the noise of his fruitless ambition would cease and they could all go somewhere else in the morning, somewhere silent, cleaner and more serene.

Or she could stay here. They all could. There was food, there were swimming pools, and in the theater were stage magicians with frosted hair wearing pancake makeup and smiling permanently.

Here she was, briefly alive, and into the long gray fall of time hopes were folding.

❧ He was not as desperate anymore: he had come to a tranquil stand, or felt as though he had. It might be temporary, but still it lightened his step.

We may be born with a predisposition to personality, he thought, but as for the rest, it is ours only because we touch it.

The world gives us our soul, he went thinking lately, and it opened him.

3

❧ Plutonium-239, the isotope best suited for nuclear weapons and most often used in them, has often been called "the deadliest substance known to man." Yet in the years since Trinity, underground nuclear tests have left more than eight thousand pounds of plutonium in the ground, while aboveground tests—with a total yield roughly equivalent to twenty-nine thousand Hiroshimas—have put at least nine thousand pounds into the atmosphere.

Scientists estimate that a single pound of the substance, if it were distributed directly and uniformly among all the people of the world, could induce lung cancer in everyone.

Glenn Seaborg, who discovered plutonium in 1940, later had six children with a woman named Helen.

❧ It was Fermi who first noticed the gray sedan parked down the street from the mansion. They were on their first break of the morning, drinking the strong coffee he had brewed and poured carefully into his small thermos.

—You know that car has been there three days in a row, he said to Ben, and nodded toward the road beyond the high wall as he sipped from the thermos lid.

—So? Isn't it the neighbors'?

—But there's always someone *in it.*

After that Ben found himself watching the long car often throughout the morning, walking with studied casualness across the mansion's flat roof to get a glimpse of it. He would kneel on the roof as though tying a shoelace or bend to fish a tool out of his five-gallon bucket, which he had set down near the edge. Once he climbed into a tall spruce and pretended to be pruning the cottonwood beside it.

Fermi was right: there was always a man in the driver's seat, his face indistinct behind the tinted windshield. The silhouette was visible and he seemed to sit without moving. Occasionally the tilt of his head changed slightly, or he lifted his hand to his head and Ben imagined he was talking into a telephone.

—You think he's one of the ones who threatened you or Oppenheimer? he asked Fermi finally.

—How should I know? asked Fermi, and shrugged.

Ben crept around the corner of the house where he could not be seen from the car and called Ted the lawyer on his cell.

—Are you still being followed?

—I'm not sure. I haven't seen them in a while, but I guess they might just be doing a better job of staying out of view.

—The guys who were following you, he said. —Do you remember what they were driving?

—You know, a car you don't really notice. American-made, of course, said Ted.

—Do me a favor, said Ben. —Would you drive by and take a look at a car that's parked here? I'm at work.

—Shit, said Ted. —I mean, if it *is* them I don't want to piss them off.

—Borrow someone else's car, said Ben. —Wear a disguise.

❧ From the informational materials of the Nevada Test Site: *Pregnant women are discouraged from participating in Test Site tours because of the long bus ride and uneven terrain.*

The bus that takes tourists to the test site, however, is merely a comfortable, air-conditioned chartered bus, equipped with a bathroom and compact video monitors for watching movies. Visitors may watch old propaganda reels, transferred to video, on the way to the Test Site, or they may watch something less educational, purely for their viewing pleasure. *When Harry Met Sally,* say, or *Saturday Night Fever.*

The ride to the Test Site, which is not unduly rough since it travels smoothly along the interstate at a high and steady rate of speed, lasts a little more than an hour each way.

❧ —OK, said Ted, calling back a while later. —I'm pretty sure it's them.

—Shit, said Ben.

—Is it them? asked Fermi, leaving his trencher behind and approaching.

—What can I do? asked Ben. —Call the cops? Is there a legal basis for that?

—You have nothing.

—Ben! called Lynn from the back door. —The crane's coming!

—Thanks, Ted. I should go, and he snapped his phone shut.

—It'll be here in fifteen minutes.

—What crane?

—Didn't Yoshi tell you?

—No, he didn't.

—They're bringing a crane over to drop the boulder.

He studied her for a second, noticing her lipstick. It went outside the lines of her lips.

—So, he said slowly, —exactly how big *is* this rock?

❧ —Ladies and gentlemen, said the elderly tour guide, standing at the front of the bus talking into a mike as they pulled away from the Bechtel parking lot. —Welcome!

He was a small man, wearing a black cowboy shirt embroidered with white eagles in flight and sporting a large belt buckle that said NEBRASKA. —Thankya very much for taking the time off your busy schedules to visit the Test Site with us today. I'm Virgil Williams. I'll be showing you around. I used to work in the testing program, in fact I worked in the program for fifty years starting the first year of the program back in 1951. I worked at the Test Site till I retired and started volunteering here on the tours. Give some young fella a chance, is what I said! I been present at over seventy atmospheric nukular explosions. These are the explosions that tested the weapons we need for the defense of our country.

Szilard, sitting in the very front row on the right, pulled out a small silver laptop Ann had never seen before, flipped it open on his knees and powered it up.

—I make no bones about it, said Virgil Williams, ignoring the laptop next to him. —I'm just a little hard of hearing, so speak up you folks in the back if you need my attention. I do apologize to you, ladies and gentlemen. I *am* a little hard of hearing.

Ann noticed that his two hearing aids sprouted thin filaments of wire like the stamens of a flower.

❧ Ben watched the crane lower the rock with Lynn standing next to him, arms crossed. She was touching the side of her body to his in a way that suggested she was merely huddling close for convenience. As she leaned toward him she was pretending, he suspected, that the point of the exercise was to lean away from Yoshi, who stood on her other side.

He remembered moments like this from high school and he allowed her lengthwise flirtation because to move away from the contact abruptly would be obvious. A sudden movement would be construed as an insult. He was planning for the future: as soon as someone else spoke to him, say when a worker called him over, then he would separate quickly and neatly, a tuck of air between them and he would be gone.

It had rained earlier and the day was cold for late August so they were both wearing layers. This protected him but he was still aware of the slick nylon of her jacket as it brushed against the grainy beige canvas of his own. It was a steady distraction.

The rock loomed above the size of a modest home, and his stomach actually turned over as it dropped lower, lower, lower in small, jerky increments.

—It'll be a focal point! said Lynn excitedly, and Yoshi gave a small, tight nod Ben could barely see when he leaned forward to glance past her profile at Yoshi's. The boulder swayed slightly, whether because of its weight or because of a breeze Ben did not know. It was close to the crown of the aspens. He feared for them.

He wished he could leave: he wished to stop working at the mansion instantly. He wanted to get away from Lynn and her whims and move to a different job, start anew. Bad taste is not a crime, he said to himself, even though it should be.

That was it: if the world gave us our souls, why were the souls so impoverished? Most of them were so thin you could see right through them.

We have *obscured* the world, he said to himself as he stared up at the rock, taken it over with our flesh and nests and leavings, and all we see is our things. We have forgotten what the world is.

We believe we are it.

We can't see past ourselves to the world, he thought.

—What? said Lynn.

—Did I say something?

—You whispered. Were you telling me a secret?

—I don't have any secrets.

—Oh, come on, said Lynn slyly. —We *all* have secrets.

❧ Across the interstate from the Test Site gate was a cluster of small tents and beat-up cars, a few motorcycles and an old Airstream, people camped out on what looked to Ann like a long-term basis.

—Pull over, would you? said Szilard to the bus driver, as though he was the boss.

—No sir, I'm afraid the tour does not stop here, said Virgil the tour guide, smiling.

—I said stop!

—If you want to talk to the protesters you'll have to do it on your own time, sir, said the driver.

Virgil the tour guide nodded.

—We're due at Badging, he said. —I make no bones about it: the Test Site *does* arrest those people sometimes. Peace groups, Indians, A-bomb survivors from Japan and so forth, your religious folks, nuns and priests and so forth. They protest what we do here, testing the nukular weapons that we need in America to defend our country. We put them in that jail right there.

As they turned into the Test Site gate she saw where he was pointing: a fenced-in enclosure on bare sand, bisected by another fence and decorated only with two blue port-a-johns.

—Sometimes around Easter—that's when they like to come out, you know, that's when they mostly come protesting here—we sometimes got three or four hundred people in our little jail there. We got a ladies section and a gents section too. See? Company named Wackenhut does the security. Now ladies and gentlemen, they're a private company. We don't do it ourselves. You know, it's these guys that arrest the protesters. It's not us personally.

—Criminal thugs, said Szilard loud and clear.

—They also give you your badges, here at Badging, said Virgil as the bus pulled over and parked. —OK ladies and gentlemen, just come on off the bus and follow me. You'll need just your ID here ladies and gentlemen. Remember, no cameras, recording equipment, or binoculars with us today. That's the deal. I do appreciate your cooperation here folks. OK? And now folks, please follow me.

In the plain concrete-block building marked BADGING they waited in line beneath fluorescent lights. Behind a formica counter men in brown-camouflage, proto-military gear signed them in.

—Fascists, man, said Clint. —You know what these guys are famous for? They beat the shit out of people doing civil disobedience. They work for like the IMF and Three Mile Island.

—Just sign here, said a uniformed man with a crewcut, impervious.

Back on the bus Virgil described the rigors of life as a security guard.

—These guys have to be able to run an eight-minute mile, or they won't be employed here too much longer, he said. —See? There's the track they run on.

They passed a nondescript track and crept down a low street of ugly, temporary buildings. It looked like a small gray city, except that no one had bothered to plant any grass or trees. Everything was drab and barren, official sterility.

—Now I personally, ladies and gentlemen, I never worked security. However, ladies and gentlemen, I *would* like to tell you, I *did* have the honor and privilege of escorting some Russians around. They visited here in '92 to see the facility. Unfortunately soon after that the moratorium went through under President George Bush Senior. So we didn't have more tests after that, and I never got to go to Russia and visit them. I'll tell you one thing those Russians told me, ladies and gentlemen: a family in Russia gets only one half-pound of beef every week. That's for *the whole family.*

—Leo, said Oppenheimer, leaning up from the seat behind Ann, —how long is this going to last?

❧ Fermi had packed a lunch for them: egg-salad sandwiches cut diagonally. But Ben wanted to patrol the street. He needed to know whether they were still under observation, whether the dark sedan was hulking somewhere nearby waiting for them. He talked Fermi into coming with him.

After the crane had rolled off, ponderous and tanklike, they changed their shoes, washed their hands and set off down the hill toward Canyon Road, toward a café where Ben knew the staff.

The sedan was nowhere in sight, but as they were walking Ben's cell phone rang. It was Ted the lawyer.

—They came to see me again, he said. —Tell Leo I'm off the case. Would you? From this day forward I'm not working for him. It's giving me too much grief.

—You should tell him yourself.

❧ The passengers got out of the bus at the lip of Sedan Crater, a vast and yawning conical hole in the dirt.

—This was a one hundred and four kiloton blast, said Virgil, leading the crowd behind him to peer over the edge from a white metal platform. —That's about seven times the explosion at Hiroshima. I would call it an underground blast but as you see it did cause a large subsidence crater, what we call them, and yessir, ladies and gentlemen, it did release some small amount of nukular radiation at that time. It was part of Project Plowshares as we called it, which was the peaceful use of nukular weapons.

—They were going to blow up Panama City to make a new Panama Canal, announced Szilard, turning to their group of twelve to orate as the other passengers rubbernecked. —One of my old friend Edward Teller's pet projects. Single stupidest idea the AEC ever had.

—Now we *do* have some opinions here, ladies and gentlemen, said Virgil, smiling broadly. —I personally, as a layman, I think it definitely would have worked. Do you know how much earth we moved here in just a matter of two seconds? Ladies and gentlemen, it was twelve million tons.

❧ Project Plowshare was Edward Teller's baby, a plan he pursued with funding and approval from the Atomic Energy Commission between 1957 and 1962. The idea was to re-engineer the earth using nuclear weapons. They would be exploded to build canals and harbors, change the climate, redirect ocean currents and in general, as Teller put it, "change the earth's surface to suit us."

Teller—with the full support of the U.S. government—planned eventually to use three hundred and fifty megatons of hydrogen bombs to blow open a new Panama Canal. To practice for this, for years he pursued a project to set off a five megaton blast in Alaska, near a native community called Point Hope. This sub-project of Plowshare was called Project Chariot. Ostensibly the massive blasts in remote northern Alaska would be meant to create a harbor, although there was no need or use for one in the region since there was nothing nearby to export. Between Point Hope and oil that might be shipped out of the new harbor was a massive range of mountains.

A handful of Alaska natives finally stopped Project Chariot with the help of powerful friends in Washington. But Project Plowshare's "nuclear excavation" program—a multimillion dollar effort that resulted in no excavations—lasted until 1970, when it became illegal.

❧ Roger came in for a bagel while Ben and Fermi sat eating. They sat quietly, reading the newspapers that were spread out on the table between them. He was sweaty from squash, carrying his racquet.

It occurred to Ben that the courts were nowhere near. Roger was carrying the racquet ostentatiously.

It also occurred to him that if he faced down and appeared to be reading Roger might not notice or speak to him. Consequently he peered hard at a story about a young girl who was raising money for abandoned pets by collecting recyclable bottles.

—Hey man, what's with that giant fucking boulder?

—Roger, how are you? The rock was your wife's idea. We didn't feel it was the best choice for the space, but we're here to please the client. She didn't discuss it with you?

—I was on a business trip. That thing's fucking huge. It's right where my putting green was going to be.

—Yes it is.

—She did this just to piss me off, said Roger.

—Yoshi objected but she overruled him, said Ben. —She said it was feng shui.

—It's a fucking boulder.

❧ Virgil Williams gave a nod out the window, smiling and deferential.

—There on your right we have the tower we built for the last bomb we were going to set off, back in the Year of Our Lord 1992. That was going to be an underground blast, since of course we weren't doing the air blasts anymore by then, ladies and gentlemen, due to the Limited Test Ban Treaty we got back in the sixties under President Kennedy. So this was going to be an underground blast.

—Look at that, Jimmy. Is it some kind of a prairie dog? asked the woman in the row behind them, pointing out the dirty bus window and raising her camera. The shutter clicked.

—It's like a ferret weasel, said her husband.

—Folks, that there is a squirrel, said Virgil.

—Oh! said the woman.

—Unfortunately, the moratorium was issued before we could fire it up. The moratorium came at midnight the very day before we were going to fire off this shot at 4:30 in the morning. So, and this is unfortunate, the shot never went.

Ann gazed out the window across the bleak valley, its brown and beige flats beneath the low mountains. It was a deader version of Trinity, the dark hills in the distance surrounding the dry used-up land, the land burned and in this case pocked with craters that were reputed to be visible from space. It looked like the surface of the moon now but once, many thousands or tens of thousands of years ago, it must have been fertile, home to a river and grassy wetlands that spread out across the valley, home to birds and fish and mammals long gone extinct.

—But it's just waiting there ladies and gentlemen, said Virgil, smiling and adjusting his glasses on his nose, —and if we ever get the go-ahead from the president for a new round of underground testing, well, we're more than ready. And that right there will be the first shot we fire.

❧ By two o'clock in the afternoon the crane was back, setting up to hoist the rock out again. Roger called Ben and Yoshi over to watch it with him, removing a cigar from his pocket and lighting up like a proud father as the crane maneuvered into place. Lynn was reported to be sulking and did not put in an appearance at first. But just before the rock lifted off she bustled past them with her arms full of dresses and coats and got into her car, flashing a smile at Ben as she gunned the engine.

—Dry cleaners! she called brightly, and the tires spat gravel.

❧ —I'm going to vomit! Let me off the bus, said Szilard loudly as the bus turned out onto the interstate outside the Test Site, the tour finished. He held his hand over his mouth.

Ann thought it was an obvious fake.

—Sir you can certainly make yourself at home in the rest room there at the back, said Virgil, as the bus driver looked up at Szilard, considering whether he was serious.

—Stop the vehicle *now,* said Big Glen, towering from his seat.

The bus heaved to a stop on the side of the road and the front door opened as the driver shrugged at Virgil and shook his head. Szilard descended onto the bottom step and waved them forward.

—Oppie! Larry! Everybody off now!

—We're getting off *here,* Leo? asked Oppenheimer. —In the middle of nowhere?

—No sir, said Virgil in protest, —ladies and gentlemen?

But Big Glen loomed over him at the front and the group surged past and down the steps, Ann and Oppenheimer lagging behind.

—Leo? called Oppenheimer again. —Please. What *is* this?

—We have business here, said Szilard, looking up at them as they dismounted. He stood on the dirt shoulder of the road with a yucca behind him, brown and ragged from the long drought, and craned his neck to wave up at Virgil through the bus door. —Thanks for the tour, but we're done.

—Business? asked Ann. —I mean how long are we staying here for?

—As long as it takes.

—Who decided that? We don't get input into where we're going?

—This isn't a democracy, said Clint, as he jumped to the ground in front of her. —Or hadn't you noticed.

—You didn't consult me, Leo, said Oppenheimer severely.

—I didn't have time. We had to act quickly, said Szilard. —It'll be fine. We'll rent a couple of RVs and some minivans. You'll still be sleeping in comfort, Oppie.

When all twelve of them were standing on the shoulder of the road the bus's doors wheezed closed and the bus pulled away, Virgil shaking his head at them sadly from the dark interior. Ann felt they had gravely disappointed him, and looking at the others she saw ambivalence on their faces.

As the bus receded she thought of Virgil inside it, disappointed. His pride was a giant thing, surging inside a small man.

Here they were. It was bright and clear and the sky was a hostile white.

—Let's go see what we got, said Szilard, and they followed him in twos and threes as he trudged back up the shoulder of the road toward Peace Camp. Larry talked to Oppenheimer about irradiated sheep near the Test Site, which he claimed had given birth to lambs with more than one head. A number of calves, he told Oppenheimer, had been born without any heads at all.

—They were just lumps of flesh when they came out, he said.
—*But with hair.*

Ann lagged behind them, half-listening, wrestling with her discontent as Webster the contortionist slogged along quietly beside her. Suddenly he was tugging with frantic haste at his bright-yellow drysuit, in a rising panic.

—Help me! I gotta get this off!

His face was flushed.

—Don't worry, she said, reaching out.

—I'm going to suffocate! I can't breathe!

She stood and helped him to wriggle out of his jacket, pulling it over his raised arms and off his head. Beneath it his cotton undershirt was soaking wet.

—Oh my God, he said. —Lord! I thought I was going to die in that thing.

The ground was hot against the thin soles of her shoes as she waited for him to fold the bulky jacket into his small fanny pack, a task he performed with fastidious care. An eighteen-wheeler thundered past them and she fumbled in her bag for her sunglasses. It blew grit and dust into their faces as it rumbled off down the road. She blinked and rubbed her eyes and wished she had eye drops with her and remembered her suitcase in the room at the Luxor. She wondered what the cleaning staff would do with her toiletries left spilled over the counter, her dirty clothes left crumpled on the bed, whether they would handle her box of tampons and her still-wet toothbrush with the same attitude.

It was hot and dry, hot and dry, in her mouth as well as on her cheeks, nose and arms. It was bright. She wanted water sweeping over her to make her clean. She wanted dark and smooth privacy.

—What about my tampons, Szilard? she felt like saying

belligerently, but could not. She was trapped in his spontaneous, inconsiderate bullshit.

Skin smelled different in the desert, she thought, lifting her hand to her nose. It smelled as though it might taste good.

❧ —If you wanna know the truth, said Roger, sucking at his cigar as the rock lifted, —we just decided to get a divorce.

After a long pause, the boulder wobbling as it ascended and the first cool air of early fall rising around them, Ben offered condolences.

—Oh—I'm sorry? he said, confused at the sudden and casual disclosure.

—Yes, said Yoshi, —very sorry. Painful for each person.

Fermi nodded.

—I mean, I'm sure it's a difficult time for you, said Ben.

—Are you kidding? It's time to *celebrate*, said Roger. —Ding, dong, the witch is dead. You hear me?

—Excuse me, said Yoshi. —The house?

—You mean who's getting it? We're selling. I wouldn't mind staying here but you know how it is. We don't have a pre-nup so I'm pretty much fucked. But it's worth it. Shit! It sure is. I'd give up the Taj Mahal to get clear of this.

—Do you still want us to—?

—Yeah, go on, finish the job. Raise the resale value.

—OK, said Ben, and nodded slowly.

—All I want is hot young women. I mean it, man! It's all I think about these days.

—Midlife crisis? asked Ben, forgetting to edit.

—Call it whatever you want! I call it a goddamn party.

❧ —Blessed be, said the woman who had first greeted them. She had a plump, kind face and eyes set wide apart. Behind her people were drumming softly. —I'm Loni. And we got food cooking under the big tarp. There are vegan-friendly options.

☙ —One week maximum, said Yoshi, and raised his water glass to toast.

They were eating dinner together to celebrate the end of the mansion job. Roger had dropped the putting green from his list of demands; native vegetation would be planted in its place, and they would soon be moving on.

The waitress had just delivered a second basket of rolls when Ben looked past Fermi's slumped shoulder and saw a man across the room staring at him.

It was rare that men looked at him, he thought. It was rare that men looked at each other.

Next he thought: It's one of them.

He was just rising from his seat when Ted the lawyer appeared in front of him holding a napkin and chewing. He wiped his mouth.

—Hey. You talk to Szilard yet?

—No. I don't talk to Leo unless I have to, said Ben. —But turn around. Behind your back. Is that one of the guys who was harassing you?

When Ted swiveled to look Ben saw an empty table.

—Damn it! He was watching us.

Ted nodded. —Listen. I left Szilard a message. Even though I'm off the case, you know? I figured I'd let him know what was happening. The DOD lawyers finally filed their brief. It's a motion to dismiss for lack of standing. There's also a mootness claim.

—Mootness?

—Mootness, said Ted, louder.

—I'm not a lawyer, Ted. I'm a human.

—They're arguing that the case shouldn't be heard because Szilard doesn't have the legal right to sue. They're saying that because Szilard, Oppenheimer and Mr. Fermi here are dead, they got no standing. Will you tell him from me?

—The guy was I don't know, about six feet. Medium brown hair, kind of receding a little?

—Look, said Ted. —My fiancée's sitting there with her food in front of her and we just got engaged. I mean like five minutes ago. So I don't want to be rude. I just thought he would want to know.

When Ted was gone Yoshi turned to Fermi with a worried look, and bowed his head to ask a question earnestly. —Henry. Someone says you are dead?

☙ —Many thanks, said Webster politely to Loni over the campfire, when she handed him a sharp stick. —But I do not eat marshmallows. They contain gelatin, extracted from the hooves of dead cows.

—Hey man, I thought we left Albert back in the hotel room, said Clint, waving flying cinders away from his face.

—Ad*al*bert, said Leslie.

—I'm sorry, said Webster. —I don't mean to be a problem. I try to eat macrobiotic, is all.

—I completely understand, said Loni. —I used to avoid processed foods, but now I embrace them. I had this revelation. Everything is part of the world, you know?

—That means you gotta eat it? asked Clint. —What, next I gotta eat dogshit? Cause it's part of the world?

In the dark their faces were orange, and behind the smoke Ann blinked away floating ash and watched Szilard ushering activists toward the Airstream. A few feet away Oppenheimer stood with a cigarette watching two young girls in front of him twirl glow-in-the-dark balls on ropes around their heads. The balls made blue and green streaks through the air like the tails of comets.

Nothing, she thought. Nothing to do but spin balls of color. It must be nice.

—Finally! Here they come, said Larry, and deposited his cup of beer on the sand as he rose.

Two mammoth recreational vehicles were pulling in from the highway.

෴ Ben woke up in the middle of the night from a dream in which black bears had been playing soccer standing on their hind legs. All they did was run sideways, and finally their awkward sideways motion, like dancing on crutches, disturbed him. He woke up thinking Don't move that way.

But it was them talking. They were talking to him.

෴ They had all slept on the couches and floors of the so-called recreational vehicles, which Oppenheimer declined to refer to by that name and insisted they call simply the buses. —There is nothing recreational here, he said. —What a ridiculous moniker. It is a house on wheels.

She was standing outside one of the buses in the morning, drinking coffee and trying to shrug the kinks out of her neck, when she looked up to see a man getting out of a car on the side of the road. The car pulled away and he swung a duffel bag over his shoulder and began to walk toward them.

She couldn't recall what made him so familiar till he was just a few paces away from her, from the shade of the gray tarp over the scarred particleboard table with the two propane stoves, the coin plate for contributions to the food bill and the crowd of plastic Thermos mugs. By coincidence Oppenheimer was descending from the bus behind her in his wrinkled dress shirt and pants, yawning and stretching out his arms, as the man approached them.

—No fucking way, said Ann under her breath.

—Ann! Language! rebuked Oppenheimer, shocked, and then followed her gaze as she reached to push him back toward the trailer.

It was the weeping man from the hotel lobby.

෴ The desert and the far north were both popular sites for nuclear testing. Even after Project Chariot was abandoned, Alaska was not forgotten by the men running the American nuclear testing program. In the Aleutians, in 1965, 1969, and 1971, three massive nuclear tests were conducted on Amchitka Island. Cannikin, in 1971, was the largest underground test the U.S. ever conducted on domestic soil at five megatons.

Cannikin was detonated with such force that thousands of animals were killed and whole lakes on the island were drained. Seabirds standing on the beach when the ground rose beneath them had their legs driven upward into their bodies, and the eyes of sea otters and seals exploded out of their skulls.

❧ —If you'll just stay quiet, reasoned Larry, —you can hang out, OK? But don't be messing around with my man Oppie. Else Big Glen will have to pick you up and throw you out. And believe me, you don't want to deal with Big Glen.

The weeping man slowly nodded his assent. He was sitting at a picnic table with Glen standing behind him, arms folded, and the others in a semicircle around them. His head was bent and his eyes downcast, as though he was ashamed.

—And what was your name, if you don't mind? asked Oppenheimer warily, standing a few feet away.

—David, Lord.

David lifted a squirt bottle to his lips—Ann noticed the word *Speedracer* was printed on it—and delivered a jet of water into his open mouth. His duffelbag, beside him on the table, was covered in buttons. *On a Recon Mission from the Kingdom of Heaven, Soldiers of Christ: Armor Up!* and *The Bible: It's a Spiritual .357 Magnum. Last Day Warriors. I Don't Know About You, But Heaven's MY Neighborhood.* Also *Viva! Reagan, Reagan-Bush Pioneers, Reagan-Bush: Cut Taxes, Not Defense, Bush/Cheney.*

—And as far as you thinking he's Jesus goes—

—The new messiah, said David quietly. —The deliverer of the righteous, the messenger of the Rapture. *The reaper.*

—Whatever, said Larry. Ann could tell he was relishing his role as mediator. —I don't care what your fantasies are. What I'm saying is, try to keep a lid on it. We've got work to do here, you know? These guys have a mission.

—World peace, said Ann drily.

—Exactly, said Larry, and nodded.

—I did not come to bring peace, but a sword. Matthew 10:34. I am coming soon; hold on to what you have, so that no one will take your crown. Revelation 3:11. Jesus did not know he was the son of God. Dr. Oppenheimer, you do not know you are the herald of the end of time.

—No indeed, said Oppenheimer.

—You think your earthly work is peace, but your work has always been war. Your work is oblivion!

—Hey Lar, is there any soy sausage left? called Tamika, coming toward the kitchen area in her bikini and flip-flops.

—It's in the cooler! yelled Larry, and turned back to his prey.

—So David, man, we need you to pretty much keep a lid on the fire and brimstone if you want to stick around here.

—And please, said Oppenheimer, —no touching.

❧ Ben was rinsing the egg off his plate when there was a loud knock on the door. He crossed the room with plate in hand and opened it to two men in uniform, one of whom he recognized from the restaurant. He wondered if he could slam the door but felt frozen, and meanwhile they flashed their badges too quickly for him to read.

—You're the ones that are following me.

—We apologize for the inconvenience. Is Dr. Fermi in?

Ben was ready to shake his head when Fermi came up behind him and peered out over his shoulder, fully revealed.

—I am Fermi, he said flatly.

—*Enrico* Fermi, is that correct sir?

—Wait, said Ben. —Show me your badge again before we answer any more questions. Who do you represent?

He leaned in close to read it.

—USAIC Fort Huachuca? What's that?

—Army Intelligence.

—And what do you want with Fermi?

—We need to take him in for questioning.

—Just a moment, said Ben.

He closed the door on them and reached for the telephone.

∽ The drumming started up before 10 a.m., a solemn and dirgelike thumping in the background. Wind moved the yuccas and the sage-brush and every few minutes a cloud of dust rose and swept through the camp, flapping tents and blowing clothes off the laundry lines.

A few feet away from Ann Tamika was doing jumping jacks. She had cut the legs off her jeans, and now they hung in strips above the knees. She also wore a bikini top that featured the Stars and Stripes. Ann watched her jumping.

—I'm Father Raymond. Would you like to join us at the prayer circle?

It was a gentle, stooped man with a weak chin, a small button nose and a clerical collar, standing a few paces away from them and clutching to his concave chest a *Book of Common Prayer* and a sheaf of sheet music. His faded baseball cap bore a peace sign.

—What kind of prayer circle? she asked warily, and lifted her metal coffee cup to her mouth for cover.

—We're not into that, said Larry.

Tamika was breathing hard as she jumped, dreadlock ponytail and breasts flopping. She scissored her legs and raised her arms as she waited for her answer.

—I'll come, said Ann, shrugging. She had been hunched on a rock for the last half hour listening to the faint drone of Szilard in-citing the Peace Camp crowd to join his campaign and staring glass-ily at Tamika's movements. She was sore from the deep ridges on the sandstone.

—All are welcome to worship in their own way, said Father

Raymond in a near-whisper. —What joins us together is a fervent wish for an end to conflict all over the globe.

—Are you guys gonna sing? asked Tamika, still jumping.

Her flag bikini seemed to stun him: he gazed at it with an expression of wonder.

—We will sing hymns, yes, said Father Raymond. —All are welcome.

Under the gray tarp of the kitchen tent people sat in a circle on blankets and cushions. A couple beat drums with their hands, and a teenage girl half-heartedly shook a tambourine.

—Uh, the tambourine? That's not really working for you, honey, Clint told her. —No offense. What's your name?

—Nikki, she said, and let the tambourine rest as Clint sat down beside her and she smiled up at him.

—Big Daddy gonna—*whoooo!*—show *you* how to play, said Clint in a hearty voice, leaning in close.

—She's real shy, said Loni, in a warning tone.

—All right! announced Father Raymond, and smiled beatifically. —I'd like to open our prayer session today with a tribute to Mahatma Gandhi.

—*Per*vert!

Nikki turned to Clint and punched him in the face.

❧ —I can't believe you have the gall to come into my clients' house, said Ted. He strode into the room officiously, suit jacket flapping for all the world, Ben thought, as though he was high-powered. —This is an egregious violation of their civil rights. Ever heard of *Posse Comitatus*?

—Calm down, sir, said the Army Intelligence man. —We're here under the authority of HR 3162, Uniting and Strengthening America by Providing Appropriate Tools Required to Intercept and Obstruct Terrorism.

Ted turned to Ben.

—The PATRIOT Act.

The other man smiled hopefully, as though offering up a gift.

—He's not under arrest. We just want to question him in a secure environment.

—You've been following us for days and that doesn't constitute coercion? squeaked Ted. —It's ridiculous. And you argued in your brief that my clients are dead. Now you're here asking to take a dead man in for questioning? Here's what I'm going to do. I'm going to call a friend of mine at the FBI Field Office in Albuquerque. Find out the Bureau's position on this.

He picked up his cell phone and dialed.

—That won't be necessary, hurried the second man. —We will leave.

Ben let them out the front door and as he was closing it behind them the first man turned and whispered, far too close to his face, —But we'll be back.

❧ —All we are saying, is give peace a chance, sang the prayer group, swaying with arms raised over their heads.

Ann was mouthing the words without emitting a sound and her hands were at her sides, hanging uselessly. She looked over the shoulders of her swaying companions to Szilard, who was pacing with his cell phone beside the bus. On the threshold of the bus Oppenheimer sat smoking, porkpie hat shading his face, shirt-sleeves rolled up to the elbow. She stepped out from under the shade of the tarp and walked toward the scientists.

A freckled, broad-faced woman stepped in front of her, wearing glasses. She was frumpy in cargo pants and a pair of well-worn leather sandals, but she carried a small, neat laptop slung over her shoulder, and held a sleek microphone.

—I'm an oral historian affiliated with a larger research project, she said. —A group of archaeologists that are studying this site. Name's Dory Greer. May I talk to you?

❧ A few minutes later Ted the lawyer had Szilard on speakerphone.

—They're not Army Intelligence, said Ted. —At least, Fort Huachuca had never heard of them when I called. They may be connected or they may not. My guess is they wanted to take Dr. Fermi into custody to use as a bargaining chip.

—You need to come join us, Enrico, came Szilard's voice over the speaker. —You won't be safe until you do.

—Why would he be safe with you, Leo? asked Ben.

—We're hiring bodyguards.

—Anyway, I just came when Ben called me as a courtesy. I'm off the case, said Ted.

—I am now in a position to offer you a fifty-thousand-dollar retainer, said Szilard.

—Oh.

❧ —Enrico's coming, announced Szilard, pocketing his cell phone as Ann approached the bus with Dory the oral historian. —Who are you?

—Dory Greer. We're working with the Shoshone and other tribes, studying the rock art and graffiti. In the culverts?

—Our work is what you should be documenting, said Szilard. —I will be glad to grant interviews.

—Szilard, I don't think that lawyer is competent, murmured Oppenheimer, his face shadowed in the dark doorway. He was sitting at the top of the step, cigarette ember glowing and metal glinting on his knees. Szilard's laptop was balanced on his lap.

—I hired him for his face, said Szilard. —He looks honest.

—Ted? asked Ann. —He looks like Jim Nabors. You know. Gomer Pyle?

They stared at her blankly.

—Whatcha doing? she asked Oppenheimer.

—Email.

—Since when?

—Leo's teaching me.

—He has responsibilities, said Szilard. —To his fans.

—You're kidding me.

—Szilard started a web page, said Oppenheimer, as Ann craned her neck to look over his shoulder. —See? There's a picture of me!

Szilard shrugged. —Larry bought us a digital camera.

Dory drifted off toward a tribal elder hovering at the food table and out of the corner of her eye Ann saw David creeping slowly nearer, stopping periodically to lift his binoculars and scribble.

—He's getting closer, she said.

—It's OK, said Szilard. —We established a minimum allowable distance. Big Glen's monitoring it, and he has a sidearm.

—What?

—A gun.

Ann gaped at him.

—I can't believe you, she said finally.

He pointed. Big Glen stood beside his coffin-shaped one-man tent with a bulge at his hip, concealed under a windbreaker.

—I thought he wouldn't lift a hand in anger, she said.

—He has to look the part though.

A roar of noise pulled along the road toward them and Ann squinted past David, hunched down and turning with his specs to the noise, to make out a long column of bright all-terrain vehicles approaching along the road shoulder, clouds of dust in their wake.

—Oh no! cried Loni, coming up to the bus with a crowd behind her and a wadded dishtowel in her hands. —It's the off-road vehicle guys! They're very violent. They act out. And I mean, sometimes there's hundreds of them.

—Even thousands, said Clint.

He had a swollen, red-black eye where the teenage girl's fist had landed.

—This is public land, said Szilard pompously. —We welcome all of our fellow Americans.

—I don't mean to be unloving? said Loni. —But they're pigs.

—I got a cousin who's into it, said Clint. —Every year they go to these dunes in California to party and they get drunk and high and run over their own kids by mistake till they're dead.

Before she could retreat the all-terrain vehicles were pulling into the camp, around them on both sides, coming in further, in hordes it seemed to her, more and more surging past, sending up dust clouds that choked her and filled her eyes with stinging grit. Some of the drivers were children.

—I'm going in, she said, and Oppenheimer got up with his laptop and stepped back inside the bus. She followed, closing the thin door behind them and failing to shut out the noise of roaring engines.

❧ After Ted left Fermi sat on the couch for a long time, his hands clasped politely in his lap. Finally Ben sat down beside him.

—We have to go now, said Ben.

—I don't want to, said Fermi.

—I know.

❧ Peace Camp was a hub for civil disobedience actions while the Nevada Test Site was in full swing. Between 1986 and April 1994, for instance, government documents indicate that five hundred and thirty-six American Peace Test demonstrations took place near the Site. They involved more than thirty-seven thousand participants and resulted in nearly sixteen thousand arrests.

When testing in Nevada went subcritical the settlement at Peace Camp dwindled. Soon after that it was more or less abandoned.

❧ Ann curled up on Szilard's bed, the wall unit air conditioner humming beside her.

When she woke up the sun had set and she could smell smoke and barbecue and gasoline. Competing musics played, thudding boomboxes and pounding drums. She looked out through the bus bedroom's small sliding window and saw fires dotting the desert in the dark, tall pyres with ORVs parked around them and men hunkered down beside them in silhouette, glittering beer cans rising in slow arcs from waist to chin.

—It reminds me of Burning Man! said Tamika, bursting in the door clad in a flowered shawl, balancing three paper plates. —Aren't you totally starving, you poor girl? I saved you a soy dog.

—I *am* hungry, said Ann. —Thank you.

Sitting up she turned off the blasting AC and took one of the plates gratefully as Tamika sat down beside her on the flimsy mattress. They huddled close in the refrigerated air and ate with legs crossed on the foam, sinking. On the dingy light-blue carpet stood a tortoiseshell floor lamp. Ann leaned forward and pulled its cord, and warm light shone down on her paper plate through green and brown panes.

—They're having a protest tonight, said Tamika. —You know those people from the Marshall Islands? The ones whose parents and grandparents got bombed and all that? They called and said they're flying here in a plane! Larry's getting kegs delivered from a party place. Kegs and ice. Plus there's a bunch of Indians coming too.

—What kind of protest? asked Ann, reflecting that she had never liked sauerkraut as much as she did now.

—What did Leo call it. That thing that debutantes have? Like a coming-out party?

—In the middle of nowhere? asked Ann with her mouth full of dog.

—See but Leo's got all the local TV stations coming in!

❧ Fermi hardly spoke as they drove and Ben could not bring himself to break the silence. Ahead there was Ann, who needed him to keep driving.

—How about we stop and get dinner, he said finally.

—That will be fine, said Fermi politely.

—You know, I would have let you stay back at the house if I could.

—Why couldn't you?

—You're not safe all alone, Enrico. You know that now. You could disappear overnight and we might never see you again.

—It would not be a tragedy, said Fermi quietly.

❧ Ann followed Tamika out of the bus only because it was cloying. She had started to feel she was breathing her own recycled breath, sweating into her own skin. She did not want to be outside with the crowds, the off-road vehicle enthusiasts and Deadheads and bikers and spinners with their colored balls, but unless she decided to hitchhike she had no other choice. She would look for a beer of her own to drink, she decided, and maybe she would ask Oppenheimer for one of his cigarettes. Maybe she would come to understand why he liked them.

She felt a lift at the thought.

A big truck was pulled up beside the bus, open at the back, and stocky men were unloading beer kegs. In the distance, beyond a row of campfires, a firework burst in the air. White rockets showered down above a row of ATVs and Harleys. Someone was stringing Christmas lights across the food tent and Big Glen was standing in a guard stance outside the bus, his feet wide apart, hands on hips. Beside him sat Webster on a yoga mat, meditating beside a flickering votive candle, and a few feet from him she could make out David, squatting in the dirt in his usual stance, a scope lifted to his eyes.

—Can he see through that in the dark?

—It's a night-vision scope. Infrared. He keeps it on Oppie even when there's a tent in between them.

—Huh.

—Oh and hey, he called after her, —could you tell Szilard we got the sat phones in?

—Sat phones?

—Satellite phones.

By the time she made it past Big Glen and was heading up the steps men were howling and hooting around one of the pyres. She turned and saw them jumping and smashing something at their feet.

—They're like baboons at the zoo, said Webster from his cross-legged stance, without opening his eyes.

—Yeah, said Big Glen. —Getting ready to hurl their own shit at tourists.

Inside Oppenheimer and Szilard were both typing on laptops, seated on folding camp chairs. Between them was Dory, sitting close to Oppenheimer on a stool and looking over his shoulder as she typed on her own laptop. Laptops were multiplying.

—So let me understand, said Ann, —you're going to be giving a talk on world peace to these ORV guys?

—They're just our studio audience, said Szilard. —Of course, the broadcast will reach a broader public. The primary purpose of this particular—

—So the answer is yes, she said impatiently, and then turned to Oppenheimer. —May I have one of your cigarettes, please?

—Certainly.

He moved the computer off his lap and stood up, his long legs awkward.

—You don't smoke, Ann, said Szilard primly.

—Right now I do.

Outside the door there was a single floodlight hanging off a nearby tree. Webster's candle had blown out in the breeze and Big Glen was holding the flashlight on the candle while he tried to re-light it.

Oppenheimer extracted his cigarettes from a pocket as she poured them plastic cups of beer from a keg. Behind him she could see and hear too many people, speaking loudly, laughing with a grating raw edge and stamping their crushed cups into the ground. Leslie and Clint wandered over, grizzled heavyset men beside them.

—When's the speeches starting? asked Clint with beer foam on his mustache.

—Ask Leo, said Oppenheimer. —He's the master of ceremonies.

—Not till the TV cameras get here, said Ann. —You can bet on that.

—What we need is lighters, said Clint, nudging hard against Ann's side as he leaned over her to talk to Oppenheimer. —For people to hold up, you know?

—Can I talk to you privately for a minute? Ann asked Oppenheimer, and pulled him away

—Thank you, said Oppenheimer, as they hunkered behind the food tent in darkness with Joshua trees framing them. —Wherever I go they're all there.

—There isn't room for us anymore, she said.

He lit her cigarette and then, as she inhaled, his own. She put it in her mouth, a cool and papery cylinder. She liked the feel of that, but when she breathed in it tasted bad.

—Have you considered, you know, asked Ann, exhaling through her nose. She remembered the plumes from high school, how they had made her feel like a dragon lady when she smoked to be cool. —Quitting?

—Never, said Oppenheimer.

—Not the cigarettes, the campaign.

—I promised Leo, said Oppenheimer.

—I don't know what I'm supposed to do, she said. —I mean should I help? Or am I—I mean do you even want me here?

—Of course we do, said Oppenheimer.

He took a deep drag and looked around, then leaned in.

—I don't know if you've noticed, but many of our followers are mentally—

—Hey Oppie!

Someone was intruding rudely around the edge of the food tent, a head sticking out at them. It was Larry, three sheets to the wind, his face redder and puffier than usual. It shone like a beacon.

Behind him was Dory, with her microphone raised. Oppenheimer smiled at her and Ann noticed how quickly she smiled back.

—The TV people are here!

❧ Each atmospheric test in Nevada, of which there were one hundred and twenty-six, released more radiation than Chernobyl. It has been estimated that fallout from American atmospheric testing between 1945 and 1963 has caused or will cause fatal cancers in between seventy thousand and eight hundred thousand people in the United States and around the world. Soviet testing likely has yielded a similar number.

❧ Szilard and Oppenheimer disappeared into the swallow of crowds and buses and lights, people and news vans. Suddenly she could see no one she knew.

She had the half-drunk cup of beer in her hand and the stale taste of the cigarette in her mouth, but around her all the familiar people had been replaced with others who alarmed her. She saw a man with a shotgun and a man with a crossbow, and wondered where they had come from and what they planned to do with their weapons.

❧ During the decades of bomb testing in Nevada, ranchers for hundreds of miles around watched their cows and sheep give birth to mewling creatures with the wrong number of limbs. In small Mormon towns downwind of the test site, pregnant women discovered they were carrying hearts that beat slowly in shapeless bundles of tissue; the children they did have died of leukemia far too often.

Later, the Centers for Disease Control determined that cancer hot spots from fallout existed as far away as New England. But for years, indeed for the lifetimes of many of the victims, the government had denied any link. Also the people themselves, the Mormons and others who lived in the area, had so perfectly trusted their government that they had denied the effects of the mushroom clouds and black rain on their dead children and mutant cows. It was God's will, some said.

A quarter of a million soldiers, known subsequently as atomic veterans, had bombs tested on them. They would be lined up to watch such explosions as Shot Hood, which at seventy-four kilotons was the biggest atmospheric test ever conducted in Nevada. Hood was puny compared to the tests in the Pacific, but it was still about six times the size of Hiroshima. Just a few years after the tests they had witnessed many of the young soldiers came down with cancer, lost legs or were found to be sterile. The government denied any connection with the nuclear tests, and hunkered down for decades to wait out its victims.

People who lived near the test site and were exposed to fallout from it—often called downwinders—almost always described the clouds that rose on the horizon after a bomb went off and then passed over their houses and towns as "pink clouds." Some said the clouds were evil, and they hated and feared the clouds. Others were not interested in the clouds and believed the leaflets handed out by the government, which said the clouds were harmless.

After all radiation itself cannot be felt, and it cannot be seen.

But most people who saw them said the pink clouds had a transcendent beauty they were at a loss to describe. The clouds moved like great crafts over the small dark towns huddled beneath them.

❧ Oppenheimer had certain tasks and took pride in performing them dutifully—public speaking, for instance, because Szilard had insisted on this pitiful effort. He had the full-time job of impersonating himself, a service he had never dreamed he would be called upon to provide.

But quietly, all the same, the turmoil of it had driven him far away. He had come to see himself as an observer in the late world, less a part of anything than a shade on the edge of the sun. If he was nothing more than perspective, nothing more than a fixed point outside the realm in which the action swirled, noisy and rude beyond his reach, he would not have to feel the pull of it, the tension and hope of being a participant. He would not have to contend with anger or disappointment.

He was not a fighter anyway, and he never had been. He described and he synthesized: he saw through the dirt to the skeletal roots of ideas. But he was not a politician. A diplomat, possibly. He could manage finesse, and a polite and civil distance. But he would not join in battle. He would speak and listen, he would do his best, but as far as he was concerned all that was before him now was a tapestry, the world after it had been mortally hurt, only moving slowly, feebly, the way an animal suffers in the undergrowth, left by a careless hunter.

To be released from desire was in fact a privilege, and when for moments or for hours he forgot how he had come to be alone here in this late, new world, forgot the absence of his wife and his children, of his own life, then he could sometimes breathe freely. Although he had made a promise to go through the motions, and he would be faithful to that on the off, off-chance there was still hope to abide by, still purpose, in fact, in the end, in the base of himself he knew everything was already over.

It was only a faint afterimage, printed on the eye.

4

❧ —Why do they give you so much food?

—Because people demand it, said Ben.

Fermi was defeated by the imposing presence of his omelet, inert in a puddle of melted cheese. They were sitting in a diner across from their motel.

—If a man can put that in his stomach then he must be very fat, said Fermi, staring down at his plate.

The cell phone rang and Ben excused himself to answer it, going outside to shelter under the awning as he pressed the TALK button. In the distance a row of pines stood against the white horizon, and the parking lot was vast.

—It's me, said Ann on the other end, faint and windy.

—Where are you?

—Someone shot Szilard in the arm. The DEA came in and did a mass arrest, she said.

—Pardon?

—But they didn't take the scientists. They took some bikers with a portable meth lab. And that Belgian food activist.

—Are you bullshitting me?

—We're still here, outside the Test Site, she said. —Szilard has a broken arm. He's got some interviews lined up with TV. He thinks someone tried to assassinate him.

The connection was uneven.

—. . . Szilard . . . challenge to the Army, she said. —. . . them to show . . .

—I can't hear you, Ann. You're breaking up. Were these DEA people connected with the military?

—. . . he's going to get them to exhume Fermi's body and do a DNA test. It's for PR.

—What?

—Yeah.

—*Fermi's* body? Why not his?

—He and Oppie were cremated. Remember?

—Did Fermi authorize this?

—Szilard claims that he did.

Ben turned and looked in the diner window at Fermi, who was delicately smearing grape jelly onto a piece of toast. On the other end he heard static, and what sounded like a long wail in the distance.

—You're breaking up. I have to go, sweetie.

—. . . don't know what to . . . , said Ann. —. . . waiting for you to save me.

—It would be my pleasure.

❧ —We do not have good intelligence on the culprit yet, said Szilard to the tabloid reporter. He squinted in the morning sun slanting into the food tent and stuffed pieces of stale-looking bagel into his mouth with his good hand.

Ann sat in a folding chair nearby, arms crossed on her chest, watching. Beyond Szilard, in the bus, Oppenheimer was sending out a press release. The door was closed and locked: he needed privacy. But he had opened a small window to let out his cigarette smoke, and she could see his dark head bent inside.

—Are the police investigating?

—Good question, said Szilard. —They took statements from us, but they did not seem overly concerned.

—Someone tried to kill you and the police aren't even concerned about it?

—They seem to be taking a laissez-faire attitude.

—Do you have, uh, enemies?

—Elements of the military-industrial complex, clearly.

—You're telling me that two men claiming to be resurrected A-bomb scientists—

—There are three of us, actually. Myself, Oppenheimer, and Enrico Fermi. He's not here yet, but he's coming.

—pose some kind of threat to the U.S. military, which has the largest weapons arsenal in the world?

—Exactly.

—The most powerful array of nuclear weapons known to man? And this Army would be threatened by—you?

—You said it all when you said it, broke in Larry.

Ann turned away and wandered past the breakfast picnic table, where Clint and Tamika sat discussing Adalbert's incarceration.

—It's because of the French accent!

—They probably don't know he's Belgian.

Over their shoulders Loni dealt out fried slabs of tofu on a spatula. Ann slid by her and walked out past the bush toilet, on which a small child was perched, blue sweatpants around his ankles, and wound through the dead-gray clumps of bursage beyond. The offroaders had decamped leaving piles of milk and water jugs, juice cartons, crushed beer cans, cigarette butts, plastic bags, dirty rags of twisted cotton underwear and balled socks, and the odd rash of birdshot cartridges, bright red on the brown sand.

Three of them, fat as pigs, ate pancakes off a Coleman stove balanced on the tailgate of a truck.

The drum circle had formed again and she steered around it, walking out toward the road again, free and clear. Across the freeway in the distance she could see the Test Site buildings, a dull concrete pile. A dark van sped in her direction and then screeched to a stop on the road shoulder, raising dust, and behind it a bus had to brake hard, driver leaning on the horn. She turned away again and walked out into the flat of the desert, keeping the low mountains in front of her, her back to the road and the site, with Peace Camp on her right.

A few minutes later she stopped and sat on a rock. She could see back over the encampment, its makeshift tents and the trailers and trucks and motorcycles. Between her and it there were cholla trees with their toxic spines alit, awkward and sharp against the sky.

She watched people move in the camp, watched the drum circle and the stream of small crowds back and forth, cars pull up and drive away. A phalanx of cyclists in bright blue and yellow clothing approached along the freeway and passed by the camp without stopping.

She felt far away for a very long time.

❧ Ben did not break the news to Fermi until they were almost there. He held off because he was reluctant to be the bearer of bad tidings: but then Fermi had to hear it now, in private, not later when there were people around them.

As the sprawl of Vegas hove into view he finally told him. Fermi said nothing for a long time, looking out the window. His fingers worked a frayed cord he had dug out of the glove compartment when he cleaned it.

—I mean, said Ben slowly, —he did ask you again since you refused initially, didn't he?

—No, said Fermi.

If Fermi was not Fermi he would not care about Fermi's family. Ben wondered how much he knew, whether he had covertly researched his descendants and learned the names of his grandchildren.

—It may not hurt them, said Ben softly.

—There's nothing I can do, said Fermi.

—You can intervene.

—I'm not worried about exhumation, said Fermi. —That is nothing to me. I'm worried about what happens after. Will they contact me? The family?

—Don't worry, because they won't prove anything, said Ben. —So it won't come to that. Szilard will be laughed out of court, if that's where he's going. Ann says it's just a publicity stunt.

—I want him to succeed, said Fermi, —but this is not nice.

૭ When she got back to camp, thirsty and sweating because she had taken no water with her, it was still and quiet. The wind had died down and the tents and the metal of the cars and motorcycles baked placidly in the sun. She saw hardly anyone anywhere until she noticed the crowd spilling out of the buses, lined up beside them, craning toward something within.

She went over but could not get through them to the front of the ranks, so all she could do was listen. It sounded like local news, except that Oppenheimer was speaking. She realized it was his speech from the demonstration, and behind his voice fireworks popped and engines gunned. She wished she could see the footage.

Then Szilard's voice.

—. . . establish our identity through forensic pathology, which has made great strides since 1945, and with the apparent anomaly of our presence here widely acknowledged and recognized by the scientific community—

—I don't get what he's saying, whispered a woman next to her in a lime-green tube top and bellbottom jeans. —What's he talking about? Can you explain it to me?

—I want to listen, said Ann sharply.

The woman sniffed and turned away from her, disapproving. Ann stared for a while at her mango-shaped breasts in the tube top. They were bigger than her head.

—. . . begin both to investigate the phenomenon in greater depth and pursue our campaign against the proliferation of nuclear weapons.

—I understand that, along with a student group from Albuquerque, you are planning to sue the Army, said the reporter. —Under the Freedom of Information Act?

—We filed suit already and we go to court the day after tomorrow, said Szilard. —Our case is finally being heard. The Army tried to get it dismissed but they failed. We know they have the records.

—Have you seen Robert? whispered Larry urgently, pushing past two men in net tank tops and the tube top woman to sidle up beside her. —None of us can find him!

—I was hiking, said Ann. —I haven't seen anyone.

—Would you help me look for him? I mean why wouldn't he be here watching this?

—Sure, said Ann, and they scooped around the back of the crowd, looking for Oppenheimer's head above it. Around the back of the bus were some teenagers in lawn chairs taking bong hits as Father Raymond hovered nearby trying to convince them to stop, saying —It's very important to build a community where people feel safe saying no.

Then they were up to the next bus, and crowds gathered there too. Larry was agitated.

—I already looked here, and at the port-a-john and the food tent, and over there where all the one-man tents are?—and behind the generators, and near the firepits.

—He might have gone for a walk like I did, said Ann. —He likes his privacy.

—But he's not supposed to go anywhere without Glen. I mean he's his full-time bodyguard till the hired guns get here! Glen took a five-minute break to separate these assholes that were fighting, and when he got done Robert was just gone.

—David! called Ann.

Always under cover, he knelt in some bushes in front of the second bus, fiddling with the knobs on his spotting scope's tripod. His hair was loose from its ponytail and flew out around his head, and he had a cut on his cheek.

—Excuse me, she said. —Have you seen Oppenheimer?

—The rich, the mighty, and every slave and free man hid in caves and among the rocks of the mountains.

—So what are you saying, Dave? asked Larry.

—Revelation 6:15.

—Dave man, I just need the info, OK? Where is he?

But David shook his head and shrugged. They walked past him and continued their aimless search at the outskirts of the camp.

—Where did he get that cut? asked Ann. —I mean it, Larry. Was it Big Glen?

—Glen will not lift a hand in anger, said Larry.

A dirty little girl in jelly sandals drove a purple ORV in circles around a yelping dog tied to a yucca tree.

❧ Atmospheric tests were halted in 1963 by the global Limited Test Ban Treaty. From then on they went underground.

Underground tests continued for decades, until 1992 when they were stopped. Then in 1997 the underground tests resumed, having gone even further underground by becoming "subcritical."

Subcritical tests do not involve a completed nuclear chain reaction; rather they use chemical explosives and a small amount of fissile material. Like conventional nuclear tests, they are conducted underground to contain radioactive byproducts.

❧ —Kidnapped, said Szilard. They were huddled inside the bus with the cell phone lying on the table between them. Big Glen paced in the cramped kitchen with his hands in balled fists and his face crumpled into a scowl. —They left a message on my cell phone.

—Should I call the cops, then? asked Larry.

—Are you fucking kidding? said Clint. —Give the pigs another opportunity to persecute us?

—Chill out, man, said Larry. —They got better shit to do. You're kind of paranoid.

—Yeah. After that massive DEA raid, I'm really *paranoid*.

—Clint? Did you ever consider using, like, a non-aluminum

herbal deodorant? asked Tamika, who was standing near his left armpit. —There's an oil that works really good. Tea tree.

—I'm not putting a corporation on my body, said Clint, and pulled the wrapper off a Twinkie.

—Leo, I need to talk to you, said Ann. —Now.

Alone outside she slid one of Oppenheimer's cigarettes out of a crumpled pack.

—So is it them? she asked Szilard. —The military?

—I don't know yet.

—But what do you think?

—I'm waiting to hear right now.

—Leo! What could they do to him?

His phone beeped and he raised a cautionary finger.

—Szilard. Uh huh. Really.

He turned around and paced while he listened, saying finally, —I think we can do that.

She watched closely, shifting her weight from one foot to the other.

When he flipped the phone closed again the muscles of his face were looser. He was clearly relieved.

—It's just kids!

Larry leaned out the door of the bus.

—What is it with you guys?

—Coming, said Szilard.

She followed him into the bus again.

∾ —I do not want to see them, but they are my only friends, said Fermi.

Ben fixed his eyes on the lane divider ahead of him, the dash-dash-dash of white that was so hypnotic.

—From the old world, I mean, went on Fermi gently. —My only friends from the world that I knew.

❧ —The good news, announced Szilard, —is it's only a bunch of juvenile delinquents.

—What do they want? asked Larry impatiently.

—Fifty thousand dollars.

—Whew! said Larry, and grinned. —No problem.

—They're going to text-message me saying where and when, said Szilard. —In a few minutes, they said.

—It'll be cool, said Clint. —No sweat. I'll beat the shit out of them.

—Won't be necessary, friend, said Larry. —All we gotta do is pony up the money.

—Still, we need more security, said Leslie. —No offense to Big Glen.

—No offense taken, growled Glen, and twisted a wet dishrag until Ann thought she could hear it tearing.

—Now that we're in the media spotlight? said Tamika. —We're targets!

—I got Frank to call a private company with an office in Vegas, said Larry. —They're going to meet us when we get to the city. We got eight guys lined up.

—Did you talk to Robert, Leo? asked Ann.

—They put him on for about ten seconds.

—What did he say? Is he OK?

—He said he was out of cigarettes.

—I got kidnapped once, said Larry. —Back when I was a kid. They just want the money. It's no big deal. I ate Tootsie Rolls the whole time.

The bus door swung open. It was Ben and Fermi.

Neither of them spoke until Ann broke the ice.

—Hi, honey, she said. —Some kids have kidnapped Robert.

❧ Larry packed up his marijuana and lay with his head on Tamika's bare stomach, sucking on a grape popsicle. Ben watched Big Glen lay out a game of solitaire on a card table beside them, a task he performed slowly and with great care. He was wearing a kerchief tied around his head.

Ann had said he was a pacifist, but Ben did not believe it. The guy had scabs on his knuckles.

—Wackenhut, Larry? You gotta be kidding, said Szilard, hanging up his cell phone.

—What do you mean? asked Larry.

—That's who you hired to take care of us? Those people are the enemy!

—Not when we're paying them.

—Isn't it a conflict of interest or anything?

—I don't think so, said Larry. —I mean, they do what they're told. They're security.

—They're thugs. We should not support that corporation. Or while we're at it, Larry, why don't we just go ahead and send Raytheon a fruit basket.

—OK Leo. If you want to book security yourself, feel free. Just call 411.

—I don't have time for those details, grumbled Szilard. —Ann. Can you do it?

—No she can't, said Ben, and then quietly to Ann, —Let's just take the car off the trailer hitch and get the hell out of here. Fermi's begging me. Don't you want to go?

—That's not what I meant by *save me,* she whispered back. —Oppenheimer's been kidnapped—

—By teenagers!

—and you want me to leave? You *know* that's not what I meant! I need to be here, I have to see it through.

—What is *through*? Follow these idiots around for the rest of our lives like groupies with nothing better to do?

—Don't be like that, OK? I just don't want to be useless. I want something to *do.*

He looked at her for a few seconds, her blandly stubborn face.

—Now you're pissing me off, he said, and got up and walked to the back of the bus, to where Fermi was sitting fumbling with his shaving kit.

When Ben sat down beside him he pulled out a bottle of Ibuprofen and struggled with the childproof lid.

—It is very annoying, he grumbled.

—I'll get it, said Ben. As he lifted the lid off the bus turned sharply and pills flew onto the carpet. —Damn!

—Look there! said Fermi. —It is a truck stop named Love.

Ben knelt on the carpet gathering pills as the bus pulled jerkily up to the gas pump. Motorcyclists putted around them, a jagged frenzy of noise.

❧ In the truck stop convenience store Ann found Dory puzzling over a dazzling array of beef jerky. Her hair was greasy and there was a pen stuck behind her ear. Without her laptop or microphone she looked lost.

—I wouldn't get the Spicy Hot Texan BBQ if I were you.

—Ann! Do you think they're *hurting* him?

—I think he's going to be fine.

Dory flushed behind her glasses.

—He's just, you know. Such an *intellect*.

They browsed beside each other along the rows of gum and novelty candy, edible necklaces, gummy bears, gummy fish, gummy worms. Behind them Clint and Ken stocked up on caffeine-loaded energy drinks and planned for their rendezvous with the kidnappers.

—Should we take tasers with us?

—What are those, like stun guns?

—Non-lethal weaponry. In case the kids try something.

—You're kidding, right? said Ann, glaring at them. When they ignored her she turned back to Dory. —I didn't know you were coming with us.

—I decided at the last minute. I have to admit I was, you know, worried about Robert. I mean he really misses his wife. Kitty? I'm so sorry for him.

—So then—you believe he is who he claims to be?

—I'm not here to make judgments, said Dory. —I'm a social scientist! I'm just here to observe and record.

—So you're sorry he lost his wife but you don't believe he lost his wife?

—I'm sure that he lost *something*. He's lonely.

Ann stared at her from the side as she placed her items on the counter and lined them up carefully. There were strands of gray in her hair at the temples, and the fake-tortoiseshell arm of her glasses was deeply scratched.

—Lonely, she said softly. —He probably is.

She looked down at her hands, realized she had nothing in them to buy, and left Dory standing there.

Outside the bus Ben was standing talking to a biker chick, a woman in her fifties with a stumplike torso and flyaway dyed-black hair. As Ann approached them the woman handed him a cigarette.

—Do you think I could have one too? asked Ann, but the woman stared at her without blinking or smiling. —I'd be happy to pay for it.

—My wife Ann, said Ben. —You probably already met? She doesn't smoke either.

—Why dontcha just buy a pack.

❧ Back at the Luxor she left Ben in the shower and went down to the lobby with Larry and Szilard to put the ransom money in a hotel safe deposit box.

—We're supposed to meet them in Pharaoh's Pheast, said Larry.

—What's that? asked Szilard.

—It's a buffet, said Ann, and pointed. —Over there.

—Do you think the food there is actually Egyptian? asked Szilard eagerly.

—Sure, said Larry. —Egyptian hamburgers, Egyptian Coke.

They found the two felons lounging at a booth near the back. They wore baggy jeans and flimsy gray witch masks with long hooked noses. One of them was sipping soda through a straw inserted into his mouth hole. His T-shirt said in large block letters FUCK OFF YOU FUCKING FUCK.

—So you *are* kids. Just like we expected, said Szilard, as he and Larry slipped into the booth beside them. Ann stood at the end of the table with her arms folded on her chest, waiting.

—And you fat.

—Pardon me?

—Let's skip the small talk, said Larry. —Where is he?

—First I gotta go get the money, said the first witch.

—I stay here with lardass, said witch number two, and then elbowed Larry. —Hey, hippie. Got the key for the box?

When the first witch had gone off in the direction of the safe deposit box, Ann swiveling to watch him as he wove across the floor between rows of slot machines, Szilard reached out and grabbed his untouched soda.

—I'll have this, he said to witch two, and then sneezed on it.

—Gross, said the witch.

❧ Fermi knocked on the door and when Ben let him in he was wearing a suit with loosened tie and carrying a bucket of ice.

—Where did you get that?

—Leo made me wear it. He says we have to do a press conference later.

—And you agreed to do that for him?

—I just move when somebody pushes me, said Fermi, and sat down heavily in a chair. —The tap water tastes dusty.

❧ —You go get him, said Szilard. —It's the women's rest room. When she knocked on the first stall a woman shrilled *Occupied!* at the top of her lungs, as though facing an inquisition.

—Robert? Are you here?

The next stall was empty so she knocked on the handicapped stall at the end. A body bumped against the door. She shook the handle but the door was bolted so she got down on all fours. Luckily the tiles were clean, and she smelled only disinfectant when she wriggled underneath.

Anyone else would have looked like humiliation, but Oppenheimer leaned gracefully against the wall as though he had been daydreaming. Except for the gray duct tape across his mouth he was as usual.

—Don't worry, she said, and scrambled upright to face the duct tape. —This may hurt a bit, though, and she began to peel it off.

—Quickly, not slowly, said Oppenheimer through stretched lips, when she was halfway through.

—Sorry, she said, and ripped off the rest. —You OK?

—I just need a cigarette. The hands, please, said Oppenheimer, and turned so she could unwrap him, his hands together at the small of his back, duct-taped lavishly.

—At least they left you in the handicapped, she said.

—Roomy.

She finished unwinding the tape from his hands and he touched his wrists gingerly. Then they exited the stall together, surprising only an overtanned young woman in pumps and a white suit. When they walked up behind her she was leaning forward over the sinks to apply purple lipstick, pouting at the mirror.

—Oh! Is this unisex? she squeaked as they passed her, and Ann shook her head.

—They took my cigarettes away, said Oppenheimer. —Those pipsqueaks smoked joint after joint the whole afternoon and then had the temerity to lecture me on the evils of tobacco.

❧ Ben and Fermi lay on the double beds in the hotel room, watching the news. Ben drank Japanese beer.

One of the local stations was running footage from the peace protest, and watching it he had to admit he almost wished he had been there. It seemed stupid and grandiose, a rock concert from a bygone era with its wild throng of hippies, bikers, longhairs, and disgruntled off-road vehicle guys. Occasionally a peace-loving priest or nun stumbled in front of the camera, apparently lost.

—Shouldn't we tell them it's on? asked Fermi.

Ben said nothing and both of them stayed where they were. Fermi had removed his shoes and set them neatly beside his bed; he had removed the bedspread and folded it neatly.

The camera panned across tacky posters of the three scientists, looking like the Three Tenors, and then a reporter stepped into frame beside a teenager wearing a T-shirt with a line drawing of Oppenheimer in his porkpie hat.

—This is Ron Stubac, a tenth-grader from Reno. So Ron. What brings you to this Peace Camp protest party?

—Op*pie*! My main man!

—Tell me, Ron. Do you believe the man calling himself Dr. Robert Oppenheimer is actually the famous scientist from World War Two?

—Totally! Time travel! I mean I read Stephen Hawking. Do you?

—Well thanks Ron, that's quite a vote of confidence, said the reporter, and smiled terminally. He turned away from Ron and gave a different smile to the camera. —We certainly have some fans here!

—Apoca*lypse*! yelled Ron Stubac, popping back into frame.

—Don't you wish he was wearing a T-shirt with *your* face on it? Ben asked Fermi.

Fermi turned and picked up his water cup carefully, not spilling a drop as he lifted it to sip.

—I am not a T-shirt.

❧ The witch got up from the table and took off running as soon as he saw Ann and Oppenheimer heading over. He passed them at a jog and Ann could hear the *fft-fft-fft* of his baggy jeans rubbing to-gether. She turned to watch as he knocked a plate off an old man's table with the tail of his heavy plaid shirt and then was out of view among the slot machines.

At the table sat Ted the lawyer, between Larry and Szilard, pen-ning into a palm pilot.

—Think he thought we were going to try to have him arrested, said Larry when she and Oppenheimer sat down, and clapped Oppenheimer on the back heartily. —How you doing, brother?

—I am fine. Thank you for paying the ransom.

—Please! said Larry, and raised his hands. —Of course!

—If you hadn't obliged I'd have been forced to watch them play Grand Theft Auto until I slipped into a coma.

—That one kid was a dick, said Larry.

Oppenheimer raised his eyebrows slightly, signaling his assent. —I did not warm to him.

Szilard was reading a legal brief, his arm in its cast on the table beside him, and spooning an ice cream sundae out of a parfait glass with the other hand.

— Grand Theft Auto?

—I thought *you* were the expert on teen culture, Leo, said Ann.

—Lar, said Szilard, —are the Wackenhut guys starting today? Because from now on they're on both of us twenty-four seven. Oh, and there's Enrico too. Put two of them on him. I think he's in the room with Ben.

—Nice to see you too, Leo, said Oppenheimer, with a raised eyebrow. —So tomorrow's when the trial begins?

Larry got up to make the call on his cell phone, wandering away from the table.

—We need to make it to Albuquerque by ten in the morning. We have a press conference.

—If you'd like to hear about our legal strategy, said Ted to Oppenheimer, —I can brief you.

—If I must, said Oppenheimer.

Ted flipped through documents across the booth from them.

—Here's the deal, he said. —What we're doing is we're arguing the No Records response the Army gave us is false. They haven't been too smart about this. What they should have done is just denied us the documents, which is fully legal. Instead they just flat-out lied and said No Records. Plus the letter was signed by someone way high up, not the FOIA coordinator, which means the peons are covering their asses. They know there's bullshit going on and they don't want to put their careers on the line.

—Uh huh.

Ann studied the way Oppenheimer's cigarette smoke curled toward the vent above them, and how Ted's ears shone pink and scrubby under tendrils of hair. She could smell onion rings.

—So we're going to ask the judge for something called Discovery and Document Production. We've already submitted the request in writing, and then the Army challenged it. The judge asked for a hearing.

—I see, said Oppenheimer, but his eyes were beyond Ted, on an electronic billboard advertising Keno, with angry red digital letters that moved too fast.

❧ Fermi slept in his clothes, tie loosened and suit jacket hung in the open closet behind him, stretched out on top of the sheet on his bed. A sharp rap on the room door woke Ben from a dream of suffocation, and he watched Fermi sleep until the knock came again and then dragged himself off his bed.

Answering the door blearily he came face to face with two large men. They were beefy and small-eyed and wore uniforms that made them look as though they wished to be important.

—What can I do for you?

—We're Dr. Fermi's security detail.

—He's taking a nap.

—We will need to make sure that the room is secure. Then he can continue sleeping.

❧ The Wackenhut force had its own vans. One drove ahead of the bus and the other followed, flanked by motorcycles, and a lone Wackenhut man was posted inside the bus with them, wearing a brown uniform. He did most of the driving, taking breaks every two hours during which he drank diet soda in the corner with his radio squawking intermittently. Ann noticed that sometimes he seemed to be caressing his handgun in its holster. There was a longer gun propped beside him.

—It's a pump-action shotgun, Clint said when he saw her staring at it. —A Remington 870.

On television they watched a videotape of the demonstration, McDonald's food spread out in front of them. Szilard was fond of it. A contingent of vegans had attempted to boycott the lunch stop but had been overruled. Behind them knelt Dory, with her camcorder resting on her shoulder, filming both the television and the three of them watching it. Her left hand, on the back of the couch, brushed against Oppenheimer's shoulder. Ann watched his face to see if he noticed, but could detect nothing.

She moved closer to Ben, who was reading.

—I'm sorry for before, she told him. —I don't mean to be selfish. This is like an addiction.

—Thank you for saying that. I'm sorry for the way I spoke to you.

But he said it evenly with a dutiful tone, and without looking up from his book.

—I can't stop until it's over, she said.

—And when will you know when it's over? Is there going to be a sign that pops up on the road and says THE END?

She glanced past him and out the window just as they passed a billboard for a brothel, well-lit in the dark. Over its yellow background was a woman's disinterested face, with a stiffly shaped helmet of hair and glistening lips.

The convoy was even longer now, Ann realized, the lights of all their vehicles stretching far ahead into the dark of the desert and trailing off into the distance behind them.

She was struck by the endless shimmer of the procession. It had happened overnight: they were legion.

—Leo, she said to Szilard, who had gotten up to get something out of the refrigerator, —I hear Enrico isn't happy about your plan to exhume his body.

—Sacrifices must be made, said Szilard, leaning down and scrutinizing the refrigerator's contents. He pulled out a chocolate milk.

—What if the body's not even there? I mean, how could it be? He's here!

—Don't worry about the logic, said Szilard. —It is complicated.

He trundled back to the couch with his chocolate milk carton open.

—He still treats you like a servant, said Ben, looking up from his book quickly and then returning to it. —Doesn't he.

❧ It was a book about mystical lights. The jewelry maker from Santa Barbara had lent it to him eagerly, with a heartfelt recommendation. It told of mysterious floating lights, lights over ancient burial mounds and modern cemeteries, lights over swamps and fields. It described a ball of light that had been photographed in a zoological garden near the beginning of the twentieth century and a mysterious fireball sighted in a French barn in 1845.

There were moving lights that chased truck drivers and balls of lightning that attacked young girls as they sat at the dinner table and then escaped up the chimney. There were corpse lights that hovered over places where people were soon going to die in accidents, a light for each victim.

Ann left while he read and went to sit beside the scientists, watching TV. Ben raised his head and looked at her across the room, and then out the window hopefully. What if there was a ghost light out there in the dark?

All he saw was a dipping and rising power line.

᠉ They ate breakfast early in a cafeteria-style Mexican place near the university, famous for its chili. Szilard's student volunteers had come to meet them, and four Wackenhut men sat rigidly in booths on either side. They wore headsets and consulted their watches periodically as though they were the Secret Service.

Dory was along at Oppenheimer's request.

—She's documenting this for a paper she's writing, he said by way of explanation, but then he smiled at Dory with a tenderness Ann had rarely seen.

One of the students, a thin Pakistani man, had brought along a copy of his script for the press conference. Szilard marked it up generously with a red pen, his large cast resting on the table beside him, as the student ate his refried beans delicately and talked to Oppenheimer.

—I saw a very interesting film about you! he told him joyously. Ann wanted to listen to his flowing accent but Dory was talking near her ear about the convenience of digital video. —When I was quite small! Of course you looked a good deal older then.

—Are you a Pakistani?

—Yes sir.

—We didn't have them back in my day. Pakistanis that is. There was only India and you were all Indians. And Mr. Gandhi. I liked his creed. I embraced it myself: *Ahimsa*. Nonviolence.

—Yes sir.

—A very good man, Mr. Gandhi.

—Yes sir.

—They shot him to death, didn't they.

She watched sidelong as he and Oppenheimer faced forward beside each other and forked up their eggs.

❧ Outside the courthouse there were news vans parked at hasty angles and crowds flocked on the steps.

Approaching along the sidewalk with the Wackenhuts flanking them Ann felt a stab of fear in her stomach. What if there was someone there with a gun again, and this time they shot something more important than the fat part of an arm?

But she was pushed back from Oppenheimer and Szilard and Fermi as they started up the steps and the crowd closed in. Ben was up ahead and she could barely see him.

—Wait! she called, but a tall man was in front of her and a boom hit the side of her head.

❧ What surprised Oppenheimer about his kidnapping was the fact that he had not been able to bestir himself to anything more than a gentle amusement at his captors' precociousness. He had every reason to hold them in contempt, but he could not summon it. He had been irritated, certainly, when they took away his cigarettes, but part of him had been content to watch their antics.

He wondered after the fact whether it was because he missed his own son, whom he had not seen grow up. But on reflection he did not think this explained his strange tranquility. Rather he was fond of them for the eagerness of their absurdity, how even as they tried to be criminals they were still infants. They used foul language and were clearly infatuated with their play violence, but even so he had a feeling of overwhelming benevolence toward them, as though if they turned on him and killed him savagely he would still be unable to stop smiling.

✍ —Are you OK?

It was a young, clean-shaven man in an expensive beige suit and red tie, a cell phone in his hand.

She rubbed her head where the boom had bruised it, watching the last of the crowd swallowed up by the courthouse.

—Fine, thanks, she said.

—Ann. Isn't it?

She stared at him.

—Do I know you?

—Jonathan Lynne, he said, and reached out smoothly to shake her hand. She had no time to hold back. —I represent a group of Fortune 500 companies. I'm here on their behalf.

He took a card from his wallet and handed it to her, and glancing down she saw he worked in public relations.

—What for?

—Listen. Can we discuss this over a coffee?

—First tell me what this is about.

—My clients are interested in your friends the physicists.

—Interested?

—They're considering investments and what they need is someone to consult with on the subject. Someone with firsthand experience of what these guys have to offer.

—I don't get it.

—They'd like to hire you as a consultant.

She stared at him but could detect nothing in his steady gaze and reasonable tone.

—Basically as they make a decision on whether to invest, they'd like the best information available. And there's nowhere to go for that but the source.

For a minute she did nothing but look away from him, at the street stretching away from the courthouse and the dusty haze of the sky over the far mountains.

—You want me to spy on my friends?

—Of course not! What my clients are looking for is just a first-hand testimonial to these guys' aptitudes, scientific interests, and future plans where any creative work is concerned. They know Dr. Szilard, in particular, is a great innovator. And believe me, he and the other two could come out of this very, very well if my clients give this investment the green light. I mean your guys could be set for life.

His phone rang in his hand but he ignored it, looking at her earnestly. He was trying hard and his proposal was well-rehearsed but she still knew him for a liar. His tan was too smooth, his words too fluid, and she would never be a candidate for industrial espionage. She was a librarian.

—What would be in it for me? she asked, hoping she sounded as though she meant it. —And what exactly would I be doing for these clients?

—Can we go get that coffee? said the young businessman. —Please, I'm jonesing. My car's right around the corner.

She wondered fleetingly if he was dangerous and then dismissed it. He was here to get something.

For the first time, filing into the courtroom beside Fermi, Ben felt he was in a solid position, among purposeful agents. At the base of the courthouse steps he had seen a delegation from Nagasaki. They stood solemnly watching and waiting, dressed in gray and black suits. Behind them were the people who had flown in from the Marshall Islands, also wearing suits but with brighter ties. Oppenheimer had pointed them out to him from the bus the night before, looking out his own window into the windows of their chartered bus. They had waved at him, smiling, and their faces had stricken him.

To these people Szilard was not trivial. It was possible there was a truth in his bustle somewhere, and where was truth elsewhere, anyway? Almost everything was a circus. The circus turned and flashed around him and around them all.

He turned and looked at Fermi, who seemed prematurely aged, and then at the survivors from injured places, crowding into the courthouse seats. He was sorry for them and distracted by his own recognition. He was not aloof anymore; he was giving up and giving in. He had been wrong. Who knew what was fact? And more than fact was the faces of the sad people, and no one should treat them callously.

He wanted to find Ann to apologize, but he could not see her. This is the world, he thought. I have to let it rest on me.

❧ The young businessman drove a black BMW. She had to admit to herself that she liked the soft black leather of the seat; she sat with her palms flat against it as the businessman drove.

But there was nothing in his car to help her discern his real purpose in approaching her. It was like new, factory-clean and un-marred by telltale hints of personality.

—. . . so what we're talking is probably the figure I gave you up front plus say two percent of whatever contract my clients finally offer your guys. Which believe me is a generous offer.

—And these reports I would have to make, she said, —what kind of information would they need from me? I mean I'm not a sci-entist. And Leo barely even talks politics to me.

—Your husband can help you there, said the businessman without pausing. Clearly he was already familiar with Szilard's habits. —He can work together with you. Remember, down the road this will all be in your friends' best interests.

Annoyed at how stupid he must think she was she stared hard out the window, watching as they passed a seemingly unending row of American flags outside a Ford dealership.

—My clients would ask for a report on every other day, deliv-ered by telephone, he said.

She looked at him sidelong as he drove, pretending interest as she ran her fingers over the stereo controls, and for the first time she noticed a heavy gold ring on his finger, bearing some kind of illegible emblem. Probably from his fraternity, she thought, and then noticed his heavy gold wristwatch. The dark bronze of his skin was so even it had to have been sprayed on.

—Let's just go to that café, she said abruptly, and pointed. Suddenly she was sickened at her position, sickened by him. —I need air.

He pulled over right away and this might have given her confidence in him, she reflected later—confidence at least that he was not threatening bodily harm, that his pretense of respectability was seamless. But instead it brought an almost hysterical note to her throat as she threw herself out of the car.

While he was in line awaiting his cappuccino she went to the bathroom and then out the back into a parking lot. Abruptly, when she stepped out the door, she took a deep breath and then ran full-out, away, her arms flailing.

A few minutes later, winded, she was scrambling over a fence when she stepped wrong and twisted her ankle, hearing the knuckled pop as it turned. Her head hit a concrete piling as she fell.

❧ The Comprehensive Test Ban Treaty to stop nuclear testing was signed in 1996. To date, sixty-three states across the globe have ratified the Treaty.

The United States is not among them.

❧ —Who found me? she asked him blearily. Her tongue was thick in her head. There were good drugs now, which made her feel as though everything was the way it should be. But she was confused beneath the light feeling.

—It was some kid from the neighborhood. What were you doing back there?

He leaned over holding her hand. Then someone grabbed her gurney and pushed, and he was walking alongside.

She was not interested in questions. —This is what heaven is like.

—What, honey?

—Nothing is bad anymore.

—What do you mean?

—When they let me go, I want more of these. The drugs they gave me. The city of God on earth.

He smiled and leaned down close, smoothing her hair. —You're a little delirious, he said. —Or it might be the pain meds. You asked for them. Remember?

—But I mean it! Drugs are the city of God on earth.

—OK, sweetie.

He was still smiling when she felt herself drifting again. Buoyancy was with her, and the absence of care. Choice could be taken away, she saw, and then you became an object: but far from being dangerous that moment when choice disappeared was when danger also vanished, and there was nothing you could do but submit. She felt the slow draw of contentment over her, and the relief of a great submission.

For after all it was not ego or a conviction of your own importance that made life worth living but whether you could see how perfect the world had always been without you. It was not to despair at this thought, not to run, not to fear, not to fight; it was if, instead of running or fighting, out of the overwhelming nearness of the world, you could finally make something that could be glimpsed from afar.

IV

A VAST INFANT

1

ᕰ During the Cold War, when nuclear weapons were proliferating most rapidly, Americans were treated to many educational film strips on Civil Defense. One of these, released in the early 1960s, was called *You and the Atom*. It offered very straightforward advice, namely: "The Atomic Energy Commission says the best defense against an atom bomb is to BE SOMEWHERE ELSE when it bursts."

ᕰ As the caravan pulled out of Albuquerque she only wanted to go home. She wanted to be alone in her house, on its calm earthen floors; she wanted to feel once again the deliberate coolness of walking across the clay tiles on bare feet. When she told the scientists why she had run they had looked at her as though they were sorry for her, nodding and smiling but condescending. She could tell that behind their kind words they were sure she had acted irrationally. Szilard's mouth said Don't worry, don't worry, but his face said hysterical woman. Even Oppenheimer remarked gently that he doubted the young businessman had intended to hurt her physically.

She herself did not regret running. She regretted falling—her agitation and the blur of her vision as she rushed against the wind—but she did not regret running. There had been something in the young businessman, something in his perfect tan and perfect calm and the soft leather and the quiet purr of the BMW's engine, that made her cold. In the company of the young businessman, she realized, sitting on the buttery seat, she had felt an insidious lull, a laxness spreading through all her limbs, as though all her will and desire was draining out through her skin.

Oppenheimer's pity for her was rare evidence to him that he could still bend from his detachment. Something in the haste and odd triviality of the episode made her seem more fearful and attention-seeking than she would have seemed as the victim of a grosser infraction. Yet he knew these were unworthy associations and he was sorry. He had rarely felt protective since he came to the new life from the old one, and he was not exactly protective now— more sorry than anything, pulled toward her by a sense of paternal longing that he could not distinguish from remorse.

❧ While they all fell asleep together inside the bus sympathy was in the air like warmth, bringing a humility that Ann did not remember from the rest of her life. People were sorry for her not because of her injury, which was minor, but because they suspected her of needing. She needed, they felt, to draw the scientists' attention, and her tactics were desperate.

But it was not as bad as she had thought it would be living in a well of pity. In fact it had a bracing quality. They felt sorry for her because they too needed, and they too could be desperate. She always dismissed the urge toward pity because it seemed condescending: but now she saw it for what it was, the most immediate and close of contacts.

The touch of it almost hurt.

❧ As the convoy traveled east unruly crowds pressed in; whenever the bus had to stop for gas or groceries the scientists stepped out the door and were swamped. People pushed in close to them, demanding responses and proclaiming their loyalty. They wanted to give or receive: they wanted to be involved. But there were hundreds of them.

Szilard was less disturbed by the crowds than Oppenheimer and Fermi because he cut off questions that did not interest him. Many of his followers could not pronounce his last name and merely called him "Dr. Leo." When they followed him around, badgering him with questions, he merely flapped a hand over his shoulder impatiently to dismiss them. He did not seem to feel any adverse effects from the pressure but Oppenheimer and Fermi resorted to evasive tactics. When Oppenheimer stepped out to smoke a cigarette Dory walked two steps in front of him and brandished her camcorder, barking out —Please respect Dr. Oppenheimer's personal space!

No one paid attention and people were all over Oppenheimer, clamoring.

Fermi told Ben that when the mob crushed in he felt he could not breathe, that panic was raising his heart rate and he was a candidate for a cardiac event. He took to locking the bus as soon as they pulled over to camp for the night, and at regular intervals he would feel for his pulse on his wrist, timing it.

But Fermi was gaining in popularity, surpassing Szilard through sheer mystique. The crowds seemed to understand that he did not like to converse and his silence became the object of fetishists. —Dr. Fermi! Dr. Fermi! Can I just get my picture taken with you for my web site? Dr. Fermi. Can you just autograph my shirt here?

His silence gave him added value.

❧ Ann saw how men approached Oppenheimer, their bodies braced and receptive at once. They seemed to admire him even more than women did, the command and modesty of his presence. She watched them seek his approval with a needy and often misplaced pride, both the old and the young. —Oppie, this is my girlfriend Jojo? She's got a mushroom cloud tattoo on her butt.

Ann felt the urgency of the crowds and the trespass of them when they pressed too close. She felt the chaos of their nearness, how it panicked Fermi. People were coming to her all the time to petition for time with the scientists, pumping her for information and handing over messages for Oppenheimer or Szilard or items of clothing and pieces of paper for Fermi's signature. Fermi made it clear that he did not give autographs but hope seemed to linger that he would reverse his policy.

The followers allowed no space and submitted to no rules. Near a town called Vaughn a bespectacled girl in a wet T-shirt flung herself at Fermi while he was drinking his espresso, saying she wanted to "feel his magic." Fermi was horrified at the sight of her large, soaking breasts through the cream-colored cotton emblazoned with NO NUKES NOW. She was only fourteen, he told Ben.

Later Ben told it to Ann, how he had watched the girl throw her arms around Fermi, eyes squeezed shut, smiling. He wondered if she was retarded, her childish face was so blissful and free of worry. She had been swimming in a motel pool near where they were parked and had come running across the street when she recognized them. He had seen her thin arms encircle and clutch and her breasts balloon and squash against Fermi's shirtfront, soaking the fabric.

It made him feel paternal, Fermi had told him, but also deeply embarrassed.

❧ —Hey Ben? I really need to talk to you, said Leslie one night at a campsite outside Roswell.

Larry had insisted on making a side trip. Beyond their own camp sprawled other camps, teeming with people captivated by aliens. Ann had walked away with Oppenheimer to visit a vanload of Tibetan Buddhists.

—Oh? said Ben. He was sitting on a white plastic chair, reading a day-old newspaper under a hanging halogen lantern.

—Can I sit down?

—Sure.

He folded his paper with reluctance and leaned over to pull off the lid of the styrofoam cooler. When he looked up he saw that Leslie was wearing a purple scarf around her head and a pair of bone earrings, which he recognized as Ashlee's work, dangled from her ears.

He took out a beer bottle and twisted off the cap. —One for you?

—No thank you. Alcohol is a carcinogen.

—Oh, I didn't know that.

It was already up to his lips so he took a quick swallow.

—I just wanted to say, because I believe in being honest and getting it out in the open will help me conquer it I think?—it's just, I have feelings.

—Feelings?

—For you.

He held the beer in a long gulp.

—Sorry. Are you pulling my leg?

Her lips pursed.

—It's just, he said quickly, —I didn't think you even liked me. When we were on the airplane coming back from Tokyo you called me a cynic with a bad attitude. You said I didn't have respect for the, uh, healing process.

—I think I felt your attraction to me and I was trying to repel you.

—*My* attraction?

—Don't worry, you don't have to say anything.

—Uh, OK then.

—I know how you feel. You don't want to be attracted to me but you are.

—Huh.

—I wanted us to clear the air. I figure once we admit it we can move forward, you know? I realize you're married.

He almost still thought she was joking. Maybe she was wearing a wire, taping his responses to play back to a mocking crowd. He realized he was sitting in shadow and was glad it was her face, not his, that was illuminated.

—Yes I am.

—And I have a lot of respect for the institution of marriage even if it has completely exploited women.

He wondered if it would be insensitive for him to take another swig from his bottle.

—Well. Thanks for your, uh . . .

—Marriage actually shortens women's lives, did you know that? But guess what, it makes men's lives longer. Surprise surprise, right?

—Figures.

—Anyway. I just, I think you have this incredible sex appeal.

He drank and waited, afraid that anything he said could make her come nearer.

—Well. Thank you.

—OK. I guess I should be going.

She got up slowly and then swooped scarily close. He almost jerked back in his chair, but stopped himself.

—So goodnight, Ben.

She said his name with a sensuous slowness. It was not good. He thought of an aunt he barely remembered, who knitted and wore green pantsuits.

—See you, Leslie.

When she stood back up and moved away he exhaled at length.

❧ Outside a huge weapons-building complex called Pantex in Amarillo, Texas, the scientists held another press conference. Ann was shocked at how many reporters attended, the black forest of cameras and microphones. Ben shook his head along with her, staring.

—It must be a slow news week.

Newspapers and magazines began to use the term *A-bomb pretenders*, but not without fondness. Oppenheimer had been featured in an apocalyptic Christian newsletter, which called him "a soldier for the Rapture"; Szilard was spurned by Christian publications because of his insistence on political screeds and his relentless promotion of the United Nations. The mainstream media used terms like *mad scientists*. When that quotation was read aloud to him Szilard shrugged and said that all publicity was good publicity.

But the Amarillo police were not happy to have the circus in town. They did not like protesters. Protesters represented the rabble, the underclass, while the police were advocates for Pantex. In their view citizens like Pantex were the kind they wanted more of in Texas.

So when the cavalcade rolled out the next morning it had a police escort. Many of the followers waved their flags as the motorcycle cops rode beside them and some had spray-painted their car windows with slogans. Oppenheimer spotted one that read FUCK THE POLICE and became distressed.

—Leo, he said gravely, —can't you control them? The obscenities!

Fermi, still miserable from his encounter with the buxom girl in the wet T-shirt, informed Larry and Szilard with quiet resolve that he was leaving right away unless they instituted a crowd control policy.

—I'm sorry, he said, —but I can't stand it.

—I'll take care of it, man, said Larry. —No problem. Scout's honor.

The next day Big Glen established a strict hierarchy of access. Ann and Ben, Larry and Tamika, Dory and Big Glen traveled with the scientists in the first bus, guarded by a surly Wackenhut named Kurt. Kurt communicated by cell phone with the other Huts in their vans. He used codes and jargon and was always gruff and businesslike, which Ann liked to ridicule silently. Kurt felt that he was authorized to take charge; Kurt felt it was only right and fitting that authority had been conferred upon him.

The groups from Tokyo and Peace Camp traveled in the second bus and pitched tents outside at night. They had to make appointments if they wanted to see the scientists privately.

—I mean what makes Glen so special that he gets to be a right-hand guy? asked Clint bitterly. —I been around longer than he has. I mean Vegas? Hell, I been with you since Tokyo!

—It's not like that, OK? said Larry. —The scientists just need some time for themselves. The cutoff is arbitrary, man. It's just the way it has to be. It's a numbers game. Leo's call.

The followers traveled in the chartered buses and trailers and their own cars and trucks, and between the buses and their vehicles was the contingent of Huts in their vans. When Big Glen was put in charge of conducting a census of the convoy he came back with a figure around two thousand.

After eleven at night there was a noise rule. *This is not a party,* read Szilard's first edict, which was handed down on pieces of green paper passed out by volunteers, one to each vehicle, outside a McDonald's west of Oklahoma City. *This is a mission. Those unwilling to submit to the discipline of a curfew and other limitations (see below) are encouraged to work for peace and nuclear nonproliferation on a separate and wholly independent basis.*

❧ Pantex was once the end point for assembly of most of the nuclear weapons manufactured in the U.S. It was later largely stripped of this function and became a weapons repository.

During the heyday of Pantex the majority of the workers who staffed the plant were Born Again Christians. For the most part these Christian Pantex employees were not disturbed by any moral contradictions in their work building bombs, because there were none. Their convictions told them they were doing God's work, for building nuclear weapons was a noble task that would serve to bring the glorious Rapture closer.

❧ The simple return of his marriage released him from other worries. Ann was nearer than she had been for months and between them was a sure bond of relief, a comfort that flowed over everything. At times when he caught sight of her ankle he felt shamed; but then he looked at the rest of her and the warmth swallowed them both again. During the day when the bus was moving he stacked cushions beneath her foot and brought her drinks and books to read, and she thanked him and gazed at him with eyes that absorbed, as though nothing had ever been wrong after all.

One night in Oklahoma he pitched a two-man tent for them in a copse of beeches and dogwood.

~ —People, said Oppenheimer to Ann one evening, when Dory and Ben had both gone to bed early inside the bus and the two of them were sitting outside with a campfire in front of them, smoking and drinking decaffeinated tea. They were near the Ozark National Forest. —The more of them there are, the worse it is.

Even then, in a moment of tranquility, there were Huts on the perimeter, patrolling at a forty-foot radius around the campfire, outside the rent-a-fence they always erected when the bus pulled in for the night. Ann wished they were invisible. She did not trust them and it was hard to forget they were there. Sometimes she watched them and wondered what sordid punishments they had endured to become who they were. Or maybe, she thought, she was wrong and the Huts were not violent: maybe they were just doing their job.

But she did not believe this. They gave the impression of always waiting for violence, not out of vigilance but anticipation.

Camp was quiet: even the followers had gone to sleep.

Tomorrow was going to be her first day without crutches. She would still have a bandage and wear homely sandals, but the ankle could bear weight, slowly, tentatively growing strong again.

—Did you hear about the gospel group? asked Oppenheimer. —They're from a church in Alabama. They joined the convoy yesterday. Their specialty is songs about the Apocalypse.

—Zealots and deluded people are the only ones who believe in you, aren't they, she said.

—And you.

She cuffed his arm. There was nothing untrue.

—They asked Glen if they could give a public concert to raise money for the campaign. Leo made him turn down the request, of course. He doesn't want that kind of attention. He doesn't want us connected to Armageddon as though we're celebrating it.

—No kidding.

—He says we'll leave that up to the president.

They gazed out past the rent-a-fence. A group of teenagers were drinking and smoking and staring at them, leaning against their cars. Some of them, Big Glen had told her the day before, smoked Dunhills to emulate Oppenheimer. They would save up to buy Dunhills instead of their usual brand. They would accept no substitutes.

❧ In Roswell the caravan had picked up a urologist from Santa Cruz who offered to write prescriptions, and Ben began to take pills at night to fall asleep. He could rarely find a comfortable position on his sleeping pad. He was a light sleeper and the movements and exhalations of others woke him; he did not want to hear what the others did when their guard was down and it tended to repulse him, but he could not help hearing. And camped in the Ozarks, around one in the morning, he heard Dory get up from her futon and tip-toe into Oppenheimer's room.

Alone among them Oppenheimer had his own room. Szilard and Fermi slept in the space next to it, on the other side of a thin wall on a foldout bed. Szilard was snoring and it obscured Dory's whisper, but Ben thought he heard her say —Is this OK? Do you mind?

Then the springs creaked and he heard the sound of her settling onto the mattress, a rustle of sheets and—he was grateful—silence.

Near Little Rock, beside a campfire, the gospel chorus gave a special performance. They were large black women with one elderly white man, and stood in purple robes holding hymnals with small lights on them. They sang "The Battle Hymn of the Republic," and another hymn that went O that will be glory for me, glory for me, glory for me; when by His grace I shall look on His face, that will be glory, be glory for me!

The followers gathered as the sound of the hymns floated over the camp. They stood silent outside the rent-a-fence while the songs were sung, listening respectfully. *I will know my Savior when I come to him, by the marks where the nails went in.*

—It's beautiful, said Ann to Ben, who had come out of the bus to listen with a sheaf of membership applications in hand.

—With music it doesn't matter what they're actually saying, said Ben.

Ann was thinking that even what the songs said was beautiful, but she added nothing. *Shall we gather by the river, where bright angel feet have trod? With its crystal tide forever, flowing by the throne of God?*

❧ Ben watched the singers in the dark and wondered how they had decided to come here, what brought them away from the rest of the faithful.

❧ —This is the march on Washington, said Szilard to reporters in Memphis, Tennessee.

He wanted to make the speech outside Graceland, because, he told Ann earnestly, it had once been the home of a well-known dead singer named Elvis Presley.

The others dissuaded him.

—And what do you plan to do when you get there?

—As we tour the country we make an average of six stops a day. Campaign volunteers gather signatures for our petition, which we plan to present to the president and Congress. And there will be a demonstration, said Szilard. —We are planning a spectacular event.

Later she asked him what he meant by that, but he would not tell her how spectacular the event would be.

But Szilard insisted on visiting Graceland, trouping through the house's narrow halls with the rest of the tourists, marveling at the gold records on the walls and the meditation garden. And that night, in a rare digression from his usually narrow focus, he sat outside the bus reading a book about Elvis that detailed the singer's exploitation and victimization by Colonel Tom Parker, who had managed his career.

—A very charismatic individual, said Szilard admiringly as he read. —And surprisingly intelligent.

—Elvis?

—Of course not! The colonel.

❧ They were eating lunch in a diner in Nashville when they heard Szilard from all the way across the room.

—They said yes to the DNA! he whooped, jogging over with a crumpled fax in his hand. He leaned over and clasped Fermi's shoulder in a rare display of emotion. —Your family!

Fermi paused in his eating and looked up into Szilard's face for an instant. Then he nodded, looked down at his food again and continued to eat.

—In return for very generous compensation, of course, went on Szilard. —Thanks to Larry.

Fermi nodded and refused to meet his eyes again, focussing on his hamburger. He was cutting it up with a knife and fork and chewing slowly, with distaste.

—The logistics are extremely challenging, said Szilard. —We have to send out the samples to multiple labs, the whole testing and comparison process has to be overseen by neutral parties for verification purposes, and when they collect your present sample, Enrico—Glen's setting it up for Greensboro—there will be a lot of witnesses, some of them probably hostile. But don't worry. It will go quickly.

—I will submit to this, Leo, said Fermi curtly. —But I don't wish to discuss it further.

Ben watched as Szilard stood crestfallen. Then his hurt shifted to disappointment, and he trudged around to the other side of the booth and slid in.

—Do they have ice cream? he asked quietly, and reached for a menu. —I want a sundae with hot fudge and whipped cream.

Watching as he trailed a finger down the menu selections, looking over the glasses that were perched halfway down his nose and pretending to concentrate on what he was reading, Ben felt a rare pang of affection for him.

Later Fermi said, —They paid my family to let my body be dug up.

—Don't judge your relatives for it though, said Ben. —I'm sure Larry offered them so much they couldn't refuse. They may be giving the money to charity, for all you know. They may be endowing a physics program. We don't know.

—It's not that I care about my body, said Fermi. —It's that Larry knows more about them than I do.

—It's best for them, said Ben.

Fermi nodded. —But not for me.

❧ Ann discovered a lack of order in the office of the bus. Big Glen's approach to filing was whimsical: he piled all file folders of the same color together, reds with reds, purples with purples, moss-green with moss-green. But the colors were not a code. They had no meaning.

As she labeled the files and arranged them in the drawers the bus traveled east from Knoxville at its usual sluggish speed of forty and it struck her that she had turned into a secretary. She had demoted herself from librarian to executive assistant, a groupie with secretarial skills.

She sat down heavily next to Oppenheimer, who was reading the news off his laptop, and thought: I joined a cult.

Next came the Kool-Aid and the mass suicide.

❧ Fermi wished that he could isolate himself, Ben could tell. But he did not want to be alone with no tasks. He wanted work to do; he wanted to keep busy. And in the bus there was nothing for him to do except respond to his public—which duty he refused—or endure Szilard.

He educated himself with gardening magazines and a few books on contemporary physics. In general, he told Ben, he found them highly speculative, all math and no mechanics. Physicists ceased to value experimentation, he said, and had apparently begun to think of themselves as philosophers or high priests, due in part to the ascendancy of their field of study.

Many of them were concerned with the origins of the universe, said Fermi, and because of this they confused mathematics with theology.

❧ During the decades of the Cold War there could never be enough nuclear weapons, yet there were always too many. For any practical purpose up to and including global annihilation, there were simply far too many.

At the height of this frenzy of production in 1960, before it refined its arsenal for accuracy instead of brute force, the U.S. alone possessed twenty thousand megatons worth of bombs. This was the equivalent of 1.4 million Hiroshimas.

❧ —The test was a match, said Szilard softly to Oppenheimer and Ben. —Fermi's DNA and the corpse of Fermi. I haven't told him.

For a few moments Ben considered the possibility that Szilard was lying, that in fact everything Szilard ever said was a lie, with elaborately fabricated documentation. Then he realized it did not matter what he thought.

—No one's going to believe it, Leo, he said.

He was standing with Oppenheimer beside a picnic table at the rest stop, smoking. Two burly Huts guarded them, telling loud racist jokes. Szilard sat on the table, his feet on the bench, his laptop on his lap, fingers on the keyboard.

—We have independent third-party verification, said Szilard, eyes scanning the screen rapidly. —From four different sources. We subcontracted four separate analyses at four separate labs. There was oversight. They all got the same results!

—It doesn't matter, Leo, said Ben. —No one's going to buy it. It won't mean anything to them. You can't prove what no one wants to believe. If some guy stepped up to a microphone and claimed there was proof that little green men had come down and killed Elvis, people would just laugh. Even if he had the proof. You see?

—But that's ridiculous.

—I'm telling you, the media won't buy it and neither will the public.

—That's where you're wrong, said Szilard. —People want to believe. Didn't you ever see *The X-Files*?

❧ —So, you still stoop to talk to the little people, said Clint.

—If you resent it all so much why don't you just take off?

Exasperated was the best she could do, though she still wanted to slap his face. If she had been the bitch he thought she was, she thought, she would have called over the nearest Hut and had him dragged off screaming.

—I mean no one is keeping you here, she went on. —And you can stop with the attitude, too. None of this was my idea. I'm not the boss.

—Come on, I'm just pickin', he said, and punched her arm with a gesture that was supposed to pass for light. But it hurt and she felt the sharpness of his hairy knuckles and put her hand on the bruised-feeling place. He leered. He had taken to wearing a white ribbon on the end of his greasy ponytail, tied into a bow. It hung down his chest now, a bizarre complement to his greasy black leather cap. —Dontcha even got a sense of humor?

He was mean. That was the risk of an ungenerous nature, she thought, whereas adoring made people spill with life. It was a talent to love, to adore and worship, and it was how they adored that made them tender, made them live as though life was a gift instead of a right. She did not mean religion when she thought of adoration: religion was a place that feeling went, but it was not feeling itself. She meant something that was not religion and also was not love, because there was no reflection of the self in it. At least there was no enlarging of the self.

In the face of the unnameable the self became very small, and then it turned buoyant.

❧ In eastern North Carolina Szilard did campus recruitment, taking Oppenheimer along for a mascot. Together they made the rounds: the University of North Carolina at Chapel Hill, North Carolina State, Duke University. Often Szilard would make his stump speech and then Oppenheimer would step up to the microphone and pronounce a sentence or two. It was all that was required of him.

The caravan gained in numbers, camped out in a moist small-treed private forest outside Durham. Permission had been given by a wealthy local landowner with ties to a fast-food chain, so the caravan waited with its generators and satellite dishes for Szilard to decide it was time to move on.

—His press conference about the DNA was a failure, said Ben, coming back to camp after a day in downtown Raleigh.

Ann was entering phone messages into a database on the computer in the bus while Dory opened fan mail for Oppenheimer. *You rule the starry night king of Kings lord of Lords. Pray for my son he has spina bifida. Can you sign this piece of cloth with Ballpoint Pen and send it back, I will keep it with me every waking moment.*

Having Dory help her with menial tasks made Ann feel like a *little woman,* like one of a huddle of submissive females enlisted to back up the great men. For that reason she preferred to work alone. But lately Dory came toward her in the morning saying —How can I help?, asking questions and bustling around till she was given a task.

—How do you mean, a failure?

—There was a good turnout but I don't think anyone's going to take it seriously. I mean how could they?

❧ Fermi decided to lead a weekend hike along the Appalachian Trail. He would not be dissuaded: it was all he wanted.

The leaves of trees were beginning to turn yellow and a coolness descended at night. He had read that there were wooden cabins to sleep in up near the peaks and bright waterfalls flowing over smooth stones.

While the other scientists went to court in Albuquerque he would be breathing the air of the rolling Blue Ridge Mountains, he told Ann. But then Oppenheimer wanted to go into the hills too and Szilard was forced to fly out West by himself.

Four of them went to hike the trail, the two scientists and Ben and Dory. Ann had to stay behind at camp because of her ankle, which was not yet strong enough for mountains. Szilard had insisted that the hikers take Huts along themselves for protection, but once he was gone Fermi ignored the suggestion. —I do not hike with bodyguards, he said resolutely.

She watched them get ready to leave, feeling left out. Ben packed two day's worth of nuts and dried fruit and Oppenheimer took a walking stick with a carved wooden parrot's head for a handle. Fermi was sporting an absurd pair of Bavarian lederhosen he'd found in a vintage clothing store. Apparently the lederhosen reminded him of the Tyrolean gear he had worn for his Alpine hikes in the 1930s.

❧ They had walked for hours and were sitting beneath a canopy of oak and hickory trees a few paces off the trail, eating sandwiches and apples, when Fermi looked up, vigilant, his head cocked.

—We are not alone, he said. —Be quiet.

Ben followed his gaze and saw a deer in the shade of thin, close-growing trees, and then a fawn beside it. As he stared they moved a little closer: then there was a faint shout and they bolted. He turned and squinted and could barely make out a figure a few hundred yards down the trail. Soon he saw more of them, a dark mass of figures behind the first one. The noise was growing.

They were legion.

—Oh no, said Oppenheimer. —It's them.

Dory lifted her camcorder and pointed it at the far-off crowd.

—Let's get out of here, said Fermi, stuffing the lunch remnants into his backpack. —I have a compass and I think I can get us to the cabin bushwhacking.

They took off after him through the trees and down the hill of a steep ravine, leaving the trail and the crowd behind them. Ben looked at his feet as they descended, sidestepping. He watched his stiff industrial running shoes crushing leaves, stomping through mountain laurel. They were out of place there.

❧ Ann sat outside the bus by the fire, her lame foot up on a folding chair. She stared up at the stars, obscured by artificial light.

Clint and others from Tokyo were playing cards at a small table outside the second bus, parked inside the perimeter fence. They hunched over, shutting out the world with their backs. Out of necessity they maintained a respectful attitude toward Larry and the scientists, but the others in the first bus had become objects of their scorn. A bunker mentality had settled among them.

The wind shifted and she had to lean out of the column of smoke, move her weak foot off the chair and then rise. She hobbled away from the ring of fire coughing and squinting and saw someone waving from across the highway, so she lifted an arm and waved back briefly. She wished she was up in the mountains of Virginia with the others, far from the trailers and the fences and the Huts patrolling.

She limped slowly outside the fence into a fringe of trees. She wanted to be clear of the lights of the road and the camp, of the fluorescent seep of the Wal-Mart parking lot. It was impossible to walk far on the weak ankle but she wanted to see the sky straight above her, to make out the stars and guess how many eons away they were, how deep and far in time.

The give of soil and pine needles beneath her feet was a relief from the parking lot.

—I brought this for you, said a man behind her, and she shrieked, jumping as she turned. But it was Webster, smiling and apologetic, holding up a frayed lawn chair. —Sorry!

—No, I'm just—

—Of course you're nervous, I'm really sorry. After what happened to you I shouldn't have surprised you like that. Anyways. I thought you might want to rest.

He bent over and set down the chair carefully in the humus and dead leaves, grinding the aluminum legs into the ground for stability.

—I heard your divorce came through.

She sat down in the chair as he shuffled around to stand in front of her.

—Oh, yeah, he said softly. —She was a nice lady. I mean, she is.

—Are you sorry?

—You know, she found another guy she liked better, said Webster, and shrugged. —People choose.

She looked up at him but could not see his face well in the dark. The trees barely swayed above them.

—Anyways, I'll be getting back, he said. —You can just leave the chair here when you're done, I'll pick it up in the morning.

—Thank you, she said again, and did not watch as he walked past her and out of the trees again.

She could see the stars now, faintly, through the gaps in the branches above.

❧ Sitting in the dark could not go on forever, even if, Ann thought, it was better than being at camp surrounded by the others. She touched the frayed straps of the chair beside her thigh, the frayed nylon threads stiff and sharp at the end, and reflected that she would not know this chair by daylight: she only knew it at night. Its colors were a mystery to her and yet they pressed against her cool skin.

❧ Fermi had not found the trail or the cabin again and they had not brought their tents, so they unrolled their sleeping bags onto the dewy grass in a small meadow.

—We will find it tomorrow, promised Fermi.

Dory wandered off into the trees with a flashlight, leaving the men to arrange themselves around the pile of backpacks and boots.

—So, said Ben to Oppenheimer when they lay down, —where is this all going?

—After the march on Washington, said Oppenheimer, —I don't know. I just follow orders from Leo.

—What's it for?

—What's anything for? We're here. We have to do something with our time. We don't have our families anymore.

—That must be the hardest.

—It is. That and the world gotten old and ugly.

—I'm sorry you have to go through this.

—I'm just waiting, said Oppenheimer softly.

—What are you waiting for?

—I don't know yet.

❧ The morning was newer when you slept outside than inside, Ben thought as he woke up to birdsong from the meadow edge, his back aching from the hard ground, the edges of his sleeping bag wet with dew. Each morning was the only morning.

❧ Shaking her awake, stooped over close, Big Glen was too big, mammoth, rough and stubbly. She pulled away from his grip on her shoulder and sat up and back, clutching sheets. Oppenheimer's bed was comfortable. It had cradled her. She was not used to comfort recently.

—What?

—It's Dr. Leo on the cell phone. He says the Army has the documents after all and the judge said it has to hand them over. The Army has Oppenheimer's and Fermi's fingerprints but not Dr. Leo's but he says he expected that because he wasn't exactly an employee of the Engineering District when they started the fingerprinting plus he wasn't ever at Los Alamos. But so anyway the Army has five business days to give them to us. He says we won!

—Good, said Ann, and slouched down in the covers again.

—That's good but why does it mean I have to be woken up at—

She glanced at the digital clock on the indoor-outdoor carpet.

—6:13 in the morning? Isn't it like 3 a.m. where he is?

—He wants you to start organizing the press conference. He wants you to fax him a list of all the numbers—

—Tough, said Ann, and turned her face to the wall. —It can wait.

Glen breathed slowly for a few seconds beside her and then got up and walked away.

❧ They got back onto the trail in the early afternoon and it was late afternoon when they reached the cabin, a wooden building beside a waterfall with bunk beds, a dining room and a kitchen with a stone floor. There was a cook, a tanned, muscular college girl and an older man who did the cleaning and heavy work, emptying the cans from the outhouse and hauling out garbage.

—We have a very large group staying here, said the cook, —but there are thirty-five of them so there should be enough beds left for the four of you. The others will be back around dinnertime. It's spaghetti. Make yourselves comfortable and just set up your beds wherever you find an empty bunk.

When the first sounds of the crowd reached his ears Ben was sitting beside Oppenheimer and Dory on the front porch. Oppenheimer was wearing his porkpie hat, smoking a pipe, and cautiously perusing a dog-eared romance called *Sweet Jezebel*. He had found it on the cabin's one shelf of books.

—It's them, said Dory.

—We can go, said Ben urgently. —We still have time to get away, if we grab our things and head down the mountain on the other side of the falls.

—I'm tired, said Oppenheimer, shrugging, and continued to read *Sweet Jezebel*.

But when the followers caught sight of them and teemed onto the porch—first a tall man with a blond beard carrying a cooler, then some chunky frat boys in T-shirts stamped with pictures of bikini-clad women—they were feverish. It was a euphoric mass with a tinge of hysteria, less a crowd than a mob, exuding a frayed energy that made Ben nervous instantly. The edges of the mob felt raw and uncontrolled, spun out by afternoon drinking and testosterone. They knew the names of the scientists, even Ben's name and Dory's, as though a mythology was in place and they had studied it. But the scientists did not recognize any of them and neither did Ben.

Fermi had been napping on his bunk but suddenly he was with them, borne aloft on the shoulders of two large men. Ben looked up to see them coming out the front door with him, the screen banging behind them. Fermi looked anxious, even panicked, clutching their shirt collars and shaking his head in protest as they whooped and spun him around.

Ben could hardly tell what was happening. Was something happening? There was motion but he did not know how to interpret it. The followers were clustered so tightly around Oppenheimer that he was hidden from view, and Dory, clutching her camcorder and filming with shaky hands, was huddled in a corner of the porch beside the door. He saw the cook inside, peering out through the screen with a yellow apron on, holding a wooden spoon.

—OK, let him down now, he said to the men carrying Fermi, and grabbed one of their arms to get their attention. —Put him down! He's not a toy.

But they didn't seem to hear him. Instead they were bounding off the porch, Fermi precarious above them, and heading toward the waterfall with others streaming after, cheering. Then the people around Oppenheimer lifted him up too, and before Ben could even reach out to try to stop them they were taking him off away. Its front cover ripped off, *Sweet Jezebel* was left face-down, mashed, spine broken on the wooden slats of the porch where Oppenheimer had been. His pipe was still perched precariously on the wooden railing and his hat had fallen into the shrubbery.

After a panicked glance at each other Ben and Dory went jogging after them, stunned and speechless at first. Then Dory let her camcorder fall to her side to call after the men: —What are you doing? You can't do that to him! We can call the police! Are you even listening?

Ben caught up to the men carrying Oppenheimer but could not catch Oppenheimer's attention, and pulling on sleeves and jabbing at ribs had no effect: no one even turned to look at him. Then they were scrambling over a flat, jutting slab of slate-gray rock, looking down at the whitewater a few feet away to the left, watching it course down the mountainside, sparkling in the calm light of dusk. There was a purple cast to the water, reflecting the eastern sky.

—Here! There's a shallow pool over here! called a woman in a broad straw hat with a polka dot band, and the men bearing Fermi splashed over to the right, stepping on a chain of rocks through shallow rivulets. The others followed them.

—What are you *doing*? yelled Ben, but the sound of the rushing was loud and no one was listening anyway. He reached up and grabbed at the back of Oppenheimer's shirt, tugging it and saying, —Just kick out at them! I'll help you get down! but Oppenheimer did not seem to hear him. Instead he seemed to be calmly gazing at the horizon above all their heads, where the sun was setting dimly behind a thin streak of gray cloud. He gazed as though there was nothing to be done, as though all he could do was look at the sky. Fermi was twisting on the shoulders of his captors and hitting their shoulders, trying to get down.

—Let's put them in! called the blond man.

The scientists were being lifted down and carried, more hands on their bodies than there was room, and then dropped in the shallow pool of water above the falls. Fermi looked rigid with fear as they put him down but Oppenheimer's face was tolerant, as though nothing anymore had the power to surprise him.

—Repentance is yours! I herewith baptize you in water, said the blond bearded man, and dripped water from his hand onto Fermi's balding head.

—Oh no, said Ben.

But he saw that Fermi was relieved: at least no one was trying to drown him. He stood in the rocky pool blank-faced, staring through the legs of the crowd around him.

Dory hesitated but then raised the camcorder to record the event, apparently satisfied that there was not going to be further violence.

—Verily, verily, I say unto thee, except a man be born of water and of the Spirit, he cannot enter into the kingdom of God, said the blond man, and tipped water onto Oppenheimer's head as the woman in the straw hat poured water on Fermi.

There was no escaping it, thought Ben. He was glad Ann was safe at the bus.

—Now you are ready! In the light of your repentance we hereby baptize you Enrico Fermi and Robert Oppenheimer, in the name of the Father, the Son and the Holy Spirit, said the woman in the straw hat, and then the crowd was clapping and hooting, and Fermi and Oppenheimer stood beside each other in the shallow pool, soaked and tired.

A bell rang and the cook's voice called them faintly to dinner. The people wandered away leaving Ben and Dory alone with Fermi and Oppenheimer, still standing in the pool where the baptists had left them. Ben went and knelt on the rock ledge, leaning down to offer them a hand up.

—I don't think we brought any towels but you can wear my big sweater, said Dory to Oppenheimer as he stepped out.

He shook his head.

—No, you need it yourself, he said, his teeth chattering. —I'll be fine.

—It's fall, said Dory. —You could catch a cold!

—Americans are mentally disturbed, said Fermi, wiping the back of his hand over his wet forehead. His long nose was dripping. —All of them. They have mental problems.

—You may have a point there, said Ben.

—They are hysterical, said Fermi.

—Drugs, said Ben.

—Should we leave? asked Dory.

—I'm not going down the mountain in wet clothes, said Oppenheimer. —I want to be warm. And sleep.

—Let's eat some spaghetti and talk about it, said Ben.

—Do you want to press charges? At least we could sue them in civil court, said Dory.

—Forget it, said Oppenheimer wearily, as they headed toward the cabin. His wet leather shoes squeezed water onto the rocks.

❧ By the turn of the millennium, nuclear weapons production facilities occupied over three thousand square miles of U.S. territory.

❧ Szilard was flushed with victory when he got in from the airport, striding up to the picnic table flanked by two Huts who were carrying his briefcase and overnight bag. —This is the linchpin! he told Ann. —We will be triumphant!

—Aren't you counting your chickens?

—The only remaining hurdle to our widespread acceptance has been jumped.

—I don't know, Leo, said Ann, and drank from her mug of wine. —They can still claim forgery, I think. Most people aren't going to buy that you guys were transported in time, or rose from the grave, or whatever.

—The anomaly? said Szilard. —Yes they will. With the fingerprints and Fermi's DNA test—Glen, did you set up the next press conference yet?

Big Glen, hunched over the campfire with a cup of coffee, glanced up guiltily.

—We were waiting to get more direction from you, he said gruffly, shooting an accusing look at Ann.

—You're kidding! We have to move on this *immediately*. Are you joking with me?

—Without you, Leo, said Ann, —we're just useless.

Szilard looked slightly mollified as he gestured imperiously at the Huts to take his luggage inside. Then he sat down at the end of a picnic bench and grubbed around on the table until he found a mixed bag of cookies.

—Of course, we may want to combine it with the march on Washington, he conceded, and discarded an oatmeal raisin carelessly to grab a chocolate chip.

Later she brushed her teeth at the edge of the trees because Szilard was monopolizing the bathroom. She rinsed her mouth with water from a plastic cup and was standing staring at nothing when she noticed Father Raymond in the distance, saying an evening prayer with a small congregation kneeling in the grass in front of him. She walked over slowly, toothbrush and plastic cup in hand, skirting the chain-link fence that surrounded the bus.

—Once again, as the end of the day falls upon us and upon all of God's creatures under this wide, great dome of a sky, we beg to gain strength in our sleep, to fortify us for the new dawn. We beg for the will to help make peace a shining force in all of our lives, for the fortitude to keep steadfast in our faith that all is not lost and that brotherhood and goodness can still reign on this sad and battered earth. And now please join me in the Lord's Prayer.

She mouthed the words with the rest of them, looking at their closed eyes, and was reminded of a saint Ben had described to her. It was a saint his mother had made a pilgrimage to see when she was a little girl, whose sparkling image she had brought home depicted on a postcard and kept to show to her son many years later. The saint had been exhumed on the whim of some potentate in the church who had seen a vision of her purity. Miraculously it was found that her body never decomposed: her face and body were pure and unlined. She was buried and exhumed again and still there was little decay.

Finally the corpse was coated in wax, laid in a glass box like Snow White and put on display. This was in a church in southern France. The saint's large white eyes were closed but still luminous, and she was known far and wide as an incorruptible.

—For thine is the Kingdom and the Power and the Glory, forever and ever. Amen.

The congregation rose with wet patches on the knees of their jeans and skirts, said quiet goodnights to Father Raymond and wandered off toward their tents and cars and vans.

—I have noticed, said Father Raymond to Ann, closing his book and zipping up his pale windbreaker against the evening, —that more and more of the followers here are turning to God. Have you noticed that?

—What I see is more and more of followers joining us because of their religion, said Ann. —It seems to me the tone has changed, the new people are on some kind of crusade. The scientists don't understand it and neither do I. I mean these are secular men.

—Would you like to walk and talk?

—I have some wine over at the picnic table if you'd like a glass.

He was patted down by the Huts as they passed through the gate in the chain-link. When he raised his right arm, holding the Bible, its pages fell open and dried flowers fluttered out.

—I'll get those! said Ann apologetically. She lent down to pick them up off the grass, but they were old and turned to dust in her fingers.

—Don't worry, said Father Raymond, —there are plenty more where those came from.

—This red one, said Ann, —what is it?

—I never learn the names of flowers.

They sat down across from each other at the picnic table and she poured him wine into a chipped mug. He took it gratefully.

—My feeling is, he said, —the names people give to things are their own names.

—What do you mean?

—For example, you say that the scientists are secular men. This is what they say to themselves, but it is not necessarily the way that others see them.

—I guess not, she said. —I guess they can't choose how other people see them.

—None of us can, said Father Raymond, and drank. —It's an illusion we live with, that we can control the way we're seen. But in fact the way we feel that we are and the way we exist before others, these phenomena are distinct. They are separate apparitions.

—That's sad.

—It is sad only as long as you are afraid of it.

Ann decided to pour herself a glass of wine despite the taste of toothpaste in her mouth. It had already started to fade anyway.

—Raymond! Working for the cause these days? called Szilard from the bathroom window. His face was framed as though by a porthole: he was a man in a ship, out to sea. Darkness surrounded him, tossing.

—Always, brother Leo.

—I'll be with you two in a minute, said Szilard, assuming that they, like all people, were waiting for him.

❧ After dinner Oppenheimer smoked a cigarette, since his pipe had fallen off the porch rail and broken. He announced he was going to take a shower and walked back into the building; and a few minutes later Ben wandered past the shower room on his way to the outhouse. Turning his head he caught a glimpse of Oppenheimer sitting hunched on a bench beneath a showerhead, naked and thin, the water coursing over him.

On the tiled floor knelt a woman, washing his feet. Wet dirt streamed down into the round grate of the drain and Ben watched the brown grit carried, swirling. He thought he could hear the woman crying, but he was not sure.

Not stopping, walking past and seeing this only in a quick flash of perception, embarrassed by the intimacy, Ben was thinking only a few seconds later that he must have imagined it. After all Dory had been on the cabin porch, reading with a sharp-scented citronella candle burning on a small wicker table beside her.

On his way back from the outhouse he peered into the shower room again, but this time it was dark and both Oppenheimer and the washing woman had disappeared.

❧ Over breakfast Szilard announced they would tour the eastern seaboard before turning back and making their way to the capital.

He insisted on bacon with his pancakes and the bus was filled with smoke and the smell of bacon grease. Ann opened the door for fresh air and saw Big Glen approaching at a rapid clip, sweating, with four Huts arrayed behind him.

—We got problems, he said, stepping up into the bright-white vinyl kitchen.

—What problems, man? asked Larry, who was rolling a joint.

—There's a situation developing with the Christians.

All of them looked up at him then, waiting.

—Which Christians? asked Szilard.

—The Fundamentalists, said Big Glen. —They sent a representative to bring a message to us. I just met with him. Guy with a prosthetic arm?

—Go on, said Szilard, forking up bacon.

—They want, uh, what did they say. "A Christian voice in the leadership."

—What? asked Szilard.

—They say they make up 85 percent of the followers. That's what they claim. And they say that as the majority they deserve representation in the leadership of the campaign. Which they call the mission.

—Tell them if that's what they want they can just leave, said Szilard. —They can clear out today. There's no way.

—But it's most of the followers, said Glen, and pulled a small notepad out of his breast pocket. He flipped it open and traced a finger down some figures scrawled on the page, Ann craning her neck to see over his arm. His printing was careful and labored, all in capital letters. —According to them, it's now about twenty-three hundred out of three thousand. And they say the percentage is growing.

—I will not be blackmailed, said Szilard.

—At least meet with them, said Ann. —Show them some respect.

—Exactly, said Tamika. —People just want to feel included, Dr. Leo. You know? It's probably a cry for help.

❧ They went down the mountain at dawn while the mob was still asleep. With the weakly lit sky below them they crossed a bog by teetering on rotting logs between hummocks and jumping from mound to mound, feet sinking into the wet turf.

Ben looked into the brown water and saw insects dimpling the surface with their hair-thin feet. Then he glanced up at the trees on a ridge in front of them, where the ground would be dry again. When the mud sucked at his feet and he had to pull them loose from the suction he looked ahead to the dry ground and tried to think he was already there.

Later he sat on a damp tree stump batting at mosquitoes while they waited for Dory to finishing peeing, just out of their line of sight.

—Robert, he said into the silence, —excuse me, but I want to know if something I saw was real. Was there a woman in the shower with you last night?

—I think there was! said Oppenheimer, as if it had just occurred to him as a possibility. He pondered the question further and nodded vaguely, at a memory far too ancient to be clearly recalled.

2

❧ The Christians had set up a large, square pavilion of pale orange. Walking up to the tent with Szilard, Huts marching alongside, Ann thought of medieval battlefields she had seen in movies, of the French Foreign Legion, the temporary quarters of generals and sheiks.

In front of the tent coolers of drinks were arrayed, and fabric folding chairs with cupholders built into the arms.

The door of the tent was furled open, and they went in single-file. At a table sat a row of white men in sweatpants and pastel-colored windbreakers, pasty-faced and middle-aged.

—Please, Dr. Szilard, have a seat. And y'all other folks too.

—Ann, said Ann, reaching out her hand, —and this is Larry and Glen, and they shook hands it in turn.

—Steve Bradley, said the man in the center, who had a fat, ruddy face and a comb-over on his balding pate. He was the one with the prosthetic arm, and it did not have a hook. Ann looked at the prosthetic fingers discreetly. —I'm with the Love of Christ Redeemer. This is Rob with Sixth Pentecostal, and then the fella with the Confederate flag tattoo on his arm—

—Indiscretion of youth!

—that's Denny with the Baptist Collective. There are almost five hundred Baptists with us today. We are richly blessed with Baptists!

The men laughed heartily.

—So, said Szilard. —You wanted to talk to me?

—We have a proposal, said Bradley.

—Yes?

—What you need to realize, said Bradley, —is that for most of the people here, this is not a political campaign. This is a holy crusade. It is a pious journey, a sacred pilgrimage. It is a pouring forth of faith, a sacrament in blood.

—In blood? asked Ann.

—Blood, sweat and tears, said Bradley, looking only at Szilard. —Let me tell you something. These people have given up jobs. They have taken their *children* from their *schools* and away from their *homes*. They have left everything that they know, they have sacrificed the guarantee of the lives they gave up back there, just to join up and to march behind the three of *you*.

—Why? asked Szilard.

—Because these people *believe*. These people *know*. They know the last hours are at hand, they know the Rapture is almost upon us, and they also know why.

—We are working for peace, said Szilard. —Is that what you're talking about?

—What I'm telling you, said Bradley, wiping at his forehead as the sweat trickled down, —is that our people have their own vision of the mission here. They have a powerful vision. Some of them even believe in the Trinity.

—Trinity? The test?

—The Father, Son and Holy Ghost. To some of them, you are the Father. Dr. Oppenheimer is the messiah who died for us and comes back bringing the revealed truth of God. And the spirit, often invisible, the Holy Ghost, is of course Dr. Fermi. This is what many of the followers believe.

—As long as they want to work for peace, said Szilard, —we should be able to coexist. Do they want to work for peace?

There was a silence, oddly long.

—We are not interested in worldly matters, said Bradley. —We are interested in the Rapture. Our people will work for you. They want to see you attain your rightful stature. They believe in your divinity.

—But not peace? asked Ann.

Bradley shot her a sidelong look.

—I did not come to bring peace, but a sword. That's gospel. My people believe you are the ones who will bring the kingdom of God to earth.

—What Steve means, said the small man to the right of him, with a pinched face and a pink polo shirt, —is we feel, and the people we speak for feel, that they should be able to express their vision as part of the parade. That there should be a more democratic thing going on here, where people can express their own faith.

—Way it is right now, said another, —you folks decide everything. Which, if you consider you're only three guys, plus your staff, and we're maybe twenty-five hundred and growing all the time, isn't real fair.

—Janey! Could I get a Coke in here? bellowed Bradley, and a woman came bustling in with a plastic jug.

—I enjoy Coca-Cola, said Szilard.

—I'll have some too, said Larry.

—We in the Redeemer Conference, said Bradley as his wife poured Coke into plastic cups, —have felt very frustrated by the lack of Christian guidance in this mission.

—The reason there hasn't been Christian guidance, said Szilard, —is we're not Christian. I myself am Jewish, as is Oppenheimer.

—What I'm saying, Dr. Szilard, said Bradley, —is the mission *is* Christian. Now.

Szilard lifted his plastic cup of Coke and drank deeply.

—I'm not sure I follow you, he said finally, when he set the cup down.

—The numbers speak for themselves. And we feel it is a moral imperative for the Christian following to take a leadership role. If there's no effort made by management to include us, we will have to take action.

—When you say leadership role, said Szilard, —what exactly do you mean?

—For example, when you talk about the mission on TV, said the man in the pink polo shirt, —the name of Christ is hardly ever mentioned.

—Of course it isn't mentioned, said Szilard irritably. —Why would it be?

There was another silence, and the men at the table looked at each other and then faced Szilard again.

—We didn't want to have to put it this way, said Bradley, —but what the situation is here? Unless we get a Christian person in management, with decision-making power, we're going to have to break off.

—Break off? asked Szilard, picking up his empty cup.

—Take our twenty-five hundred followers in Christ and leave the mission. We know what we know, but we have to work to spread the word in a Christian way.

There was a silence. Szilard studied the cup, turning it in his fingers as though it contained an answer.

—Well, said Szilard, putting the cup down again, pushing his chair back and rising, —thank you for your frankness. We'll certainly think it over.

Ann felt he had been uncharacteristically tactful.

❧ The Christians sent them a note later that day at a crowded fuel stop. They had received permission to camp in a vacant business park in a suburb of Baltimore for the next week. The CEO of the landlord company was a believer, the note said, and the business park was between tenants. There was a map included.

When the buses pulled into the parking lots in the dark, a chain of concrete lakes around an island of sleek glass buildings, Oppenheimer and Fermi were already asleep. They parked at the edge of the lot, beneath a tall lamp, and got out to explore as the Huts set up the perimeter fence and the other trailers began to pull in after them.

One of the buildings in the complex was standing open so that the followers could use the toilets. Its interior lights had been left on too, glaring out through plate-glass windows and flooding the parking lot with an eerie fluorescence. As cars and vans streamed in the eeriness was lost and the park became gritty and glaring, a dirty fairground at night.

Walking with Ben down a gravel path that skirted the building, Ann was slow and careful on the bad ankle. Behind them followers set up their tents with a streamlined efficiency and were quickly roasting hot dogs and singing prayers.

—Look at that, said Ben, and pointed to a pile of trash cans beside a service entrance. A family of raccoons moved among them, two adults and five young.

—They're beautiful! said Ann, as they purred and hissed and tore at garbage with their sharp teeth, their black eyes wide and vigilant, having known her presence before she knew theirs.

—Scavengers, said Ben.

Above them a bat flitted and swooped near a lamp post, and Ben followed it with his eyes as it vanished in the dark again.

—Do you think you know what's happening anymore? she asked him.

—I have no idea what's happening.

—How about when we get to D.C. and they do the demonstration? Is it over then?

—It's already over, said Ben.

❧ In the morning Szilard took the other scientists aside to discuss the request from the Christians. Ann and Ben were not privy to the conversation but afterward Oppenheimer came and sat at the picnic table and told them what his contribution had been.

—There's no harm, he said, —in including them. To let them have a voice is not to submit to their direction.

—I think you'll find, said Ben, —that is a naïve conclusion.

Oppenheimer exhaled smoke and cocked an eyebrow at him, mulling it over.

A few minutes later Larry and Big Glen came back from a second meeting in the orange pavilion.

—It's going to be Bradley, said Glen.

In the bus office, combing through newspapers for stories about them and watching his wife sort mail as Tamika and Dory filed faxes in the scientists' inboxes, Ben said softly: —This is going to change everything.

—I know, she said.

When he looked up from his stack of papers he saw Dory had the camcorder on her shoulder and was filming them, *documenting their role*. That was what she said when people asked her why she was taping them changing their clothes or applying deodorant. "Documenting your role," she always said.

He knew the answer already but a mean impulse drove him to ask: —That wasn't you, was it Dory? With Oppenheimer in the shower?

—What?

As his phone rang and he slipped his hand in his pocket to get it she snapped at the bait. —There was a woman in the shower with him?

❧ —The first request was banners, said Big Glen gruffly.

Ann and Ben pitched their tent beside the trees that flanked the rest room building and he came to talk to them there, where they sat in folding chairs eating sandwiches.

—Banners? asked Ben.

—It used to be against Szilard's rules so now they want to decorate their vehicles with these, uh, testimonies to Christ.

She tossed away the last crust of bread and walked through the crowds camped out nearby. There were arts and crafts projects in progress, followers kneeling on the ground on long rolls of news-print, painting signs.

Back West the women traveling in the church buses had worn skirts and low-heeled pumps every day. Their hair had been freshly permed in tight curls around their heads and they had smelled of cheap shampoo, girlish perfume and cloying deodorant. Now their hair hung lank, tied back in rubber bands, and instead of skirts and blouses they wore T-shirts, once-white sneakers and dappled acid-wash jeans with elastic waistbands that might have been briefly in style sometime in the early 1980s. They could not bathe often enough on the road and so they cleaned themselves with baby wipes, their faces and armpits. She had seen the evidence walking past their campsites, toiletries laid out on folding tables: razors for the men, plastic tubs marked *baby powder scent* and basins full of gray soapy water.

One or two of them recognized her and waved as she passed, leaning over them to look at their signs and banners. She read ALL HAIL THE NAZARENE as well as quotations from Scripture: THE GOOD SHEPHERD LAYS DOWN HIS LIFE FOR THE SHEEP. THE END OF ALL THINGS IS AT HAND; KEEP SANE AND SOBER FOR YOUR PRAYERS. CHILDREN, YOUR SINS ARE FORGIVEN. LEAD ME TO MOUNT ZION!!!

❧ When the caravan moved on Ann and Ben decided to drive their own car. They sat on the hood in the clear chill of the morning, drinking hot drinks as the rest of the cars pulled out.

It took hours and Ann counted the banners and signs until she got bored. BE NOT AMAZED; HE HAS AGAIN RISEN. OPEN THE GATES, SAVIOR, WE ARE READY. HAIL THE REDEEMER. GOD'S LOVE GOES ON FOREVER BUT THE HUMAN RACE WILL END. There were Jamaican flags, Jews for Jesus, doves of peace and eagles clutching machine guns. There was a family in a station wagon, whose children made faces out the windows as they passed.

She was stunned by the numbers.

—Szilard must be livid, said Ben.

When all the cars, vans, motorcycles, and buses had passed Ann walked around the parking lot. Garbage was piled everywhere and there were puddles of liquid on the concrete, yellow, blue, coffee-colored, rainbows of gasoline. Crossing the lot to use the bathroom she noticed a window pane in the building was broken, cracks spidering out from a bullet-sized hole. She followed trampled cups and food debris down the corridor to the women's bathroom, where a toilet was spilling water onto the floor and water was also running in a sink filled with wet cornflakes. She turned off the tap and looked at broken soap dispensers that had left pink pools on the counter, used tampons bursting from a metal box on the wall and one long bulb flickering over open stall doors that revealed mounds of sodden toilet paper wadded and trailing on the footprinted floor.

On her way out she passed a raccoon slinking along the wall of the corridor, leaving bloody tracks behind. Outside the door a smashed whiskey bottle lay on the concrete and she wondered if it had stepped on a piece of broken glass.

❧ In terms of the sheer number of nuclear warheads, Cold War proliferation peaked for the U.S. in 1966, when the country had thirty-two thousand warheads active.

By 1967, when China detonated its first high-yield nuclear device at Lop Nur, that number dropped to a mere thirty thousand and continued to descend until it reached about ten thousand stockpiled weapons in 2003.

The Soviet Union's stockpile did not peak until 1986, when it reached over forty thousand.

❧ Oppenheimer had become more and more passive. He was not distressed but content.

—I have a feeling these days of being carried, he said to Ann as they walked by the river. —I'm lying on my back being carried along.

૭ Szilard was waiting impatiently near the reflecting pool in Rittenhouse Square when they got there. He grabbed Oppenheimer by the shirtsleeve and pulled him aside. Ann could hear his stage-whisper as they retreated: —They want a press conference. They insisted. They had the nerve to claim that while we are "still *management*," they are the *leadership*.

She did not want to be part of the press conference so she took Ben's hand and guided him to a nearby fountain where they could sit down. The followers had not been alerted to the occasion except for the Christian leaders, who huddled together with notes and cordless microphones.

Then the network news vans arrived and before Szilard could speak Bradley had called the press to attention and with the other leaders arrayed behind him had begun to pace back and forth talking about the Second Coming. Feedback crackled.

Ann and Ben were sitting too far away to hear every word, but beside her Ben shook his head. She had a feeling of detachment from everything, of something lost and dispersed and replaced by the strange.

But they were shaded and comfortable where they sat, and the trees were tall and broad and old.

—What are these? she asked him idly.

—There's maples, of course, and oaks, and those are locusts. That one there is a plane tree, said Ben, pointing.

Bradley launched into a passage from the Book of Revelation and Ann looked at the reporters, expecting them to turn away. Instead they watched him with unchanging faces, their cameras rolling. Behind Bradley the three scientists stood in their Sunday best, proper in suits and ties, Oppenheimer cutting his usual old-fashioned and dignified figure in the porkpie hat. Their hands were clasped in front of them, except for Szilard who was rifling through a sheaf of papers.

The other two waited with patient expressions, as though they were not consciously present but dreaming where they stood.

Paper snagged on her leg. Sheets of it were fluttering across the square, caught by the breeze. Szilard had passed out press packets full of documents and reporters had dropped them.

—. . . What we say, said Bradley, —what Scripture says, that now is the time for the armies of light, for the lifting up to the final days. We will build this army greater and greater. All Christians everywhere should join us, and the unsaved too. This is a call to arms: join our quest for peace and salvation in the risen Jesus Christ Our Lord!

—Amen, chorused the Christian leaders behind him, nodding.

Ann saw a reporter near her mouth the word *Amen* silently, as though it was a reflex.

Bradley relinquished the microphone to Szilard, who snatched it from him with a flick of his wrist.

—We welcome volunteers and advocates of all kinds, he said through gritted teeth. —All that you have to believe in is peace. And now to the substance of this press conference. You have in your hands the proof that Dr. Enrico Fermi, standing here to my right, is who he claims to be and none other. This has been rigorously verified and attested to by a panoply of DNA experts and neutral third-party observers who monitored the testing process, including the chain of custody of all DNA samples during transportation and laboratory guardianship . . .

The reporters looked bored, moving their feet restlessly and making adjustments to their cameras and microphones.

—Look at Fermi, whispered Ben, and she stood up and leaned around the shoulder of a reporter for a better view.

Beside Szilard Fermi was turning round and round where he stood, his eyes wide, his arms raised slightly from his sides.

—. . . at that time, said Szilard, —we will press for recognition of our special status by the president and Congress—

—What the hell? whispered Ben.

Reporters were craning their necks too, squinting to try to see what Fermi was doing. When Oppenheimer noticed Fermi's movement he leaned behind Szilard to whisper something to Fermi, but Fermi shook his head and kept turning.

—Something's wrong with him, said Ben. —Something is *wrong*. I'm getting him down.

She watched as Ben pushed his way through the crowd, up to the front, past Szilard who was talking about reaching out through the United Nations to all the countries of the world. He took Fermi gently by the arm, leaning in close to whisper in his ear. Fermi nodded and Ben led him toward the street.

She skirted the throng to catch up with them.

—Enrico, are you OK? she asked softly when she reached them, touching his shoulder.

—OK, he said distractedly, but she caught Ben's eye and he shook his head.

—What were you doing up there?

—The updraft, he mumbled.

—The updraft?

—You just need to rest, said Ben. —I think we'll get you a hotel room for a couple of nights. It's so crowded in the bus. Would you like that?

❧ When the other scientists paid them a visit at the hotel that night they were confused.

Ann and Ben had taken a room next door and called Larry, who came with Tamika trotting beside him, ready for the hotel pool with her bikini over her arm.

—He's not himself, Ben told Oppenheimer, who had requested

a meeting in the cocktail lounge where he could smoke. Szilard was coming later. —He's not here.

—I don't understand what happened, said Oppenheimer. —Did something happen to him?

—Nothing that we know of, said Ben.

They went up to Fermi's room together, the two of them with Oppenheimer, along a long dim corridor with a striped carpet in blue and beige and framed prints of flowers on the walls. Ann knocked lightly. For a long time there was no answer, and then she noticed the door was not clicked closed and pushed it open, calling his name.

—Enrico?

Fermi was sitting writing on hotel stationery at the small round table beside the air conditioner, under his window. The window behind him was open to the pool enclosure, a few lights looming tall over the shifting blue of the kidney shape.

—Enrico, said Oppenheimer, and walked ahead to the table while Ann and Ben sat down on the edge of the bed, a few feet back. —What's happening?

—I'm writing them a letter, said Fermi, and Ann noticed that his face was sallow and he was sweating. At the corners of his mouth were flecks of spit. He wore only a button shirt with the sleeves rolled up to the elbow, and boxer shorts and his socks.

He was usually fastidious in his neatness, but there were wadded balls of Kleenex on the carpet beside his feet.

—Whom?

—The ones who love the birds.

—You mean bird watchers? asked Oppenheimer softly, and sat down in the chair across from him. —You used to be a birdwatcher. Remember when you knew all the birds in the forest near the mesa?

—They love the birds, said Fermi. —They don't *watch* the birds.

—Oh, said Oppenheimer, and nodded slowly.

After a few moments of silence Ben asked quietly, —What does that mean, Enrico?

But Fermi said nothing, only began to whistle between his teeth. Ann knew the tune from somewhere but could not place it.

—Where's the paper? asked Fermi a few minutes later, impatiently. He had come to the end of the page and there were no blank sheets left.

—I'll get you some, said Ann, —let me call the front desk.

When the bellhop came with fresh stationery Szilard was behind him, but Fermi had eyes for nothing but the paper, snatching it hungrily.

—What's the matter with you? asked Szilard abruptly. —Snap out of it! I don't believe this. You're full of shit!

—Leo! barked Oppenheimer. —Don't you dare to speak to him that way!

Fermi ignored them both, sitting down to write again.

—Can I take the pages you've already written and maybe put them in an envelope for you? asked Ben.

Fermi nodded absently. Ben picked up the sheets of paper and sat down beside Ann, leaning over her to flick on a bedside lamp.

—It's in Italian, he said under his breath.

Szilard rummaged in the minibar and pulled out a bag of peanuts.

—I need to talk to you, he said to Oppenheimer, still seated at the table opposite Fermi, gazing out the window.

—And you too, he said to Ben, and the three of them rose and slipped out the door, closing it behind them.

Ann went to sit where Oppenheimer had sat and watched Fermi write, the blank pages secured under one arm for future use. He guarded them jealously.

She could not keep looking at him so she averted her eyes and looked out the window as Oppenheimer had, fleeing from contact. She tried to make out shapes in the dark beyond the room's reflection. At the far corner of the pool enclosure Tamika sat in a hot tub. Only her head was visible above the water and the hot tub rim, dreadlocks piled high. She looked buried up to her neck. Nearer the water in the main pool moved dancelike, swaying and glittering with new emptiness. On the cement deck early autumn leaves had already fallen, gathered in narrow piles at the base of the white metal fence whose sign bore the words SWIM AT YOUR OWN RISK. Tamika seemed not to mind that it was night, growing cold, already fall.

Beyond her were the lights of other rooms across the way, past the swaying water. Most of the curtains were closed and only thin bars of light slanted out. On the third floor Ann could see a man standing stock-still and staring outward over his balcony, staring in her direction or possibly down at Tamika's body in the water below. It was only his silhouette and the silhouette was of a big, thick man with no arms. Then he moved and the arms became separate from the body. They seemed to blur as he raised them over his head, as though they were not two arms but many.

Then he pulled the curtains together and disappeared.

She watched this with Fermi very slight on the other side of the table, pen scratching.

❧ The next morning he would not come out of his room, which Kurt the Hut was guarding. They ordered him room service but he showed no interest in eating.

—We need to decide what to do about this, said Szilard.

Larry tried to hand around a joint, but heads were shaken.

—I think he needs medical care, said Oppenheimer. —Isn't it that simple?

—The problem is, said Szilard, —we have a lot of business. He's our biggest asset, DNA *and* fingerprints. We need him.

—He's not an asset, Leo, said Oppenheimer.

—Why don't we just get him some peace and quiet, said Ben. —He needs a rest from all this.

—And then there's the publicity, said Szilard. —Are we going to issue a statement?

—Absolutely not, said Oppenheimer.

Szilard gave a distracted nod.

—I know this one place a friend of mine got sent to, said Larry.
—It's in New Jersey. It's like a five-star hotel with hot and cold
running shrinks. Swear to God, it's not a bad place to be. Plus they're
totally discreet. No one will ever find out he's there.

—Does it have gardens? asked Ben.

—With roses and these long paths. It's got this kind of imitation of that French castle, what's it called? The one with the king that
got his head chopped off. And his wife with the blond curly hair
piled up high on the top of her head. She wore those big-ass skirts.

—He would want more than anything to have his mental faculties restored to him, said Szilard. —We should put him where the
treatment is highest rated and most aggressive.

—The shrinks at this place are cool, said Larry, nodding
reassuringly.

—Why don't you ask *him*? said Tamika, from a chair in the corner where she was painting her toenails.

They looked around at each other.

—If we can get through to him, said Larry.

—It should be either you or Ben, said Ann to Oppenheimer.
—He trusts the two of you.

❧ He would not say much so they asked a series of questions, trying to narrow down the options.

—You don't want to stay here, in the hotel, do you? asked
Oppenheimer.

—It's OK, said Fermi eventually.

—But you'd probably rather be somewhere else, said Ben.
—Somewhere with a garden.

Fermi said nothing to this, writing steadily.

—Would you like a garden? asked Ben.

—Garden, said Fermi, in a tone of neutrality.

—We're thinking of taking you to a clinic with a garden, said Oppenheimer, —where there would also be doctors. Would that be all right with you?

Fermi shrugged and turned over his piece of paper.

—Doctors, said Ben, —but we could try to get you gardening privileges, if you wanted.

—Do they have the birds there? asked Fermi.

Ben and Oppenheimer looked at each other.

—There are *some* birds, said Ben slowly, —but it might be mostly sparrows and doves and pigeons. I can find out for you if you want to know.

—See if they have the birds with the long legs, said Fermi enigmatically. —Then ask me.

—Ben? Would you go call about the birds, please? said Oppenheimer. —I'll stay here.

Ben went out the door, past Kurt the Hut who was swigging soda and into Larry's room again, where they all looked up at him. It was only Ann's face he noticed. She looked sad.

—He wants to know if there are birds at the facility.

—Birds? asked Larry. —Like pet birds? Canaries and shit?

—Wild birds is what he meant. What he said to me before was flamingos or storks or something, waterbirds with long legs, is how he described them.

—I don't know, said Larry. —Glen, get me information.

While Big Glen dialed Ben sat down beside Ann on the couch. She put one hand on his leg, resting it, and with the other traced the outlines of flowers on the sofa arm.

—How did he seem? she asked softly.

—The same.

—Hey, I'm interested in bringing a patient there, said Larry. —But he needs to know if you got birds. Wild birds. Yeah.

Back in the room with Fermi Ben told Fermi he would have to see for himself what birds there were.

—There are loons though, he added, —I know that. Sometimes you can hear them calling in the morning and at night.

—What do you think, Enrico? asked Oppenheimer. —It's up to you. Are you willing to give it a shot?

Fermi said nothing for a while, but finally collected his papers and stacked them, tapping the sides for perfect alignment.

—Get me the case, he said in a businesslike tone. —Get me the big suitcase.

—You don't have a big suitcase, said Ben. —How about a regular suitcase?

—I am ready, said Fermi, and clasped his hands in his lap, waiting stiffly in an upright and regal stance.

❧ The place was like a warm tomb, all silence and marble.

—You wanna know why it's so quiet? said Larry, as they walked down a shining hall. —Because no one can afford it.

Fermi's room was spacious, with a tile floor and vast windows that gave him a view over a lake. Oppenheimer waited in the corridor, smoking. Ben put Fermi's bags down on the floor, Larry checked the bathroom and Ann gazed out the window at clumps of rushes growing at the edge of the water. Salt-smelling wind blew over his face, as though the lake was briny. Behind the black pool of it she could make out a row of low hills, hazy blue with distance.

—Are you going to be OK here? asked Ben, leaning over Fermi where he sat on the side of the bed staring.

—See you later, said Fermi carefully.

❧ With Enrico gone he was more alone. But where we take refuge, thought Oppenheimer, pacing the slick hall, tapping his ash onto the shine at his feet, after all, where we take refuge is where our home is. Fermi had a new home now, in long scrawls on hotel stationery and a distracted absence.

I hope he's happy there, he thought.

He did not want to resent his friend: he wanted only to be concerned for him. But Fermi had left him abruptly, with no warning—an offense for which, in this late, cold world, there could be forgiving but no forgetting. And Szilard was no real company because he had no weakness save gluttony. He was only marginally human. He had the capacity to reason but not to weep. At least, this was what Oppenheimer suspected. It was all Szilard had shown him.

Of course he himself was human in form only these days so he should not fault it in Szilard. Even he could tell he had become reduced to a symbol of himself, because while he still felt, he still shivered in the chill of morning, he also saw himself as others did. Increasingly his impulses were defined by what he sensed they should be, and his movements were guided by a view of himself from over his own shoulder.

❧ Ben wanted to stay with Fermi but there was nothing to do. He got into the bus reluctantly, with the letter and an Italian-English dictionary. When they left Pennsylvania they were heading for Rhode Island, bypassing New York since it was not on the schedule yet.

—It's beside the sea, yes? said Oppenheimer, as they sped along I-80.

—Why? Do you want to go to the seaside? asked Ann.

Ben was staring out the window at sprawling industry.

—I would like to see dunes, said Oppenheimer pensively. —With dune grass growing on them.

—We can go for a walk on the beach, said Ben.

He also needed a book of Italian verbs, he realized, with conjugations. There were too many words he could not find in the dictionary. When they stopped in Providence for dinner before they made camp, he drove to a bookstore and bought one.

His translation of the first paragraph was awkward and he had to change the order of the words so that they read more fluently. *The crane that makes the noise of a trumpet has a graceful white body, a head that is red and black and long wings with black ends. Once it lived on the lands of grass in the West but when all the people went there the crane disappeared. Now there are almost none left.*

—How's it coming?

—OK, he said.

His was the only light in the bus. While the others slept he sat at the counter on a tall stool and translated.

—Go back to sleep, why don't you, he went on softly.

—What did he write about?

—Birds.

The great cranes nest in marshes among rushes and cattails. They eat insects, fish, mollusks, frogs, and small rodents. In the winter they perform their dances of courtship, and after that they mate for life.

—I can't sleep with that light on, she whispered from a few feet away, where she lay in her sleeping bag.

The great birds have been killed by the draining of the wet places where they nest. These places have been made into fields. The birds have been shot by hunters. They have been electrocuted by power lines. They have died of lead poisoning, cholera, and tuberculosis. In 1941 a last flock of fifteen flew north for the summer. They were all that was left of their kind. They followed the paths of their ancestors.

—It's been half an hour, she whispered.

—OK! OK! he muttered, and tucked away the originals in a manila folder.

He lay down in the dark beside her but could not fall asleep.

—Are you feeling bad you couldn't do more for him?

—I'm still trying, he said.

Falling asleep he thought of the crane in Fermi's letter, a letter that had been addressed to no one. He thought of the black and red face and the long slender body. *Crane that makes a noise like a trumpet,* he thought. Must be a whooping crane. They were highly endangered, if he recalled correctly.

He would ask Oppenheimer if Fermi had ever said anything before about whooping cranes.

☙ Early in the morning Ann and Oppenheimer were leaving to walk on the beach, their coffee mugs in hand, when Szilard bustled out of the bathroom in his striped pajamas and insisted on going along.

—Wait! I have to talk to you about our message! he called to Oppenheimer, so loudly that others began to stir and turn over in their bedding.

On the wet sand two Huts walked behind them, though one of them had wanted to walk ahead. But Oppenheimer refused to have him ruin the view.

Ann took her shoes off and hooked them over her fingers. The others kept their shoes on.

—My research indicates, said Szilard, —that almost half of all Americans call themselves either *Evangelicals* or *Born-Agains*.

—You're kidding, said Oppenheimer.

—Approximately forty-four percent of two-hundred and eighty million. We're talking about a hundred and twenty-five million.

—Where do you get your information?

—I can show you the citations, said Szilard impatiently. —I do have a source that reports Protestant Evangelicals as low as 23 percent but that's a different accounting system. To be conservative, we can estimate a quarter of our countrymen at the low end to almost half at the high end.

—I know it didn't used to be that way, said Oppenheimer. —In our day. People were Christian, of course. But not fanatical.

—Seventy-seven percent of Americans claim to be Christians, said Szilard. —But the Born-Agains and the Evangelicals are the ones in our following.

—What are we talking about here? asked Ann.

—Belief in the literal truth of the Bible, said Szilard. —Some Born-Agains do not hold themselves to such strict standards, but most tend to insist.

He was fatter than when she first met him. His stomach was almost bursting the lowest button on his shirt. But his face was bronzed and healthy, despite the jowls. It struck her for the first time that he looked like a working man.

—For the dogmatic, he went on, —requirements include a belief in the physical and bodily return of Jesus at the End Time, a belief that Satan is an actual being of flesh and blood, and the conviction that good works have nothing to do with salvation. Oh!

He stepped over a jellyfish, dying on the sand. Ann leaned in close to see if it was still breathing. The tentacles appeared to be gone: it was only a mass.

—Ann told me some of the followers believe we're the Holy Trinity, said Oppenheimer.

—A certain contingent holds that view, said Szilard, nodding. —But I have recently learned that most of them are not interested in the tripartite nature of God and therefore do not have a religious interest in Fermi or me. They believe chiefly that you are the risen messiah.

—Robert. Could I have one of your cigarettes? asked Ann.

They stopped and stood still as a wave broke and rose almost to her feet. She stepped out of the way of the skirt of water and watched as he shook a cigarette out of his case for her and then lit it. When she cupped a hand over the lighter flame she noticed how Szilard's eyes moved quickly beyond her and Oppenheimer to the Huts behind them and, far down the shore, smokestacks trailing black smoke.

—Is that a pelican? asked Oppenheimer, and pointed to a white bird flying slow along the crest of the waves.

—It is! said Ann, and they watched it plummet in a steep dive and then rise again, a small fish in its long bill. —They have herons here too, at least on Block Island. We should look for them.

—My point, said Szilard, —is that in terms of winning the hearts of Americans it may not be a mistake to allow the followers to identify us a religious movement.

—That seems a little cynical to me, Leo, said Oppenheimer, inhaling.

—Not at all, said Szilard stoutly. —We are not claiming to be believers ourselves. We have a task before us. We have a message. That is all. People are free to interpret our work as they choose. That is both their right and their privilege.

They started walking again, Ann feeling her feet to be almost equally solid as they sank into the wet sand, the weak foot forgiven. The sand could not tell the difference.

She wondered if she could live entirely in sand.

—Keep in mind, Robert, that science is an idea to these people but religion is a belief. I learned the hard way. It has taken me a long time to realize, because initially I had assumed this country was civilized.

—You won't make that mistake again, said Ann.

Szilard ignored her.

—But in fact it only has a thin veneer of civilization. It is a country of ignorant cultists. They are grossly illiterate. Most of them cannot pinpoint New York or Los Angeles on a map. They still believe Iraq bombed the World Trade Center. Why? Because they believe anything the powerful tell them.

The tide had left a mustard-colored foam at the waterline, bladders of kelp and plastic tangled in the froth.

—In short their lack of education makes them easy pickings. These people are savages, manipulated by demagogues.

He glanced down at his watch.

—Wait! I have to get Kurt to make a call to the *Boston Globe,* he said, and backtracked.

Oppenheimer was looking at the tideline too as he walked

slowly beside her, both of their faces turned down. Then he stopped, stricken.

—That this will all be *gone,* he said, stifled. —The tides will keep rolling in, but there will be no life in them. When the tide goes out nothing will be left here but old bones.

She held his arm and leaned against his side, her eyes watering. A wind came up and she closed them.

Now and then she thought she dreamed his dreams, that his dreams had been entrusted to her. Why else had she seen him before she even knew him, kneeling in the sand? Before she had even met him, when she had barely heard of him, she believed, she had been infused with his sentiment, as though it had bled from him. And here they were on the sand again, the ocean instead of the desert, on the sand with dry mouths and wet eyes, yearning.

A wave came in and wet his leather shoes, soaking a dark line across the toe.

☙ Ben left early the next morning to visit Fermi. It was chill and quiet before the others at camp had begun to get up and Ann liked it then. There was the smell of smoke from fires the night before, dew on the tree limbs and the clean sharp cold.

—I don't know, he said to Ann as he hunkered over the engine checking fluid levels, —I still feel it's dangerous, leaving you with these people again.

—I'll be fine, she said, and smiled.

She watched him sling the duffel bag over his shoulder and dumped into the passenger seat and the Toyota was pulling away. She waved at the back window and made her way back to the bus, where Larry and Tamika sat at a picnic table eating granola bars and drinking orange juice.

—Don't even get near Leo, said Larry. —He's pissed.

She sat down and poured cereal out of a jumbo box as Big Glen set down a carton of soy milk.

—How come?

—The Christians are having this tent revival at a fairground tonight, said Tamika. —They advertised it real big and Leo just found out about it this morning. He read a fax that came in yesterday from some sheriff's department.

—What's the problem? asked Ann.

—He's pissed because they didn't ask his permission.

—Where is he?

—He and Oppie went to meet Bradley to talk about it.

After she finished her cereal she wandered out of the bus enclosure toward the pavilion where Bradley had set up his office. Two Huts stood outside guarding it, but beside them were other men in camouflage gear, each holding a rifle across his chest.

—Who are you guys? she asked curiously.

When they said nothing a Hut leaned in close to her.

—They won't talk to anyone but Bradley.

—Are you kidding?

—They're not professionals, said the Hut, while the men in camouflage stared straight ahead of them pretending to ignore the conversation. —They're volunteers. Let's just say they're enthusiastic.

She looked closely at the nearest rifleman, whose pale skin was tinged red with acne. His hair was cut short and military and he wore a black belt stuffed with gear over the green uniform.

—So can I go in? Tell them it's Ann.

The rifleman lifted a cell phone and speed-dialed. Ann heard a faint answering ring on the inside of the tent.

—Are you kidding? You're calling someone who's ten feet away?

—Got an Ann here wants entry, he said into the phone. —Caucasian female, light brown—yes sir.

He pocketed his phone and nodded sharply at her and she

went between the two of them into the shade of the tent, where the scientists and Bradley and two other men were clustered at the end of the long table.

—But how will we handle all of them? asked Szilard.

—Hello, Ann, said Oppenheimer.

—What's with the guys with the guns? she asked Bradley. She sounded belligerent and she liked it.

—We have been forced to call in some recruits. For protection.

—They don't want to be at the mercy of the government, said Szilard, and looked at Bradley. —Right?

—Not exactly. Parts of the government are friendly. We have friends there. But in the broader establishment we have powerful enemies.

—Like who? asked Szilard. —The Jews?

—Come sit by me, said Oppenheimer to Ann, and patted a folding chair beside him.

She moved over toward him and stood. She was reluctant to sit.

—Whatever, went on Szilard impatiently. —We're not happy that you're playing with guns. But the matter at hand is this potential influx of new bodies.

—Believe me, we know how to handle it, said Bradley. —I assure you.

—The Baptist Collective is highly organized, said a thin man wearing thick-rimmed glasses. —We're used to dealing in volume.

—Now if you'll excuse me, said Bradley, —I have to make this call now, and he lifted his cell phone with his good hand. —I got organizing to do.

❧ Fermi was in art therapy.

—Would you like to go visit him?

—Yes I would, said Ben.

—Follow me.

They walked quickly along the sleek halls hung with muted

landscapes and medieval pastures. All he could hear was her heels clicking and somewhere a piano.

—Is there anyone who can tell me if there's a diagnosis?

—You'll have to speak to his doctor when he gets in tomorrow, said the nurse, —since you're not family. But I think what you'll hear is, it's too early for anything definitive. He's only had two full sessions.

The art therapy room was vast and flooded with gray daylight, with one whole wall a window. In the distant sky clouds were massing, silver and heavy over a land of trees and far-off office buildings. It was going to rain.

He could see no one. Easels and chairs were grouped around a platform but there were no painters behind the easels and no models on the platform. It smelled of turpentine.

—Where is he?

—He stays in the darkroom mostly. It's the door at the end, you can't miss it. Two doors in a row.

He knocked on the inner door so that Fermi would not be startled. Inside was red and black and his eyes adjusted slowly.

—Enrico?

The darkroom was simple and old-fashioned, with enlargers hunkered down on a counter against a wall and three shallow plastic basins of chemicals on a waist-high plywood table. Fermi stood at one of these, dunking a print in the liquid with a pair of tongs.

—Enrico, it's Ben. You can probably see me better than I can see you.

Fermi said nothing, only lifted the print out of the chemical bath and clipped it onto a line.

—You've already had time to take pictures?

He moved closer to look at it, but the paper was blank.

—It's blank, he said flatly.

—So, said Fermi, and moved to the first basin. Ben leaned over it too, and was relieved to see an image forming.

—Is it the lake outside your window?

—It's them, said Fermi. —But they're small.

Ben watched the reeds by the lake grow into contrast, their fine, sharp lines darker and darker. The picture was black-and-white and the lake itself grew black against the light sky.

—I don't see them, said Ben slowly. —Can you show them to me?

Fermi ignored him at first so he repeated the request.

—Here, said Fermi, jabbing with a forefinger. —And there and there and there.

He seemed to be identifying invisible points above the lake, where there was nothing.

—I'm trying to see, said Ben, leaning in close. He could detect no marks on the paper's porous surface, no texture but whiteness.

—They're flying south for the winter, said Fermi.

—Oh! Is it—the whooping cranes?

Fermi stepped back suddenly, as though slapped.

—You know them?

—You wrote it down, said Ben. —Remember?

Fermi looked at him for a long time and then stooped down to pick the print out of the developer with his tongs.

—So are you liking it here?

—I can show you the pond.

They left the darkroom and walked through the studio. Fermi led Ben down the hall to a stairwell but once they were going down the stairs he changed his mind and turned around, and they were going upstairs again. Ben followed without questioning until they came to a door marked FIRE EXIT EMERGENCY ONLY.

—But we can't go out this exit, Enrico.

—Don't worry, said Fermi, and pushed on the bar. The door opened easily and no alarm sounded.

The roof was a garden, planters of herbs and flowers in individual plots with names on them.

—Do they let you have your own garden? he asked, pleased.

—They will if I ask them, said Fermi, and shrugged.

He walked through the tables of basil and rosemary toward the edge of the roof. This made Ben nervous so he stayed close.

—That's where we are going, said Fermi, and pointed down at the lake. On the surface large white birds sat and appeared to drift.

—It's beautiful up here, he said gently.

Fermi was standing with his arms crossed on his chest, scanning the sky. Ben looked up also and saw the clouds were low.

—We should probably go now if we're going, he said. —Before the rain begins.

❧ They watched the revival from Bradley's trailer, on a live feed. It was a minimal trailer, unlike the bus, without wings that opened to make it broader, without even a full bathroom. In the closet-sized space between the main room and the bedroom there was only a flimsy blue toilet, and the strong smell of disinfectant. On the back of the toilet there was a basket of fake flowers and sitting among them a yellow chick made of felt. Its beak held a leafy sprig.

The walls were fake wood-panel dark and there were piles of papers spread over the table, flyers, leaflets, even grim religious comic books in black and white, and against the wall a case of prayer books, Bibles and Concordances.

Oppenheimer lay back on the couch and stretched out his long legs.

—And now we have the beautiful Crystal Night to sing for us, said Bradley, onstage with a microphone.

The picture was fuzzy and handheld, jogging up and down.

—Let's give glory to the Lord for the first song she's going to perform for us tonight, "Come for me, Jesus."

—I think I'll take a walk, said Oppenheimer, and disappeared into the darkness beyond the steps.

—Potty break for me, said Larry.

❧ Fermi waded into the marshy edge of the lake in his good leather shoes, suit pants rolled up to the knees. Overhead the bank of clouds was a heavy bruised color, brown and pending.

—You can look for them from the water, he announced, beckoning.

—Do you see the swans, Enrico?

—Swans are everywhere, said Fermi, dismissive.

Ben liked to look at the swans, gliding out calmly toward the horizon and away from them.

Fermi was up to his armpits now and Ben thought: What if he goes under and doesn't surface again? *Stay with him. Stay with him.*

He took off his own shoes and waded in behind. The cold was stunning.

—I'll look for them with you for a minute, he called, gasping and curling his fingers with the freeze rising up to his thighs, —but then we need to go back in. There could be lightning.

Fermi stopped with the water up to his shoulders and tipped his head back to squint into the sky. Coming up behind him, teeth chattering, treading water because he had to hold his feet off the slimy lake bottom, Ben leaned back too.

Even with the clouds massed over them the brightness of the sky was still too much for his vision, so he closed his eyes and felt the first light raindrops on his cheeks and forehead.

—It's raining, he said. —We should really go in.

—Wait! said Fermi.

Now the rain was audible on the water and Ben looked around him at the pinpricking of the surface, spread out around him in a gray and complex infinity.

—Do you see? said Fermi solemnly, and pointed up at the clouds, rainwater coursing down his long nose and dripping off the end. —They are everywhere! Everywhere!

Ben followed his finger but there were no birds visible overhead. It was only a silver blur.

—What? asked Ben.

—The cranes! crowed Fermi, smiling. —They cover the sky. Can't you see them?

—I don't see them at all, said Ben sadly.

❧ In the early 1950s, while the Cold War was accelerating and Congress was considering the details of a new Air Force budget, Representative John Rankin, a Democrat from Mississippi, stood up to speak in the House. Rankin supported a massive increase in Air Force spending, which the Air Force had requested. To explain his position—which was a popular one—he said: "We have reached the time when our Air Force is the first line of defense. The next war will be an atomic conflict. It will be fought with airplanes and atomic bombs. It may mark the end of our civilization. I shall vote for the top amount offered here."

❧ —Dr. Oppenheimer! said Mrs. Bradley, at the open door to the trailer. Ann recognized her: she had brought them Coca-Cola at the first meeting.

She stepped inside and reached out for him shakily.

Confused, he extended his right hand and took hers.

—Remember, said Szilard drily, —you're the risen messiah.

—Seeing you up so close! said Mrs. Bradley. —Mercy! I think I need to sit down.

She stumbled over to the sofa and perched on the arm, where Ann saw her arms were trembling, thin and brought out in goose bumps. She clasped her hands onto her knees but the trembling went on.

On television Bradley had brought a man on stage to testify. Behind them was a black-and-white photograph of the porkpie hat.

—When I met him, when I saw the light that hovers around him, said the man into the microphone, —I knew the truth!

—What is he talking about? asked Oppenheimer, straining to see the television.

—And no matter what the demons of doubt tried to whisper in my ear, I knew this was him!

—What does he mean, he touched me? asked Oppenheimer. —I've never met the man in my life!

—They have pieces of your clothing, said Mrs. Bradley, and they all stared at her.

—What are you talking about? asked Ann.

—Articles of his clothing get passed around. They have a suit they keep in this clear plastic box. It travels in a special car, you know, one of those black ones for funerals.

—Leo? Did you know about this? asked Larry. —How come no one told me?

—First I've heard, said Szilard.

—They have one of my suits? asked Oppenheimer vaguely. —I didn't notice there were any missing. Must be one of the old ones.

—There's also pieces of things you've touched, towels, glasses, cigarette cartons. When you're in public they pick up your cigarette butts. The followers touch those things and then they can say they've touched you. They call them articles of worship. Some people have displays.

—Fetishistic, said Szilard. —Primitive superstition.

—It's faith! said Mrs. Bradley, shocked.

—Where do they get these things? The glasses we *drink* out of? asked Szilard.

—I think maybe some of the guards, you know—pick them up and sell them.

—Come with us, said the man on the stage, —join with us and be redeemed. Join and be gathered up in the arms of Jesus.

—Can I ask you what you prefer to be called? asked Mrs. Bradley.

—Robert's fine. What do the rest of them call me?

—Just, you know. He. Or Him.

❧ Fermi had instructions to go to bed early but he asked Ben to play chess with him instead. They sat across from each other at a table by the window in his room and said nothing as they played, cups of tea at their elbows, the rain falling outside steady and light. Fermi did not touch his tea.

Ben had bought a pack of cigarettes after they climbed out of the lake and occasionally he smoked one in the corridor, thinking of Fermi who waited inside. Fermi was always in the same position when he came back, sitting with his elbows on the table, staring at the board.

But he seemed content.

Back in his motel room, the television droning in the background, Ben put in a call to Ann. She said she was watching a tent revival, that on the screen there were pictures of Oppenheimer, and that on the stage at the revival there were people testifying to Oppenheimer's holiness. He laughed at that. They laughed together and in the background he could hear Oppenheimer laughing too.

Then he took out his Italian books and foolscap pad and went back to translating Fermi's letter. It continued to detail the life cycle of the whooping crane, its migration patterns and strange-sounding call, its downward spiral toward extinction and recent efforts at recovery, which pulled its global numbers back into the low hundreds.

When he got tired of his clumsy translation he went to bed and with the covers pulled up to his chin thought of Fermi looking up at the sky from the murky water, Fermi's invisible birds and the birds that Fermi called *common,* the birds he did not love because they were not rare.

He thought of these great, white, and common swans leaving their spreading wake behind them as they drew away from him.

❧ In the morning he stopped at the desk, where a nurse told him none of the doctors would have time to talk to him before he left. She was sorry.

—As long as you know, he told Fermi in the darkroom, —that whenever you want to get out of here, all you have to do is call us. You have the cell phone, and all the numbers are programmed. Even the sat phone in the bus and Glen's number, in case of emergency. I just want you to understand that you're only here now because you want to be.

—I know, said Fermi, nodding. He hesitated, and then said softly: —I like it. No one bothers me.

For a split-second Ben caught his eye in the dark and saw lucidity. It struck him that all of this could be pretense; and for a long time Fermi had longed for privacy.

He watched him, speculating, locked in place. Fermi picked a print out of the basin and his hands seemed deft. They moved with subtle authority.

—I wish I could stay with you, he said, testing the waters. —It's good here. It's like a high-end hotel. And maybe Ann could come too. It would just be us three.

Neither of them said anything for a while and Fermi did not make eye contact.

—Do you like this? he asked finally, and held up the new print. But it was dark and blurry and Ben had no idea what he was seeing.

Then he thought: nothing, of course. The content is irrelevant.

He couldn't help smiling at Fermi, but Fermi did not smile at him.

❧ There was disgruntlement. No one felt they could live with the new crowds.

—We're at seven thousand, said Larry, perched on the side of Oppenheimer's bed with Tamika seated behind him massaging his shoulders. Dory had got up long before and Oppenheimer was holding court in the bed alone, sitting with his back to the wall, drinking coffee. Big Glen leaned heavily against the wall opposite, his arms folded, next to Ann and Szilard at the door. —More than twice what we had before. You can't move with that. I don't know what Bradley was thinking. They may be used to handling volume at these tent revivals, but that's not the same as camping out along the interstate. The guy's clueless.

—We may want to split up, said Szilard.

—What else? said Larry. —We can't have this. I'm the one that has to deal with the cops, me and Glen.

—I'll talk to him.

—You do that! The guy's an asshole. Four *thousand* converts?

—There may be accretion, of course, said Oppenheimer. —They may have been brought into the spirit by the preachers, but that doesn't necessarily mean they're with us for the long haul.

—I need you with me, said Szilard to Oppenheimer. —But no one else.

Ann watched them go with a hand shading her eyes, their dark suit tails flapping. Beside them walked the Huts in lock step. When they first came to work for Larry they had lounged around without guns in the shade; they had spent their breaks smoking and drinking beer from cans they crunched afterward and left in piles. But since the arrival of Bradley's army they had sharpened their attitude, standing straight, practicing target-shooting, jogging in formation in the early mornings. Now they kept their weapons polished, their hair buzzed and their cheeks shaven.

Bradley's soldiers did not smoke or drink and these were the sole habits that the Huts retained, as though to showcase their toughness against the goody two-shoes.

—Did you see this? Larry asked her when the scientists were gone, and steered her inside the bus again, to a stack of magazines on Szilard's desk. —Look, and he opened a magazine and slid it across the table.

A-BOMB SCIENTISTS GARNER HIGH RATINGS, read the headline.

She sat down in Szilard's small wooden desk chair and bent over the glossy pages. The story told of a cult following for the scientists, which collected news clips about them from television stations and posted these on a slew of web sites. A one-hour news show had showed video footage and advertised it in advance. It showed the vastness of the crowds at a speaking engagement, with stadium lights in the distance.

Ann did not recognize the scene. She had never been there.

But more than a million viewers had tuned in.

Fan clubs had sprung up across the country, holding meetings to discuss the scientists' progress, writing to their representatives in Congress, conducting educational campaigns and collecting funds to "promote the public image, and foster greater understanding, of the scientists and the anomaly." There were slick digital pictures of Oppenheimer from the present day beside grainy photos of him from the 1940s. The center photo was of his porkpie hat, sitting alone on a stage behind a microphone, casting a shadow.

❧ Driving away Ben felt light. He popped a CD into the player and cranked up the volume. At a gas station he spoke to the cashier about her son, whose mullet-headed high school photo was taped to the side of the cash register.

The rain had stopped but grass and bushes were still wet and the sky was still gray. *Something new!* he thought.

Something new.

❧ Szilard came back angry, Oppenheimer indifferent.

—I'm not dealing with them anymore, said Szilard.

—What happened?

But Szilard was already in the bathroom, shutting the door behind him.

—Leo and Steve couldn't come to an agreement, said Oppenheimer. —In fact Steve accused Leo of exploiting me for his own selfish purposes. He said Leo was putting words in my mouth, making me talk politics when I should be speaking Scripture. He said his flock believes that Leo is a profane influence interested only in expansion and monetary gain. He sullies my purity. They feel Leo is one of—how did he put it, Leo?

—The bad Jews, said Szilard, banging out of the bathroom again with a wet face. —The Christ-killers.

—I spoke strongly against this sentiment, said Oppenheimer, —and all that it represents, but they did not listen to me. They seem to have developed a real hostility toward Leo. Almost a vendetta.

—But not against him, because he's one of the good Jews, said Szilard.

—Assimilated, they mean, said Oppenheimer.

—We're leaving for New York tonight, said Szilard. He lifted a dishtowel off the counter and wiped the beads of water off his forehead and cheeks. —While the rest of them are sleeping.

❧ Ben was relieved, and the relief felt like a victory.

After Ann called he went swimming in the motel pool in the dark, floating on his back in the future, full of a pent-up joy. The caravan would be gone and the world would shrink in scale and become his again: he would be free.

First Fermi had fallen off and away, a lost soldier. Now the parade was ending at long last, and they would all be able to stop waving their flags and go home.

Eventually Oppenheimer and even Szilard would follow in disillusion, and he would be alone with his wife again. They would go for long walks in the forest, beneath the soft redness of ponderosa pine. A breeze would sweep through the high branches and they would shed their memories of all this and be filled with a new momentum, the sense of a hopeful enterprise, the air around them not static but moving.

❧ After she had talked to Ben she tried to go to sleep, but she was too nervous. Anything by stealth set her on edge, made her alert and wary.

The last lights around the camp went out at two but it was not until almost 3 a.m. that Kurt the Hut finally turned the key in the bus's ignition. All of them waited together in the darkness of the interior.

The Huts packed up the perimeter fence without flashlights, in the dark, and the second bus idled close behind them, its head-lights off. Their tires crunched over the gravel as they pulled out of the lot, two dark hulks nose to tail with a guard van ahead and another behind. Ann stared out the window at the trucks and tents spread out beyond them, and as they pulled away felt relieved.

At fifteen miles an hour they left the camp behind them and crept slowly up the gravel access road to the Interstate.

—No headlights till we hit the on-ramp, said Szilard to Kurt. —I want to be sure.

—I feel better already, said Larry to Ann. —Don't you?

Then there were bright lights around them, dazzling in the windshield. It was a circle, and Ann narrowed her eyes against the glare as she picked out the headlights around them. They burned at all the windows.

—What *is* that? asked Tamika, dozing fitfully with her head on Larry's lap. —Turn it off!

—It's not us, said Big Glen grimly, and the bus rumbled to a halt.

Ann put her face against the window. The night blazed and blurred and she could barely make out shapes.

—It's Bradley's men, said Szilard. —Their guns are drawn.

Kurt the Hut lifted his headset to make contact with the guard van, adjusting it against his mouth.

—Two of our guys are stepping out of the advance van to talk to them, he told Szilard. —Without their weapons.

They waited until he spoke into his headset again. The lights outside were harsh and unwavering. Ann looked down at her cold hands and saw they were shaking.

—They say we're not leaving, he said, turning to face them.

—What, they're holding us prisoner now? We can just call the cops! said Szilard. —What are they thinking?

Oppenheimer stood in his bedroom doorway in plaid flannel pajamas, blinking.

—What is this?

—Now we're hostages, said Szilard.

—They want to talk to you again, said Kurt. —Szilard. Not Oppenheimer. They don't want to put Oppenheimer in jeopardy.

—That's nice, said Szilard. —But I'm not going out into a battle zone. Get Bradley on the phone.

Kurt spoke into his headset again and then shook his head. —No, they say they want a face-to-face. They say he's coming in.

❧ When I wake up, he thought, she will be here without the other thousands. The crowds will be gone again.

He felt his mouth smiling.

❧ They stared at Bradley sullenly from their seats as he stood near the door with his arms crossed on his chest and a pair of night-vision goggles strung around his neck, a soldier on either side of him.

—What it is, he said, —is we can't just have you clearing out like this without addressing your responsibilities. The disciples will feel abandoned.

—We have no responsibility to you, said Szilard. —But what we do have is the capacity to call the police. Tell me why I shouldn't dial 911 this minute.

—The duty I'm talking about is not worldly, said Bradley. —It is a higher calling.

They sat in silence after that, Larry shaking his head and Tamika reaching into a cupboard and pulling out a bong.

—Tell me why I shouldn't call 911, repeated Szilard, and touched his cell phone where it sat on the desk in front of him.

—Because we'll do media that will make you look like the moneylender you are, said Bradley sharply.

—Anti-Semite! said Tamika to Ann.

—Please don't conduct illegal activities in front of me, said Bradley suddenly to Tamika, who was firing up the bong.

—I'll do whatever I want, said Tamika indignantly. —I don't even know you. And so far I think you're a major asshole.

—If there is anything here worth saving, said Oppenheimer softly, drumming his fingers on the table and raising his eyes to Bradley, —it should be saved by grace, not violence.

—What our position is, said Bradley, —those of us that are the faithful, is if you are going to betray your flock you owe them at least an explanation. You owe them the truth about what you're doing.

—Why do we owe them anything? asked Szilard. —I have to tell you, you lost me there, Steve.

—Because they can ruin you.

—I don't understand, said Oppenheimer, still mild-toned and soft-spoken. —What can they ruin? We have nothing to hide. We are who we say we are. I am Oppenheimer, Julius Robert. He is Leo Szilard. Our colleague is Enrico Fermi. These are facts that science has proven to our satisfaction, even if others do not wish to credit them. We have a message of peace. We wish to speak to the president about nuclear nonproliferation, and the dangerous precipice on which this country stands. That is all. And I do not claim to be a messiah. I have no wish to be a religious figurehead. I am a physicist, plain and simple.

—The people don't see it that way.

—The people are laboring under a misapprehension. If they wish to have it corrected, I can certainly speak to them.

—Nothing you can say will convince them you are not the risen Savior. Your protests will only further convince them.

—Fine, said Oppenheimer, —let them believe what they wish.

But it does not make us beholden to them. I never asked to be made into a god.

—I think Dr. Szilard here may see things differently, said Bradley smugly. —Am I right, Leo? You have PR to think about. You have a media image. Bad press won't help you right now, right before the whole climax and the march on Washington.

—Leave, said Szilard. —We will talk about it.

—Of course, we don't care if the rest of you leave, said Bradley, looking from Tamika to Ann. —Dr. Oppenheimer is who we want.

—No way, said Ann. —We're sticking with him.

—We'll give you some time to yourselves.

—How generous, said Ann.

—Would you turn off all those headlights when you go, please? said Tamika. —It's like we're under interrogation by Nazi pigs.

The soldier nearest the door went out first, followed by Bradley, with the second soldier scoping all around the bus, rifle up, as he stepped down behind them.

Kurt the Hut closed the door in their wake and leaned against it, shaking his head.

—It has gone too far, Leo, said Oppenheimer. —These men are dangerous.

They gathered on the couch and around the desk and table, waiting for the blinding lights to be extinguished. It was a full five minutes of waiting until they went out.

—Their guns are still on us, said Larry. —You can bet. Pass me that, would you? I got a headache.

Tamika passed him the bong and lit a votive candle of the Virgin Mary.

—I think we need the Lady right now to watch over us, she said, and then into Szilard's scowl: —It's not a Christian thing, OK? It's like more mystical. *Womyn* power. Heard of it?

Szilard opened a window.

—Our security forces are no match for theirs, he said, shaking his head.

—You're telling me we're *outgunned*? asked Oppenheimer, coming back from his bedroom with his cigarette case.

—In the final analysis armaments are irrelevant, said Szilard. —The outcome will be determined by tactics. But it's worth keeping in mind that we have twenty guys with guns and the Christians have five hundred.

—And they don't limit themselves to legal weapons, either, said Larry, nodding. —Some of them got their AKs converted to full-auto.

—Someone must have ratted us out, said Tamika. —Or how did they know we were leaving?

—Are you kidding? They got guys whose whole job it is to watch us twenty-four seven, said Big Glen, who sat on the arm of the couch with his large legs spread wide and his elbows on his knees. —I thought we had a distraction set up, but obviously it didn't work.

—You didn't mention a distraction to me, said Szilard.

—We had some guys blow up a port-a-potty near Bradley's tent, said Larry.

—What? cried Oppenheimer, and fumbled the cigarette he was lighting. —*What?*

—There was no one *in* it or anything, said Big Glen.

—My God, said Oppenheimer.

—I didn't see any explosion, said Ann.

—Maybe that was the problem, said Big Glen. —Far as I know they were just using the gunpowder from a few M80s. You know, wrapped up in packages. Maybe Clint screwed it up.

—I can't believe I'm hearing this, said Oppenheimer.

—You got *Clint* to do it? said Ann.

—I say we call the police, said Oppenheimer. —I refuse to be held hostage by these people.

—Here's the problem with that, said Szilard. —It's one thing to go off on our own. It's another to be completely repudiated by the Christian wing of this movement. I mean, a public breakup with Bradley would have national reverberations.

—Still, said Oppenheimer, sitting forward and puffing more rapidly on his cigarette. —Why do we need them at all? What we have here is a peace mission. We want an audience with the president, Congress and the United Nations. Do we need a following of thousands to get those things?

—It helps, said Szilard. —And FYI, Robert, it's not just the thousands that are with us on the road. These people have drummed up a following for us in the hundreds of thousands.

For a second Ann heard nothing but the wall clock ticking, and outside one of the soldiers calling across the night.

—You're totally bullshitting, said Larry.

—No way! said Tamika. —That's so wild!

—What do you mean by *following*? asked Oppenheimer. —People who think I'm the Second Coming?

—People who say they're willing to show up in D.C. and march for peace, said Szilard.

—I don't believe it, said Oppenheimer.

Moths fluttered against the window. One of them was huge, inches long with dark, dappled wings. In the dark outside Ann heard a series of mechanical clicks.

—What's that?

—Someone racking the slide on their gun, said Larry.

They were all quiet for a while, until a light went on a few feet outside the window and the moth fluttered away. It was a Hut with his flashlight, walking over from the second bus.

—Get the door, said Szilard to Big Glen.

When Big Glen opened the door and leaned out to hold it open, Ann saw him for a second as a broad, ample chest, *a man not yet shot.*

—They still got their weapons trained out there, said the Hut, when they let him in. He and Kurt did a handshake. He was nervous and sweating. —These people are freaks.

—You got news for us? asked Larry.

—Message from Clint, said the Hut. —Apologies. He says they were stopped before they could do it. They didn't pat him down so they never knew what the plan was, but he couldn't get close. That was the message. He didn't tell me what the hell he was talking about.

—Oh, *we* know, said Oppenheimer, and glared at Larry.

—Let the people in the other bus know they're all free to leave if they want to, said Szilard. —We may not be leaving ourselves, but we encourage them to take the opportunity.

—Yes we do, said Oppenheimer. —It's probably in their best interest. Bradley has no need for them. For him it's all about me. All the others are free to go. Please assure the others they are free to go, won't you? I encourage it. It's not safe here anymore.

—We'll still be in contact! put in Szilard quickly. —They can work on the campaign from a remote location!

—I don't even like walking around with their infrared scopes trained on me, I tell you what, said the Hut to Kurt. —They got itchy fingers out there, I just got a feeling.

—I know, man, said Kurt, and clapped him on the back as he turned to leave. —They're fuckin' psychos.

❧ —No, said Ben, —no. This is not happening.

Outside his window in the motel parking lot a family was packing up their van. A girl and a boy chased each other in circles as their mother, in a blond ponytail and a hooded sweatshirt that read RUTGERS, stood watching them sleepily, holding a blue-and-yellow beach ball in her arms. It looked like the end of a vacation but it was almost October and beside the van a spindly maple already had red leaves. He wondered if they had been to the beach, if they had walked on the sand with a cold wind springing up, in jackets and sneakers. *A family.*

—We weren't forced to stay, said Ann, a small voice on the other end of the line. —But we're staying anyway. I mean Glen, Larry, Tamika and me. And Dory. The people in the other bus already left. They pulled out right before dawn.

—You're staying there when these guys have guns pointing at you?

—They're not pointing at us anymore.

—So now they trust you? Now they're just going to let it go back to how it was before?

—Leo made a deal with Bradley. We can ride ahead of the crowd as long as the leadership van is with us.

—*Leadership* van?

—The Christians. You know, Bradley and some of the others. I don't know who exactly. Plus some of their soldiers I guess. The soldiers have their own jeeps.

He sat down in front of the window as the mother ushered her children into the back seat, leaned in to fasten her daughter's seat belt and then set the beach ball on the girl's legs. As the mother slid the door closed she looked up and saw him watching them, but looked away again, barely noticing.

—So where should I meet you then?

—I can't hear you!

—Where should I *meet you then?*

—You can stay put. We're still heading for the Jersey Shore sometime after breakfast. We'll be there tonight.

As the van backed out Ben saw a colorful plastic cup wobbling on the hood and falling off. It spilled a purple liquid on the gray metal and then fell and rolled on the ground, but no one in the family seemed to notice, their faces behind the windshield already preoccupied, already turned to the prospect of a next event that would never be known to him.

◦ The crowd would be managed by Bradley's army and would maintain a safe distance behind them. As Bradley assured Oppenheimer over breakfast at the picnic table, his army was full of *actual retired Army guys* and *National Guardsmen.* —There's guys with us that actually got drafted, way back when, he told them as he spooned up stewed prunes. —There's guys that came to Jesus in Saigon.

—Tell me why any of us need guards, said Oppenheimer, —if we're traveling alone. Because I'd like us to get rid of our weapons. I'd like us to divest ourselves of the trappings of violence. Since after all we're a peace movement.

—There is purity in your heart, said Bradley, —but sadly, we live in a world governed by the whore of Babylon.

—Good gracious, said Oppenheimer testily, and got up from the table to light a cigarette. —Dory, is there any more coffee in the thermos?

—We still want privacy, said Szilard, —in case you were wondering. Just because we're traveling with you and your thugs doesn't mean we don't need our space.

—Believe me, said Bradley, as Oppenheimer and Dory and Ann walked away from them with coffee and cigarettes, —we need time alone too. Time to pray and worship.

—Dr. Oppenheimer! called out a woman behind them.

When they turned it was Bradley's mousy wife, carrying a small white umbrella.

—Can I walk with you?

Huts tagged along behind them as they went through the gate, keeping their distance from Bradley's men who stayed vigilant alongside the bus. Outside the perimeter fence Bradley's sentries stood guard, each with a rifle held vertical against his shoulder, each, Larry had told Ann, wearing a silver cross on a chain around his neck.

Some of the soldiers, Larry had said, had their old dog tags around their necks too, and these nestled against the crosses over their hearts.

—I wanted to ask a special favor, said Mrs. Bradley, trotting along beside them as they walked down a pebbly path toward a small public park tucked into a cul-de-sac. Ahead there was a swing set, empty of children. —I have a women's prayer group, and we meet for special worship twice a week. There's a meeting tonight. And it would mean so much to them if you could speak. You don't even know how much it would mean. They worship you! They do!

—These women are under the impression that I am the Second Coming of Christ?

—They believe in you.

—I don't know what I would say to them, Mrs. Bradley, said Oppenheimer, patience strained. —That's the problem.

—But all you have to do is be yourself!

—Myself is a Jewish physicist from New York, said Oppenheimer drily. —I enjoy a nice bourbon and reading the classics of Eastern philosophy.

—We know all about you, said Mrs. Bradley warmly. —We are bathed in the light.

And she opened her umbrella suddenly and raised it over his head, though she could barely reach.

—It's not raining!

—It will be, she said.

—Can I film you? asked Dory. —For our records? I record oral histories.

—Oral? asked Mrs. Bradley uncertainly, and Dory raised the camcorder.

—I can give them half an hour this evening, Mrs. Bradley, said Oppenheimer finally, —but this will be a one-time event, do you understand me? And for future reference, I don't do children's birthdays.

They sat down at a table beside a seesaw. Ann wanted to sit on one end of it and go up and down but none of them would sit at the other end. She looked around at the still objects of the park, the red and blue slide, the yellow roundabout, a jungle gym in the shape of a rocket ship. Empty and motionless, they called up the same feeling.

Without play there was only getting old.

A few minutes later the rain was falling. While Oppenheimer smoked placidly beneath his dome of white, Ann and Dory stood under the tin overhang of the rest room roof sharing one of his cigarettes between them. At the table in the middle of the playground Mrs. Bradley sat beside him, holding the umbrella over his head and talking to him in a low constant patter whose words they could not distinguish. She was soaked.

🙘 At a rest stop in Connecticut she came out of the bathroom and wandered toward the back of the lot, toward a straggly grove of trees and dried grass where she could stretch her legs. But before she reached the corner of the building she was hearing a private conversation between Dory and Oppenheimer, standing a few feet away behind a rhododendron. Dory was crying raggedly.

She jerked back from the corner but then she had to listen briefly. She looked behind her, furtive, to make sure no one else could see her lurking. She was shamed but compelled.

—It's nothing about you, said Oppenheimer, —I'm very fond of you, as you know. And you have been a great comfort about losing Kitty.

—So you wouldn't—with anyone?

—I don't have it in me, said Oppenheimer. —There's something missing. I don't know how it happened, but it's the way I've always been since I got here. I simply have no capacity. I'm sorry.

—Are you saying you don't—what, you don't even get erections?

Ann turned away cringing, her hands coming up involuntarily, fingers spread in horror, as though someone was speaking lewdly about her own father.

—I have turned from all that, she heard Oppenheimer say

painfully as she walked toward the rest room doors again, anything to shut herself in and be out of the way. —It was taken from me.

In the bathroom she stood over the bank of sinks without moving. The room was empty and she was glad. She looked in the smoky mirror, and could barely make out the features of her own face. It had been embarrassing: she had been embarrassed for Dory. But there was an element of relief.

Poor Oppenheimer had no secrets.

❧ Ben was sitting on a white plastic chair beside the motel pool when the two buses pulled into the parking lot. Bradley's army dismounted through the back doors of a van, hitting the ground hard in their black boots, armed to the teeth.

Szilard and Oppenheimer stepped down from the bus, followed by Ann and Larry, and Ben walked across the pool's herbaceous border, bent down and kissed Ann over the top of the wire fence.

—How are you, he said, —are you OK? and she smiled up at him.

—I'm not bad, she said. —It's good to leave the crowd behind. You'll see.

—Where are they?

—They're something like sixty miles behind us. Whenever Leo has an event staged we'll allow them to catch up, but the rest of the time we have privacy.

—Except for Bradley and his boys.

—Except for them.

❧ Bradley had ceded his hotel suite to his wife while he met with Szilard. It was already dark outside and the room was sepulchral and dim, lit by bedside lamps and candles and camp lanterns. The overhead was not on.

Ann and Dory sat in the corner quietly on folding chairs while the women filed in. They had promised they were there only as observers and would not interrupt the proceedings, and Dory had brought her camcorder. Ann thought she was paler than usual, flatter. But she lifted the camcorder dutifully and taped the women as they milled around eating shortbread cookies, drinking sugary lemonade from a plastic dispenser and waiting for the arrival of Oppenheimer.

Each woman had brought her own pillow to sit on, and Ann noticed that several were U-shaped.

—Hemorrhoid cushions? whispered Dory.

Oppenheimer was late.

—Would you like me to go check on him? Ann asked Mrs. Bradley finally.

—It doesn't matter. I know he's coming, said Mrs. Bradley, and held out the platter of cookies. —We can wait for as long as it takes.

It was almost nine when Oppenheimer stepped through the door, hat in his hand, trailing two Huts with their hands on their sidearms. One of the women crumpled onto the carpet as soon as she saw him, and Ann ran over to help her.

—Is she OK?

—She just fainted, said another woman quietly, staring past them at Oppenheimer, who was apologizing to Mrs. Bradley for the delay. —She is overcome.

The Huts stationed themselves in opposite corners, pulling chairs over to sit on and setting their rifles down across their laps. Standing under a camp lantern suspended from the ceiling Oppenheimer looked older than he had before. At the same time, as always, he looked like a child; his face was lined but his eyes were large. She thought of children with an aging disease. She had seen a documentary about these children, with deep wrinkled pouches under their large eyes.

Against the sliding door that led to the narrow balcony, two older women were holding hands and weeping as they gazed at him.

—I see it, I see it, said one of them, a black woman wearing a flowery dress. —Do you see it?

—I see it, said the other woman, and they both looked at him with tears streaking their cheeks, the white woman shaking her head.

—No involvement! said Dory to Ann. —You promised. Let them take care of her.

The woman who had fainted stirred and opened her eyes as Ann stood up.

—You'll be OK, said Ann, trying to reassure, and moved back to her chair as the woman moved her head back and forth dizzily.

—I apologize for my lateness, he said to all of them, —I was held up. I plan to speak briefly on our proposal to slow the global proliferation of nuclear weapons and bring about their eventual elimination.

❧ Ben left Larry and Tamika with a pizza box open on their bed and wandered out into the parking lot with his cell phone to call Fermi.

—Room 410, he said, and then waited for what seemed like a very long time.

—He's not answering, sorry, said the switchboard operator when she came back on.

—Can you try the darkroom?

But Fermi was not in the darkroom either.

—This worries me, said Ben. —Is there someone I can talk to, a nurse or someone with oversight?

When the nurse came on she told him Fermi had the run of the grounds and had not been seen since three.

—You're not worried? he asked.

—If he's not in his room by curfew we will send staff to locate him. And if we do not, of course, we will notify you.

—When's curfew?

—He has another two hours. As you know, we allow a lot of latitude here. The patients who choose to stay with us depend on that.

—Any idea where he could be?

—All these big white birds came down from the sky, she said. —I guess they're flying south for the winter. He went out to see them.

—Big white birds? There?

—Beside the lake.

—What were they?

—I think he said cranes.

—There are no cranes in this part of the country.

—Oh.

—They could have been herons, maybe. If they had long thin legs?

—Oh, I didn't actually see them myself.

—I thought you were saying—

—I just took his word for it. He described them to me.

—Yeah. It's what he's been saying since he got sick. All about these whooping cranes, these birds that are nearly extinct. He always thinks he sees them.

—I see.

❧ The women started singing before Oppenheimer was even finished giving his speech. He paused to step out onto the balcony and smoke a cigarette and they joined hands and begun to sing a hymn.

Ann stood outside on the balcony with him and smoked and listened. When she glanced in at the women, standing in the cramped space between the sofa and the kitchenette, she thought they shone with contentment.

—*Must Jesus bear the cross alone, and all the world go free? No, there's a cross for everyone, and there's a cross for me.*

—Nothing I say can change their opinion, he said to Ann, shaking his head, voice pitched high in disbelief.

—It's not an opinion, she said. —It's faith.

When she first met Oppenheimer, she realized, she had been one of these women. In fact she was one of them still, except for the matter of doctrine. To her he was a dead scientist, to them he was a living messiah. The only difference between her position and theirs was that she and Oppenheimer happened to agree.

—The way you look at science, she said, drawing on her cigarette and then sipping from her cup of lemonade and taking note that she did not like it, —that's the way they look at you.

He glanced at her quickly and then turned, nodding, and looked out over the parking lot, where Ben was pacing and talking on his cell phone under a street lamp. Near him a truck pulled into a space and parked, and men began to unload rifles. She wondered if they were reinforcements for Bradley's army.

She waited until Ben's face was turned her way and then waved down at him. He raised a hand back and kept talking.

—What point is there in speaking to them, went on Oppenheimer, —if they have no interest in what I'm saying?

—They do have an interest, she said. —They just don't hear what you think they should hear.

—OK, he said abruptly, —fine. Let's get it over with.

When the hymn finished they stubbed out their cigarettes and went back in. On the coffee table a series of items was laid out, including a bandanna, several rings and necklaces, a rosary, and a small glass vial.

—These are for you to bless, said Mrs. Bradley, with a slight bow of her head.

—I don't know how to bless things, he said brusquely.

—All you have to do is touch them, she said.

—Even better is if you could kiss them, said one of the other women, her voice trembling, and picked up the rosary. —It belonged to my mother.

Oppenheimer looked at Ann helplessly. Dory was squatting down panning along the row of belongings with the camcorder.

—He doesn't feel comfortable with that, said Ann after a long silence.

—I feel as though I'd be pretending, said Oppenheimer. —I don't wish to take advantage of your credulity.

—Please! said the woman who had asked him to kiss her rosary. —All you have to do is pass your hand over them.

They were gazing at him and waiting. Ann thought they would wait forever.

Oppenheimer stood indecisive at the end of the sofa with Ann next to him, trailing his nicotine-stained fingers along the over-stuffed arm. Finally he bent and touched first the small glass vial, and then the rings.

—What is this for? he asked, holding up the vial.

—It's for holy water, said the black woman who had been weeping at the beginning. —A Catholic friend of mine asked me to bring it.

An older woman with dark roots in her red hair leaned forward from her seat on the couch and clasped his arm with both hands.

—And those are our wedding rings.

—No touching! snapped a Hut from the nearest corner, and stood up, his hand on his gun.

—Sorry! I forgot! I'm so sorry!

—No, *I'm* sorry, said Oppenhcimer gently, and took the woman's hands in his own as the Hut sat back down. —He didn't mean to alarm you.

Ann followed Dory's camcorder up from his hands to his face, and then saw that all the women in the room were gazing at him, still, their faces fixed in a single rapt expression.

❧ Increasingly he was allowing the literal to recede. He was be-coming figurative.

It seemed to him more and more than the world was composed of abstractions, himself another among them. His field of view was no longer restricted to what could be or what should, no longer fixed to an insistence on logic. Instead he had begun to see himself as an impression on the minds of others. What was seen and felt, that was all that there was anymore, impressions, convictions, acquiescence. He was less a self-determined organism than outside views of him and so it was easy for him to defer to the perceptions of others.

Instead of reason anymore there was only movement. It was the movement of crowds, to whom faith substituted for education, to whom facts were only a competing myth and the subject of mockery. It was the movement of those who believed.

3

❧ In the morning Ben left Ann in the motel room shower and reported to the bus. It was packed with men in well-cut suits. They sat in a row with their laptops, typing silently.

In the corner lay a gray mound of coats. Even in a heap he could tell they were expensive.

—What happened here? he asked Szilard. —The clock struck midnight and the soldiers changed into attorneys?

—Leo, Al here wanted to give you his report, broke in one of the lawyers. —He has a plane to catch in a few minutes. The situation with the Army.

—Did they make the concession? said Szilard, turning to a black lawyer wearing a purple tie.

—What it looks like, said the lawyer, removing his laptop from his knees and standing, —is now they've lost the suit they want to turn a blind eye. They don't want anything more to do with us.

—Why would they? asked Ben. The lawyer's eyes flicked over him, disinterested.

—They wanted to try to have us arrested under the Patriot Act, said Szilard. —You didn't know about that?

—On what basis? asked Ben. —What have you done that's illegal?

—Apparently they claim we're terrorists, said Szilard.

—Not per se, said the lawyer in the purple tie. —A national security risk, is how they put it.

—Undermining American foreign policy with our outreach to other countries, said Szilard.

—Probably because we're not campaign contributors of the president's, said Larry.

—I can't speak to their intentions, said the lawyer. —What I can say, Leo, is it looks like they've dropped us. We've made a couple of disclosure requests to them in the past couple of weeks and they complied gracefully, but with no fanfare. The consensus is, they want to disappear out of this.

—Fine, said Szilard. —There's no place for the military in this question anyway. This is an issue for the civilian government.

—Leo? Can I talk to you?

Bradley stood at the door.

—Gotta go, said Szilard, dropping the melon rind in the sink and wiping his fingers on his pants. —Be right back.

Larry was sitting with Tamika at the table, writing checks.

—I like the ones with the dolphins on them, she murmured. —I think you should order those.

—When are we leaving? Ben asked Larry.

—I think a couple of hours. Don't worry, though. We'll send a Hut to come get you two in your room.

—For New York?

—For New York.

On his way out he glanced along the row of lawyers. Ted the rookie had become a small cog, deferring to the big guys from large firms in New York and Washington. The Christian leaders retained their own counsel but the Szilard legal team refused to work with them, citing potential conflicts of interest. The two teams did not fraternize.

—We need the Ninth Circuit on this one, said a thickset middle-aged lawyer to a young thin one, and Ben shut the door behind him.

❧ There was a reception for Szilard and Oppenheimer before their speech to the United Nations Security Council. It was a few blocks away in a penthouse garden owned by a thin, aging heiress who wore long flowing dresses and bulging jewelry. When the old woman took Ann's hand in her own pale claw the fingers were spread wide by thick rings, and her eyes were blue and rheumy but her smile was gentle.

The garden wrapped around three sides of a venerable building that overlooked the East River. Ann wandered along the balcony with her wine glass in one hand and Ben holding the other.

—Fermi would have liked this, he said, and touched the rim of his own wine glass to a bush of yellow roses.

He said it as though Fermi had faded away.

Scientists and diplomats milled around talking to news cameras and wealthy patrons, jabbering away in languages Ann did not know. She ducked inside to find a bathroom and heard Oppenheimer tell a man in a tweed suit that the stone carving running along the ceiling of the dining room looked like a *Babylonian frieze*.

—Very astute, Dr. Oppenheimer. In fact it's from the palace wall of Ashur-nasir-apal at Nimrud.

She left them nodding speculatively at the fierce stone angels and walked along looking at photographs. One was a sepia-toned portrait of a young bride and she assumed it was the ancient patroness, with clear and unlined skin, beautiful.

When she came out of the bathroom again Szilard was speaking in the garden, booms swinging over his head. —. . . of course require a rigorous system of inspections . . .

Just inside the French doors sat the old lady on a needlepoint chair, listening.

—It's very kind of you to open your home to us, said Ann, leaning down close.

—Anything for the cause, said the dowager weakly, her chin trembling. It took her a while to muster her next words, while Ann waited and felt awkward.

—Thank you.

—I believe, she went on softly and with difficulty, her voice quivering, —that by the time that our great-grandchildren are the age I am now, everything that we think is beautiful will be gone.

Ann lowered herself down beside the chair, squatting.

—Can I get you anything?

The old woman shook her head.

—I was sorry that Dr. Fermi could not be here, she said. —I met him, you know. When I was a young girl.

—You did?

—And now he is—sick?

—He is sick now, said Ann softly.

In his farewell speech of 1961, President Dwight D. Eisenhower famously warned of the growing power of what he called the "military-industrial complex." Said Eisenhower, former war hero, general and Republican, "We must guard against the acquisition of unwarranted influence, whether sought or unsought, by the military-industrial complex. The potential for the disastrous rise of misplaced power exists and will persist. Only an alert and knowledgeable citizenry can compel the proper meshing of the huge industrial and military machinery of defense with our peaceful methods and goals . . . disarmament, with mutual honor and confidence, is a continuing imperative."

They walked the few blocks to the United Nations complex with the crowd of scientists, stately streets lined with old doorman buildings and tall wide-limbed trees. The leaves on the trees were yellowing and Ben thought the years of his life would have been different had he spent them ensconced in one of these restrained and elegant buildings, in rooms with high ceilings and gleaming wood floors and windows that gave a view of these large and venerable trees.

Finally they turned a corner and saw the scenery change and the building was looming. Ben stopped and held Ann's hand, watching with the cameramen as the crowd of scientists flowed past them and disappeared inside. As Oppenheimer was swallowed by the doors Ben felt he had watched him vanish over and over again. This was something Ann had known for a long time but Ben had learned recently: Oppenheimer was always in the process of vanishing. He was present only in faded effigy.

Larry was drinking with some friends at an old bar near Union Square and Tamika had promised to meet them. They had no plans of their own and so they let her lead them down busy streets and followed her like sheep, rubbernecking at the sights, the stores and the traffic and the pedestrians, all bustling and full of direction.

❧ In the bar the wood of the counter gleamed and the ancient floor tiles were pleasantly worn, but the air was rancid with stale cigarette smoke and spilled beer.

Big Glen was wearing a mustache of Guinness.

—I thought you were AA, Glen, said Ben.

—No, man. NA and OA. Not AA. Not my thing.

—I see.

—Hey Clint! Over here!

—You didn't tell us Clint was coming, said Ben.

—Sorry, said Larry. —He just called and asked us.

—He's an asshole.

—Yeah, but you know. He's kind of a nice guy.

—What?

—I want to go, whispered Ann into his ear, but then a waitress descended with a pitcher of beer and Clint was already sliding onto the bench beside her. —Damn it!

—Hey little lady, said Clint, affecting a devilish charm that did not exist. He nudged her shoulder with his own. —Whatcha been up to?

—We've been steering clear of you, said Ben. —Weren't you supposed to blow up a toilet or something?

—Oh man, is *that* a story, said Clint, and helped himself to a stein of beer from the pitcher. —So we were supposed to get Bradley's guys' attention diverted, right? And we had the powder from all these M80s, and you know, we packed it real tight. That's the key. So we've got this stuff in my pack and we're going through the trees at night without even a flashlight, right? All creeping and shit.

—Another couple of pitchers here, please, said Larry to the waitress.

—But we figure let our eyes adjust to the dark and all that and we'll probably do OK. But what we weren't banking on is fucking Bradley's guys actually have this high-tech surveillance bullshit that takes readings off your body heat. You know, like they use to track animal migrations from planes and satellites and shit? I mean, Lar, we're talking these guys got serious money. I thought *you* had money till I saw the gear Bradley's got.

—They took you somewhere you could see it?

—Their satellite truck. You know, like the shit the TV news people have. You wouldn't believe the setup they got in there.

—But they went easy on you, said Ben.

↜ Ann wished Clint would not breathe on her as he told the story. She turned and looked at the wall on the other side of Ben, which featured a faded photograph of a softball team, circa 1920.

Today wherever she turned she saw old photographs, pictures of old people when they were young.

—Yeah, so what happened? Suddenly we got like eight guys descending on the two of us. The only reason they didn't do a full cavity search is we had our IDs from the buses. If we'd been regular followers without ID badges? I tell you, man, we'd have been up shit creek. Those guys pistol-whip people. I've heard stories.

—Get outta here, said Larry.

—No, I swear. This guy Adalbert knew? Bradley's soldiers found him stealing shit out of one of their tents and they broke all his fingers on his right hand.

— I told you, Lar! said Tamika. —Total Nazis.

—So then they took you into their van? asked Larry. —Without patting you down?

—They patted us down, they just didn't search our things. We didn't have guns, just the powder in the pack. We told 'em we were on our way to go smoke a joint with some chicks. So then this one guy got into showing us their whole system. And you know what? I was fucking impressed.

—Excuse me, said Ann, —can I get by there, Clint? I have to use the bathroom.

—You ladies, said Clint, getting to his feet slowly as though it required a Herculean effort and hefting his beer as he rose. —You and your peanut-size bladders.

—How do they get the images? asked Ben.

—They had these special thermal cameras rigged up in the trees and telephone poles around Bradley's HQ. These people give new meaning to the word *paranoid*. I'm telling ya.

She left them behind and lingered in the hall outside the bathroom looking at more old photographs, black-and-white images from the bar's heyday. There was a faded group picture of kitchen and wait staff, the kitchen staff in chef's hats, the waiters in tie and tails, holding trays and looking austere. Underneath was marked the date, in spidery handwriting: *1936.*

Oppenheimer could have been here then, she was thinking, Oppenheimer or even Szilard.

Back then they could have been patrons in their thirties, young and debonair.

❧ Szilard was pleased with the coverage in the New York Times.

—Our case is laid out succinctly, he said over breakfast.

—Can we move to a hotel where there's somewhere other than that diner to eat at? asked Tamika. —The stuff's all cooked in lard here.

—We're leaving today. We're going to Washington this afternoon, said Szilard. —Can I take one of your sausages?

—You know what Leslie told me? It was old Mrs. Purcell that got them to run that big article, said Larry, and dropped a sausage onto Szilard's plate. —She pulled some strings. Someone in her family used to own the paper or something.

—Don't be ridiculous, said Szilard. —We're talking about the *New York Times* here. The UN talk was an historic event. *That's* why they ran the story.

—So when's the march?

—Friday, said Szilard. —So many people are coming, there's all this coordination. But we don't have to worry till the day before. Bradley's people are handling it.

—That doesn't seem wise, Leo, said Oppenheimer, slipping into the booth. —You want them calling the shots?

—They're not doing the message, said Szilard. —Just the logistics.

—You mean they're *organizing* the march, said Ben.

—Not the speakers, said Szilard. —Glen lined up the speakers for me weeks ago. There are peace advocates from all over the world flying in. We have several Nobels.

—You've been hijacked, Leo, said Ben. —Why are you kidding yourself?

—Don't be ridiculous. We're letting them do the legwork. It's called delegating authority, said Szilard haughtily.

❧ In a suburb of Washington called Greenbelt the scientists received a heroes' welcome. When they pulled into the hotel parking lot veterans stood on the wide lawn next to the hotel, saluting them in full uniform. Oppenheimer got out first and moved along the line slowly, shaking hands and bowing his head. Szilard and Ann followed after him and heard the testimony of a man wounded by shrapnel, whose head was misshapen as a result.

—I'm Lenny Wren, I'm an A-bomb veteran too, I head the group out of Baltimore, said the wounded man, holding onto Oppenheimer's hand for too long. Ann was standing right beside him and could see Lenny's own thin hand had bitten-down nails and a tattoo that read LAKOTA. —We got about three thousand A-bomb veterans coming in for the march, overall. Including your widows and your kids. You know, the next of kin.

—Great, said Szilard.

—I'm riddled with cancer all over the place, said Lenny, turning to Oppenheimer and grinning affably.

—I see!

—You name the organ, I got tumors there. And more than half of them qualify for federal aid.

❧ Under the presidential administration of George W. Bush steps were taken to begin research and development of so-called "usable nukes." (Other nicknames included "bunker busters" and "mini-nukes.") These weapons, it was argued, might be employed in the battlefield to take out hardened targets.

At the same time the White House and elements in Congress pressed to lower the threshold for using nuclear weapons in conflict. To ensure the military supremacy of the United States, proponents of nuclear weapons development at Los Alamos and Lawrence Livermore National Laboratories urged the U.S. to build nuclear weapons small enough not only to deter, but to use.

Because weapons left over from the Cold War were too big to be used against rogue states, the argument went, and therefore would not have a deterrent effect—since no one could possibly *believe* the U.S. would use such powerful weapons against weaker adversaries—the American military must have smaller weapons at its command, weapons whose use would not be unthinkable at all.

The construction of small nuclear weapons would therefore close the door on pure deterrence and open the door to practical, feasible, and convenient nuclear war.

❧ The first night in Greenbelt the hotel room felt close and airless. Ann got up in the middle of the night and tottered toward the air-conditioner to turn it on, stubbing her big toe on the bottom of the metal bed frame. In the dark she could not see the knobs on the air-conditioner so she flicked on the lamp on the table. Then she thought she heard something outside, so she looked out the peep-hole in the door.

Nothing was visible on the catwalk, and she was still half-asleep. She forgot about the air-conditioner, turned off the light and went back to bed, where she dreamed that she and her mother were finding yellow fruits growing in clumps of long reeds. Then they were stealing them, and the reeds became the aisles of a supermarket.

Awake again, when the bedside clock read five in the morning, she tried but could not fall back to sleep. She wondered if the windows opened, and when she went to find out she pulled back the heavy drapes and saw a figure slumped in front of the window, on the concrete of the walkway.

—Shit, she said, —Ben? There's someone here.

He turned and muttered something, waking up and raising himself on one arm.

She opened the room door and looked out. A balding man in a trench coat was sleeping against the wall beneath their window, curled up in the fetal position. She recognized the slope of his high forehead and was concerned.

—Are you OK? she whispered, and knelt beside him, reaching a hand out to touch his shoulder.

He rolled onto his back and opened his eyes.

—Ben? It's Enrico!

Then Ben was beside her and both of them were leaning over. Between them they lifted him up and helped him into the room, let-ting him sag onto the second double bed.

—I'm OK, he said. —I'm just tired. It was a long trip.

They took his shoes off for him and covered him up. Under his trench coat he wore only pajamas.

—I'm going back to sleep too, said Ben when they had tucked him beneath the covers and watched him pull the coverlet over his head. —If I can.

But she was not tired anymore. She dressed quietly in the bathroom and brushed her teeth quietly at the sink. Then she put on a sweater and left them both on the beds and went outside, to breathe in the chill and walk down the stairs from the concrete cat-walk to the parking lot. There was frost on the grass and the bushes were coated in a thin wax of ice.

Nothing was open, she realized, there would be nothing for her to do but wander through the suburbs. It was still dark and the sun would not come up for almost two hours. She wanted to explore the hotel but the lobby door was locked, and the water in the pool was flat and unmoving.

༄ When Ben woke up later and saw she was gone he was worried and called her on her cell phone. This woke Fermi, who sat up on the edge of his bed and stared at his feet, his face haggard. Ben hoped he was a new man, or at least his old self, but all he would say when they got up was that he had come because Leo had wanted him to, that for the march on Washington all three of them had to be together.

—After that, said Fermi, —I'm going home. Can I have a glass of water?

Ben went to the sink and poured him one.

—It's going to taste like dust, he said as he handed it over. Fermi was still looking at his feet.

—I need slippers, he said, taking the glass with fingers so limp Ben was afraid he would drop it. —They are cold.

Ben was thinking how he had always had a daydream of hotels. He and Ann both had a dream of hotels, about a time in their lives when they would live in a succession of these hivelike buildings, small self-contained cities with grand lobbies and fountains and restaurants. They both had a dream of being eternal tourists, living in buildings with yellow walls and trellises of climbing vines, where responsibility lay with the authorities and the authorities were dis-tant, kind fathers, seamless in their trustworthiness.

❧ As she walked the sky lightened in the east and cars began to pass her on the street, first few and far between and then in a steady stream. Commuters freshly washed for morning sat at their steering wheels and drank coffee at stoplights as she passed.

She had been asked, she remembered, what she was waiting for, what the point was of this long and ceaseless trip. Ben had asked her repeatedly until they agreed to leave it, and more recently she had begun asking herself. She thought of the fact that she was always waiting for something to happen, that she was here because of some unpredictable reversal, some new marvel that was always supposed to occur in the future.

Was there a difference between waiting for enlightenment and waiting to be entertained?

❧ Ben called Oppenheimer's room and invited him to have breakfast. He did not mention Fermi.

But then a few minutes later he led Fermi into the restaurant, and the hostess pointed them to a leatherette booth at the back where Oppenheimer was waiting. They passed Kurt the Hut and another bodyguard two tables away, no weapons visible on them, sitting rigidly and watching the few restaurant patrons with gimlet eyes as though each one could be suspect.

Oppenheimer rose as they approached, smiling with his arms raised, and Ben was surprised to see the depth of affection in his face when he stooped to clasp both of Fermi's hands in his own.

—You're with us again! he said shakily, and Fermi nodded awkwardly, his head bowed.

—He joined us for the march on Washington tomorrow, said Ben, and they slid into the booth. —He's planning on going back after that.

—I understand, Enrico, said Oppenheimer quickly. —You still need your R&R. But it's so good to see you.

❧ The morning air had a sharp, clear quality that made her think she could answer questions. For once she had a chance of knowing why she was walking down the street in Greenbelt, Maryland in the fall, thousands of miles from her home, why she had left her job and everything she knew and why her husband was in a hotel with brown shag carpets eating breakfast with a balding and delusional Italian.

For the chance of finding out she kept walking. There was nothing to see but the wide suburban intersections and the residential streets with their rows of neat lawns, fake-Tudor bungalows and Victorian facades climbing up to her left and her right, and the commuters, whom she stared at in their cars with growing longing.

People needed the comfort of routine and she was one of them. That was all.

She had been waiting for something to happen for months now, yet nothing ever did, nothing on a grandiose scale. Events were swiftly part of the past, receding, and the wait was thankless. But more than that it was misguided, she had come to suspect. You could wait for an event all your life but once it came it would only slip into history and be gone. Oppenheimer and the others had come from the past, she thought, and yet she stayed with them because of what she believed was the future: but they were not the future. They were something that had already happened. They were the past bleeding into the present and further, all three tenses collapsed into one.

There was nothing to touch in the future but the past, and so there was nothing to be waiting for. It was not what was going to happen, she saw in a shiver, but what already had.

She knew what she knew, now, she thought, walking back to the hotel. She hoped she could remember the way.

❧ —Enrico! Are you better? crowed Szilard, finding them at a table beside the pool.

Oppenheimer and Ben were both smoking and Fermi sipped

gingerly at his coffee. Beside them the pool was covered in plastic, dead leaves and brown water collected in the slack.

—He came because you wanted him to, said Ben quietly. —But he's going back after the event tomorrow.

—Well, said Szilard, and coughed into his hand. —Thank you, Enrico. Would the two of you like to come with us to see the floats for the march? They're in a warehouse about twenty miles into town.

—They've been building them for months but we've never seen them, said Larry, coming up behind Szilard dangling his car keys. —I've spent tens of thousands of bucks on these things. Dr. Fermi! Hey!

—Tomorrow is soon enough for me, said Oppenheimer, and sipped from his own coffee. —Anyway, I have a TV interview this afternoon. Glen is driving me to the studio.

—Soon enough for me too, said Fermi, and nodded sagely.

❧ Bradley's army did exercises that night, first marching around the block, then turning and moving in elaborate formations in the vacant lot behind the hotel while a drill sergeant barked out orders. Ann watched them from the balcony at the back of the room while Ben ordered room service from a menu of deep-fried foods and Fermi sat at the table near the window, poring over a book. It was a large book depicting birds of all kinds and Fermi turned the pages slowly, scrutinizing each bird as though it was a long-lost relative.

She counted the neat rows and calculated there were about four hundred soldiers, all in camouflage, all with rifles, all stone-faced and rigid as though facing the enemy. From the balcony she could look down on them and pretend their ranks were hers to command.

—You shoulda come with us, man, said Larry, and she heard the door close as Ben let him into the room. —That shit was awesome. These things are fucking huge and they look totally real.

—What looks totally real? she asked, pushing the sliding door open.

—The floats, man!

—Look, an ibis, said Fermi, and held up his open book to a large photograph of a bird with a thin curved bill. —A straw-necked ibis. *Threskiornis spinicollis.*

—The zucchini sticks and a Caesar salad, no chicken, said Ben on the phone, and hung up.

—This is a roseate spoonbill, said Fermi, and pointed to a graceful bird with pink feathers.

Larry raised an eyebrow. —That thing looks like a freak.

❧ It was still dark when they rose, following Szilard's schedule. The schedule read *5:00 a.m. Meet in parking lot. Granola bars, water bottles, and hot coffee will be provided. Attire: comfortable jogging shoes or cross-trainers. (Oppenheimer/Fermi: suits, ties, and hats. NB: ORIGINAL @ 1945! Better for the cameras. Makeup artists will be provided on our approach to Washington but BE CLEAN-SHAVEN.) 5:20: Leave for first meeting point in six vans including security.*

—I do not wear makeup, grumbled Fermi as Ann tied his tie for him, standing in front of their open hotel room door.

—It'll just be pancake makeup, I'm sure, said Ann. —You know, like the TV reporters and the newscasters wear.

—They wear makeup? The men?

Outside the door Bradley's soldiers were posted along the catwalk. He had insisted that the Wackenhut bodyguards come under his jurisdiction for the day and shunted them into menial jobs where they would be invisible. Szilard's instructions on this point read *For the day of the march the Wackenhut guards will be under the command of the Righteous Army. A special corps of Bradley's men will be assigned to guard S, O and F. O/F: Go to them for any of your security needs and once we exit the vehicles at Meeting Point 1 <u>always keep at least four (4) per physicist</u> within a ten-foot radius. NB You will be able to recognize the special detachment by their yellow armbands. Each of them has sniper training and martial-arts expertise.*

Bradley did not approve of the Huts and called them rent-a-cops. In turn they hated him and were humiliated by their demotion.

Ann and Ben and Fermi went down to the parking lot and stood waiting in the dark beside the van, drinking coffee from a thermos. When Szilard rushed over laden with clipboard and portable computer and at least two cell phones he was wearing a baseball cap squashed flat on his head and a T-shirt with his own picture on it.

—I thought your dress code was suit and tie, Leo, said Ben.

—I will be changing en route, said Leo. —Teller died.

—Edward? asked Fermi blankly. —I didn't know he was still alive.

—Alive and ancient, said Szilard. —My old friend. But as you may know from your reading, Enrico, he became a militarist after the war. After we knew him. Incidentally, he turned Oppie over to the McCarthyites. Biggest hawk physics has ever known.

—Poor Edward, murmured Fermi, and looked over Szilard's shoulder, unfocused. —Where is Robert?

—The president gave him a Medal of Honor, mostly for loving the bomb.

—Robert?

—Teller.

—I want to see Robert, said Fermi.

—Anyway, he died a few days ago, said Szilard. —Now I regret I didn't pay him a visit. Anyone want donuts?

☙ The vans pulled into a downtown parking lot as dawn was breaking, beside an array of trucks with their rear doors open. Floats were being assembled under tall floodlights behind a blue nylon barrier erected to block the view.

It was a poor downtown block with winos sleeping in doorways, stains on the sidewalk and litter collecting in the gutters. Piano wire was strung up along the walls of the parking lot.

Fermi was shocked by this and declined to get out of the van.

Beside a folding table, pouring coffee into styrofoam cups and piling donuts on a paper plate, Ann watched Oppenheimer stand under a floodlight in front of the blue screen talking to reporters. Around him paced Bradley's special corps in their yellow armbands, wires trailing down their necks from their Secret Service earpieces and weapons bulging under their flak jackets.

—Can they do that? she whispered to Ben, leaning back into the van. She handed Fermi his donuts and stepped out again, and Ben clambered down to join her. Back in the van Fermi chewed and stared out the window. —Just have guns in the street in D.C.?

—They all have concealed weapons permits, said Szilard, who was having his makeup done nearby by a makeup artist with long kinky hair.

—How did they swing that? asked Ben.

—I think he looks kind of orange, Darcy, said Larry, edging up to the side of the van with a camera in hand and snapping a picture of Szilard. —You don't think he looks kind of too orange?

—Trust me, said the makeup artist.

The crowd from Tokyo pulled up in its own vans and Clint and Leslie walked past Szilard's makeup station toward the nylon wall that hid the floats from public view.

—Sorry, no entry, said a guard, and Clint swore loudly.

—Lar! Larry! he bellowed, and Larry rolled his eyes and walked away from them toward the blue wall. Tamika put her hands on Szilard's shoulders and stared into the mirror in front of him.

—You look so *cute*! she said. —You're like a teddy bear!

Fermi emerged from the van carefully, looking both ways before he stepped down onto the pavement.

—What are they doing? he asked Ben, and pointed to a group of Righteous Army soldiers clustered along the fence.

—Praying, said Ben. —They say prayers several times a day.

—I will go there, said Fermi, and walked over to the circle of praying soldiers, his own guards trailing him.

Ben watched as he stood on the outskirts of the circle gazing in.

◑ In 2003 North Korea, named by President Bush as one of the three "axis of evil" powers inimical to the U.S., revived its nuclear weapons production program and planned the production of five or six weapons.

Also, reported the chief of the International Atomic Energy Agency, between thirty-five and forty countries beyond those who already possessed nuclear arms had become capable of producing them. Should any of these countries choose to withdraw from the Nuclear Nonproliferation Treaty, they could have a weapon ready in months.

In 1998 India and Pakistan exploded their first nuclear weapons, with the exception of a so-called "peaceful" bomb India had tested a quarter-century before. Pakistan declared itself willing to sign the nonproliferation treaty if India did, but India declined.

The physicist Abdul Qadeer Khan, who headed Pakistan's atomic weapons development program for years, was lauded as a national hero in Pakistan, where he was often called *the father of the atom bomb*.

◑ Most of the reporters did not have difficult questions, rather their questions were repetitive and superficial and required nothing but rote responses. Because of this Oppenheimer found himself distracted as he talked to them. He gazed beyond them, his eyes skimming over the people he did not know until they rested on someone he recognized.

In the corner of the walled lot Bradley's wife stood staring back at him, clutching a handkerchief he recognized because she had asked him to bless it. Beside her Dory was filming, crouched with her camcorder on her shoulder. Above them a sign on crumbling brick read *$7.99 Early Bird Special*.

Seeing the two of them together he could not help but consider them in the same light, two faithful camp followers, humble and submissive, deferring. Dory had begged for service, and thinking of it made his bones feel cold as steel. He flinched without moving.

He could perpetrate any insult or injury against them without provoking anger or outrage. And yet of course there was no injury he wished to give them. He was without urges of any kind, mean or lustful or disparaging. He had first seen his pity as a relief from neutrality, but since then it had become a burden. It was the only thing he knew how to feel anymore. And the fact that he was left with pity, one sad small shade from the broad spectrum of emotions, seemed pitiable itself. Wherever he looked over these past few days he saw something worthy of condescension—a repulsive inclination. In theory he rejected everything about it but in practice there was nothing he could do. Pity was simply how you felt when everything around you was mortal.

But when he first came here, he remembered, he had cried. He had had feelings then. How quaint he had been. He recalled himself sitting at a bus stop in Los Alamos, the crisp air of the high plateau around him, weeping for his lost house and neighborhood and wife and children as though he was human.

❧ Ben first became aware of the noise while he was walking around the block with Fermi, bodyguards behind and in front of them. They had both gotten cold and needed to walk to generate heat, despite Fermi's alarm at the squalor of the street, which he said he could hardly believe was actually a street "in the downtown of America's capital city."

—What is that? Sounds like someone humming, asked Ben. Fermi only shook his head.

—It's the crowd, said one of the bodyguards. —They're meeting up about a half-mile away.

As they walked around the block the faint hum grew louder and Ben could see that streets were cordoned off, crowds massing at the ends of them, banners held and megaphones blaring.

—I'm afraid of it, said Fermi suddenly, coming to a dead stop. His lips were blue. —I prefer to go back.

—You'll be fine today, said Ben. —And you can go back tomorrow. OK? Right now we need to get you warmed up.

After a few moments Fermi seemed to forget his alarm.

—We used to wear long underwear, he mused, and picked up his stride. —Woolen. I had a red pair. In those days we kept warm.

❧ In 2001, the George W. Bush administration withdrew from the long-standing anti-ballistic missile treaty of 1972 and began to agitate for the placement of a "Star Wars" type anti-ballistic missile system in California and Alaska, though such a system, since it did not yet exist, was still only science fiction.

The following year, when it made its argument for small, usable nukes, it published a "Nuclear Posture Review" that recommended expanding the U.S. nuclear program. The paper outlined a plan to deploy a new type of intercontinental ballistic missile by 2018, a new submarine-launched missile by 2030, and a new heavy bomber by 2040.

Knowing how much the public likes to see reductions in nuclear weapons, however, the American and Russian presidents made a great public show three months later of agreeing to reduce their stockpiles of strategic weapons by several thousand by 2012.

This so-called historic agreement was actually non-binding and in fact set the same levels of reduction already outlined in old treaties. In the meantime, the men in charge of the American government were dreaming of a future where nuclear weapons loomed large once again.

❧ Szilard and Oppenheimer would make their opening speech from a balcony that overlooked a square, with Fermi standing behind them. The rest of them would not go upstairs with the scientists but would watch from the ground with the crowds.

The van pulled into an underground lot and let them out, and bodyguards led Oppenheimer and Szilard and Fermi and Bradley to an elevator. When the doors closed behind them other soldiers in the Righteous Army led the rest of them up a car ramp to the street.

—Is Bradley going to talk too? Ann asked Larry.

—Say some of that Christian shit? I don't think so, he said.

She looked sidelong at the soldiers but their faces betrayed nothing.

—So why is he going up with them?

—He has to be where the action is, said Tamika.

They were on the street then and walking toward a police barrier, behind which crowds were teeming. Ann saw a wavering, dipping handmade sign that read HAIL THE SAVIOR. In small print beneath this was written INTO YOUR HEART WELCOME HIM.

The square was packed and further out, down the streets that fed into it, there was no end of people. It struck Ann as they moved along the margin of the crowd with their bodyguard escort that the marchers were very well-behaved, even orderly.

—Can you hear me? boomed a voice over their heads. It was Szilard, but his voice was deeper than usual, a rich baritone. They had come to a concrete barrier and Ann looked up at the balcony, almost immediately overhead. All she could see was brick, and all she could hear was the drone of conversation, now dropping off around her as the crowd began to clap. Behind her someone was singing in a high, off-key voice. *Glory, glory hallelujah, glory, glory hallelujah.*

—Thank you all for the effort you've made to be here today! We couldn't have an impact without you!

—We can't even see them here! complained Tamika to one of the guards. —Can't we move? We're like right under their feet!

—Instructions. This is the most secure location, said the guard, and turned away to speak into his headset.

—This sucks, said Tamika.

—Secure location my ass, said Larry.

—But Dory's taping it, hon, said Tamika. —She wangled a deal where she can be up there with the network news people, where she has a good view of the mall. At least we can watch it on tape later. Right?

—This is a day that will herald the dawn of a new age, came Szilard's distorted and magnified voice.

Around them people cheered and screamed, and more voices took up the hymn the single voice had been singing. Ann turned around to see who it was but could not pick out the singers from the crowd.

—How many people did they say were showing up? Ben asked Larry.

—Somewhere around three hundred thousand, I think they were telling me, said Larry, and turned to Tamika. —Is that right, honey? I know it's more than they had at that million-man march way back when.

—Today we march for an end to warlike things, said Szilard, and the crowd screamed again.

—Where are the floats? said Ann into Larry's ear.

—They're coming. Should be here any minute.

❧ Szilard spoke of "the imperative of ridding the world of the nuclear menace" and below the balcony where he and Oppenheimer were standing Ben could see nothing, only hear. Around him he read the signs of the marchers, which did not refer to peace but rather to the Rapture, not of the *need to bring together the community of nations* but of the *final annihilation in which God's justice will be done.*

Bodyguards flanked them. When he looked past a burly shoulder he could see down a wide boulevard: over the crowds loomed a missile, easily the size of three eighteen-wheelers. It pointed straight up like a rocket.

—Oh my God, said Ann beside him, and Larry grinned.

—That's the lead float, he said. —It's a reproduction of an ICBM!

—Very lifelike, said Ben.

It was white and written on the side in somber black were the words *U.S. Air Force.*

❧ —And I give you my colleague, said Szilard, —Dr. Julius Robert Oppenheimer.

The crowd surged hard against Ann's back, all of them pressing forward, the pitch of their cries rising into a scream. She raised her hands to her ears and leaned against Ben.

—The king! The king! chanted a group nearby, and she turned to look at them. They were teenagers, holding signs that bore pictures of the porkpie hat.

❧ Oppenheimer was not surprised by the crowds. If there was anything he was used to by now it was multitudes. Whether in their vastness they were only a dream of crowds or actual crowds he was not sure, but he would give them the benefit of the doubt. *Pretend the world is real.* This had been his creed at the very beginning and lately he had returned to it.

But lately it had been a stretch because the dreams stayed with him when he was awake. Their tone lasted throughout the morning, haunting him as he drank his coffee and smoked his cigarettes and even talked to the people around him, the dreams covering their faces. All the dreams were of multitudes. There were multitudes of people or multitudes of things, but they were all multitudes.

One of them was of women weeping, the kind of abject women he had begun to see everywhere and feel beholden to, women to whom he could give nothing. In the dream he owed a debt to all women and all children. He was guilty before them, guilty even before animals of which he did not know the names: he was guilty before the world of the living.

Now all of them, these living animals and men and women and children who would soon enough cease to live, converged on him. They drew themselves along the ground, moving in crowds across the land, slow and sightless and wishing for something he could no longer offer. One day he had done a thing that could not be undone and now he basked in the sickening afterglow. It was a glow like a needle, the edge of a flashing knife.

Another dream pressed down on him with the hard white burning of the sun, and under the sun the water: there were cars under the ocean, all the cars he had seen in the world since he got here, the thousands or hundreds of thousands of them. They lay side by side at the bottom of the sea, covered in water, overgrown with seaweed, rusting in peace. The ocean was dark around their bodies.

This last dream was a good dream. Ever since he had come to the new life he had hated the cars.

But his one wish was for simplicity. He would be satisfied to live without what he had prized most all his life, namely intelligence. He considered the small mammals burrowing under wet leaves, the long-legged graceful ones running across wide fields. Most likely they did not know the prospect of their own death or the end of history but only moved about their business when the sun rose or set. He wanted to be one of them, or even a man still but without faculties, one of the slack-jawed and smiling, one of the bumbling and grinning and always childlike. Ignorance was what he wanted, and he saw now what a beautiful thing it could be and always had been.

He saw how the crowds looked up to him worshipfully, as though one man could mean anything. He envied them even as he pitied their simplicity, hating himself for his own condescension, an anthropologist among the pygmies.

I see it now, he thought. All my life I held up the ideal of learning, but I was wrong. We all were wrong, he thought. It is not learning we need at all. Individuals need learning but the culture needs something else, the pulse of light on the sea, the warm urge of huddling together to keep out the cold. We need empathy, we need the eyes that still can weep.

After a point learning is useless, he thought, useless because it has been swallowed by technology and instead of compassion has brought the end of it.

He felt grief in him but it was not a flowing grief; rather it was the grief of a stone, always solid and gray and unmoving. That's what happened to me, he thought. I became an abstraction. At first, he thought, we tried to learn about the universe, and for a while we were still safe. But then we tried to learn about ourselves before the universe, not because we were curious but because we had something to prove. We wished to prove we were made in the image of God. And then the universe and ourselves became one in our eyes.

All of this he thought in a flash as he stepped up to the microphone beside Szilard; all this was gone as the people massed beneath them roared and Szilard, for once completely silent, instantly crumpled at his feet.

For a second he barely registered it, and then, when he did, he could not believe what he saw bending over his fallen colleague. Of all the unreal matters to fly before his eyes since he had come from the old life this was the most obscene: and Szilard, who despite his formidable genius had always been, at base, a figure of fun to him, would never be funny again.

↝ The crowd beyond them pressed forward with a shriek of hysteria and Ann was screaming too, into Ben's ear this time: —What happened?

She had not been looking upward because she had no vantage point, had not seen whatever caused this last vast movement, in fact because their part of the crowd had no view of the balcony all around them was confusion as people strained to see and hear.

—He was shot! screamed someone else to someone else, across her. —Szilard was shot in the face.

She and Ben turned and stared at each other, strained and unwilling. She felt her face and arms tingle and the hair raise, but she would not believe.

—We have to get out of here, he said, grim, and she said, —We have to get to them! But the throng was packed far too closely.

—You! called Ben to one of the bodyguards, but he was moving away, pressing through the crowd himself with a raised gun, which allowed him easier passage. He did not even turn. The other body-guards were also leaving, talking into their headsets, weapons held up and plainly visible, plowing through bobbing heads.

They had been abandoned.

❧ Bradley's soldiers pressed in around him, lifting up Leo's body—for there could be no doubt that it was now a body—and bearing it inside, and at the same time Bradley himself was at his elbow, pulling him along, curiously calm and certain. Others of the Christians were close by also, flanking them.

—It can't be, murmured Oppenheimer, —what is it? but Bradley only steered him with a firm hold on his arm, saying words he could not pick out above the din. Beneath the balcony the crowd was still screaming.

—You are pure now, he thought he heard Bradley whisper. —You are free.

Death was the realest thing, he was thinking as they pulled him, and part of him resisted; but was this death or was this vio-lence? It was a curious sensation: as they towed him through the rooms, as they towed him past Leo, or where, at least, Leo had used to be, *in that skin*—oh! being laid on a table, splash of flesh on a bright blue tarpaulin, which someone had already laid out—he turned and looked at him, looked at his poor friend. And he real-ized this at the same time: Leo had not been merely a colleague but a friend, moreover no mere friend but a hero, for heroes are not movie stars but worker bees. The farmer in the field, he thought: man, not the image of man.

He saw what had once been Leo's face and understood that the hole in the back of the head was neat and the ragged exit wound, the terrible injury of the bullet leaving, was what had torn out poor dear Leo's eyes.

And so, because Leo had stood right beside him, he knew with certainty that the shot had not come from the crowd but the inside, not from the masses out there to whom such an act of madness could easily be ascribed but from the ones right here. They had done it, these men misled to worship him. They had killed his friend.

❧ Later Ben would remember the day as though he had not lived it but only been handed the memory. He would not recall a chronology, only a series of impressions and how, after a while, his body had become too tired to react to events, and his senses were dulled by the tiredness of his limbs. He would recall Ann hanging on his arm, the people around them, one woman with her child on her shoulders, the child crying snottily in the chaos, and her husband beside her wearing a tattered brown robe and a dirty pair of running shoes.

He remembered the pace of the walk—too slow—and how formless the crowd was, and how impossible it was to know anything with certainty. He remembered confusion and Ann asking him if they could please get somewhere, please sit down, anything but what they were doing. He carried her for a while, carried her piggyback because there was no way out of the crowd to find a place to sit down. They were packed in too tightly and the crowd stretched too far. The restlessness of the crowd was alarming from the moment Szilard fell, a moment they had missed, being too close beneath him.

He remembered what happened later, the men in riot gear teeming, the visors through which faces were not visible, the burn of tear gas on his eyeballs and in his throat and the wail of sirens.

All of this was overshadowed in his memory by what came before and after, but neither of those, in retrospect, seemed real.

❧ In the lobby downstairs Bradley's men held Fermi waiting for him, Fermi who knew nothing of what had happened, a lost man.

Still, as they stepped closer he could see on Fermi's white face a growing fear, and he turned to Bradley, gripping his one good arm with sharp fingers.

—You will tell me who did this *now*, he said. —Tell me!

—Dr. Leo was executed because he was using you, said Bradley, and gazed unblinking past Oppenheimer's shoulder. Oppenheimer felt swiftly infuriated and almost as swiftly resigned. —He would have betrayed you for a handful of silver. He was a shackle holding you to the earth and keeping the faithful from their due. He refused to admit to your divinity.

Behind Bradley's head Oppenheimer noticed there were soldiers staring at him, staring and waiting for what he would say to this. Against such ignorance nothing could be said. He thought of Leo eating a lettuce leaf coated with sugar, nibbling at it with bulging eyes. When desserts were not available he had often rummaged in Ann's refrigerator until he found a head of lettuce; he had peeled off the outer leaves and into a tender, pale inner leaf he had poured white sugar.

He thought of Leo looking at him over his sweetened lettuce leaf and *refusing to admit to his divinity*. It made him smile.

—But you knew that, went on Bradley gently.

Oppenheimer was called back to him.

—So were you the ones who were threatening us? Were you behind the warning in the Marshall Islands?

—The Marshall what?

One of the soldiers leaned forward and whispered in Bradley's ear, distracting him.

—Was that your people too? persevered Oppenheimer.

—I don't know what you're talking about. Move along, OK? We gotta be going now.

—We were under surveillance. An officer threatened me in Micronesia. Men threatened Fermi in Tokyo. Someone shot a cat.

—Why would we threaten you? You are the final sign. No, that had to be them. They are afraid of the End Times, for they know they will never be saved. We do have some believers in the armed forces who have joined us in the cause, in fact we have many thousands, but they are enlisted men. Many of the civilian and military leaders belong to *them*.

—Them?

—The ones who do not want the Rapture, said Bradley solemnly.

—The high priests of Mammon.

Oppenheimer stared.

—And now, said Bradley, lowering his voice to a vicious whisper, —you will do your duty.

For the first time, strangely, looking down at Bradley's prosthetic arm, Oppenheimer thought of the sameness with his mother: she too had only had a single good hand. She had been lovely, and Bradley was grotesque, but still he saw now that both his mother and this man had made him what he was. In that moment he was conscious of repulsion: he was repelled by Bradley, he reviled him. At the same time a shadow passed over his head and he knew that Bradley was right. He was the worst kind of man, but he was also correct.

For Oppenheimer himself was nothing but history. He had loved the world and wanted to build something to honor it, and all he had ever known said this was a noble quest. But instead it was human. It was human but it was not noble, for men are only noble in humility.

So he had built the wrong thing, and his was both the last and the original sin, the tower of Babel.

And all he could do now was to give himself up.

❧ In the distance the missile was still vertical, looming over the trees beneath it, rivaling the nearby Washington Monument. Behind it were the dark low floats of Fat Man and Little Boy, its primitive ancestors, and around her on the mall the crowd hushed as

Oppenheimer ascended the stage. Ann could not tell where the song began because it seemed to come from all quarters, and far from calming her or inspiring her it made her itch. Amazing Grace, how sweet the sound, that saved a wretch like me.

It was then that she began to look around at the crowd more desperately, trying to discern a way through it. She wanted a path to open in their ranks to lead her away to freedom. But there was none.

The hymn got louder and louder, more and more oppressive in her ears as Ben lifted her up and she saw Oppenheimer standing patiently at the microphone. Fermi had joined him, head bowed, and then Bradley stepped up behind them and she felt sick to her stomach. Behind them was a screen that showed their faces large and looming. Bradley looked like a fat cat, smug and proud, and Oppenheimer looked sad.

Finally the song trailed off and people clapped, rhythmic claps she thought would burst her eardrums.

— Our dear friend has fallen, said Oppenheimer, and the crowd screamed. Oppenheimer shook his head and they trailed off again. —I ask for a minute of silence for him.

The multitudes hushed. Ben put her down and on the wide screen she saw that Bradley's face, occasionally visible between Oppenheimer's and Fermi's bent heads, was still smug.

— So it's true, whispered Ben.

Before her hands and face had tingled with fear and shock even when she was not sure, but now they felt leaden. Szilard, she thought, gone: she could not allow it.

The crowd swayed and all she could see was the head of the man in front of her, swirls of thinning dark hair on a white scalp and dandruff above a bright blue T-shirt bearing the loosely drawn white outline of a dove. Even when she went up on tiptoe briefly the blur of the stage came into view too quickly for details, and she was too exhausted to jump, could barely stand straight but was reduced to slumping, shifting her weight off the weak ankle.

Ben was riveted on the stage and she could not ask him to lift her up again. Instead she watched a woman next to her, who was crying softly and scraping her keys along her bare arm, drawing blood.

Then the minute ended.

—At first I did not believe, said Oppenheimer, and the crowd fell abruptly silent. —At first I could not see what was seen by many.

—The king! The king! chanted someone Ann couldn't see.

—But then I started to see the world through other people's eyes, went on Oppenheimer, in a despair tone. The woman cutting her arm next to Ann let out a wail and Ann elbowed Ben to look over at the thin line of blood on her forearm. Then the screen behind Oppenheimer lit up with the image of a mushroom cloud and she could not see him but she could see the screen, and the cloud was enormous.

—In Biblical prophesy the end of time was brought by a man. Half man and half God, the messiah who began history returned again to end it. Half man and half God: what does that mean? God is omniscient, as science pretends to be. God has the power of creation and destruction, like the atom. God is also a crucified body who died for our sins—

The song started up again, softly this time. *I once was lost, but now am found, was blind, but now I see.* But Oppenheimer's voice could still be heard clearly over the strains.

—. . . in the West we now have crucified brains. Take Einstein, the benevolent genius who could do nothing to effect peace in his time, no matter how hard he tried. And in the anomaly of our presence here, from the moment the bomb first went off, we have, too, the elements of the Trinity—symbolic elements, of course, but we are a symbolic race, and we always have been. It is no coincidence that the test was called Trinity, and that we came here then, in a split second: Szilard, the one who started it all, I, who was sacrificed by men hunting down Communists, and Fermi, the spirit that moved the bomb by transmuting matter into energy. The Father, the Son and the Holy Spirit. All of this I have come to see, and I assure you: we are not gods, but we are something else. We are the end of man.

—He's lost it, said Ben into her ear, barely audible over the crowd.

—. . . and why? Because men and God have become indivisible. We see gods in the mirror, but we are ignorant. We have the power of gods but we do not have the wisdom. This is our tragedy.

—Look at Bradley, said Ben, and hoisted her up, fingers digging painfully into the skin on her hips.

Bradley had his arms raised to the sky behind Oppenheimer and she thought she could see his lips moving. Other men ascended the stage from behind as she watched, and they too raised their arms and were swaying. She did not recognize them. She let Ben hold her up till she could not stand the bruises on her hipbones, the jabbing fingers.

—There are more of them up there now, she told him. —Who are they?

—I think it's the others, he said. —The other Christian leaders.

—Sadly most of us do not yet know what we have seen, said Oppenheimer. —We have not recognized the end of time.

The woman beside her was crying so hard Ann was afraid she would hyperventilate. On the other side a woman was taking off her clothes, peeling off her pants and leaving them in a heap on the ground, then peeling off her coat.

—She's stripping! yelled Ann to Ben, incredulous, and he looked over and gaped.

—Some of us have seen it but are afraid to say what we behold, and live in a state of paralysis—

—Over there! said Ben, and pointed. —That guy too!

Past the woman a man had also begun to take off his clothes. Ann looked around her, feeling a frantic elation that was mostly fear. Behind Ben a middle-aged man was scraping his arms like the woman, scratching them with his fingernails and drawing beads of blood. His lined face was streaked with salt from dried tears.

—What *is* this? she asked, and pressed herself against Ben, her arm around his waist. She did not want to be separated, and for once she found herself wishing Larry were there, Sheila or Tamika or even Clint, anyone. —Why are they doing that?

—Now listen, listen to me, said Oppenheimer urgently, and stepped forward to clutch the microphone. —Leo was a sacrifice to these men here! and he turned to look behind him at the Righteous Army.

Ann gazed up at the screen but none of the Christians had looked at Oppenheimer after he spoke: they were still swaying with their eyes closed and their arms up, as though he had said nothing about them.

—But these men here are not the final threat, went on Oppenheimer. —These men are only pawns. You have to stand and fight, you—all of you! and he looked around at the crowds, —take up arms against your true enemy. Peace will no longer work for you. Peace is a dinosaur. It is the end but no longer the means.

The man beside Ben whined and nodded as he scratched at his forearms. Ann gazed at the sallowness of the skin with the shadow of green veins behind it.

—I beg you: take up arms against the true enemy. For the true enemy is not men, these men or any others . . .

—What the hell? asked Ben, shaking his head. —What is he—?

—The true enemy is the institutions that men have made. And all of you: you have to be willing to give your lives up in the fight.

Silence spread over the far-flung legions of the crowd and Ann looked around hastily, confused. She leaned close to Ben to whisper.

—What is he talking about?

—Didn't I tell you? He's lost it.

—You may have thought before that there was something you

were willing to die for, and you may have assumed the question was academic. But it is not.

There was a pause and the sound of breathing over the speakers. On the screen the roiling mushroom cloud vanished abruptly and in its place there was blurred, jerky video of Oppenheimer's serene countenance, and behind it Bradley's face over his shoulder, smaller because it was further away, skin sweaty and pink, gaze fixed on Oppenheimer. He raised his arm and gestured at someone off to the side, and then nodded impatiently.

—This is the time, said Oppenheimer, still serene and smiling faintly, —this is the moment at which you are called upon to choose.

Ben was staring at his shoes.

—You can live for yourselves or you can lay down your life for the sake of what is beyond you. Either give up the future or lay your bodies down. Because it is not the bombs that are killing the world. It is the mind that made the bombs. For that purpose the bombs are not needed.

The sound from the microphone cut off abruptly and the great screen went gray. Beside Ann the man with the bleeding arms looked down at his turned-up wrists, seemingly confused. In front of them someone tittered nervously, and then a man holding one end of a banner that read ENTER THE KINGDOM OF THE LORD began to wave it singing. Later she clearly remembered looking at the man ahead of her again, staring into his dark greasy hair above the blue T-shirt with the outline of the dove just as she heard the explosion. Nothing had ever shocked her as much as the sound, the sudden concussion. She felt the shock at the base of her stomach, a jab of fear. Bright lights were streaking into the sky, trails of smoke behind them and above her and from the crowd near the missile issued a different screaming.

—What is it? she asked Ben.

He was propping himself on the shoulder of neighbors, jumping to see.

—It looks like . . .

—What? *What?*

—It looks like the cops. Hundreds of them. They're plowing through the edge of the crowd with shields and gas masks on.

The crowd began to move and a panic rose through it. They wanted to get out but could not: there was no way out and the crowd was pressing and surging, moving forward.

—This is going to get messy, said Ben. —We need to get out now.

—I want to, said Ann, —that's all I want.

—Did you see Fermi up there?

—They must be taking care of him, she said, —aren't they?

They could move in only one direction, the direction of the crowd. Bradley's voice was telling the crowd to *Keep calm, keep calm,* but they were not calm, they were moving and shrieking and Ann tripped on someone else's foot and twisted her bad ankle slightly and tried to keep walking but the pain jabbed and brought tears to her eyes.

So Ben had to lift her again and put her on his back, even through his exhaustion. From there she could see the missile and beyond it a bare part of the street with a line of men in black pushing people away from the missile with their convex shields, pushing them toward her and Ben and the stage, compressing the crowd. Past the trees she could see the roof of the White House; or possibly she was imagining.

❧ Ben knew the danger was real and a stampede was imminent. He felt the threat of it in the back of his throat and the muscles of his arms. His back ached but the only way to get out of this was to stay with the crowd. There was no use struggling against it, in fact any attempt to move against the close-packed throng could be lethal. He could feel hysteria mounting in others around them, discerned the edginess he had felt the afternoon at the bright waterfall. He would not let himself cave in to fear though he sensed it all around him, warm and sweaty.

His lower back was hurting so he enlisted the aid of a guy next to him and they hoisted Ann all the way up onto his shoulders, still moving the whole time, pushed along. As they pushed her up she winced from the pain in her ankle. It was precarious but she could not walk and there was nothing he could do about it.

—Can you see where the crowd thins out? he yelled up to her, and repeated it when she did not hear him. She looked around and then pointed past the stage to his right.

—Up there! she said. —Go that way!

It was with the crowd, just a slight veer, and he leaned into it, packed in by other shoulders as they half-walked and were half-carried by the momentum. His neck felt strained, the cords standing out and pulling at his chin and throat, and his mouth was parched. In front of him was denim, a sign bobbing that threatened to take out an eye with its sharp corners, *Can You Hear the Voice of the Dolphins?*

—Just stay calm, he called up to her, because her hands on the tops of his arms were squeezing too hard.

He stepped on a shoelace and stumbled when it was pulled out from under his foot, but was held up when he fell against a big man beside him.

—Keep pointing me in the right direction, he yelled up to Ann, —you're the lookout!

That was when the tear gas billowed near the base of the missile, at the far edge of the crowd.

❧ Oppenheimer had felt the explosion, though he had not been looking in the right direction to see it. But from his high place he could see the aftermath: the missile was burning. Smoke rose in columns at the edges of the crowd: tear gas, he thought, most likely, or perhaps some more lethal chemical agent. Was it sabotage, or was it a direct attack?

Then he was pushed backward on the stage and Bradley's soldiers were surrounding him. Others among the Christian leadership were close—all of them, he thought, so recently euphoric, so recently beyond themselves and ecstatic, now babbling and squawking so loudly among themselves that he could barely make out the words of those nearest to him. Nearby he could see Fermi, but not near enough to address.

Bradley's soldiers were more frightened, he thought, than they should have been by fireworks and tear gas; certainly they were far more frightened than he.

—It's gotta be them! yelled one of them to another—Denny, if he recalled correctly, with the Confederate flag on his arm, a thick-necked Baptist from the deep South. Past him stood the soldiers with their rifles raised.

How, Oppenheimer wondered belatedly, had they been permitted to bring their rifles to this public place, in this time of supposed peace? These rifles, one of which had surely killed his friend?

—How do you know it's them? said Rob, who resembled a well-heeled golfer but whose working-class congregation, he had once told Oppenheimer, enjoyed the handling of snakes. —It could just be the D.C. cops. They're nothing!

—It's not the D.C. cops, said Denny, and Oppenheimer noticed the color had washed out of his florid face.

—It's a private security force, said one of the soldiers, a middle-aged man with furrowed brow who spoke near Oppenheimer's ear. —Either that or Special Ops.

—It's theirs, urged Denny, —I'm telling you.

Oppenheimer looked off the stage beyond him. In the crowd people had to be fleeing from the tear gas, and yet the crowd was so dense and wide their movement was barely perceptible.

Then there was Bradley again, jogging over from a huddle with his lieutenants, the small mouthpiece of his headphone blocking his mouth.

—This is your fault! he said to Oppenheimer. —We didn't care what you said about us. We have nothing to hide. But they do. They don't like to be named. And now they're coming. We have spotters in helicopters and they've seen them. They're on their way in from all sides and they want to kill you.

Then he was swamped by the others, as overhead a small helicopter hovered and dropped a ladder. Rob from the Pentecostal church was the first to climb up it, shimmying up with a face red from the effort and his thick beige-clad legs clutching awkwardly; but then there were other helicopters above them too, dark, flat-bellied and sinister, ponderous and massive. They were edging the small one out and forcing it away. The noise of them was deafening.

Oppenheimer looked away from them, down and around him at the crowds beyond the stage, beneath the smoke and the screen of gas, which seemed to him a turmoil. He looked up again just in time to see Rob clamber into the blue helicopter as it began to retract its ladder. It occurred to him that Bradley could not hope to get clear in this way, one-armed as he was, with only the rope ladder to assist. But anyway it was not going to be the way out for any of them, for the small blue craft swooped jerkily away flanked by the military choppers.

Surely even Bradley and his soldiers would be overcome by the tear gas; surely they did not have long to formulate their plan. Surely the so-called high priests of Mammon were closing in.

And yet he was perfectly calm: and he knew.

❧ To look down around her at the sea of heads made her queasy and dizzy and she was willing herself to stay strong, stay upright and not fall off of Ben's shoulders. She kept her eyes on the horizon, the stage and the burning ICBM.

Onstage Bradley was shouting past the microphone inaudibly, shouting with soldiers arrayed behind him, their faces projected on the screen, strained, confused, panicking. Over the crowd she could no longer hear them and she could not see Oppenheimer either. If she knew how to read lips she would know what they were saying, she thought, and wished she knew how to read lips, but she did not. She had never known a deaf person and had never interested herself in deafness.

She regretted this with a sudden anger.

—I should have had an interest in the deaf, she repeated as they moved. But of course no one heard her. She could be panicked but instead she was dumb; there was nothing she could do. It frustrated her that she could not see Oppenheimer or Fermi on the stage anymore and her eyes stung. She turned toward the missile and saw white smoke billowing there again.

—Oh no! she said, and looked down at Ben. —Smoke! Did something else explode?

—Tear gas! he yelled.

—What?

—Tear gas! It moves fast! Get your water out of your bag!

The bag was hanging off his shoulder. She leaned down and fumbled with it one-handed, slipping out the near-empty bottle and spilling candy bars and her watch onto the ground. She let them go. —Are you thirsty?

—Soak the bottom of your shirt in it and then hand it to me! The gas is going to drift over here! Any second!

She poured the water on her shirt and handed it down to him.

—Hold up your shirt to your nose and mouth, OK? Breathe through the wet cloth. It's going to catch up with us. We can't move any faster than the rest of them.

She held it over her nose and mouth but could still feel burning start there, and her eyes and nose were running. Around her people stumbled and fell against Ben and she felt a clutch of fear rising through her body. Even her feet trembled. They would fall and people would step on them, boots would crush their windpipes, their necks would snap like dry twigs. Her legs trembled all the way up to her crotch and her stomach was like water.

—Can you see the physicists up there?

—Only Bradley, she said, muffled through the T-shirt, —on the screen.

Then the burning grew and was stifling and they had to stop talking at all. It was all they could do to keep going forward. He had his wet shirt over his nose and mouth and she had hers, holding onto each other with their free left hands, people whimpering around them, now and then a shriek or a hoarse yell. When she finally felt herself falling, felt both of them toppling over pressed from the side, she closed her eyes because there was nothing else she could do. The fall seemed slow once it was in motion and because they landed on a cushion of bodies there was a softness to it, but at the same time it was almost impossible to breathe because she had to let her hand fall, her shirt was wrenched away from her nose and mouth and instantly the burning was far, far worse. A man was on top of her and she kicked out her legs, trying to unscissor them from Ben's head, afraid of crushing him. It was black and hot and she wanted to scream but could not, the burning and her closed throat, the thickness and the suffocation, and her eyes and nose streaming.

❧ Oppenheimer saw the riot police pushing their way through the crowd, absurd with their shields and masks like boys playing at war with pots and pans. He saw them before he noticed the SWAT teams, though the SWAT teams were far nearer, barely a hundred yards away, past the cordons and the crowds with nothing in their way, converging on the stage around him.

When Bradley's soldiers fired warning shots into the air—in doing so finally, he thought, seeming somehow almost innocent— the SWAT team opened fire on them. He stood among their falling bodies confused more than frightened as the SWAT team moved up the sides of the broad stage; he stood watching without bending, without taking cover, as though bullets could not penetrate him.

A few feet away Fermi sat in similar passivity, on a folding chair that had once been placed behind the podium, as usual gazing up at the sky.

Oppenheimer thought at first that the SWAT team was firing on Bradley's soldiers only but had to admit, as a trail of fire seared his forearm, that they were also firing on him. It was a grazing wound and did not bother him, but he was caught up in curiosity, gazing down at the bloom on his shirtsleeve like a man drugged or detached, as the SWAT team cut down Bradley's soldiers. They fell jerkily, one by one, with a surprising lack of protest.

Then like a man moving underwater he stepped up to the microphone. It would be the last time, he knew. He could not tell if the microphone was working. His arms moved slowly and stiffly as he reached and held onto the thin metal stand; he spoke without hearing his voice in the gunfire around him, persisting deafly.

—These men shooting at me now, he said, —Ann! Can you hear me? They are the ones who were hunting us! The other ones want heaven on earth. They shot Szilard! But it's the institutions that want to kill me. They have no use for the Rapture. They want their empire to last forever.

His vision was blurred, and he could not tell if he was speaking out loud. Grayer and grayer until the world is all gone, he was thinking: money and a vast machine.

—But the question is not, who is the enemy, he said, or thought he said. —The question is not even, why is the enemy winning? Those are the questions people ask but they are the wrong questions. The right question is: What is it in me that delivers the world into the hands of my enemy?

Amid the chaos everything had ceased to be separate, and inclining his head slightly he gazed at the simplicity of his red and white sleeve, alarm softly frozen. Just then the last rifles were lowered and sighted on his chest and head, and before they could fire the great white birds were coming down around him.

He had not seen their shapes against the sun, their shapes

move out of silhouette and turn from black to white as they drew near. Then now, descending, they were a density of lightness, and they enfolded him.

❧ Bones prodded her, sharp things poking, before the pressure abruptly let up and she was lying on the ground with no one above her and none beneath. She was astounded at this and the quick silence, a silence that fell as though a wind had dropped, and there was serenity.

Afraid and relieved at once she opened her eyes in a quick painful blink and saw white above her, white with small flashes of black but almost all white. In the silence she heard calls but did not know what they were, and then the white mass above her was rising and falling everywhere. Beside her on the ground was Ben, and near them was the crowd, not on top of them anymore but standing.

She pulled herself up, feeling scraped knees faintly against the fabric of her pants and blinked at the whiteness, which was moving. The wings were longer than she had ever seen, seven feet or eight feet together, vast. Feet dangled on long black legs.

—What *are* they? she whispered to him finally, incredulous, tears wet on her cheeks, and wiped her nose with the back of her hand, wiped her whole face with her wet shirt to clean it. The eyes and nostrils were still stinging hard and Ben was doubled over coughing from the tear gas still. Her throat burned and the other people were coughing too, there was coughing above the silence and the strange calls.

—It can't be, he said, standing up. —This is impossible.

She looked at him and saw him squint blinking into the sky above them.

—There aren't that many of them in the world, I mean look, there must be thousands, *tens* of thousands! he said, and his tear-wet, dirty face was turned up to the white in the sky. He bent quickly and choked and coughed into his hand.

—But what? she said.

—But they *are*, he said to himself more than her, staring.
—They have the black wing tips, see that? The dark legs . . . I can't
see their heads from below but it's them. They're huge. There's
nothing else it could be.

—Than what?

The screen was obscured by the birds, flying so low they had
darkened it. Her vision blurred with new tears from the gas and she
could not see whose face was on the screen anymore, whether
Bradley was looking up at the whiteness above him like everyone
else, the coughing and weeping crowd, standing motionless now
beneath the thousands of wings and gently sloping undersides. The
air was so thick that the sky was not visible and underneath the
white feathered slopes of the undersides of their bodies was a darkness not like night but shadow. The wings moved slowly, so slowly
she was amazed they could stay airborne, and the black legs
dangled beneath their bellies like afterthoughts.

—Whooping cranes.

She turned and saw them flying past the Washington Monument so that the peak could not be seen, and over long parallel rows
of trees. She kept turning in place and saw them flying over the
Smithsonian castle, the Capitol, the reflecting pool, over the Grant
Memorial and the Museum of Natural History, all of this in snatches,
all of these behind the birds and subsumed.

—It's a mass hallucination, whispered Ben, stunned. —The gas
maybe? Some obscure neurotoxin that makes you see things? Because these birds don't even exist anymore. Not in these numbers.
They're practically extinct.

—They must just be something else, said Ann. —Like storks or
swans or something? I mean—neither of us knows anything about
birds.

Deaf language and birds, she thought, of both she was sadly
ignorant.

—No they're not, said Ben. —Fermi wrote about them and I did the research. There's nothing else they could be.

—They have black heads, sometimes you can see them, she said, as the film on her eyes cleared for a second. —See? You can catch a glimpse . . .

She was noticing the missile, which had a pointed black tip on its white body.

—They look like the bomb, she whispered, and pointed. —See? All white on the body, and black at the top.

—Ann? Why are you whispering?

—Everyone is, she whispered back after a few seconds, and it was true, no one was talking, only coughing and wiping the tears off their faces and blowing their noses, only recovering and staring up above and occasionally leaning in close to each other to whisper or rasp from their burning throats. —They're so graceful, she said. —What are they doing in the city?

They came to get us, thought Ben, but he knew it was not his own thought: it was Fermi's. *Finally.*

—I think they came for the scientists, he said slowly. —I think that must be why they're here. I think they came to save them.

The birds swooped lower and lower over the stage, and at last she could make out figures there. There were the dark figures of men on the stage, but the birds swooped and flew over and covered them. When she saw a dark man uncovered, fleetingly, he was running and waving his arms, and then she heard the shots again.

—They're shooting at them! said Ben. —The cranes!

He was straining to see past other people's heads, people still standing in place and watching the great flock of birds above them, their faces turned upward.

—They can't be, she said, but then another shot rang out and she saw a flash of white as a bird fell near the stage. —Who?

—The military, said Ben. —Or whoever's up there now. It doesn't look like Bradley's men.

There was something on the screen again, flickering: a slight man in a suit, his hairline receding, reaching out at the birds as they swooped around him.

—Look, she said to Ben, —Fermi! It's Fermi!

—What is he *doing*? Doesn't he know they're shooting?

The birds were flying in wide arcs over the stage, back and forth, turning gracefully and returning. Fermi spun around and around among them, smiling. His smile was visible on the screen as a faint line of white teeth, and he was walking so near the screen that his silhouette touched the image of himself behind him.

—Oppenheimer! said Ben, and she saw him beside Fermi, bending over as though he was bowing; for a split second she thought he had tipped his hat at them. Then the flurry of the birds hid them, and the birds were diving and swooping, and the crowd was quiet.

Then were other shots and other birds fell.

—I wish they would stop it! she said urgently, voice shaking, afraid she was going to break down. The birds were beautiful and shocking in their nearness, the wide white wings with end-feathers like long black fingers and thin legs hanging down as they flew past.

She saw the eye of one of them, the deep and lovely eye.

❧ Ben had lost sight of Fermi in the white blizzard but then he caught sight of him again, briefly; and the last split-second he saw him he had to blink and squint, muttering under his breath What?— because he could have sworn Fermi was being lifted off the ground.

❧ The birds swooping low over the stage hid the screen now but still vaguely she thought she could see the dark forms of the physicists against it. On the edges of the stage she could certainly see other men, soldiers or police she could not tell, trying to shoot the birds as the birds dove at them, almost, she thought, fighting, diving at them, being shot and then others diving again.

More and more birds flew low over the stage until she could not see anything else anymore, though she strained to make out the shapes past their blurred and shifting bodies.

All of them watched, she and Ben and the people around them they did not know, watched as the birds, banners of white in the wind, musical and rhythmic, flew thicker and thicker among them and anything that was not the birds—buildings and trees and the further reaches of the crowd itself—could not be seen. After that they lifted up in a series of fluid motions, in waves and lulls, and their calls began to grow faint. Rising into the sky the cover of their bodies slowly lifted, the dense white of the flock grew sparser and revealed the mundane and usual below it, concrete and brown, the city and the people, the derelict stage littered with a dark mass that she guessed had to be Bradley's soldiers. They lifted to reveal the Washington Monument and the burned husk of the ICBM.

—Is that—can you tell what that is? she asked Ben, and pointed.

In among the white birds, somewhere above the stage and to the west, there were small dark shapes. But he shook his head and told her he could not see what they were.

The flock thinned as it moved away toward the horizon, thinned as the birds spread out and flew. Finally they were few and far between enough for the light of the sun to filter through the gaps in their ranks. For a while as they receded people watched them endlessly, still silent no matter how far away they grew, for a time that felt closer to hours than minutes.

And then abruptly the crowd seemed to feel it had kept silent for too long, and was embarrassed by this. Whispers broke out, and then normal voices, pedestrian, vulgar, returning all of them to the business of being who they had always been, saying trivial things in the usual way. But Ann would think later only of the silence, and how the patience of the crowd had seemed infinite, watching the birds vanish in the distance.

She had the feeling she had been left behind.

When she finally looked away from what were now black flecks, low and fading in the red western sky, and tried desperately to pick out the physicists on the stage—recalled to the danger in which they had been, the men shooting all around them, a lurch of panic in her throat—she saw bags from the stage being piled into trucks parked behind it, being carried on stretchers and loaded away from sight. She could not be sure at the time but to her they looked like soldiers in camouflage.

Not bags, she thought later: bodies.

Not ambulances, she thought later: trucks.

The work was conducted swiftly and with great precision because almost before she knew it the stage was bare. Yellow and brown leaves skittered over the concrete in front of her as dusk fell.

And the scientists were gone.

❧ Oppenheimer finally knew as they rose how he had come to this. He dismissed the precision of sums for the last time, let go of calculation. The birds had him now. Their wide wings were beating as they carried him, and it was good with them.

Only the dead have seen the end of war: and it was such a relief. He did not need to look for Fermi for he knew that Fermi, too, was out in the white somewhere beyond, shedding worry, skin turning to feathers, turning lighter than air.

He could shed everything now because in the end there was nothing more for him, he had done his best and finally it was nothing to what his worst had been. He could almost laugh now at the smallness of his good intentions, how paltry they had been against his mischief and the mischief of the neighborhood boys he had played with. He thought of Groves's fat, smug face and the beady homespun ignorance of Truman. Governments were gangs of boys, he thought, roaming the best neighborhoods and kicking puppies with their steel-toed boots; but their henchmen in the private sector were far, far worse. What a fool he had been: but all men were fools. His problem was to know it.

And he saw what it was that had brought him here in the first place, moved all of them from the first life and into this one. He understood finally. It had looked like desire, how it shaped them and sent them away from the blast, sent them wishing with such a piercing will from the moment of ignition that they left themselves behind.

But it was not desire, not exactly, though it flared like desire, flared and burned out. It was both more and less. It was regret.

And he could offer no more of it. He was tapped out. He had come to the end: he had done his best to undo himself. But his efforts were those of a child, frantically trying to bring back to life a small unknowing animal that it had killed in play. He was tired and ready for sleep, and alone on the road time was waiting for him.

But for a moment now they were together again, the birds and him and Fermi and even poor Szilard: they were adrift in infinity, where all became nothing.

❧ How they made it back to Larry's limousine Ben could not recollect shortly afterward. It was a slow blur. Those sad and limping moments would come back to him unexpectedly, without context, in the remaining days and years of his life as those days and years spun out and away from him.

They sleepwalked through the crowds, dispersing in a weary haze. People were saying little even after the birds vanished; an exhaustion settled over them and it was unmistakable; it was the tiredness of defeat.

The crowds left a trail of signs and litter in their wake, trampled cardboard and broken bottles. He could walk without touching the shoulders of his neighbors now, and swing his arms again. There was air around him. He thought, for no purpose he could know, *I am free but I am also useless.*

Near the edge of the mall they passed a dead crane, lying shot on the concrete. There was not much blood but its neck was bent at a wrong angle. He looked away because he could not stand to see, and then a few paces further he turned and ran back and squatted down beside it, full of a grief that almost choked him. Even Ann standing beside him almost vanished in the sight of the bird.

He moved his eyes over the red spot on the crown of its head, along the dark thin beak, and stroked its soft white feathers with a hand. Finally, with Ann swaying in fatigue beside him, about to collapse into sleep, he picked it up in his arms, its long, graceful neck flopping, and carried it away with them, cradling it like an infant.

—I'm going to bury it, he said when Ann pressed him.

The birds, he knew, had somehow won, had been not the vanquished but the triumphant: but there were those among their number who had been sacrificed to the men with the guns.

People stared at him as he walked, the man holding his crane; they stared as though they had no idea where the crane had come from, as though they had already forgotten.

Once they had reached the limousine, parked a block down from the ruined ICBM—cordoned off and teeming with police—Ben laid the dead bird out in the trunk on a blanket, and Tamika, suddenly dressed in a sari with a diamond on her forehead, dropped dry leaves around it.

Before he let the chauffeur slam down the lid he smoked a cigarette. He stood at the corner of the trunk and glanced down at the bird now and then, almost furtive, leaning against the fender and drinking a cup of stale, tepid coffee someone had handed him. Ann slipped inside the car and lay down on one of the long plush seats.

Neither Oppenheimer nor Fermi had returned and neither of them had been seen since the birds rose into the sky and flew away. Almost all of the Huts were assigned to the search by Larry but Bradley's men did not show an interest in searching: they were massed nearby, praying and weeping for those of their number who had been shot and killed, swaying with their arms around each other and huddling for prayer. Now and then one of them would break away from the circle to drink water or wipe the grime off his face, but mostly they were impregnable, a fortress of backs in camouflage, heads shaking as voices intoned.

Bradley sat off under an oak tree on what looked like a wooden crate, talking on his cell phone as the other leaders conversed in low tones nearby. When Ben approached and asked him what had happened, who had attacked them, who the dark men had been who ascended the stage right before the birds covered them, he would say nothing; he merely shook his head and turned away from him. In fact he would say nothing about Szilard's death either, nothing about any of it.

—You were there, weren't you? asked Ben belligerently, gesturing freely with the hand that held his lit cigarette. —Oppenheimer blamed it on you.

—We have nothing to say, said Bradley stiffly. Others rose with stern faces to warn Ben away and Bradley watched as he was forced to back up, the ranks of the believers closing against him.

When Oppenheimer had fingered Bradley he and the other men had been carried away, there on the stage behind him, swaying. They had not denied the charge and they had not rushed him. Possibly, Ben decided, they had thought at that moment that the Rapture was upon them; possibly they had thought they were already home free.

Now they were back in the world and their mouths were sealed shut.

Soon after this Bradley and his friends in the leadership called together the soldiers who were praying and crying, climbed into their black jeeps and drove noisily off down the street.

The rest of the travelers from the buses perched in and around the limousine with the doors standing open, wiping their faces with paper towels and napkins and thirstily gulping water from the bottles in Szilard's cooler. Their eyes were red and puffy and still streaming from the tear gas, and they held ice from the cooler against their faces. They were quiet.

—Who did all that shooting? asked Tamika, but no one knew the answer.

Without Szilard no one knew what to think. He had been the source of all information, and now he was gone and there was no more. They turned on the radio and sat there waiting, and Ann laid her head down and fell asleep on Ben's knees.

But the radio reported nothing.

❧ The scientists could not be found, and Larry's men came back alone.

It was dark when the limousine pulled away from the curb and Ann felt closed off, extinguished. She had nothing to say and she wanted no one to talk to her. She wanted only to sleep in the dark hearing nothing; she wanted the past to be changed.

—There's gotta be news reports on TV, said Larry, aggrieved. The car moved through the dim streets, stragglers crossing in front of them and slowing their progress, and Ann gazed up into the glow of yellow and orange fall trees as the streetlights winked on. —We can watch the news in the hotel, he went on. —Whoever did this, they can't get away with it. There had to have been arrests. There's probably reporters all over the story now.

Maybe the scientists had been arrested, maybe they would call in later, maybe they would have to be bailed out, said Larry. Maybe they had been jailed as insurgents. The men who had murdered Szilard, the men who had shot and killed Bradley's soldiers and brought down cranes, where were they now and why were they free?

—Where is Dr. Leo's body? asked Webster, teary-eyed. —He deserves to be buried.

—How could this be allowed to happen? said Tamika, and shook her head in wonder.

None of them had any comment after that. Finally someone changed the radio station and country music played. They sat stunned, barely speaking. Now and then someone fumbled with a water bottle or a shoelace.

As Ann was dozing off again, her head still aching from the effects of the gas, Father Raymond turned and whispered into her ear. Before she heard him she had not even realized he was beside her: she was barely noticing anything.

—They still don't know what happened, he murmured. —Any of them.

She opened her eyes with an effort, looked at him and saw his face was solemn. As she looked she felt a jarring in the world, in her position, as though she had not moved but magnetic fields were shifting and her coordinates were uncertain.

It did not matter. It had no consequence.

What a baby she had been, she thought sadly, about meaning.

—The birds were beautiful, though, she said dreamily.

—You thought they were birds? asked Father Raymond.

She sat there without moving as he stroked the Bible on his lap with trembling fingers, gently, comforting. He was kind: she had always liked him.

When other things were gone, that was all there was left.

—What do you mean?

—Such a hopeful book, in its own angry way, he said, and smiled fondly.

—The Bible?

—Always hopeful that at least some of us would be saved. But when all was said and done none of us were, were we?

—What are you—

—None of us.

She sat looking at him, his bowed head, thinning hair and double chin.

—Saved, saved, saved, he murmured. —We never knew what it

meant but we wanted it anyway. For our children and our parents if not for ourselves.

—It had to mean something good, she said vaguely, too tired to converse.

They sat there for a minute.

—Those were not birds, he said, and looked up at her with watery eyes. —Or put it this way: they were not *only* birds.

—What do you mean? she whispered.

—They brought us a message, he said sadly. —Didn't you know? The end has already come and gone. And here we are.

❧ Ben looked around the tired circle, their collapsed and inward faces suffused with failure, and thought how less they seemed than they had been. Without the scientists they were only strays, gathered together for warmth.

❧ When they reached the hotel Father Raymond sat without moving while the others filed out of the car. She reached out and touched his hand but if she was waiting for something it never came. He did not look up at her so she slowly roused herself to step out the open door of the limousine after Ben.

—Was it a moral failure? he asked as she stood up. —Did the spirit fail us? Or was it never in us at all?

She could tell he was talking only to himself.

—Ann? called Ben from the motel door, holding it open as he looked back at her. —Coming?

She said goodbye to Father Raymond, who sat shaking his head as though he had not heard. Then she turned and slogged across the parking lot in a tired daze, noticing nothing but her own exhaustion.

Later she woke up thinking: But they *were* birds. They were gone birds, gone birds who had taken the gone men.

The birds had forgiven them.

❧ He buried the dead crane in the woods the next morning, beside a trail in a state park a few minutes off the highway. He had nothing to dig with but a crowbar he found in the trunk of their car, so he used it to hack away at the dirt at the foot of a dead tree. When the hole was deep enough he laid the crane inside, filled in the hole again and covered the freshly turned earth with rocks and dry leaves.

Ann was watching him from a boulder a few feet away, where she sat drinking beer and smoking a Dunhill from a trampled half-empty pack she had found on the floor of the limousine.

He showed her photographs of whooping cranes to prove the bird's identity, even showed her printouts of its population numbers to illustrate the impossibility of the mass descent they had seen, but she only nodded, smiling sadly and tolerantly but showing little interest.

Now she said, across the air between them, —The Christians had it right all along.

He laid the bird down in the dirt.

—History is over.

When they got back to the hotel it was snowing lightly, at a slant. It was early for snow and the large flakes melted as soon as they touched the ground. In the hotel parking lot were Larry and his friends. The Christian leaders and all their thousands were already dispersing far and wide, but failure had not yet quelched Larry. Despite the fact that the massacre had not been reported on television or newspapers, that a sudden and complete radio silence had descended on everything they were doing, that television and newspaper reporters did not return the calls he made to them, Larry and his friends were still waiting for the scientists to return. They had not given up. They huddled in groups, drinking hot chocolate and coffee from plastic travel mugs covered in stickers, rubbing their hands in thick woolen mittens and discussing the situation in urgent voices as snowflakes alit on their shoulders and hair. They had sent out electronic alerts and volunteers all over the city were tacking up MISSING posters.

Ann and Ben did not join them. They only walked past with their faces set in pleasant neutrality and raised their hands half-heartedly to wave.

The day after that they were listless and did not know what to do. While they waited in line to see a movie, standing outside a multiplex at a mall in the suburbs, she said it.

—We'll never see them again.

He could not contradict her so he lifted his cardboard cup of tea to his lips and sipped. He liked the narrow pressure of the rounded white rim.

—They came and went, she said. —They did what they had to do but it was no use. And now they're gone from us.

—The birds took them, he said.

She nodded vaguely and looked away from him into the mall's food court, where a man dressed as a hot dog hopped first on one leg and then on the other.

He wondered if there would be an end to the effort to understand. What would happen in the future felt more known to him than what had happened already, though both were elusive. The scientists had flown into the sunset on the wings of birds he was sure could not exist anymore. Had Fermi known? Either he had known or he had summoned them.

First he had come, and Oppenheimer and Szilard, and they had stayed a while. This was impossible. Then the impossible birds had come, the birds long gone extinct.

And finally they had disappeared together.

❧ Larry knocked on the door of their hotel room that night while Ann was in the shower. Ben let him in and watched with moderate interest as he sat down at the small round table to roll a joint.

—So Clint disappeared after the event, said Larry. —Never saw him again. You notice?

—Good riddance, said Ben.

—Thing is, said Larry, —someone saw him loading bodies onto the trucks.

—I don't get it.

He looked at Larry's face then, which was haggard in the yellow cast of the table lamp. For once Larry seemed as old as he was, not a rugged boy surfer with sun-weathered skin but a sad man in his middle forties trying to cling to youth.

—He was with the Covert Ops guys, the Green Berets or whoever they were. He was talking to them like he knew them, all familiar, you know? He had a weapon in a holster and he was dragging one of Bradley's guys across the ground by his feet. He slung him in the back of a truck like garbage.

Ben gazed at him for a time, his crisp blue irises beneath the lined forehead, until Larry lifted a joint to his lips, inhaled, held his breath, and then handed the joint to him.

—What does that mean?

—I think, said Larry slowly after he let out his breath, —he was working for them the whole time.

—Clint was undercover?

Larry nodded and Ben closed his eyes as he held the smoke in his mouth. When he opened them again he asked, —Undercover for who?

—Glen warned me, man. I shouldn't have trusted him. He always wanted money. He was all about that. They probably paid him a lot to spy on us.

—Undercover for who? repeated Ben, impatient with his own confusion.

—You know, said Larry, and looked away from him to the bathroom, where Ann was standing wrapped in a towel. He lowered his voice. —The ones who were going to kill Oppenheimer. Before the birds took him.

❧ Between the invention of nuclear weapons and the turn of the twenty-first century the U.S. spent over five trillion dollars building and maintaining its nuclear arsenal—about one-tenth of the country's total spending since 1940. In America, annual spending on past and present military activities exceeds spending on all other categories of human need; approximately eighty percent of the national debt is estimated to have been created by military expenditures.

The so-called "military-industrial complex" about which Eisenhower warned is thus, in a sense, the single largest consumer of the country's resources. It might fairly be seen as the prime mover of the U.S. government.

4

On the high plains of San Augustine west of Socorro, New Mexico, is a small town named Magdalena. About a half an hour's drive farther west is a row of telescopes called the Very Large Array.

To the untrained eye the Very Large Array looks like a row of satellite dishes, extending for many miles in a long line across the desert. They can be seen from the highway. The dishes can be moved, so that sometimes they stretch for great distances and sometimes the formation is neatly compressed. Astronomers call them antennas.

The array comprises twenty-seven dish antennas, turned up toward the sky. It is a complex of radio telescopes, devoted to observing the cosmos. Its mission is to collect radio waves from natural celestial bodies vast distances away from earth—waves that are then fashioned by computers into images of these far-off bodies, which include planets, stars, even whole galaxies. There are spiral galaxies like the one in which our solar system dwells, dwarf galaxies, even strangely shaped, distorted galaxies astronomers call *peculiar*.

Ann and Ben moved onto an abandoned ranch outside Magdalena in the winter of 2003. By that time, in the known universe, the number of stars within telescope range was estimated at seventy sextillion, or seventy thousand million million million.

Ann had learned of this estimate in the late fall, soon after they got home, and begun to comb newspapers and web sites for land for sale near the Very Large Array. She thought if she lived there she would feel the presence of the sextillion.

She found them an isolated place, an old mud-brick ranch house with a stone chimney and tile floors. It sat on a sagebrush ridge overlooking rolling valleys and hills of grass, piñon, cedar, and juniper, and at sunset purple and red clouds spread across the whole sky and nothing could touch them.

Often they looked like they were burning.

It was painful to sell the house and the garden in Santa Fe but she could not stay there. In the city there were too many smug Rogers who wanted to relive the old days, too many intimations of quiet power on the sides of trucks that passed the city hurtling down the interstate. In the country house they found a new routine, drinking wine every night as the sun set and they sat on their front porch watching the dark shapes of their low, scrubby trees bending in the wind. They ordered the wine several cases at a time, but they were not immoderate; and in the pantry, waiting to be drunk, the bottles gathered dust.

❧ Ben found work on a nearby national forest, planting trees, thinning brush, and occasionally watching planned burns. He liked the sight of the fires in the dark, all low along the ground.

At first he was an independent contractor to the Forest Service and was surprised to learn that most of his salaried coworkers did not like to work at all. Rather they drove over the old logging roads hour after hour in their government vehicles, looking for ways to waste time. One of them drank cheap beer all day long, driving over the rutted mud with his windows rolled all the way down, red dirt caking his hair, fishing the cans out of a cooler on the passenger seat of his truck as he drove. Whenever he saw Ben he offered him a can, and when Ben did not want it he shook his head with a smirk to let Ben know he did not suffer fools gladly.

But Ben was stubborn and worked hard and though they mocked him at first and even called him a "pretty boy," soon they dropped the mockery and he thought he might have won their grudging respect. They continued to do nothing themselves beyond driving around and fielding phone calls from their wives and girl-friends, but they allowed him to work without railing against him.

In return, every so often he accepted a warm can of Schlitz in the morning.

As he drove to the forest at dawn, uphill all the way, he often had a view of the peak of South Baldy Mountain ahead, looming at over ten thousand feet. He liked this and he liked the crystalline frost patterns on his windshield and watching them melt softly from the edges as he drove. Within months he had seen mule and whitetail deer, elk, a black bear, a golden eagle, and herds of pronghorn antelope running fast alongside the highway.

෴ After a while Ann went back to work too, cataloguing images of celestial bodies at the Very Large Array. She drove there every morning in their old car with no heater, her fingers and toes growing numb as she listened to the radio.

She loved the pictures of the celestial bodies and would lose herself in concentration. The images were not actual photographs, since no optical telescope could reach as far as the radio telescopes did, but rather false-color images in rainbows of yellow, green, red and violet. Because these images were all she looked at during the day she began to see outer space as the radio telescopes saw it, an infinite blackness punctuated by explosions of spectral color.

She learned about the celestial bodies as she catalogued them, but she never assumed that what she was learning was real. It was a story the astronomers liked to tell and had a singular beauty, and she found the words for the bodies as lovely as the pictures of them. We have seen these bodies, she would think, and even long after we are gone some particle in the universe will hold a memory of the words we once used to describe their beauty.

There were *galactic sources:* supernovae, star-forming regions, pulsars, black holes, and planetary nebulae. There were *active galactic nuclei,* including quasars, radio galaxies, and Seyfert galaxies.

There were also *hypernovae,* black holes that formed after the death of massive stars.

෧ Once or twice a month Ben searched news archives for word of the scientists, but as he expected there was none. They had never been seen since the day of the birds.

Some of their fan groups remained active, selling souvenir mugs and T-shirts on their web sites and reporting on the sluggish progress of various old Szilard-authored petitions through minor committees of the United Nations. Several list-serves notified interested parties on the release of videotapes of the scientists' public appearances. Obscure sources documented clearly spurious "sightings" of men meeting Oppenheimer's and Fermi's and even Szilard's descriptions, in isolated locations as far-flung as Luxembourg and Beijing.

When he told all this to Ann she did not seem interested. She neither spoke of the scientists nor asked about them, even when she caught a glimpse of what he had on his computer screen. In fact she rarely discussed any of the events of the past year and he was mildly surprised to find out she corresponded occasionally with the well-mannered, unassuming minister from Peace Camp. Father Raymond had given away all his worldly possessions after the day of the birds, renounced his U.S. citizenship and left the country. He was ministering to war victims with the Red Cross in Africa.

The worldly possessions, Ann told Ben as she read aloud from a letter, had amounted to a 1985 Volkswagen Jetta, some cooking pots inherited from a great-aunt, and a rotary telephone.

෧ It was hard to remember sometimes that history had ended. The trees and the sky felt no different unless she stopped herself from moving and listened to them. Even then they were the same: only she was different.

When the ground was so real and the evidence of solid life was all around her, it mostly seemed out of the question that anything had changed.

Only in strange moments would she be stopped as she walked or closed a car door or moved between rooms. She would be stricken then, shot through with a panic, convinced for a fleeting fraction of a second that what she was seeing would be the last sight seen.

And then she went on, back to the everyday world she could touch, which could all disappear in a flash.

❧ They were not unhappy but there was the sense between them that what was beyond their presence was shimmering and unreal. The superworld, the world of trade and great cities and daily news, was only an image of itself anymore. On television, in the magazines, nothing was said about what was real: only the surface was touched. And even on the grainy plastic dashboards of their cars and in the spidery cracks in their dusty windshields as they drove forward through the desert there were textures of loss and forgetfulness. Both of them believed that human time spun on only for the sake of a machine, and the machine was far greater and more monolithic than anything weak and living.

Inhabiting this afterlife, which was less life itself than the memory of a life passed away, it was safer to spend time in the wide open spaces of the ancient plains than the cramped roads and stores and homes of a newer geography whose end was already foregone. It even hurt her at times to be in the city, to see the weak and living animals whose time was marked, so precious and unsung, their children, their art, their gardens.

At least what was remote and wild in the country could be relied on to go on nearly forever: the sky, the curve of the earth, the sun.

—When I was a kid, she said to Ben one morning when they were afraid to get out of bed because the room was cold and the floor was cold and their feet would have to touch the floor, —I would stand in my parents' house when I was bored and wait to be told what to do. There was this static feeling right then, this feeling of being frozen. With this reluctance and at the same time a sense of anticipation. Feeling torn between doing something and doing nothing.

She pulled the comforter up to her chin and sat back against the headboard.

—I didn't recognize it back then but now I see what it was.

—So what was it?

—It was how I was going to spend the rest of my life.

❧ In a late afternoon in the early spring they walked down into an arroyo together and trailed their hands over the sage bushes to lift their fragrant fingers to their faces. A breeze moved the brush and ahead of them the sun was setting, and because there were no clouds it was a wide and vacant sky.

Stepping over rocks on the crumbling red soil he asked her if it was wrong to want to have a child when their paralysis was so clear, when they lived already in a present that could not go forward and only longed for what had already been and was gone.

—It is not wrong for people to want something, she said quietly, —but our problem is we want everything.

She was walking ahead of him by then and since she did not turn back toward him to speak her answer was carried away from him on the wind.

❧ By the beginning of the twenty-first century the men who had been central to the design and construction of the atom bomb a half a century earlier were dead. The bombs they had conceived remained, of course; the bombs in their various silos, trucks and trains, their submarines and aircraft, had been dispersed over the globe like seeds, and lay quietly waiting to bloom.

But the scientists had lived thoughtful lives, weighing their responsibilities gravely. They were not warlike men. Mindful of the moral dimensions of their work, they were inclined for obvious reasons to value reason over instinct. They were duly troubled by the implications of the first great weapon of mass destruction. They had built the first device under the shadow of Hitler, and they dedicated it to him. But finally they were driven by something far simpler than fear or anger.

They worked because they wanted to see; they worked because they worshipped the structure deep within the universe, what was sweetly unknown and could only with great perseverance be drawn into the light. As others might feel tenderness for a child or a home, so they cherished and nurtured their science.

It was love that led them to the bomb.